Life in the West
THE SQUIRE QUARTET

Brian Aldiss, OBE, is a fiction and science fiction writer, poet, playwright, critic, memoirist and artist. He was born in Norfolk in 1925. After leaving the army, Aldiss worked as a bookseller, which provided the setting for his first book, *The Brightfount Diaries* (1955). His first published science fiction work was the story 'Criminal Record', which appeared in *Science Fantasy* in 1954. Since then he has written nearly 100 books and over 300 short stories, many of which are being reissued as part of The Brian Aldiss Collection.

Several of Aldiss' books have been adapted for the cinema; his story 'Supertoys Last All Summer Long' was adapted and released as the film *AI* in 2001. Besides his own writing, Brian has edited numerous anthologies of science fiction and fantasy stories, as well as the magazine *SF Horizons*.

Aldiss is a vice-president of the international H. G. Wells Society and in 2000 was given the Damon Knight Memorial Grand Master Award by the Science Fiction Writers of America. Aldiss was awarded the OBE for services to literature in 2005. He now lives in Oxford, the city in which his bookselling career began in 1947.

THE SQUIRE QUARTET

Life in the West
Forgotten Life
Remembrance Day
Somewhere East of Life

BRIAN ALDISS

Life in the West

The Friday Project
An imprint of HarperCollins
77-85 Fulham Palace Road
Hammersmith, London W6 8JB

www.thefridayproject.co.uk
www.harpercollins.co.uk

First published in Great Britain in 1980 by Weidenfeld & Nicolson Ltd
This edition published by The Friday Project in 2012

ISBN 978-0-00-746114-1

MIX
Paper from
responsible sources
FSC® C007454

FSC™ is a non-profit international organisation established to promote
the responsible management of the world's forests. Products carrying the
FSC label are independently certified to assure consumers that they come
from forests that are managed to meet the social, economic and
ecological needs of present and future generations,
and other controlled sources.

Find out more about HarperCollins and the environment at
www.harpercollins.co.uk/green

Life in the West is dedicated to other
Distinguished Persons
Chen, David, Iris, Maysie, and Michael
by no means forgetting Felix, Elena, Derek, and Janet
to show them what one of their number was up to
before we sampled life in the East
and walked the Great Wall together

Acknowledgements

The characters and events depicted 'on stage' in this novel are fictitious, and are not intended to have reference to any persons living or dead. Some of the characters depicted as being 'off stage', such as the Shah of Persia, are real enough.

Acknowledgements for help and advice go to John Curtis, Andrea Boicelli, Hilary Rubinstein and, particularly, John Roberts.

Contents

I walked beside a sea aflame,
An animal of land. The fire
Of stars knocked at my earthbound frame:
East of grapples West, man maid, hope Fate;
All oppositions emanate
From constellations of desire.

Burning below hair, flesh, and teeth,
An image of the Bright Ones lies,
A lantern hid in bone. Beneath
That vision, teeth and hair begin
Again; wolf grins to wolfish grin
As smile I in my lover's eyes.

Too soon that love with false-bright hair
Is dead: the house stands silent. I
Fare forth across the world's despair,
Its muteness, oratory, and banners,
To seek not truth but modern manners.
The head must win what heart let die.

INTRODUCTION

When I began to write the Squire Quartet my intention was to portray something of the world I was living in, from the 1980s onwards. I found most of that world exciting – enticing to experience and to record.

This, the first volume of the Squire Quartet, brisk and chatty, was published on March 6th 1980 – as a loving card from my wife, still tucked into her copy of the book, reminds me. We were living on a quiet North Oxford street and our younger children were seriously into education. We were always moving house, depending on our fortunes.

I had been attending a conference in Palermo – a conference with a strong Communist flavour, not particularly enjoyable. It was over. I was standing on the dockside, looking north over the sea. A story began to build up in my mind: the conference; the players from various countries, where the economic blocs seemed irreconcilable; and at the same time, a man's – Sir Thomas C. Squire's – difficulties at home.

Once I returned to our house in Charlbury Road, I launched into the novel. My mother died during that period; a melancholy event recorded when Squire's mother dies just before Christmas. You have to go on, whatever happens. Maybe the army taught me that. Or maybe I had known it even as a small boy. Anyhow, Squire also has to press on. Trouble in Yugoslavia, where he is almost killed. Separation from Teresa, his wife. More human experience, more meditation. More striving to penetrate the thickets.

The novel opens with Squire in Ermalpa, Sicily, for a conference on the popular arts, dubbed 'the arts of no refinement'. He claims that the pop art of one generation becomes the classic of the next: 'Homer was, in his day, the Bronze Age equivalent of the TV soap opera.' Squire is for the new, insisting we rise up to change.

Later, back at his Norfolk house, Pippet Hall, Squire is filming and being filmed. The traditional pretty girl in a swimsuit is with him. He remarks, 'We are all symbols to each other as well as real people.'

It is the period of the Cold War – much discussion takes place. Squire and his wife quarrel bitterly.

Squire recalls a note given to him in Ermalpa, in which Vasili Rugorsky, the friendly Russian, proposes they visit Nontreale's cathedral and that Squire pay the bus fare: 'our government keeps us poor as saints.'

They get to Nontreale and enter the cathedral. Rugorsky praises the elaborate artwork. He says to the unimpressed Squire, 'Without God, I can see no meaning in anything.'

'Do you ever experience the feeling that you have come to a dead halt in your life?' Rugorsky asks.

So the questioning goes on, the faltering marriage, the symbols, the seasons, life itself . . .

Brian Aldiss
Oxford, 2012

Prelude

Spring 1977

A period in the history of the West known as the late nineteen-seventies. One of the milder inter-glacial periods, when textbooks describe the North European climate as 'pleasantly cool and damp'.

Over the European Economic Community, eight o'clock of a windy and rather chill spring evening. Television screens brighten everywhere, in flats, houses, and apartments stretching from Scapa Flow to the Gulf of Otranto. Hundreds of them, thousands, millions, the characteristic burning to ward off the terrors of ancient night. So characteristic that future historians will refer to this cultural epoch as the Rounded Rectangular. The global village enjoys its nightly catharsis of violence or *Kultur*.

The light brightens. Music, and the sight of a savage tropical landscape. The peaks of mountains covered with rain forest stand out against a fast-moving sky. The forest also appears to move, crawling across the screen as if its trunks were a myriad legs. It sweeps beneath the viewer. A river is revealed, dark-flowing, hemmed with sand.

As the viewpoint sinks, a long-boat is revealed, pulling in to one of the banks of the river. Six tourists climb ashore, gazing up at a towering and broken cliff face. From every cranny of the cliff, trees and creepers grow. At one point, tangled creepers hang down into the water.

The viewpoint moves in to reveal the boatman in close-up. He is a lean and aged Dayak, with a polished brown countenance, a wrinkled forehead, and hollows at cheeks and temples. He rests his hand upon a no less worn wooden post which marks the start of the ascent up the cliff.

Floating down, the viewpoint rests upon the Dayak's arm and hand.

On his wrist is an LC digital quartz timepiece and calculator. Its case, finished in gold and stainless steel, glints in the sunshine. With its perimeter punctuated by studs, it resembles momentarily, in the dazzle of its reflection, some armoured insect from a much earlier period of Earth's history. But a slight move of the boatman's wrist, and the six square ceaseless digits are revealed. They grow larger, writhe into red letters. The red letters come swimming forward to fill the screen, forming the legend:

FRANKENSTEIN AMONG THE ARTS

The party moves from the boat, trudging through the sand with their heads down. They climb the cliff by a winding path from which lizards scurry. Cloud shadow comes and goes. The tourists walk along a raised plank walk through dense primary forest, often having to brush creepers aside. The detached voice of Thomas Squire is heard.

'We're in some of the oldest jungle in the world, older than the jungles of the Amazon or the Congo. Successive Ice Ages, which caused so much change elsewhere, had no effect on this luxuriance. Listen to its rich silence – you can hear the murmur of antiquity. Transitory-seeming things like silences and pollen have proved themselves capable of enduring over millions of years.'

As his voice lapses to allow the voice of the jungle to take over, another legend swims into view:

Episode One:
Eternal Ephemera

The party of tourists continues deeper into the forest, emerging suddenly under a ravaged hillside. They pause; they are seen to be of mixed race, two Caucasian, the others Mongoloid; all are dressed similarly, male or female, in comfortable travelling clothes. They walk towards a strangely-shaped cave resembling a whale's mouth. Stalactites and fallen stone about its rim reinforce this impression and give the appearance of teeth, broken but still functional. One by one, the party moves into the great mouth.

'We are entering the limestone mountains of a part of Malaysia called the Tinjar National Park. Few tourists from the West ever visit here. These caves are dangerous. Not only do they shelter snakes, bats, and a spiteful variety of centipede, but there are concealed abysses on the cave floors, down which an unsuspecting traveller can drop, sometimes for hundreds of feet. Despite these dangers, when we enter here, we are coming into one of the most ancient homes of mankind.'

From inside the whale's mouth, the foliage outside appears pale and translucent, like spray off a sea. From a deep darkness into the light, bats begin to pour, more and more of them, flying like leaves in an October wind, ceaselessly.

'Human beings, homo sapiens, lived in these caves 40,000 years BC, at a time when the last Ice Age had its grip on Europe, and the draughty caves of the Dordogne sheltered our remote forebears. In that long period of time, these bats have not changed in any way, as far as we know, while mankind has changed in so many remarkable ways that we often forget that we have also hardly changed at all.'

The bats continue to pour out into the daylight, thousands upon thousands of them, and still no cease to their numbers. The rustle of their wings follows the viewpoint into the throat of the cave, which is uncertainly illuminated by a floodlight.

'In terms of centuries, a human life is ephemeral. The things we do, the things we make, our alliances and enmities, are even more ephemeral. These paintings were executed one forgotten day thousands of centuries ago.'

In the uncertain light, faces loom, bodies of men, animals, bright fish, plants, all in mysterious relationships and preserved under a glistening film of limestone. Then the light dies.Something can still be seen in the darkness; it is the liquid crystal display of the boatman's watch, on which the seconds flit rapidly by.

'These paintings were not intended to last. Perhaps they were intended to please or function – whatever that function was – just for a day. They are beyond taste. There is an old saying, it is "De gustibus non est disputandum", meaning, "It's useless to discuss questions of taste"; yet this series of programmes is designed to discover more about taste, and why and how taste changes.'

Further in the cave, the light reveals pictures of two lizards, curving their bodies round bosses of rock. One lizard is green, one red.

'Did the prehistoric painter prefer green to red? Some gentlemen prefer blondes, some black-haired beauties. There is always a reason for our preferences, sometimes an important reason. We may prefer Beethoven to Burt Bacharach; there may be a political reason why we like rock'n'roll more than Ruddigore. Are the reasons why a church moves us more than a warehouse purely religious? What makes us read one sort of book in preference to another, or flip from one TV channel to a practically identical one?'

More lizards, and a strange creature that is a kind of man with a tail, or else an anthropomorphic lizard.

'Nothing like this imaginative creature exists in the caves of Europe. Nor do we find in these paintings that emphasis on hunting which is so pervasive in the caves of Europe. It is almost as if a marked difference between the thought of the East and the West existed all those thousands of centuries ago, even as it exists today. Could the greater passivity of temperament in the East relate to the absence in this part of the world of large animals of the hunt which were common throughout Europe? We can as yet hardly formulate such questions, never mind answering them. In the middle of the twentieth century, we still stand in the middle of unfathomed mystery.'

Darkness, then light again, light moving into a larger cave, where stalactites and stalagmites come together in great folds, like closing teeth. One wall is covered with the outlines of human hands. The hands are all open, palms facing towards the spectator, hundreds of them, stretching up into the darkness, interspersed with strange squiggles reminiscent of intestines. The light moves slowly. The hands continue, palms glistening from their coating of limestone; countless hands, one gesture.

'We don't know what these hands mean or meant. They symbolize man – the prehensile fingers, the opposed digit. They reach out to us, as if in supplication. We cannot touch them.'

He places his hand against one of the painted hands. His own palm glistens when he withdraws it.

'Time and limestone intervene between us. I know nothing more poignant than this wall of hands.'

The hands thin out at last. The wall becomes rougher. The light dims. Someone's shoulder gets in the way. The music is sombre, romantic, cool, Borodin's 'Steppes of Central Asia' strained through a synthesizer, with acoustics added. Crimson, such as hides behind eyelids, fills the screen; from it, a narrow corridor emerges, and large shattered stones which could have been brought here from outside.

Bones lie in a recess, in the wall. Squire's hand reaches down and lifts up a skull from which the bottom jaw has dropped away. The forehead gleams, shadows lie in the eye sockets.

'We can admire the aesthetic qualities of this extremely functional object. However, we would be less appreciative if we knew this to be the skull of a brother who had died only last week. Why is that? Are there degrees of being dead? Perhaps there are even degrees of being alive – we all know that some people are more lively and alert than others. Perhaps the life force is less democratically distributed than we suppose.'

A bright green beetle runs out of one of the eye sockets as Squire lowers the skull to the floor.

'Let's ask no more questions for the moment. I believe the answers to a lot of trivial-seeming questions to be profound, to concern politics, life and death, religion, and to lead directly to our imaginative perception of the world. A T-shirt advertising Coca-Cola holds a key to the wearer's personality: we move from casual preference to the prevailing winds of the individual psyche.'

The viewpoint swings. Now we are returning to the light of day.

The members of the party are revealed as six blundering figures, their hands touching the walls for security. This is the throat of the whale, through which bats still whistle like a dark outgoing breath. A patch of daylight ahead is an undersea green.

'We like to imagine that the men and women who lived and died here 40,000 years ago were haunted by symbols, taboos, superstitions, omens. Yet the same must be said of us today, although our lives in the twentieth century are fortified by elaborate cultural superstructures. Interplay between superstructure and individual is complex. Do we like China because it appears friendly, fear it because it is large, mistrust it because it is communist, or idealize it because it is remote? An individual must choose between cultural superstructures.'

One of the party, a woman in jeans, has stumbled. She bends so that we see she has a badge pinned to her hip pocket. The legend on the badge reads, 'Friends of the Earth'.

'In the last two centuries, an infrastructure of man-made objects has proliferated. Mass-produced goods are everywhere, from badges to weapons of destruction, and we find it oddly difficult to pronounce upon them; their very plenty seems to ensnare judgement.'

The speaker produces from his pocket a slender box of matches. The box is black, simply embossed with a gold head in an antique-style Chinese hat and the one word, 'Mandarin'. The box slides open. Inside lie some twenty matches with white heads. They fill the screen, rough wooden shafts culminating in smooth bulbs.

'This is a give-away packet of matches from my hotel in Singapore. The matches are wood, the box plastic. It is a neat and beautiful product, and totally beyond the technology of our fathers. It is worthless. Can we then call it – beautiful? Because it is worthless, is it valueless?'

We are back in the mouth of the whale. The bats have all flown at last, the tourists have disappeared. The speaker is silent. There is no music. Just the ancient cave.

A great column of limestone stands at the cave-mouth, moulded by the forces of water. Orchestral strings wake in startlement as two figures mysteriously appear on either side of the column. One of them – she moves forward, smiling – is a golden girl in a bikini, her blonde hair bouncing about her shoulders. She goes barefoot. The other figure remains unmoving. With his back to the light, we see him merely as a brutal silhouette. He rests one arm nonchalantly on the limestone, waiting.

'*These two are our Sex Symbol and our Dark Figure. They represent the two poles of life and death, and will be with us as we explore the familiar. They both loom large in our minds, as they do in the world, and they dominate how we feel about those questions of tone, form, smell, and colour which shape our preferences.*'

The caves are left behind. Sea glints through the trees. The viewpoint rises past mountain peaks remote in their encampments of cloud. Soon we are flying over the isle-spattered sea.

'*No part of the globe is more beautiful than South East Asia; nowhere can life be more pleasant than in Malaysia. The climate is tolerable, the food good, the scenery superb, and the people kind and friendly. What's more, just south of Malaysia lies the most extraordinary city in the world – Singapore.*'

As we rush across the waters of the South China Sea, we can observe Squire for the first time. He is a tall sun-tanned man in his late forties, with grey in his thin crop of sandy hair. His is what is called a strong countenance, but there is possibly little outstanding about him. Nor does he dress obtrusively. He wears only a blue short-sleeved shirt, rather faded, shapeless cotton trousers, and a pair of sandals. His manner is cool but sociable as he speaks to camera.

'*In 1818, Mary Shelley published her novel,* Frankenstein. *It was something more than the Gothic novel it superficially resembled. It portrayed the scientist in a role we recognize today, or at least we did yesterday, as a man who strikes out for himself, discarding old authorities, caring little for the social consequences of his inventions. The result is a reign of confusion by the creature that Frankenstein, the scientist, has created. The welter of mass-produced goods which surrounds us can be described as Frankenstein's legacy.*'

Singapore and its skyscrapers glitter beneath us. The river flashes a signal from the sun, then we are down.

'This marvellous city, too, is part of the legacy. It is as much a technological product as a digital quartz watch.'

A pleasant quayside, shaded by trees. The busy river beyond. In the background barges, boats, old buildings, a jumble of roofs, glittering high-rise structures beyond. In the foreground, a statue of a man gazing inland.

'This is reputedly the spot where Sir Stamford Raffles first stepped ashore. It is decent and undoctrinaire of the Chinese to have left the statue in place when they took over from the old British colonial regime which created the city. But I find Singapore an enlightened place. Raffles landed here a year after Frankenstein was published, in 1819. He turned this island into one of the liveliest places on Earth. Just a few fishermen lived here when he landed. Now, in one of the cleanest and most prosperous of cities, there are two and a half million citizens. The principle of free trade which Raffles laid down is still observed. This is definitely a Chinese and Malayan and Indian city, not a Western one. They have our crazy worship of speed, but don't share our veneration for open space, so they indulge neither in building sprawling suburbs, which are anti-city, nor in shooting men to the Moon; the Chinese in particular live happily in high densities, and the death rate is one of the world's lowest.'

We are moving into the business centre of the city. The shops and hotels are bright, and sparkle with electronic clutter in a rapture of newness. The streets are lined with trees and flowers; they shimmer with well-nourished automobiles.

'Singapore trades with the world. It survives on the principles of hard work and strict discipline. There are fines for dropping litter, imposed immediately, fines for contravening strict laws of hygiene, and the press is censored, like the press throughout most of the world today. Some find the Prime Minister of this city state, Mr Lee Kuan Yew, autocratic, and exercise their consciences on behalf of his subjects. In my opinion, anyone conversant with the history of this part of the world must admire what Mr Lee and his energetic subjects have achieved.'

He has stopped before an open-air food stall, and eats a sizzling satay from a stick. Beside him, the Sex Symbol appears and sinks two rows of white teeth into a similar skewer full of meat.

'You can eat where you wish and not get ill from contaminated food. Good for trade.

'We in the West no longer care so much for work and discipline. That is why places like Singapore represent the coming century, the twenty-first century, while the nations of Europe sink back towards the nineteenth. Singapore is winning the economic war, as work and discipline always do. Singapore plays globally something of the role played by London in the last century. I know which city I'd rather live in.

'To my mind, Singapore is the dishiest workshop ever invented, where people are on the whole as happy and as handsome as people can ever be at our present stage of evolution. It is no utopia. What it is is a shining example of capitalism, unmatched in the communist world. It is a staggering work of man's imagination. It is also the biggest mass-produced goodie in the history of the world. Whether or not you like it is a question – the sort of question we want to explore – a matter of taste.'

We are crossing Merdeka Bridge, driving along the fast Nicholl Highway in dense traffic. The sun is going down. The city lies in front of us, suddenly insubstantial as sunset brightens behind it.

1

The International Congress

Ermalpa, September 1978

Two men were walking in Mediterranean sunlight only four blocks from their hotel.

An observer following behind them would have learnt much from their backs. One was a comparatively small-built man, with thick heels on his shoes to compensate for a lack of height. He was thin almost to the point of being emaciated, so that, as he talked, which he did with a wealth of gesture, his shoulder blades could be seen moving beneath his jacket like two ferrets working back and forth in a cage.

He wore a brown suit with a faint yellow stripe, a neat suit light enough in weight for the climate, but somewhat worn. It was shiny round the seat. It was an expressive suit, the jacket flapping slightly as its owner vigorously demonstrated a point, or looked up sharply laughing, to see if his companion was also enjoying the joke. This sideways glance would have enabled an observer to catch a glimpse of a thin yellowish cheek belonging to a man slightly on the shady side of forty, and a neat beard shot through with grey.

The feature that announced the man in most companies, however, was his flow of copper hair. As if to compensate for the meagreness of his stature, the colourlessness of his cheek, his hair blazed. He wore it amply, down to his collar. In the sixties, it had trailed considerably further down his backbone. Now as then, it showed no white hairs.

The hands, when they appeared, were small and sharp, more useful in debate than games. They were the chief illustrators of gesture, and scattered words rather than spreading them evenly. Their possessor was a Frenchman by the name of Jacques d'Exiteuil, the chairman of the conference.

D'Exiteuil's companion was taller and more solidly built than he, and stooped slightly, although he was at present walking briskly and with relish, smiling and nodding his head in a genial manner at d'Exiteuil's remarks. The observer would not have seen a slight developing paunch, although he would certainly have noticed the bald spot below the crown of the head. The surrounding hair was decidedly sandy, with a crisp dry curl to it. The white hairs in it were no more plentiful than d'Exiteuil's, though the latter was the younger of the two men by some eight or nine years.

The taller man wore slacks of light brown colour and fashionable cut, with a neat Scandinavian canvas jacket patterned with vertical stripes of red, brown, and white. The jacket fitted smoothly across strong shoulders. This man also gesticulated as he spoke, but his gestures, like his walk, were looser than his companion's and less precisely aimed. When he turned his head, a powerful countenance was revealed, tanned of cheek, with heavy lines – not necessarily misanthropic – running from nose to chin, bracketing a full, square mouth.

He was guest of honour at the conference, and he signed his cheques Thomas Squire or, more impressively, Thomas C. Squire.

Although the scene and the city were strange to them, neither Squire nor d'Exiteuil paid much attention to their surroundings, beyond stepping out of the way of the occasional more aggressive pedestrian who refused to move out of their path. They were discussing the state of the world, each from his own point of view. Both had strong and opposed beliefs, and blunted some of the force of what they had to say in order to proceed without undue argument.

The first day's business of the conference was about to start. The two men worked in different disciplines. D'Exiteuil was primarily an academic, with a good position in the Humanities Faculty of the Sainte Beuve University in Paris. He and his wife Séverine d'Exiteuil had made several experimental films. Squire was a small landowner, a director of a London insurance firm, and an exponent of popular aesthetics. He had become something of a national hero in the late sixties, when he planned and executed the Hyde Park Pop Expo in London. For that spectacular event, he had received the CBE. His more recent television work had reinforced his success.

The conference was d'Exiteuil's brainchild.

D'Exiteuil and Squire had known each other for many years. They corresponded irregularly and met occasionally – the previous New Year at Squire's publisher's home outside London, or at conferences or symposia, once in San Francisco, once in Stockholm, once in Poland, and twice in Paris.

Though they were in some respects enemies, they shared close common interests. The Frenchman recognized in the Englishman knowledge and wit; the Englishman recognized in the Frenchman integrity and application. All these qualities both admired. Because they could also be useful to each other, they had discovered a way to talk to each other, which seemed, over the years, to function effectively.

The relationship, while not a friendship, had proved more durable than many friendships, and was valued by both men.

When they came to the bottom of the side street down which they had been progressing, they reached an entry to the harbour. Before them stood a low double wall, in the middle of which had been planted bedding plants and cacti. The two men stood by the wall, looking across at a desolate area which stretched between them and the water; it was given over mainly to cracked concrete, grass, and dull square concrete buildings left over from Cubist paintings. An old lorry moved slowly among cranes. In the distance were warehouses, wharves, warning notices. Then the sea, or a section of it, tamed by a confining wall which terminated in a lighthouse. Beyond that wall lay the Mediterranean.

'Looks promising,' Squire said.

'I don't mind sitting on a beach with a book,' d'Exiteuil said, 'but I can't bear going on or in the sea. Are you a yachtsman?'

'Not really, but I did once sail right round Sicily with a couple of friends. I wouldn't mind doing it again. Shall we go and stand at the water's edge?'

D'Exiteuil looked smartly at his wrist watch.

'We'd better go back to the hotel. It is fourteen minutes to nine o'clock. You and I have to set a good international example, Tom. On the first day, if not later.' His English was fluent and almost without accent.

'As you say.' A headland crowned with palm trees stretched out into the sea to one side of the harbour, and there a white sail could be seen.

As they turned away, a boy ran up carrying newspapers. D'Exiteuil bought a copy and scanned the front page.

'The Pope sends a message to the peoples of Poland.' He ran a finger further down the page. 'Scientists forecast 20,000 cool years ahead. The glaciers retreated to their present positions about 11,000 years ago, but now the cooling is beginning again. During the next 20,000 years, we can expect that considerable depths of ice will build up over the Northern Hemisphere. They could reach as far south as Milan. The cause is irregularities in the Earth's orbit.'

He looked up, grinning.

'So says *Oggi in Ermalpa*. It means the end of England.'

'Yes, and France. Not a political collapse but a geophysical one.'

They walked briskly up a side street, where men in aprons were sweeping shop fronts, brushing water into the gutter. The first side street they had tried was entirely blocked by parked Fiats, beached like whales on either pavement as well as down the centre of the roadway. The street they were traversing held a mixture of offices, apartments, shops, and a restaurant or two. Outside one of the restaurants, men in shirt-sleeves were unloading containers of fish from a cart. They paused to allow the two visitors to pass.

The top of the street formed an intersection with the broad Via Milano. The Via Milano divided its opposing traffic flows with narrow islands of green on which palm trees grew. Traffic was thick at this hour.

13

A short distance along on the other side of the road, the Grand Hotel Marittimo faced them. It had a heavy facade of lichenous stone, with a high portico imitating a grander structure. It was set back only slightly from the uproar of the road. Despite its name, it offered its guests no glimpse of the sea from its old-fashioned bedroom windows. Last century, perhaps, it had stood where it could command a splendid view of the sailing ships in the harbour. Since then, upstart lanes of banks, offices and shops had come between it and the water.

Above the entrance, a nylon banner hung. On it were the words:

FIRST INTERNATIONAL CONGRESS OF INTERGRAPHIC CRITICISM

Of the four doors of thick plate glass set inside its porch, only one opened. The two men bowed to each other and went through it.

The heat, light, and noise of the outside were replaced by a melancholy coolness.

The foyer of the Grand Hotel was extremely capacious. Its floors and balustrades gave an impression of marble, its reception desks of fumed oak. To either side, this effect tailed off into cloakrooms or petty chambers in which a man might wait for a mistress, or smoke a cigar, or pretend to write a letter. In one petty chamber stood a glass case offering Capodimonte pottery and other objects to the tourists' gaze. A similar case (both with curly bronze feet, betraying their age) displayed a number of silk ties.

Such subsidiary matters did not detract from the chief glory of the foyer, a centrally placed white marble of Paolo and Francesca in the Second Circle of Hell, by Canova. Squire had identified it as soon as he entered the hotel the previous evening, recalling involuntarily the volume of Dante's *Inferno* with Doré illustrations, which his father had bought, and the line where Dante comments on the fate of these lovers:

> Alas! by what sweet thoughts, what fond desire,
> Must they at length to that ill pass have reached!

When he had first read the passage, he had been too innocent to understand what the lovers had done to deserve such punishment. This morning at the hotel breakfast table, between pineapple juice and bacon and eggs, he had written a postcard to his daughters, referring to the statue jokingly as 'two undressed people retreating from something rather nasty'. Whilst writing, he had averted his mind from the actual situation of Ann and Jane, who were in the care of his sister Deirdre in Blakeney.

The postcard had come from a temporary stall set up on the threshold of the conference hall. The stall had extended itself this morning, and was staffed by smiling students, two girls, presumably from the faculty of Ermalpa University involved with the conference. Prominent on the bookstall among other titles were the English edition of *Frankenstein Among the Arts*, published by Webb Broadwell, and the new Italian translation of the same, *Frankenstein a 'la Bella Scuola'* in its glowing orange jacket. Also on display was the American paperback edition of Squire's earlier book, a collection of essays entitled *Against Barbarism*. It was published when television had still to make him famous, and had not achieved an Italian translation.

Standing by the bookstall was a white board announcing that the television series had been captured on videotape and would be shown in its entirety over the four evenings of the conference, Wednesday to Saturday inclusive, at twenty-three hundred hours. In the small conference hall. No admission charge.

Delegates were crowding round the stall, which did brisk business. A number of other delegates stood about the main foyer, in groups or singly. The sight of them was enough to remind d'Exiteuil and Squire, if they needed reminding, that they were fragments of a greater whole, and they moved away from each other without a word of parting.

The polyglot d'Exiteuil appeared to know everyone here. He could have been observed at breakfast, making a courteous round of the tables, welcoming his guests. Squire, who spoke no Italian, knew few people. He moved politely among the delegates, smiling and nodding.

'Ah, Signor Squire. Good morning.'

Squire looked at the slender man who confronted him. He was fairly typical of what Squire regarded as the medium-young generation of Italians: born after the Second World War ended, but torn by the divisiveness of the peace. He had dark liquid eyes, which darted nervously about as if the foyer was full of enemies. He had a trim beard, kept his hair oiled and combed, wore a cappuccino-coloured suit, and was remarkably tidy. His manners were polite; he had a certain style; and there were many men rather like him.

This man Squire could identify. His nervous eagerness was familiar.

'Carlo Morabito,' he said, holding out his hand. 'Animal Behaviour. You remember me? How nice to see you here, Signor Squire. I never dreamed you would be in Sicily. You have taken a walk already?'

As they shook hands, Squire said, 'I was up early. I am a yoga freak.' Seeing the other's blank look, he said, 'I practise yoga.'

'Oh, you practise yoga, eh? I now work at the University of Ermalpa. Before, I was at Milan, when we last met at your Norwich Symposium, three years away.'

At that, Squire's memory grudgingly yielded a few details. With help from the University of East Anglia, he had organized a symposium on *Animals in the Popular Imagination*, which had turned into a lot of fun for the local children, if nothing else. Morabito, already making his name in his field, had been invited to contribute, and had been almost as big a success as Desmond Morris.

'That was a good occasion.'

'You know, Signor Squire, best time for me was when we finished the symposium and you kindly drove me to your lovely house. We had tea on the lawn and your wife served it, helped by another lady. It was a perfect English place and I don't forget it.'

'I remember you achieved a perfect understanding with our Dalmatian, Nellie.'

'And with your pretty daughters.'

'Ann and Jane. Yes, they are lovely.'

The Italian sighed, cleared his throat, shuffled his feet. 'One day I get married also. I also would like two lovely daughters. Your wife told me when I was at your house that every year you have a pop festival in your gardens, like Woodstock and Knebworth. Is it so?'

'They were only small festivals. Nothing grand, but great fun. We had The Who one year and they were fantastic. We've stopped doing it now, I'm afraid. It got too complicated and too expensive . . . How do you like the university here?'

'I take you round for inspection, if you like, one evening.' Morabito looked anxious, fixing Squire with his luminous eyes. 'About the delegates to this conference, I have some doubts. Do you know many of them personally?'

'Only a few. You must know many more.'

Morabito made an expressive gesture and moved closer to Squire. 'I tell you, maybe I shouldn't tell this, but I think many are second-rate, and you will be disappointed. Another thing – they have here the Russians.'

'A couple of them. We're pretty safe – they're outnumbered. You have to invite them these days if you want to seem international.'

'For myself, I don't like the Russians and just having them here will not make a crowd of provincials seem at all international. You will see how these small men bow to the Russians. Excuse my saying so.'

Squire smiled. 'I'm glad of the information. Frankly, I'm a bit lost. Are you going into the conference hall now?'

'Yes, yes. It's time for the procedure to start.' He gestured Squire in ahead of him.

'We'll have a glass of wine together later.'

'I will buy you one, in return for that tea-time in your English garden.'

The conference room was situated at the rear of the hotel, through a marble gallery lined by busts interspersed with plants – an elegant place in which to saunter. Beyond the gallery, the chamber in which all sessions were to be held was walled by mirrors framed in gilt. Three large chandeliers glittered over the green baize hectares of the table. At the far end of the chamber behind arches, a small area was set apart for any members of the general public who might wish to attend. Above was a balcony, in which some members of the press were gathering.

In an adjoining chamber, reached by wide shallow steps, four glass booths had been built; inside the booths the interpreters sat waiting, ready to translate anything into, or out of, English, Italian, French, and Russian. Behind the glass, their expressions were apprehensive as they watched the delegates enter.

The delegates ambled round the table, looking for their places, pushing politely.

By each place was a name card, a microphone, a folder and pencil, a shining drinking glass with a sanitary paper lid, and a bottle of San Pellegrino mineral water still beaded from the refrigerator. Thomas Squire found his name looking up at him, and sat down, laying his briefcase before him. He was seated at the top of the table, with Jacques d'Exiteuil on his right and the secretary, Gianni Frenza, beyond d'Exiteuil. On Squire's left was a place for a delegate from the Soviet Union, Vasili Rugorsky.

At meetings elsewhere, Squire would have taken his jacket off and hung it over the back of his chair, as much to make other people feel comfortable as for his own ease. He saw that the delegates here preferred to be formal. He sat down, content to be there before his neighbours arrived; an element of ascendancy enters into everything.

He opened his folder. In it was a ballpoint pen, clipped to a timetable of the sessions of the conference with a list of speakers. Tucked into the pocket of the folder were some foil-wrapped perfumed tissues for refreshing the face and hands, and a map of the city of Ermalpa and surroundings, presented by courtesy of the local tourist board.

A separate dossier, on variously coloured papers, presented biographies of the main speakers, with Squire's heading the list. He looked it through idly. It had been copied and abridged from *Who's Who* or some similar work of reference; he reflected on how curiously little the curt sentences told of his real life.

Squire, Thomas Charles. C.B.E. (1969)
B. July, 1929. *Educ:* Orwell Park, Ipswich, 1937–42; Gresham

School, Holt, 1942–45 (First XIV); King's College,
Cambridge, 1947–50.

Mar. Teresa Rosemary Davies, 1951. *Ch.* John, b. 1953; George,
b. 1955 (d. 1959); Ann, b. 1965; Jane, 1966.

Nat. service. Royal Mendips, 1945–46.

BIA, Belgrade, 1946; Exhib. 'Restoration of Serbian Monasteries',
Wellcome Hall, 1950; 'American Noises', Newnham College,
Camb., 1950; 'Microgroovey: Style in L.P. Record Covers',
Verlaine Gallery, London, 1954–55; 'Piranesi Goes Pop', ICA,
1962; 'On the Road Roadshow', ICA, 1965.

Regal Insurance, dir., 1951-

Lect., Univ. of East Anglia, 1958-

Prs., Anglo-Yugoslav Assoc., 1964-

Ch. and dir., Hyde Park Pop Expo, 1968. Founder, Soc. For Pop.
Aesthetics, 1969. Lect. in Pop Aesthetics at Berkeley (1971),
Bahrain (1973), Austin, Texas (1975) Univs. Ch., Animals in
the Popular Imagination Symp., Norwich, 1975.

Pubs. Against Barbarism, 1960; Cult and Culture, 1975;
Frankenstein Among the Arts, 1978.

Fellow, King's College, Cambridge; Wolfson, Oxford.

T.V., How Serbia Served the West, 1965. Frankenstein Among
the Arts, 1978.

Clubs, Travellers, Arts,

Home, Pippet Hall, Hartisham, Norfolk, England. *Tel.*,
Thursford 336.

The desiccated facts were followed by extracts from an interview
published in *The Times* some years earlier. There was also a photograph,
reproduced in green on yellow paper, but nevertheless distinct. It was,
in its way, quite a famous photograph, having served as a still to advertise
'Frankenstein Among the Arts'. Squire was dressed in a flapping canvas
shirt and swimming trunks; beside him was Laura Nye in a bikini, hair
streaming, in her role as Sex Symbol of the series; they were jumping
through the shallow waves of the North Sea. The photo, more than the
potted biog., said something about Squire's life style.

Also included in the presentation folder were envelopes and a pad of A4 paper of good quality, handsomely decorated with the name of the Faculty of Iconographic Simulation, University of Ermalpa, Sicily. Below the inscription was the symbol of the conference, five red tulips on parallel stalks – or they could be lollipops or hearts – the iconography was deliberately ambiguous – with one stalk, the longest, branching off sideways at right angles, with a spearhead – or was it a rocketship with vapour trail? – neatly piercing a red sun. At the top of the paper on the other side, was another symbol, the symbol of the organization of which Thomas Squire was founder and president, SPA, the Society for Popular Aesthetics, with the S and the A buttressing the big P with a wide eye in its centre. Squire recognized the placing of this hieroglyph as at once a tribute to him and an insinuation. They wanted his organization.

One hundred and fifty delegates from fifteen countries were listed in the programme. The seating round the table, as a rapid computation showed, allowed for only half that number to appear. Fairly standard practice.

Squire watched the delegates seat themselves, observing their various ploys. An arrangement of pens. A watch removed from wrist and prominently displayed – LCD digital quartz most likely, to judge by its brutal shape, possibly new. A manly and immediate attack on the mineral-water bottle. Earnest writing of notes. Intense communication with one's next-door neighbour. A deliberate stare towards the ornate ceiling. Someone whistling. Smiling. Frowning. Everything equally effective, really, in asserting one's individuality, if one needed to do so.

Gianni Frenza, the secretary of the conference, said hello to Squire before sitting down. He was a decent solid man with a heavy face and thick shaggy hair which curled over his heavy spectacles. Probably a good family man.

Vasili Rugorsky entered with a colleague. Both bowed formally to Squire before sitting down. Rugorsky had written a curious book on Shakespeare and Evolution, which ranged Shakespearean characters on a sort of evolutionary ladder, starting with the 'youth heroes' like

Romeo and Hamlet and proceeding through Mark Antony and Julius Caesar to Lear and Prospero. A curious work for a Russian critic. His book had been translated into French but not English. Rugorsky was a handsome man in a rather porcine way, his white hair brushed back over a good broad brow. He wore a blue double-breasted suit, with a white handkerchief protruding, neatly folded, from the breast pocket. A bit like a nineteen-forties big bandleader, thought Squire.

Rugorsky's compatriot, according to the notice before him, which he was examining with blunt figures, was Georgi Kchevov. He was listed in the curriculum simply as 'Leningrad critic'. Nobody knew his name. The editor who had been invited, a distinguished academician well known in the West, had not materialized; Kchevov had materialized instead. That too was fairly standard. Kchevov could be a truck driver, judging by his muscles and rugged looks. The gold-rimmed spectacles contributed a parody of a Weimar professor.

The Russians were escorted into the conference hall by one of the vulpine young academics from the University of Ermalpa who played some part in the organization of the conference. Squire observed that Kchevov spoke fluent Italian to this dignitary; Rugorsky maintained a watchful silence, blinking as he gazed about the room. He hardly looked up as the Ermalpan delegate bowed himself away.

When Jacques d'Exiteuil entered through the double doors, his copper hair gleaming, the chatter in the large room was slightly hushed. His arrival was a signal that business was about to begin. Slight but important, he smiled at all and sundry as he advanced, slipping easily from one language to another according to the nationality of the delegate he addressed. Even to the Greek . . .? Well, it sounded remarkably like it.

Using the biography list, Squire started to make a nationality count. Three quarters of the delegates were Italian, over half of them from the University of Ermalpa, which gave the proceedings the provincial air of which Morabito had spoken. There were ten French, five Americans, including the youthful Albert Russell Cantania, who had already made a name for himself in academic circles with his large structural work, *Form Behind Formula*. Had he been invited because he was likely to make a real contribution or because he had an Italian surname? Then a rabble of nationalities, including Squire himself, the only Englishman present. He was sorry to see there was no Yugoslav delegate.

The Americans, two Canadians, and two Australians, who were very young and studying in Ermalpa (and apparently invited along for the ride), all dressed in sloppy style, without ties or jackets; one Canadian wore an old T-shirt with an advertisement for something across his chest. They all seemed to be heavy smokers, lighting up as soon as they slumped into their chairs.

'Are we going to be too hot in here, Tom?' d'Exiteuil asked as he passed Squire and took his seat.

'Temperature's fine as far as I'm concerned.'

'No windows, you notice. Poor psychological effect. Well, we will proceed. We can always scream for ice, I suppose.'

He dropped his head, looking at his watch; his hand rested on his knee. He studied it so hard that Squire looked at his own watch. Nine four on the morning of Wednesday, 13 September. It was the same time in Britain. And where was Teresa and what would she be doing? The possibilities which swam to mind in response to that question made him sigh. He took a deep breath and held it, diverting his attention. D'Exiteuil would not be studying the time but gathering his thoughts for his opening speech.

Something like calm settled round the table.

Frenza whispered to d'Exiteuil and then began speaking into his microphone without standing up. He sounded amiable and relaxed.

Putting on his headphones, Squire twiddled with the translation box. Instructions said Dial 3 for English. He switched to 3, but nothing happened. He noted that the other English-speakers were having trouble.

Then a girl's voice entered his ear, saying in a foreign accent, 'Sorry, he is saying some general words of welcome to delegates, from a number of important people – like the mayor of Ermalpa, I think he said, or maybe – yes, the mayor couldn't be present. The Faculty of Icon – Iconographology Stimulation – well, yes, all from the great University here. The first ever of such international affairs on such a subject and of such an importance. To be in keeping with the modern age and find a way of accessing all the productions of all the mediums generally regarded as of little weight, which is in fact where culture, it begins. So first he'll let Mr Sagrado from the Azienda Autonoma di Turismo di Ermalpa e Nontreale give his address to us.'

Squire glanced covertly at d'Exiteuil, but the chairman was staring ahead, following everything without headphones.

The man from the tourist office rose to his feet and spoke at some length. He praised the conference, its delegates, its objectives. He welcomed everyone to Ermalpa, and hoped that, despite the brevity of their stay, they would be able to forget work for a short while and see something of the beautiful coastline and the city and provinces which were, he could assure them, stuffed with antiquities, not only from Roman times but Norman, Arab, and Gothic periods. On the Sunday, at the close of the conference, there would be an excursion for delegates, in special luxury coaches provided by the Board of Tourism. He also expected that they would have a marvellous discussion in this room where Garibaldi was known to have been, and was only dismayed that he was unable to stay to hear their words of wisdom. He thanked them for listening and sent the mayor's regrets.

Delegates clapped. They murmured among themselves.

The two Russians sitting on Squire's left had remained looking straight ahead, arms folded, not even exchanging a word with each other. The Englishman was conscious of the bulk of Rugorsky in the next chair, and so prepared when the Russian turned to him and remarked, in French, 'The speaker did not mention the cathedral at Nontreale, which is only some kilometres from here. Yet it is famous even in my country for its mosaics.'

'I've heard the mosaics are very fine. I've not been there.'

'Perhaps it will prove possible to go there. Perhaps one can get a coach.'

The impact of his gaze was considerable. For a moment, Squire received the impression that he recognized Rugorsky. The man's eyes were hazel, with a golden gleam at their centre; they were fortified behind marked folds beneath the eye and cheeks positioned high on the face. Looking at Rugorsky, Squire remembered the old Russian saying, 'Scratch a Russian and you will find a Tartar.'

'Possibly we may talk together later.'

'I'd be glad to. I enjoyed your book on Shakespeare.'

D'Exiteuil rose, clutching his beard.

He began to speak in English, then switched to his native language, then, with a small joke, to Italian. He spoke for about half-an-hour, about the nature of the conference and about what they should strive to achieve during the conference. He reminded delegates that they would not be allowed to talk for more than thirty minutes, because of pressure of time, but full or extended versions of their papers would be published later in the proceedings. There was tremendous interest all over the world in what had been termed 'arts of no refinement', the instant clichés and iconophilism in various media given off like radioactive particles by the bourgeois societies of the West. Whole genres were being born which invited categorization and scholarly attention, since these reservoirs of the dystopian imaginary were where we could go to learn most about the social dimensions of contemporary mondial life.

Changing tack slightly, and putting a small restless right hand into his trouser pocket, he went on to praise the University of Ermalpa for having established the Faculty of Iconographic Simulation, and for its foresight in setting Dottore Gianni Frenza at its head. Even better, the University had agreed – not without a couple of years of prompting from the present speaker in his watchdog role as editor of *Intergraphic Studies* – to host this present vitally needed conference. They had secured monies from the International Universities Foundation, for which they were most grateful. And the Ermalpa Tourist Board had been extremely helpful also. The Faculty felt that it was following parameters set down almost a decade ago by that doyen of popular culture, Thomas C. Squire, whose series of TV programmes, 'Frankenstein Among the Arts', had done much to further interest in a vital study area. They esteemed themselves very fortunate to have Tom Squire with them as guest of honour.

Squire appeared pleased at this, nodded to both sides of the table, and restrained himself from reaching for the water glass.

The small hand returned from its trip to the pocket and took a slow circuit through the air in a clockwise direction as d'Exiteuil explained that they hoped this First International Congress of Intergraphic Criticism would first of all promote deeper interest in polyvalent media throughout Italy, and then throughout the rest of the world, including the socialist countries.

He knew that the socialist countries had already begun to express interest, and even to study the subject academically.

As he said this, he turned slightly, to smile beyond Squire at the slightly bowed white head of Vasili Rugorsky.

'I feel bound at this point to inject the personal note,' the interpreter of d'Exiteuil continued. 'I have been personally involved on this issue, and I know that all my colleagues are in general compliance that we have reached significance here only because we have taking part members of one of the foremost nations or I should say states on the planet today. It's the home of most powerful coinages, achieved nowhere else, followed everywhere. Let's just say without emotion how we welcome very much the two colleagues from the USSR, Vasili Rugorsky and Georgi Kchevov.'

D'Exiteuil started to clap his hands, and most of the Italian members joined in. So did the Americans. Other delegates followed suit. Squire, sitting next to Rugorsky, joined in. The applause mounted. The two Russians rose from their chairs, and stood there smiling amiably. Everyone was clapping now, smiling and nodding in agreement to each other.

'*Merci mille fois,*' said Rugorsky. There was general laughter as if a witticism had been delivered. The clapping died. The two Russians sat down. D'Exiteuil raised his left hand, palm inward, letting it drop to a horizontal position as he inclined his head with a similar movement, and then sat down himself. It was not entirely a modest gesture, not when linked with a sly little smile which chased itself into his beard. It appeared to say, 'Well, there you are, *I* gave them to you. It's what you all wanted.'

After a pause, Frenza spoke into his microphone, and the English voice in the earphones said, 'Now our first formal speaker of our first formal session, our guest of honour, Mr Thomas Squire, will address us. Afterwards, just fifteen minutes, please. Thanks, Mr Squire, if you would . . .'

Squire removed his earphones, placing them on the table before him as the clapping died. He regarded the faces round the table. Sharp, intelligent, youthful, for the most part. An audience he, like d'Exiteuil, had worked for.

'Mr Chairman, Ladies and Gentlemen, I must address you in my native tongue, and trust that the interpreters will carry my meaning to you. Will the interpreters please stop me if I go too fast?' His mouth was slightly dry, his heart beating strongly. He was used to the effect; it gave him power and his voice resonance as he breathed deeply. In any case, it would pass as it always did when he got into his stride.

'It's not for me but for our hosts to say "Welcome to Ermalpa"; what I can say is welcome to a select band, the band of people who attack that great open conspiracy, critical contempt of popular culture. That band comprises not only critics but readers, viewers, and general doers. Everyone benefits from popular culture, and a reasoned critical view should be to wish to survey it, not condemn it. The pop art of one generation becomes the classic of the next; Homer was, in his day, the Bronze Age equivalent of the TV soap opera.

'I will remind you of the simple and seminal idea of my founding of SPA, the Society for Popular Aesthetics, which has led to our present encouraging situation here, with the Faculty enjoying IUF support. As a child in the thirties and forties of this century, I was addicted to the cinema, the great popular art form of the period. I went as often as I could in the small town in which I lived. I kept lists of the films I saw, of the actors in them – not only the stars but the minor players – and of the directors and companies who made them. I could tell by the sets and the lighting whether I was watching a film made by MGM or Warner Brothers or Gainsborough.

'All this activity was opposed by my parents. They regarded the cinema simply as a repository for trash, as too many people today regard television. In particular, they disliked the way in which I settled on two actors as my heroes. Those actors were Errol Flynn and Humphrey Bogart. Flynn was at first my particular favourite, then I shifted to Bogart. The bitter and wise-cracking character Bogart played, on whichever side of the law, spoke to me of something enduring in human nature, and personified the man who lives his life battling in obscurity, often against forces of which the rest of the world has no knowledge.

'Although I was quite inarticulate about it, I revered Bogart. For himself and for what he symbolized. My parents came to hate him. To them, Bogart was just a gangster and, if I followed him, I should go the same way. It may sound ridiculous, but so it was; nor is that kind of unthinking opposition to living symbols defunct today. There will always be a vocal minority against whatever is vital in our culture; it prefers what is safely dead.

'The Hollywood system as it was in its hey-day has passed away. In the hour of its downfall, critics suddenly found good things to say about it, where before they had done nothing more than sneer. As soon as Bogart had died, they did the same for him. They pretended they had always praised him. He became – as Elvis Presley did a few years ago – a great cult hero. He was dead, and safe. You recognize one of the themes of *Frankenstein Among the Arts*: praise only for the dead; exile, cultural exile, for the living.

'What we hope to bring about here, and hereafter, is a much wider appreciation of what it is in popular culture which had genuine vitality, and how its roots are always based firmly in the fertile soil of the past, even when that is by no means easily apparent.

'Which brings me to my paper. You will see from your programme that it is entitled "Since the Enlightenment". Because of the time limit sensibly imposed on speakers, I can give only a résumé now. The full paper will be published in our proceedings, and also in the next issue of our friend Jacques's *Intergraphic Studies*. Am I going slowly enough for you, interpreters?'

He caught a flash of smile in one of the boxes, and continued.

'The subject we study is admittedly amorphous. It must often seem even to us that we are all studying different, even conflicting, subjects. I believe that not to be the case, and expect that conferences such as this one will bind more closely together not only our interests but us ourselves. To that end, I hope you will consider a proposal that we should adopt a common term for our diverse subject matter. My suggestion is, "Future Culture". FC for short. Or perhaps you prefer "Symbols Future". SF.

'Under some such heading, we can consider the arts which interest us, the arts of today, the arts scorned by higher criticism in whatever field. You see them listed in your programmes: pinball machines, movies, prophecy, TV, pop art, rock'n'roll, the Top Twenty, science fiction, design, and the rest. Everything from make-up to metropolises. I have nothing against higher criticism, but its analytical tools are honed towards the objectives of its dissection. It has shown itself unable to discuss effectively our Future Culture.

'Because Future Culture is something, according to my definition, which has sprung up since the beginning of the last century. It is either affected by, or the product of, mass-production. The machine has transformed it. A paperback novel, for instance, can be purely a product of the mass-market, designed as a unit package with its cover to sell this month at check-out point in a million supermarkets and never be seen again; or it can be a newly edited edition of Henry James's *The Ambassadors*. What are the differences and similarities between a James novel and the latest catastrophe novel? It's rich ground for investigation.

'Some of our subjects do not claim to be art or even folk art. Car bumper-stickers. I know a man in Toronto studying them now. Are they ripe for something more than sociological study? Some subjects are simply commercial ways of doing traditional things. But are T-shirts a modern equivalent of sandwich-boards or a way of legitimizing graffiti? We have to improvise questions and answers as we go along. Virtually all arts have been touched by the change-compelling system of mass-production and mass-consumption.

'We believe that precisely in this amorphous situation lies a hope for future acculturalization. Improvisation and spontaneity are still possible, contrary to what is sometimes argued. Older arts tend always towards formalization or even fossilization, and never more so than now, as we move towards the eighties, when global change is swift. The fluidity of non-art may become one of the staples of the future. It's up to us to forge a methodology to help direct it constructively.

'I see from the noticeboard in the foyer that some ingenious person on the Faculty of Iconographic Simulation has videotaped my television series, "Frankenstein Among the Arts", and will be showing it in the adjoining small hall for the next three nights. You'll excuse me if I stay in the bar while it's showing – I lived with the series for so long, I almost know it by heart. Of course, it does relate closely to the subject of our discussions. But I must remind you, for all the kindness you have done me, that I am an amateur in a field where you are experts, and I took as my text for the series a tag from the philosopher Gurdjieff, which I discovered long ago in Ouspensky's fascinating book, *In Search of the Miraculous.*

'It's a tag which many authors could use at the front of their books as a warning. Gurdjieff says, speaking of his work, "The object I had in view was to produce an interesting and beautiful spectacle. Of course there is a certain meaning hidden beneath the outward form, but I have not pursued the aim of exposing and emphasizing this meaning."

'Nor have *I*, because I am unable to. I only know that the traditions of the West, strong and honourable though they are, are insufficient to live by. We have to embrace the new and rise up to change.'

2

Flattery and Higher Foolishness

Ermalpa, September 1978

On checking into the Grand Hotel Marittimo, conference delegates had received small books with meal vouchers in them. One voucher had to be presented at every meal, the meal being understood to include a bottle of red wine and half a bottle of mineral water.

Squire entered the dining room of the Grand Hotel a little late for lunch, and found himself with no choice of table. He had been detained by one of the American delegates, Selina Ajdini.

Following the coffee break, four speakers had delivered papers on various aspects of popular culture: Enrico Pelli on 'Psychiatry and the Popular Understanding of Prehistory', Marianne de Suffren on 'Horror Films in Catholic Countries', Geo Camaion, the Romanian delegate, on 'Symbolic Cognition', and finally Selina Ajdini on 'Aldous Huxley as Failed Prophet'.

Since only the last paper had been received in English, rather than in the language peculiar to the interpreters, and since Squire had once met the subject of the paper, and admired his writings, he had paid particular attention to Selina Ajdini.

There was another reason to attend. There were few women at the conference, and only three actually delivering papers. Of those, the most immediately striking was Selina Ajdini.

She carried herself with a defiant air, as if aware of the covertly predatory glances of the young Italians. A heavy brown leather travel bag over one shoulder gave her the air of a soldier – perhaps a soldier in a comic opera. So Squire reflected, seeing her move with the encumbered shoulder thrust forward, one red-nailed hand about the bulk of the bag. She wore a fine blue corduroy suit with a white shirt beneath. Where the blouson jacket gripped her waist, she wore a large-linked gold chain, the end of which jangled as she walked. High leather boots tight to the calf completed the comic opera soldier effect.

Ajdini's face suggested something different. Although she was slenderly built, this slenderness was masked by her clothing; the quality emerged nakedly in her face. It had a bare keenness like a hare's breastbone found on a windy headland, eroded of flesh, robbed of formed associations. The simile occurred to Squire as the woman rose to speak; there was something remote and inhuman, he thought, about that proudly sculpted profile, which the scrupulously coiffed black hair did little to counteract. The remoteness made her age difficult to estimate.

She put spectacles on her nose to read her paper. The paper proved to be littered with references from a dozen languages. Her thesis, as far as it could be distinguished, was that Aldous Huxley's life typified the end of one great strand of English and European bourgeois Romantic thought. The Huxley family typified the nineteenth- and twentieth-century culturally privileged elite, with its Darwinian connections. And that elite typified a repressive class structuralism cloaked by a veneer of scientific and humanistic enlightenment.

It was Ajdini's contention that Huxley's 'life parabola' from Eton and Balliol to the scoured coast of California represented at once a despairing attempt to escape the autocratic vengeance of late capitalist society and a further plunge into a deeply destructive hedonism masked as asceticism (but betrayed by use of drugs).

Although she spoke brightly, Ajdini's summing up was equally dusty in content. Huxley's life represented to pop culture, one of whose idols he had been, a Janus-faced bourgeois prophet with nothing to pronounce upon but the collapse of his kind. While assuming to speak ostensibly for preservation of values such as ecology, Huxley found himself forced to act out prophetically the effete culture of the West. That culture was running into suicidal acts and self-destructive deserts. Prophecy could no longer function under capitalism; there was no science of the future since that future was about to terminate. The picture of laissez-faire sexuality and technology in *Brave New World* was an inadvertent portrait of a way of life already doomed.

It was not even a clever paper, decided Squire, pencilling the words 'Higher Foolishness' on his programme; yet it was tricked out with cleverness. Ajdini's reference to Romanticism came adorned with learned references to European Romanticism, wherein was pointed out (in parentheses) that, although English and German Romanticisms were well propagandized, in reality the great Manzoni of Italy, and of course the Russians with Pushkin and Lermontov, not to mention other East European figures working in Slav, Hungarian, Romanian, Georgian, and other languages extending as far as the Caucasus and further, where the authenticity of folk poetry and (for example) the romantic letter had become truly popular, much more tellingly represented the Romantic tradition at grass-roots level.

When Ajdini sat down, a French delegate asked a lengthy but footling question, to do with the relationship between Huxley's *Brave New World* and the 'plays of protest' of Shakespeare – or, as he believed, Lord Bacon – particularly *The Tempest*, as interpreted through the monopolistic tendencies of late-nineteenth-century scientism. Ajdini answered quite briskly, smiling and making an unscripted joke, in which it was apparent that she had been misled by the interpreter and missed the drift of the question. Frenza then intervened, thanked the main speakers for their contributions, and adjourned the meeting until sixteen hundred hours.

As delegates poured from the hall, Selina Ajdini was waiting among the ferns of the marble gallery. She advanced towards Squire, travel bag thrust forward, smiling and holding out her hand. Her big blue-rimmed spectacles still on her nose made her eyes – of a much more elusive shade of blue – look large and defenceless.

'Mr Squire, we have not met and it is my great pleasure that we do so now; I attended your Pop Expo in London a decade ago, and marvelled like everyone else. It is wonderful that you came to Ermalpa. My name is Selina Ajdini and I am Associate Professor in Comparative Stylistics at the University of the Gulf in Galveston, Texas. This year I have a sabbatical in Europe East and West, with a roving commission for the Frankfurt-am-Main magazine *Die Spitze*.'

Seen close to, she looked older than Squire had estimated. Probably in her forties.

'I used to know Ted Zold, head of the English department at Gulf.'

And no less attractive for that.

'Ted's retired just this year. He's working on the Yale edition of the correspondence of Howard Dean Efflinger.' She spoke English without an American accent, rather with some kind of European intonation Squire could not place. Her voice was pleasant – if 'pure and clear as a mountain stream', then the associations with the hare bone picked bare on the headland were still present in Squire's mind. Her lips were thin and coral pink; they moved delightfully, whatever she was saying. He transferred his gaze to the blue eyes; the diatribe against Huxley had left him too affronted for any ready supply of conversation.

She was presenting her credentials in a sophisticated way, chatting about an acquaintance of his whom she had met in Budapest. She punctuated her talk with 'Thank you', and 'You're very kind' to delegates who, passing by, felt compelled to offer her congratulations on her speech. This she did without in any way dissipating the impression that she was deep in conversation with the man she regarded as most important. The leather travel bag, turning gently on the left hip, touched Squire's right thigh; the slender hand with the scarlet nails, adorned additionally with a slender silver and a fat amber ring, remained grasping the callipygous leather.

'You are part of the reason I am in Ermalpa, Mr Squire, and I hope that maybe we could get together this evening and you would allow me to interview you for *Die Spitze*? They plan a special number for the spring on Contemporary Thinkers. You probably know that "Frankenstein Among the Arts" has been running on German television earlier this summer.'

'I never give interviews,' he said, smiling to break the force of the words.

She yielded gracefully, smiling in return so that the coral lips parted on pretty white teeth. 'I understand. Perhaps we could talk anyway and I could indulge in a little hero-worshipping over a drink or two.'

'That would be pleasant.'

The slender hand came out. 'Seven o'clock then, in the bar.'

He made off towards the dining room palming his hair into place, gripping his briefcase tightly under one arm. 'Acting out prophetically the effete culture of the West . . .'

Most of the tables in the dining hall were already fully occupied.

Courtesy demanded that he should not appear to show preferences at this early stage of the proceedings. He made himself sit at the nearest table. In some respects, it looked the least inviting, in that the two Russians were seated there with the secretary, Gianni Frenza, and two other delegates whose names Squire did not know.

He took hold of the back of the spare chair and smiled questioningly, with a gesture of the hand. All five rose or just failed to rise in polite fashion. As he seated himself, Frenza introduced him formally to the two Russians, Georgi Kchevov with the gold-rimmed spectacles and rugged looks – close to, his rough red skin and blunt nose made him look even more an inhabitant of trucks rather than classrooms – and the white-haired Vasili Rugorsky.

Frenza then introduced the other two men as delegates from the Federal Republic of Germany, Frank Krawstadt and Herman Fittich. Both smiled and shook Squire's hand. Krawstadt was an untidy wiry man of perhaps thirty-two with a straggle of yellow beard and a raw spotty face, the very opposite of the spruce young Italians.

Herman Fittich was a more comfortable figure in his early fifties, with white sideboards to his hair; he wore a neat grey suit. Although his face and manner were bland, Fittich gave Squire an appraising look as he shook hands. Apparently satisfied with what he saw, he remarked in perfect English, 'This is a time when we are apt to lean a bit heavily on compliments, but I'm perfectly genuine when I say that I have long appreciated many aspects of your work. You're learned but you're also kind to your readers. You permit us the luxury of a low boredom threshold.'

'Good of you to say so. If you like whisky, never get a teetotaller to write about it.'

Fittich chuckled. 'I'm sure Humphrey Bogart couldn't have put it fairer than that. Let's call the waiter for you. The food's good.'

'It smells good.'

'The dining room is as grand as the conference hall – a token of the esteem in which the sensible Italians hold the arts of the stomach,' Fittich replied.

In honour of the conference, vases of flowers stood on small tables round the sides of the room. Carnations in silver vases stood on every table, next to the glasses containing upright packets of *grissini*.

Any formality these arrangements might have induced was dispelled by the waiters. They were encouragingly numerous, and in general broad-stomached middle-aged men with oiled black hair and docile countenances; they were supported by young eager men learning this most rewarding of trades. They moved with fatherly dignity, aware of their importance, and in no time a delicious soup was set before Squire, a roll of warm brown bread provided on his side-plate, and red wine and mineral water poured into the two glasses by his right hand.

'We met once before in the Tate Gallery in London during March of 1970,' said Rugorsky to Squire in slightly majestic French, as his Russian colleague, Fittich, and Krawstadt were picking up the threads of their previous conversation. 'It was during the Richard Hamilton exhibition, and Leslie Lippard-Milne was showing me round. You have forgotten it.'

He regarded Squire steadily.

Although he had forgotten, Squire found the memory returned, so that he said, 'Why, yes – and I even remember that we met in front of . . .' Teresa had been with him then, wearing a smart new suit they had acquired in Mayfair, where they were staying at Brown's Hotel; she had been so pleased with it that she had worn it immediately and had her old suit sent round to the hotel.

'We were introduced in front of "Hugh Gaitskell as a Famous Monster of Filmland", one of the early landmarks of pop art,' Rugorsky said. 'We talked about the insights to be derived from the common-place – as you say, the feeling behind a banal phrase, or, as I say, the sense of evolution even behind very static things such as a multinational company or a bureaucracy.'

His eyelids were heavy and fleshy, in common with his face; they descended slightly as he spoke, masking his glittering eyes which nevertheless firmly maintained Squire's gaze.

Squire remembered both the gaze and the man now, chiefly through his sly and testing sense of humour. Good mood restored, he said, 'There's also the emptiness behind a banal phrase to be considered. We may have problems, I think, in understanding the difference between banality and sincerity.' The soup was delicious.

'D'accord. Just as insight is not always found behind complex phraseology. There again we see the spoor of evolution – mankind invents all its many languages not only for communication, but also as anti-communication devices, to keep out strangers.'

It was always a good idea to test Russians out with George Orwell, whose works were banned in the Soviet Union. 'Orwell said that even the art of writing is largely the perversion of words.'

'I know it. But Orwell also says that the whole meaning of a word is in its slowly acquired associations, and that is untrue – or is no longer true, or not if you believe that it is the duty of those who still can to distinguish between true and false to do so continuously. One of the attractions of words these days – this I observe mostly in the West, by the way – is that they should be new, fresh, mysterious, and therefore carry thought forward. "Escalation" was a fashionable word last time I was in London. Now, even in Paris, "Trade-off" is very popular. There is also something called "The Crunch".'

'The Crunch is what you get from a good *grissino*,' said Squire, suiting action to words as one of the fatherly waiters took his empty soup plate away, and substituted a generous helping of lasagne. 'I seem to think that after our meeting in the Tate we had a drink in the bar.'

'Or,' said Rugorsky, again fixing a veiled scrutiny on Squire, to see how his remark went down, 'to speak more precisely, several drinks. Mr Lippard-Milne became quite merry. Remind me please of the name of his attractive wife.'

'Sheila.'

'Ah, yes.' Rugorsky smiled to himself. 'Sheila.'

'Such new words are usually generated by small groups,' said Fittich, breaking from his own conversation in German with Krawstadt and Frenza and speaking in English across the carnations to Squire and Rugorsky. 'So there is always a certain cachet in using such words, implying one is an insider. In consequence, they pass quickly through the social system. We live in a world of bottlenecks, chain reactions, different ballgames, and indeed "different ballgame situations". And we are constantly hoping that things are *going to gel*.'

Squire explained the word 'gel' in French to Rugorsky. 'A situation that has not gelled is considered to be a liquid rather like hot jelly. As it cools, it goes through a phase-change, setting into a definite form. Would you say that this conference has yet gelled?'

Rugorsky, who had turned his scrutiny on Fittich, asked the latter, 'Excuse me, you are a philologist?'

'I'm sorry, I do not speak French.'

'Then I suppose I must speak in English. We have only a few days here to make ourselves understood to one another.'

As the waiters brought in steaming dishes of fish and macaroni, which Gianni Frenza said was a local speciality, Fittich observed, 'My belief is that the cuisine is gelling into rather a success. Too much of this pasta and I may undergo a slight phase-change myself in the region of my middle.'

After the meal, the Russians excused themselves and Frenza slipped away to consult d'Exiteuil. Squire and Fittich decided to take a turn in the street; Krawstadt crossed the foyer with them and excused himself at the doors. He had no English, as Squire had no German worth mentioning.

They walked in silence along the Via Milano, or exchanged small talk about the goods on display in shop windows.

'It must be important to you that this conference succeeds,' said Fittich, as they waited to cross the next intersection. 'Although I believe – or I'm given to understand – that many of the Italians are well-known in their own specialized fields, yours is the only celebrity name. I wondered why you chose to associate yourself with the proceedings.'

'I've known Jacques d'Exiteuil for some years. And his wife, Séverine. That's one answer. Another answer is that I am not an academic so, unlike the academics here, I have little at stake. Also – third reason – well, I am rather at a loss at home.'

'I should not have thought that to be possible.'

After a silence, when they turned down a side street towards the sea, Fittich said, 'Sorry, you may have thought I was probing. Perhaps I was. My expression of admiration over lunch for your work was not idle. I forget you probably will not know of me, since my work goes on in Germany, and is in any case not on the scale of your "Frankenstein Among the Arts".

'I should tell you that I am a rather old-fashioned teacher of literature at the University of Bad Neustadt, which is not all that far from Würzburg and rather too close to the frontier with the so-called German Democratic Republic.'

'Of course I know Würzburg, and the Residenz with its beautiful Tiepolos. For that matter, I know the GDR . . . What literature do you teach?'

'German and English. Mainly old-fashioned literature, before this century. But as a matter of fact I am not averse to the contemporary forms of fiction, and have held courses on the masters of crime, such as Hammett, Chandler, and Bardin, a personal favourite. I'm also devoted to science fiction, on which topic I am to deliver my paper tomorrow.'

When they were half-way down the steep little street, Squire pointed ahead.

'There's the Mediterranean, still looking inviting. Well, I'm looking forward to hearing your paper, though the interpreters will do their best to make sure that we all hear something other than your intention.'

'Isn't it awful? The German translation is terrible. Well, it isn't even German. However, I shall do my best. You may sight a few dim landmarks here and there, through the fog. For instance, I shall have an opportunity to mention the writings of Aldous Huxley rather more favourably than was done by the American lady this morning.'

He shot Squire a quick interrogative look, a mild smile playing about his lips.

'You could hardly speak more *adversely*. "Acting out prophetically the suicidal tendencies of the West . . ."'

'Exactly.' Fittich exhaled. He walked with his arms hanging relaxedly by his side.

They came to the bottom of the street and paused. Ahead, beyond a double line of traffic, were flats, walls, and then sheds, shutting them off from the Mediterranean which, from farther up the steep side road, had been visible as an inviting strip of blue.

'The entrance to the harbour's farther along. This is about as near as I got to the sea this morning.'

'Oh well, we must resign ourselves,' said Fittich, in the tone of one well-accustomed to resigning himself. 'At least we had our sight of the sea, and a little exercise. Now I shall return happily to the hotel. I am very pleased to make your acquaintance.'

'The next session is not until four o'clock. We could walk along this way.'

'I wish to have a siesta, thanks all the same.' He smiled apologetically and tugged at his neat grey sideburns.

'Then I'll walk back with you. I flew in rather late last night, and an hour's snooze will help keep me awake through the afternoon papers.'

They turned, walking side by side.

After a silence, Fittich said, 'My considered opinion is that it really requires more delicacy to form critical opinions about the popular culture of today which we find all around us than it is to deal with the illustrious dead, such as Beethoven or Goethe. One needs an open mind and a specific vocabulary.'

'We got a lot of Marxist-Leninist vocabulary this morning, didn't we?'

'Are they only talking to themselves? Do they not enjoy what they speak about? Well, I shall console myself with your remark – "If you like whisky, never get a teetotaller to write about it."'

They laughed. 'Let's have a whisky together this evening,' said Squire. 'I have to go out for an hour or two, but will be back by about ten o'clock.'

'Fine. A great pleasure.' They had reached the doors of the hotel. 'I want to talk more with Vasili Rugorsky. He seemed a decent enough chap.'

'I thought so too.'

'Of course, the decent ones generally turn out to be KGB men, don't they?'

In the foyer, Squire checked his stride and went to look at the rack of postcards.

'We shan't see much of the island. Might as well buy a postcard.'

'Well, I will detain you no longer. Some of the more important people here will wish to speak with you.'

'Oh, don't say that, Herr Fittich. I'm delighted to have your company. Look at this, the Villa Igiea. Beautiful, eh? I'd like a villa right there, pitched on the cliff.'

He waved a postcard of the ruins of a Roman dwelling, reduced to no more than half a dozen columns, set on the edge of the sea among pines, looking out to distant islands.

'You also have a pleasant house in England, Pippet Hall,' said Fittich.

Squire turned to face him. 'Why do you say that?'

Fittich looked nervous. 'My apologies, I should not have made the silly remark. To be honest with you, in the spring I visited your home in Norfolk. Pippet Hall. It was when your television series was actually being shown and your name was everywhere. I happened to stay with an English friend who, like me, is an admirer of your series. Well, we passed by your gates. I was astonished to find such a grand house visible from the road, not hidden, and close to the village, unlike most fine houses.

'To be frank with you, I stuck my camera through your gates. You will think it a terrible cheek. And as I was about to snap, a charming lady appeared in my lens, strolling along with a young man towards the gate. It was exactly what I needed to complete the composition. I opened the gate for her. She smiled at me and said she hoped I had got a good shot. Back at my friend's car, I looked at the photograph of you with your family on the back jacket of your book. It was your wife I had passed a word with. We drove off, I in great delight. And it turned out to be a good picture. I should have had the decency to have posted your wife a copy of it.'

'I'm glad it turned out well. Excuse me, I'll see you later.'

Looking slightly puzzled at Squire's abruptness, Fittich said, 'My apologies for detaining you. But knowing you would be here as our star guest, I brought you a copy of the photograph. Please allow me.' As he spoke, he was bringing a leather wallet from the inner pocket of his jacket. He removed a colour print from the recesses of the wallet and, smiling, passed it to Squire.

The house in its mellow red brick appeared to nestle among trees and the giant rhododendron bushes which served as windbreaks on its east side. All looked serene and peaceful in the spring sun. In the foreground was Teresa Squire, wrapped in a warm coat, her head on one side with a gesture of suspicion directed at the intrusive photographer; it was a look Squire knew well. By her side, but hanging back, perhaps also in response to the sight of a camera, was a lean young man in jeans, his narrow face notable chiefly for sharp side-whiskers.

As a look of pain passed across Squire's face, Fittich said, 'Did you wish to keep this print? I trust that your wife is well, Mr Squire?'

'We were parted when you took this shot. Thanks, but I don't want it – not because of her.

'Because of *him*.'

Upstairs in Room 143, Squire locked the door and took off his shirt and trousers. He sat by one wall in the lotus position, gazed at the wall before him, and practised *pranayama*. A yogi in Southall had once told him that, through correct breathing, modern man could regenerate himself; Squire, who liked to hope, partly believed the yogi.

Nevertheless, when he rose to his feet twenty minutes later, he was left with a desire to phone England, and to be informed. He put through a call, not to his wife or his sister, but his London publisher, Ron Broadwell of Webb Broadwell Ltd.

After an hour's wait, the number rang, and Broadwell's secretary came on the line. 'Hello, Mr Squire, I'm afraid Mr Broadwell's out. Can I help?'

'Oh, I just wondered if Ron had any news for me.'

'Yes, we heard this morning that your American publisher has put a reprint of 20,000 copies in hand. So that's good, isn't it?'

'Splendid. Is Ron at lunch?'

'Yes, he's still at lunch. He should be back by four. I'll tell him you rang.'

The genial Ron Broadwell was lunching – unknown to the world – with Squire's sister, Deirdre Kaye. They lunched together once a year in the Hyde Park Hotel, Knightsbridge, and had done so ever since the fifties when, as undergraduates at Cambridge, they had consummated a brief love affair in the hotel. Since then, both had married Americans, and the affair was long over.

They remained good friends and still enjoyed their secret annual meeting. This year it was Deirdre's turn to pay. A delegation of Chinese in sober business suits was eating Dover sole in unison at a nearby table. Deirdre and Broadwell had both ordered *cotelettes d'Agneau Madelon*, and were drinking a claret with them.

'I saw your mother's obituary in *The Times*,' Broadwell said. 'Tom didn't expect me to come up to Hartisham for the funeral, did he?'

'Good God, no. But we've met since then. That was the Christmas before last.'

He looked embarrassed. 'I lose account of the time nowadays. So it was.'

'You're not having an affair with another woman, are you?'

'I promised always to be faithful to you. The lamb's good.'

'Looking back, I can see what a snob she was. I suppose that generation were. The Hodgkinses do tend to be. I remember mother's advice to me on my twenty-first. "Always look first-rate," she said. "Dress becomingly, wash thoroughly, particularly between the legs, always hold yourself properly. Keep a fit expression on your face at all times. Remember you're a Squire, gel."'

She had given a precise imitation of her mother, and Broadwell laughed. 'She was rather grand. "Always look first-rate." I like that. She did look a bit first-rate.'

'Oh yes. Those hats. Drank like a fish towards the end. Tom preferred not to notice. Tom likes to maintain the family image.' The cutlets were tiny, delicately done, and served with a *sauce Madère*; she cut one in half and raised it to her mouth.

'It's quite a relief to be married to old Marsh. As an American, he doesn't grasp all the implications of being a Squire gel, so I've escaped all that. More or less.'

Broadwell gazed at her over his glass. In her late forties, Deirdre Kaye had grown rather like her brother. There were the same strong features, the same marked lines beside the mouth, even the same way of carrying the head. He enjoyed their relationship, and was not sorry that it was no closer. He also reflected that she was more Squire-like than her brother.

'Belinda simplifies my life. "Cut out all that English bullshit," she'll say. Not that she hasn't plenty of bullshit of her own. By the way, she informs me that *The Times* may cease publication. Staff troubles – the unions, of course. Can you credit it? Life won't be the same. I'm one publisher who'll suffer if the TLS goes.'

'Belinda's fun for you, Ron. What you deserve. They are tasty, aren't they?'

'Was Tom very upset by Patricia's death?'

'You know Tom. Nothing upsets him. One of his worst characteristics. Now he is head of the family, etc. We don't see much of Adrian, except at Christmas. I guess being a Squire boy is a bit of a responsibility. Notice Tom always looks first-rate. Ideal telly fodder.'

'He came over very well on the box. More wine? How is his relationship with Teresa? I daren't ask him, not after the great bust-up at my house last New Year's Eve.'

'I'm getting such an alcoholic in my old age. It's all a mess. I suppose you know he's not actually at Pippet Hall any more? First he stayed at his club, now he's got a flat somewhere in Paddington, of all places.'

'I know. Chops were good. He could have stayed with us. The dogs are worse than children, though. Mind you, the first meal we ever had here was the best.' He wiped his lips on his napkin and grinned at her. She had grown softer over the years – not to mention plumper.

'There was a woman Tom had the hots for a while back. He thought Marsh and I didn't know, but I happened to find out. Sheila Lippard-Milne. Rather a saucy bit of goods, saucier than Teresa by a long chalk.'

She drained her glass and beckoned the waiter over.

'I know Sheila. I published a book by her husband. He's a bit of a wet, but quite a sound art historian. What about sweet? Our Hungarian tart as usual?'

'Two *Dobos Torta*,' she told the waiter. 'I think the waiters change every year. This chap's a Cypriot or something. The chef seems permanent, thank God. They'd make a good pair.'

'The chef and the waiter?'

'Tom and Sheila Lippard-Milne. He needs jollying up.'

'We'd make a good pair. Then your Marshall could marry my Belinda.' He reached out and took her hand.

'My God, Belinda'd *eat* Marsh . . .'

44

'Missed you while you were in Greece.'

'You never think of me. It was nice to escape the strikes, I suppose. The hotel on Minos is dreadful, not even picturesque. I took along my watercolours, like a good Squire gel, but never used them.'

'The sign of an irredeemable nature,' he said, beaming at her.

The sweet trolley arrived. The *Dobos Torta* looked and tasted as delicious as in previous years.

3

A View from the Beach

The world underwent one of its amazing simplifications. First and nearest was the great band of beach, decorated in bas-relief with a complex ripple pattern; then a sliver of sky-coloured lagoon left by the retreating tide; then a band of lighter sand, then a drab donkeyish strip of distant fern and grass; then a band of dark green, formed from the long line of Corsican pines which stood guard between land and beach, allowing pale sky among the colonnades of its trunks; then the enormous intense blue summer sky, sailing up to zenith, beyond capturable reach of camera.

The equipment and human figures were reduced to toy scale by the expanse of beach.

Thomas Squire was wearing a blue canvas shirt and a pair of brown swimming trunks. He was up to his knees in almost motionless sea, moving steadily towards the shore.

Beside him was a gorgeously tanned girl in her mid-twenties. Her thick fair hair streamed over her shoulders in the light off-shore breeze. She wore a black bikini with artificial white roses stitched round the line of her breasts. She was laughing and vivacious, the very embodiment of seaside girls on posters everywhere, and paid Squire no attention as he acted out his part.

'The sea is always close to our thoughts in Europe, because it has played such a part in history. It may also have played a considerable part in pre-history, if mankind reverted to marine life at a stage in its early career. I think of that theory whenever the annual summer pilgrimage to the nearest strip of beach begins. The human race then shows a tendency to cluster like penguins on the shores of the Antarctic, as if we were all about to revert to the sea again, having found life on land a little too complex.'

He and the girl were almost ashore. There were no waves, only the purest warm ripples of water which glided up the beach like liquefied sunlight.

'The sea that most possesses the European imagination is the Mediterranean, the sea at the middle of the Earth. It's the cradle of our culture, the home waters of Greece and Rome. This is not the Mediterranean but the North Sea. I love this stretch of the North Norfolk coast, and the docile summer North Sea, not only because it is much less crowded and despoiled than most of the Mediterranean coast, but because I happen to live within ten miles of this particular beach. As you see, the water in late June is entirely warm enough for our Sex Symbol to sport in.

'If I mentioned the name of the beach, that advertisement would cause it to become crowded within a year.

'Such is the power of advertising. Advertising in various media frequently makes use of the sea and, of course, of sex symbols such as this young lady by my side. If I mentioned her name, she would become a character, not a symbol; such is the power of names.

'Her skin is really white, not brown, but she has applied suntan oil to satisfy tradition. The image of brown girl in blue water has proved strongly evocative ever since sea-bathing became fashionable last century.

'You may believe that such images demean women. Perhaps you think they demean the Mediterranean or, in this case, the North Sea. I don't. We are all symbols to each other as well as real people. The experience of the imagination gives life savour.

'People have a down on advertising. Of course I can see why, just as I can see why they have a down on smoking. Yet people go on smoking and derive at least temporary pleasure from it. I derive a lot of temporary pleasure from advertising, and am practised at separating the commercial from the aesthetic side of it; it's a trick I learnt from my children, who are connoisseurs of TV advertising. Adult moral disapproval of advertising spoils our enjoyment, just as the Victorians found that moral approval of a painting enhanced their enjoyment of it.'

He and the girl were heading up the beach, splashing through a shallow lagoon. In the water lay a large beach ball with the word 'NIVEA' on it. Squire kicked the ball out of the way. Taking the towel wrapped like a scarf round his neck, he put it round the damp shoulders of the girl, talking cheerfully at the same time.

'Some enemies of advertising claim that advertisements show a too perfect, too happy world against which reality can never compete. I disagree. George Bernard Shaw said that perfection was only achieved on paper; utopia is only achieved in adverts. We need to be reminded that it exists even if it is attainable only by purchasing Domestos or Horlicks. Enemies are, in any case, blind, and have not noticed how often adverts on television show things going wrong; catastrophe has become a new sales gimmick. Here's a current advert for Andrex toilet paper or, as they put it more refinedly, toilet tissue.'

Squire broke off and the cameras stopped. He and the Sex Symbol sat down abruptly on the hard sand. They looked at each other and laughed.

'Just fine that time, Tom,' Grahame Ash said, coming up from behind the cameras and removing his ear plug. 'You must be exhausted. And you, Laura. Good day's work, both of you. At that point we cut in the ad with the little dog running into the garden with the toilet roll in its mouth. Great. Thanks very much, everyone.' The director waved his hands above his head. The crew moved nearer and doled out cigarettes.

His PA, Jenny Binns, called, 'Remember, nine o'clock tomorrow at Mr Squire's house, without fail everyone, okay?'

'We're all going over to Blakeney to a hotel for posh nosh this evening,' Ash reminded them.

'Count me out of that, Grahame,' Laura said. She scrambled to her feet and clutched her arms, rubbing them and shivering. 'Ooh, this isn't quite Singapore. I've gone all goosey.'

Squire put an arm round her shoulder and kissed her ear.

The men were talking about the good filming conditions as they gathered their gear together. Hartisham Bay stretched to either side of them, punctuated to the west by a low headland on which the window of a parked car glinted in the sun. To the east, the sand seemed to extend for ever. Some distance out to sea, a cluster of what looked like rocks were visible now the tide was low. It was the remains of Old Hartisham Priory, which had been overtaken by coastal erosion in the Middle Ages.

'Let's go,' Ash said. 'Forward march. Jenny, did you book us a table for this evening?'

'Of course, Grahame,' said his assistant, sweetly. 'Haven't I been booking you tables all round the world?'

There was still half a mile between them and the path through the dunes. Squire and Laura Nye trudged along together, she gripping the crossed ends of his towel, still wrapped round her neck. The others straggled along behind, exchanging insults and laughing. They fell silent on reaching dry sand above tide level, where the going immediately became harder. The cameras were dragged on sledges. The equipment van, the generators, and their cars were parked on the other side of the dunes, in the shelter of some pines.

As Laura went with the wardrobe girl to the caravan that served her as dressing-room, Squire stopped and waited for Ash. The four other members of the team streamed past them. Summer sun made their movements dazzle.

'That all seemed to go well. All those hours splashing about in the water, and we never even took a dip. Amazing weather for June.'

Ash smiled and shook his head. 'You can keep your dips. I would never swim in the North Sea, never. My health is precious to me.' He looked mock-solemn. Ash was a small round man, his fringe of long grey untidy hair sprouting round a freckled bald patch giving him a monkish air. By contrast, and possibly to prove he was a dedicated media man, he wore a gaudy flowered shirt that recalled Hawaii and

British Home Stores, although Squire had been with him when he bought the garment in Orchard Road, Singapore, to the derision of the camera crew.

On their many trips to locations at home and abroad, Grahame Ash had shown himself to understand perfectly Squire's material, and had made contributions they had incorporated in the script. In particular, he had proved himself visually inventive. He was a north countryman, his soft-spoken vowels adding to a general impression of comfortable command.

'It's supine, Grahame, supine, that sea, a reformed teddy bear sea, promising never to play rough again.'

'I never swim with teddy bears.' He emptied sand from his canvas shoes. 'It must be tea-time. I need a drink.'

'What's next in the script?'

'A word about advertising supporting newspapers, television companies, colour supplements, sport, pointing out its virtues in a capitalist society.'

Ash climbed into the Peugeot and pulled the script of the episode of 'Frankenstein Among the Arts' they were filming from the crammed glove compartment. Squire went to the sheltered side of the vehicle and pulled an old pair of slacks over his swimming trunks.

'Okay. Perhaps we should scrap that as a bit didactic and say instead that advertising – like the Andrex ad – reinforces a rather dangerous Western obsession with cleanliness.'

'My father served three years in the mud and trenches in World War I and was never the same afterwards, at least according to mother. Perhaps in reaction against the mud, his devotion to cleanliness spilled over into pacifism.'

'Interesting,' said Squire. He climbed into the passenger seat beside Ash. 'How much is the unpreparedness of the West due to fear of war, how much to advertisements with perpetual stress on avoidance of dirt – meaning death as well as excreta.'

'Bit difficult to avoid either if you ask me.'

'Yes, but you can avoid thinking about them.' It was seven months since his mother died, yet the loss was still with him. 'I mean, do we see the shiny packaging of purchasable objects as guardians against evil, like Chinese temple dogs? Why is packaging so often of more durable material than the object being packaged?'

Ash backed the car out onto the road. 'That would fit more appropriately into Episode Twenty, "Shiny Surfaces", where we're dealing with Jasper Johns, Warhol, Claes Oldenburg, and the pop artists' interest in commercial packaging.'

Laura Nye came over to them. She had changed into a frilled blue shirt and jeans. The blond wig had gone, to reveal her own neat crop of chestnut hair.

'Are you going to go to the pub?' Squire asked. She was staying at The Lion in Hartisham, like most of the crew, for the four days they were working here.

'No, darling, not tonight. I've got to dash to London. See you tomorrow, okay?'

Her smile echoed the note of interrogation in her voice.

He squinted against the sun in order to study her expression, shielding his eyes in an instinctive attempt to conceal his alarm.

'You've got a hell of a drive from here all the way to London. Can't it wait? We'll be back in the Smoke in a couple of days.'

She glanced unnecessarily at her wrist watch.

'I'll be in town by seven, no bother. I'm looking forward to the drive. I must go. Sorry.'

'Are you going to see Peter?'

'I must, Tom. Besides, you're going to see Teresa.'

She smiled soberly across at Ash. 'I'll be back for work on time tomorrow, Gray.'

The two men watched her retreating behind in silence. Sunlight glinted through the characteristic female crutch gap.

'Let's go,' Squire said, with a sigh. 'Pippet Hall.'

Ash said nothing. He drove.

The Norfolk coast road from Hunstanton meanders eastwards towards Sheringham and Cromer. On its way, it calls at a number of small towns which are never quite on the sea, whatever their intentions. Blakeney, for instance, gazes placidly across tidal river and marshes to its distant head, with scarcely a glimpse of the real sea. It once held fairs which were among the excitements of the Middle Ages; Muscovite ships visited it, with cargoes of silver, sable, caviar and bear grease. Three stout ships sailed from Blakeney against the Spanish Armada.

Only at Wells-next-Sea is there still clear sight of the open waters leading on to Norway, the Arctic, or Ostend. At Wells tourists can walk with their ice creams and fish'n'chips straight across the road, to view little Egyptian freighters or the modern, hammer-and-sickle-flying descendants of the Muscovites who reached Blakeney, all moored peaceably against the quayside.

Take one of the minor roads which turn southwards off the coast road between Wells and Blakeney. After a few miles' drive, you will arrive at the pretty village of Hartisham. Hartisham is set half on a small eminence, half in a small valley, through which the small River Guymell runs. The higher village contains a manor house, a vicarage, and a fine church, dedicated to St Swithun, and refaced with knapped flint in the eighteen-eighties. The lower part contains most of the village, its dwellings (mainly cottages, built blind side to the street), a few shops, and Pippet Hall, through the modest grounds of which the River Guymell flows.

The countryside is undulating hereabouts, rather than flat. It is very fertile, and must once have abounded in the deer for which the village is named. Pippet Hall estate consists of under one hundred acres since the Squire family had to sell land off to meet death duties. The modest farmhouse, now occupied by the manager of the estate, lies in a bend of the Guymell. The manager frequently eats trout for his supper. The Hall itself stands on a slight eminence. It is mentioned and often pictured in all the guide books of the area, and also in Nikolaus Pevsner's architectural guides. It was named after the meadow pipits which used to nest abundantly hereabouts.

The house is visible from the front gate, but to reach the front porch the drive curves elegantly and crosses an ornamental stone bridge over a small lake which was created by a Squire ancestor with advice from Thomas Repton. The cedars Repton planted, the blue cedars of Lebanon, still stand in a noble group of four on the north side of the lake. It is tradition that, when the weather is cold enough and the ice will hold, the local population enters the grounds of Pippet Hall and skates or slides on the frozen lake.

'I love this place,' Ash said, as he braked the Peugeot in the drive outside the porch. 'I'll buy it off you.'

A dog barked somewhere in an offhand manner.

'Let's see if Teresa's at home.'

The house was early Georgian, built of brick cornered with stone. It replaced a smaller building on the same site which had been destroyed by fire. It owed its existence to an earlier Squire, the vigorous Matthew, born in Norfolk in 1689, in the reign of King James II.

Matthew Squire bought himself a commission in Marlborough's army and served as liaison officer between Marlborough and Prince Eugene at the battle of Oudenarde in 1708, in which the French were defeated. Matthew's bravery, his dash, and his command of the German tongue, commended him to Eugene.

The bravery must have been inborn; the command of German was acquired from young Matthew's mistress, Caroline, the illegitimate daughter of a Westphalian captain of dragoons. With Caroline following behind, Matthew joined Eugene's army to fight at Peterwardein in 1716. There the Turks were defeated for the last time on European soil.

As victory bells pealed throughout Christendom, Matthew found he had lost a finger and gained a reputation. He was decorated and rewarded by Eugene. He acquired a substantial train of Ottoman booty. Whereupon he retired with his beloved Caroline to his native village, Hartisham. There in the seventeen-thirties he had the present house built and, it is claimed, was the first man to introduce coffee to North Norfolk. Despite lavish expenditures, he ensured the modest fortunes of the Squire family for the next two and a half centuries.

Caroline's sturdy Westphalian loins provided for the continuance of Matthew's line. She outlived her husband. He died, a slightly dotty old man with a cork finger, in his seventy-first year, and was buried in St

Swithun's churchyard at almost the same time as Horatio Nelson was entering the world, only a few miles away across the Norfolk meadows.

As the two men climbed from Ash's Peugeot, a Dalmatian bitch came bounding from the rear of the house and flung herself at Squire.

At the same time, a female voice was heard calling, in hopeless tones, 'Nellie, Nellie, good girl!'

A plump white-haired lady appeared, carrying a trug in one hand. She paused, then came up smiling, saying, 'Tom, your dog is quite uncontrollable.'

Squire introduced her to Ash as Mrs Davies, his mother-in-law. She was recently widowed.

'Where's Teresa?' he asked her, patting Nellie's back.

'This sunny spell we're having is beautiful, and yet you know I get so hot,' she told Ash, with the confidence of one who has regularly enjoyed the attention of men. 'I never used to get so hot. I mustn't do any more, but I couldn't resist pottering. All the poor plants need water. Tess feels the heat too, and I would not be surprised if she hasn't retired to her own room for a shower and rest. You must have found filming on the beach intolerably hot today, Mr Ash.'

'Don't forget that Mr Squire and I were filming in Singapore three months ago,' said Ash, smiling. 'It was really warm there.'

They paused on the lower step of the house, Ash slouching, smiling in his flamboyant shirt, hands in his pockets, Mrs Davies shortish but erect, her white hair carefully tended, talking but keeping an eye on Squire, who stood square-based, legs apart, twiddling his bunch of keys. The dog disappeared into the cool of the house.

The symmetry of Pippet Hall was emphasized by its red brick and its white paint, with the plum-coloured door centrally placed. The complete entablature of the doorcase, with a pediment over it, in turn emphasized the sensible centrality of this feature. It was a three-storeyed house, the four sashed windows of the ground floor running almost from floor to ceiling, but diminishing in height floor by floor. A brick parapet ornamented with recessed panels rose above the second-floor windows, half-concealing the truncated pyramid of roof. The chimneys were grouped at either end of the roof, emphasizing the symmetry of the whole.

Five shallow steps rose from the level of the drive to the front step (for the meek Guymell had been known to rise up and flood). Squire led the way up the steps to the panelled door.

'My husband flew out to Singapore,' Mrs Davies was telling Ash, 'by air in the thirties, in a seaplane. I went too. It was very comfortable and we slept on board. I wouldn't care to go now. Flights are so terribly crowded nowadays, I don't know how people can bear it. Yet I saw in *The Times* just yesterday that they're planning even bigger airliners. Where it will all end I don't know.'

Squire was edging his friend into the hall. He waited while Mrs Davies talked to Ash. The interior was cool, and silent, apart from the click of the Dalmatian's claws on the stone tiles as it circled him. This hall was Pippet Hall's grandest feature, designed to make an immediate impression on guests before they were led to the relatively cramped reception rooms. Stairs led to the upper floor in a graceful double curve; portraits of Matthew and Caroline hung in heavy gilt frames on the half-landing.

'Where are Ann and Jane?' he asked sharply.

'The girls have gone over to Norwich with Grace and their Aunt Deirdre. They'll be back later,' said Mrs Davies. 'They're wearing their jeans. I told them that dresses were more suitable for Norwich but, no, they would go in their jeans. Ugly things. Do you have children, Mr Ash?'

'I think I'll get Grahame a drink, Mother,' said Squire. 'Would you like one, too?'

'I could make you some tea if you liked, and there are some doughnuts from the Crooked Apron. Do you like doughnuts, Mr Ash? They're terribly fattening . . .'

Squire manoeuvred Ash and his mother-in-law into the living room and poured both Ash and himself large vodkas-on-the-rocks. Leaving Ash to his conversation, he went off in search of his wife.

The dog sat at the bottom of the stairs, watching him mournfully, knowing well that Dalmatians were not allowed upstairs.

Music sounded faintly along the upper corridor. Teresa had taken over the room at the south-east corner of the house. Squire tapped lightly at the door and went in.

The room was shaded. The curtain at the long south-facing window had been drawn to keep out the sun; but a thin beam, shining through the window set in the other wall, painted a line of gold across the white-and-green carpet, as if to emphasize the shadow into which the rest of the room had been plunged.

Teresa had furnished the room with rattan chairs and sofas, each with a white cushion, and all recently purchased from an artistic shop in Fakenham. There were several large plants, two *monstera delicosa* reaching almost to the ceiling, a rubber plant, and an aspidistra. The general effect was that an attempt had been made to recreate a Malayan environment, but the sofa had been pushed aside to make room for a white formica desk and a work table at which Teresa now sat.

The table was littered with rolls of plastic and wire and a cluttered miscellany of paint pots on a tray. Beneath the table were boxes and litter. On the walls hung the results of Teresa's labours, fantastic insects of all sorts, beetles with amazing horns, moths with wings of gold, butterflies with eyes in their wings. These exotic creatures of wire and plastic glowed with the light from the floor, the unusual angle of illumination giving them an unexpected and even sinister aspect.

'Tess! Are you all right?'

She had been sitting looking through the window, holding a paint brush in one hand. Although she turned to look at Squire, the end of the brush remained between her teeth, slightly wrinkling her upper lip.

'Hello, Tom, I didn't expect you back yet.' As if making a decision, she dropped the brush abruptly and stood up. Teresa was a plump, soft-looking woman of under medium height. Now in her mid-forties, she had lines under the large doe eyes which were such a striking feature of her face. Her hair was piled neatly on her head and dyed with gold tints. She had taken recently to wearing plenty of make-up and false eyelashes. Her smock was stained with plastic paints; beneath it she wore crimson slacks. Crimson-nailed toes peeped from golden sandals.

Squire moved forward, clutched her, patted her chubby bottom.

'We've finished filming for the day. Grahame's here. Come down and have a drink with us.'

'Where are the rest of them?' In her regard was the slight suggestion of squint which he had once found so attractive.

'Of the company? They're mostly putting up at The Lion. Is anything the matter, Tess?'

She looked hard at him and said, 'No, no, nothing's the matter.' With one sandalled foot she moved a cardboard carton out of the way.

'Good. Come on down then.'

'I'll be there in a minute. I can't come downstairs looking like this.'

'Of course you can. You look lovely. Grahame won't mind.'

She frowned, as if concentrating on resolving the contradiction in what he said.

'If you go down, I'll join you, if you really want me.'

'Naturally we want you. Mother tells me the girls are in Norwich with Deirdre. I thought we might all go over and have supper in Blakeney with the film crew. It would be fun and the hotel cuisine's not bad this season.'

With a lack-lustre air far from her normal manner, Teresa turned away, saying, 'You go if you wish. I don't feel like going out this evening.'

'There is something the matter, isn't there? Have you got business troubles?'

'Not at all. On the contrary.' She waved her hand over the cluttered table. 'Vernon Jarvis is convinced I can make a great commercial success with fantasy insects. He says I shouldn't bother to sell in England. He can get massive orders from Germany and New York

57

which will pay much better. He thinks we should start an export company.'

'Who's Vernon Jarvis?'

'A young man with flair *and* very good business connections. You met him before you went to Singapore but I daresay you were too busy to take any notice.'

'I think I do remember now. Funny side-whiskers? Well, if all's going well, don't be gloomy, come down and have a drink.'

Going back to his vodka downstairs, Squire found Ash still in the conversational embrace of Mrs Davies, who was showing the director photographs of the three children, John – now grown-up and living in the murkier reaches of Manchester – Ann, and Jane. Prising Ash away, Squire took him into the study, where separate scripts and story-boards of each episode of 'Frankenstein Among the Arts' were arrayed on a trestle-table brought in for the purpose.

As Ash strolled with his drink to look out of the french windows at the sweep of lawn and meadow beyond, Squire said, 'I'd better warn you that Teresa is in rather a peculiar mood. Probably her horoscope upset her this morning.'

'Mine always upsets me. "Chance of financial advantage . . ." – and a tax form arrives with the postman. Never fear, I'll be at my jolliest tonight.'

They switched on the video-cassette machine and flipped through a few items which might yet be fitted into the series. One showed a collection of hundreds of pepper-and-salt cellars, all different.

Both men laughed. 'One function, diversity of forms. Condimental evolution,' Ash said.

'This array tells you a lot about the imagination of mankind. I think it should go in, if we can fit it in.'

'It would have to go in Four, "Animals from Machines". I'll see what can be done.'

When Teresa appeared, she had changed into a summery blue dress which set off the artificial gold of her hair. She sailed into the study smiling, her mother and Nellie the Dalmatian trailing her. Greeting Ash warmly, she demanded a gin-and-tonic from her husband, and then chatted to the director. He invited her to join the party at the Blakeney Hotel.

'Do we pick up your crew, if that's what you call them, from The Lion?'

'Yes, Mrs Squire. That's where we are all staying. It's picturesque.'

She accepted the drink from Squire without a glance in his direction. 'You should have stayed with us. There's room. This place has been like a nunnery with Tom away so much . . . Is your "Sex Symbol", about whom I've heard so much, also staying at The Lion?'

'Laura Nye? She's in London overnight. Everyone else will be there. You'll like Jenny Binns – she's held us all together. Laura's a good girl, too – as sweet as she looks. The series is her first television job. She's had plenty of stage experience, worked with Ralph Richardson at one time.'

Teresa had developed a withdrawn look. Nellie flopped on the hearthrug.

'Perhaps I'll come,' Teresa said.

Squire got the Jaguar out. It and the Peugeot drove into the village to collect the crew. Then they headed for the coast. The sun still shone, though cloud gathered. The evening appeared motionless. The tide was still out. The dinner was good.

Tom and Teresa rolled back to the Hall after midnight, leaving the car outside the house. They staggered indoors and Squire chained the door behind them. He went through to the kitchen to make tea while Teresa went upstairs to see that the girls were in bed. When he carried the mugs up, slopping tea on the carpets, Teresa was already undressing. A particularly brilliant dragonfly, with outstretched wings of crimson and viridian, glittered in a block of perspex on her side of the bed. She kept her gaze on it instead of looking at Squire.

'Pleasant occasion, darling. Multo conviviality, as father used to say. I hope you enjoyed yourself as much as you appeared to be doing.'

'It was all too apparent you weren't enjoying yourself. That dreary doomed way you toyed with your Chicken Kiev . . .'

'What do you mean? You could see I enjoyed myself. It was visible to all. And I ate up all my Chicken Kiev.'

'Absent-mindedly.'

He removed his blazer, saying controlledly, 'I drank a bit more than I intended. Grahame was well away, wasn't he? Think he'd get back to The Lion safely?'

She made no answer. Instead, she disappeared behind her Chinese screen, in the shelter of which, since she had decided she was 'getting too fat', she preferred to undress.

'Oh shit,' he said, 'if you're refusing to talk to me, I'll go downstairs and get myself another whisky. You're brewing up for something – I know the expression "bottled fury" when I see it in the flesh. Tell me what the matter is, tell me what bloody mortal sin I've committed now.'

'Don't start swearing, Tommy.' Her voice, heavy with reproof, from behind the gold-limned outline of a Cathaian mountainside. 'It's always a sign of guilt.'

'Why do you damned well say I didn't enjoy this evening? Any reason why I shouldn't have enjoyed myself, apart from those hang-dog looks you kept giving me?'

'You never even glanced at me, so how would you know?'

'I did look; I was enjoying myself. I told you.'

Her face partially appeared, as if to get a sight on him, then withdrew behind the screen again. 'You know what I mean. There's enjoyment and enjoyment. Absent friends and all that . . .'

'What absent friends, for heaven's sake?' He put his blazer on again. 'You're not insinuating that we should have taken your mother with us?'

'I've long ago ceased to expect you to be decent or even civil to my mother. I mean, it wasn't quite the same for you, was it, without that – that *girl* of yours, that Laura.'

'If you're referring to Laura Nye, I've not a clue what you're talking about. You were told, she's gone to London. Grahame told you.'

'That's what makes her an absent friend, isn't it? Gone to sleep with some young stud of hers, I suppose. That's what models are all about, isn't it?'

He strode round the bed and dragged the screen back. Teresa stood there in her powder-blue dressing-gown, drawn to her modest full height, unmoving.

'Come out of there if you're going to insult me and Laura. She's not a "model", as you sneeringly call her. She has worked with Peter Brook and was in Shakespeare at the Old Vic for three years.'

'I'd never trust anyone who was in Shakespeare for three years.'

'Oh, this is just stupid, Tess. You've had too much gin. Let's get to bed and go to sleep, and perhaps you'll talk sense in the morning.'

She said, 'I suppose you were playing Shakespeare on the beach this afternoon. What was it? You're a bit long in the tooth for Romeo . . .'

It was very quiet outside. He went and peered through the curtains, over the balcony, at the garden and fields beyond, faintly visible in the starry night. Mist was gathering.

'Come on, Tess, give it up. You're spoiling for a fight and I'm not. You're just making us miserable.'

She sat down on the side of the bed and selected a cigarette from the silver box she kept there. Lighting it with a shaking hand, she said, 'How typical of you to pretend that I'm making the misery. You've been away all over the world, I've hardly seen you from one month's end to the next. You come back, and I find you've got a new girl in tow. After all the trouble we had three years ago, I thought you'd learnt wisdom.'

He made to speak but she raised a hand. 'I'm talking, aren't I? You can have your say afterwards, though I'm not sure if I'll listen. I'm fed up, Tom, utterly fed up. What sort of marriage is it? If you want to know, I drove up to the headland this afternoon and watched you with that woman through binoculars. I saw you mauling her about, cuddling her, kissing her, feeling her tits – in front of the others, too. How do you think I liked that, eh? You bastard!'

'Christ!' He ran the palm of his hand up his forehead and into his hair. 'Teresa, you're just being tiresome and exercising that suspicious nature of yours. Neither you nor I are anything to do with the world of television or show biz or whatever, and once "Frankenstein" is finished and in the can at the end of August, that will be the end of it as far as I'm concerned. I shall go back to work as usual.

'But we both know about show biz. Different pressures, different *moeurs*. Sure, I did put my arm round Laura's shoulder. It was breezy, she was cold, and she needed cheering up. Nothing more to it than that. So just drop the whole subject right here and now. Did you feel good, spying on me?

'I admit I've been away a bit, but we agreed that this was my chance and I took it. "Frankenstein" is a marvellous opportunity and a new subject and I'm proud of it. But this period will shortly be over, then we'll live a more normal sort of life. Simply let me sail through it without having emotional problems with you.'

Teresa came round the bed, shuffling her bare feet into fluffy slippers as she walked.

'Men are such bloody liars. I tell you I saw you with her through the binoculars. Now you expect to jump into bed with me and screw me, don't you? Whatever's to hand, eh, Tommy Squire? You've been fucking that bitch in Singapore and all over the map, haven't you?'

'No.' He regarded her woodenly, head down, face heavy, the flesh of his jowls creased as he faced her charge, his eyes defensive, angry.

His monosyllable – or his pose – stopped her before she reached him. She coughed furiously over the cigarette, fist to her mouth.

'You bloody liar! Sagittarius woman with Cancer man – I should have known all along it would never work out. You're a philanderer, you philander even with your mind, you're rootless, you live only for yourself, don't you? Well, why don't you go back to Yugoslavia and live the way you used to live there?'

'Don't be silly, dear, you're working yourself up for nothing. I've no wish to return to Yugoslavia. I'm too old, I want a peaceful life.'

'A fine way you go about it. I suppose you'll tell me you're undergoing the male menopause next. That girl must have loved all that sort of thing – a case of *Much Ado About Nothing*, wasn't it? Get out! I'm not having you in this bedroom with me. Go and sleep in one of the guest rooms. You're no better than a guest.'

He moved slowly, like a man in a dream, picking up his pyjamas, his brass carriage clock from the bedside table, and his mug of tea.

'The stars may be moving against us, Tess, but that is not my wish. We have to make our own decisions and not pretend we are helpless. You must behave less cruelly to me.'

'It's your behaviour not mine that's at fault.'

Squire wandered for a while through the vacant rooms of the Hall, unable to rest. He was familiar with the dimensions of the house from childhood, could walk them unhesitatingly with his eyes closed. In the dead of night, this familiar substantial presence was doubly comforting. Every room held for him a different ambience; by its temperature, its smell, its silences, the very texture of its air or the creak of its oak floorboards, he could tell which room he was in, and respond to its character.

She had her difficulties, finding her way through life. All the astrological nonsense which recently had preoccupied her was simply a means by which she tried to manoeuvre round the hidden obstacles of her existence.

He thought back to an evening only three nights ago, before Grahame Ash, Laura Nye, and the crew had come down to Hartisham to film – only three nights ago, but now, separated from the present by the quarrel, a long way in the past. It had been so peaceful, so domestic: Tess and he, and the two girls, and Tess's reliable friend, Matilda Rowlinson, sitting drinking coffee in his study after supper. Yet even then he had been dreaming of someone else . . .

Teresa was painting, copying a large butterfly. She used acrylics on a large pad, and worked deftly, occasionally looking up and smiling at Ann and Jane, who lolled by the fire with Nellie, the Dalmatian. Ann was just thirteen, her sister eleven; the sandy gene had run out with their elder brother; they had inherited their mother's mouse, and their father's enquiring nature.

'You girls ought to be going to bed,' Teresa said, as the grandfather clock in the hall struck ten.

'We're watching you,' Ann said. 'We're fascinated, aren't we, Nellie?'

'You're not.'

'What sort of butterfly is it, anyway?'

Teresa appealed to Squire. He had bought the spectacular insect in its frame in a Singapore shop as a homecoming present for her.

'It's called a Bhutan Glory.'

'You're ruining the ecology of Singapore by buying that poor butterfly, Dad,' Jane said. 'There soon won't be any left. How'd you like it if *they* came over here and bought all our butterflies?'

'We'd have to exercise some controls.'

Teresa said in his defence, 'Daddy helps to preserve the ecology of the Norfolk Broads, because they are our local responsibility, but you can't expect him to butt in on Singapore's affairs.'

'It's a pity we didn't manage to stop the council pulling down the old almshouses,' Matilda said. She was the vicar's daughter, a tall pale woman in her early thirties and, with her plain looks and self-effacing manner, an embodiment of the traditional vicar's daughter, until one became aware of her lucid way of thought.

'They were tumbledown,' Teresa said, 'but the semi-detacheds that Ray Bond is building in their place are quite out of keeping with the rest of the village.'

'I know, why don't they build houses with green bricks instead of red ones?' Jane said. 'Then they'd merge with the landscape.'

'Who's ever heard of green bricks, Stupid?' said her sister.

'Well, they could invent them . . . Only I daresay they'd fade after a year and turn the colour of dog shit.'

'*I* heard that Ray Bond was having an affair with two women at once,' Ann said. 'Both of them married. Isn't that beastly, Dad?'

'Beastly complicated.'

'It's disgusting. You girls shouldn't listen to village gossip,' Teresa told them.

Ann rolled onto her back, and pulled Nellie on top of her. With evening, a chilly wind was blowing in from the coast, and the big old electric fire was burning. She rested a slippered foot on top of it and announced, 'I think I shall have affairs when I grow up. I'd like to have people gossiping about me.'

'What, affairs with people like Ray Bond? You are nauseating,' Jane said. 'That's just about your style.'

'Oh, you can stick to your boring old ecology. You think caterpillars are more important than love, but I don't. Grownups think love is important, don't you, Mummy?'

'Yes,' said Teresa, and nothing more; so that Matilda, who sat quietly on a large Moroccan pouffe just beyond the compass of the light falling on Teresa's paper, added, 'Love can be a way of perception, like science or art, Ann, provided you don't use it for power over people.'

'To think I once used to be in love with that odious Robert Mais! I was only six then. I've got better taste now . . .' Ann thought a while and then asked Squire, 'Were you in love when you were very young, Dad?'

'I don't remember being in love at six. But I was at nine.'

Ann sat up. 'Go on, don't just stop there! True confessions . . . Who was she? Do we know her? I suppose she must be pretty ancient now.'

He laughed. 'That's true. Her name was Rachel. She lived here during the war. I loved her dearly.'

'She *lived* here!' Ann laughed. 'I smell a rat! Did you have an affair with her, Dad? I mean, you know, a real flaming *affair*?'

'Oh, shut up, Ann!' Jane exclaimed. 'You're embarrassing poor Daddy, can't you see? Nellie, eat her, go on, eat her! This conversation is getting too carnal entirely.'

They rolled together, shrieking. Teresa called to them ineffectually to stop.

'Was it carnal, Dad? Tell us, we won't tell anyone!'

He broke into laughter. 'I just loved her, that's all.'

Matilda, smiling, said, 'Even carnal love can be a sign of someone's yearning for Unity, though one can only really achieve unity with God.'

'You're bound to say that because you're the Reverend Rowlinson's daughter,' said Ann, derisively. 'I bet you've never had carnal knowledge – not even with Ray Bond, have you?'

'That's very rude, Ann. Apologize and go up to bed at once.' Squire joined his wife with a shout of 'Apologize!'

'We're only talking, Mummy,' Jane said, soothingly.

But Ann had already shifted back to her original target. Jumping up, laughing, she demanded again, 'Were you carnal, Pop – even when you were only nine?'

The noise of a woodcock roused Squire. For a moment he had a vision of happier things, imagining that his father was alive and moving about in his room; then his waking senses returned. His bladder was full. His body felt cold. Sighing, he sat up.

Light of another day filtered through the long windows. His carriage clock pronounced the time to be five-twenty. He was lying cramped on the chesterfield in his study, with a quarter-full glass of whisky standing on the carpet beside him. His head ached. His mouth was dry.

The pallid light seemed to cast a veil between Squire and a painting on the wall on which his sickened gaze rested. The painting dated from 1821, and had been executed by a nineteenth-century artist whom Squire had collected consistently over the past quarter century, Edward Calvert. Entitled 'The Primaeval City', it showed a scene which charmingly mingled the rural with the urban. A bullock cart trundled among trees into a city of thatch and domes and ruin, where figures could be seen in cameo, a bucolic pressing wine, a nun entering the church, a woman hanging out washing, a man pulling a donkey. In the background, garlanded with leaves, a gibbous moon rose like a planet above the crumbling rooftops, and a shepherd tended his sheep. In the foreground, dominating everything, stood a nude maiden in a leafy bower of pomegranate trees, having climbed from a brook. She looked over one shoulder without coquetry at the viewer, a bewitching mixture of flesh and spirit.

Recalling the previous evening, Squire turned his regard from these symbols and yawned.

Painfully, he got to his feet and staggered across to the french windows. When he twisted the latch, they opened with a squeal. He walked stealthily across the terrace, arms enfolding his chest to ward off the chill. He went on tiptoe down a gravel path and made his way barefoot over damp grass to the nearest clump of rhododendrons.

Down by the Guymell, faintly, he could see cattle standing without movement. Steam attended their flanks. All was still, artificial. The nearby cedars stood in a mist which rendered them as outlines. As a painter reduces a tree to a symbol which will function within his composition as a real tree does in a real landscape, so these outlines rendered the awakening world artificial. They and it had been sponged, as if Cotman were temporarily God.

As Squire turned after relieving himself, he saw the Jaguar standing at the front of the house, half-hidden by a corner of the building. Its two doors hung open. Something on the driver's side had fallen out onto the gravel; a travel atlas, possibly.

In the mist-blurred wall of the house, fluorescent light spread towards the garden, where he had left on the kitchen lights when getting tea.

Looking up at the damp eaves as he picked his way back to the study, he observed that the bedroom light also was burning. The bedroom curtains had been pulled half-way back. The light spread a faded orange wash across the ceiling, a glow belonging to midnight rather than dawn, an ominous shade boding no good.

So she had not slept, or would not sleep, or could not sleep. Or was already prowling about the house. It had only been a minor tiff. He must eat humble pie, reassure her. All would be well again in a day or two.

He entered the study, shivering. As he turned from securing the windows, he discovered with a start that Teresa had entered the room while he was out of it; she stood in her dressing-gown, drawn up to her full height, by the door into the rear hall, in shadow. Her motionlessness was unnatural. She regarded Squire with fixed intensity.

'You startled me, Tess. A Lady Macbeth act? Couldn't you sleep?'

In a tone different from her usual tone, she said, 'You have been getting into bed with that piece of goods, Laura, haven't you?'

'Yes. Yes, Teresa, I have. I'm sorry if it hurts you. It means very little to me but I could not resist the temptation. I have been to bed with her.'

Teresa said, as if that was the really important matter, 'You lied to me last night, you rotten bastard.'

4

Conversation with 'Drina's'

Ermalpa, September 1978

Darkness had fallen. The first-floor corridor of the Grand Hotel Marittimo was littered with silver trays, lying forlorn with a mess of coffee-pots, used cups, and tousled napkins. As Thomas Squire left Room 143, a guest was in another room playing a violin behind locked doors.

After a half-an-hour suspended in *sarvangasana*, followed by a cold shower, Squire was feeling alert and ready for the evening. Downstairs, before turning into the bar, he took a stroll in the busy street. One of the Canadian delegates, seeing him walk towards the swing doors, said, in honest horror, 'You're not going out alone in Ermalpa after dark, Mr Squire? You know this place is the headquarters of the Mafia?'

Surviving a turn in the muggy air, Squire went to fulfil his seven o'clock appointment in the bar.

Selina Ajdini was there already. Several young Italians were talking to her, pressing round her armchair. She had changed her clothes, and now wore an ankle-length white jersey dress with long sleeves and edged with gold braid, its only decoration being a criss-cross pattern of braid with loose tassels which covered the bosom. Several thin gold bracelets hung at her slender right wrist, three rings glittered on her rather cruel-looking fingers. Her neat black hair, gathered into a thick tail, hung asymmetrically to one shoulder. She still carried her bulky bag.

The bar was full of the cheerful noises characteristic of a popular time. Three barmen in smart uniforms moved freely behind their gilded pallisades, smiling, exchanging jokes with each other and their customers as they worked; glass chinked against glass; the cash register whirred; wallpaper music played softly in the background; a waitress bustled among the customers, collecting glasses; and a murmur of many languages grew from all sides. A female voice called Squire's name.

He turned and there was a small dark Italian lady he had watched earlier in the day. She was an efficient messenger for Frenza, the conference secretary, and spoke a little English. She had a minor administrative detail to sort out with Squire and, as she talked, he realized that she was Frenza's wife; her well-turned ankles and heavy gold hair were immediately recognizable. Her name was Maria. She wore a neat black dress, had one bracelet on her wrist and two rings on her fingers. The smile she gave him was tired.

When they had settled the matter, he moved towards the bar. Ajdini had dismissed her retinue and sat smoking through a long holder, awaiting him. Although the bitter herb of her Huxley speech still flavoured his memory, he could not help smiling as he joined her, sinking into an armchair facing her.

The eroded bone was softened in artificial light. She said, 'These Italians are so sociable, that we would talk with less disturbance in one of the rooms off the foyer. I have spoken about it to one of the barmen, who is very kind, and he will serve us with drinks as long as we are there.'

'Very well.'

'Let's go, then.'

The room she referred to led off the passage where the case of silk ties stood. It was small, containing by way of ornament only a large marble bust of a general, whose remarkable cranial development alone was worth commemoration. Some earlier occupant of the room, perhaps idly waiting a tryst, had pencilled in the general's pupils, making him appear cross-eyed.

'This is a privilege for me,' she said, lightly arranging the white dress as they sat down. 'I suppose that any university in the capitalist world – and not only there – would be delighted to be able to address you face to face, Mr Squire. Your television series, and the book, which is a delight in its own right, does for the culture of today what Lord Clark's *Civilization* did for the past.'

'The series was the work of a team. They made it work – Grahame Ash, the director, in particular. Ash is a genius. He has a way with people and he thinks in pictures.'

'Your work in general. Since the Hyde Park Expo – and before. What you do enables the various artists of today, and those who would not presume or care to call themselves artists, to go ahead with more confidence, as one always can when one sees oneself working within some kind of a tradition. You generously defined a revolutionary tradition. However, I must not embarrass you, a modest Englishman, with my praises, although I am aware they can have no significance for you.'

'That is a mistaken assumption. I am delighted to have your good opinion. You have a higher opinion of the series than some critics. What man does not desire the good opinion of an attractive woman?'

She smiled, and the bangles rattled as she stretched out a hand. 'Nor will I ask you if you are finding enjoyment in your world-wide success, since you must surely have become tired of such a question. Do you mind if I smoke?'

She was more striking than pretty, with a sharpness about her features which suggested wary intelligence. The sharpness, a quickness in her movements, a fleck of green in her irises, suggested wolf to Squire. He admired wolves; wolves were good to each other.

Her hair moved about her cheeks as she reached into the clumsy leather bag and brought out her cigarettes. He noticed immediately, with surprise, that they were Yugoslav, 'Drina' brand. He knew the name.

Whilst he was leaning forward to give her a light, the friendly waiter arrived. He cast an envious and distinctly unfriendly look at Squire. Squire stood his gold lighter on the table as he ordered drinks. After the waiter had left, dismissed by a brilliant smile from Ajdini, she picked up the lighter and inspected it as it lay in her narrow palm before pressing it into Squire's hand.

'What I respond to personally in your work is your humanity. It gives your criticism what the rest of us lack, a creative depth. No, I'm not praising now, merely stating. To prove it, let me be a little critical, if you will permit, and say that I find the humanity the more impressive since you do come, do you not, from a deeply privileged background?'

He regarded her through her protective cloud of smoke, admiring her breasts and thinking of the benefits her beauty must bring her, unasked.

'Almost anyone, in North America or Western Europe, must admit to a privileged background.' Seeing her expression, he added, 'And that is not intended as an evasion of your question. We must use that privileged background to carry not only our materialism but our liberalism and awareness to the rest of the world. We must hope that ultimately those values will prevail.'

'Liberalism doesn't carry much priority, even in universities.'

'No, or in an ant heap. But we have to resist the idea of the world as ant heap.' He could catch the distinctive smell of Balkan tobacco.

'Well, I know what you mean, but only people from backgrounds of privilege can afford the luxury of fine sentiments. Your series, when all's done, was admirable as *display* . . .'

He laughed. 'Display? Give me credit for keeping my politics out of it.'

She looked down at the table, sharply up at him, down again. 'I found it loaded with politics.'

Music was playing, perhaps in the room overhead. The atmosphere of the room was oppressive; having the general listening stonily to all that was said did not increase comfort.

'I don't see any worth in a world in which individuality has been lost or relinquished,' he said. 'On an evolutionary scale, mankind strove for many generations to become a conscious individual being, instead of a unit in a tribe or a herd or an ant heap. In our gener-ation – or generations, I should say, since there is a considerable difference in our ages – we have seen a menacing move in the opposite direction, and individualism crushed by the power of the state.' In fact, there probably was not more than eight years between them.

'In a world threatened by fascism, where parliamentary democracy has failed, the state must protect the individual, and the individual submits for his own good.'

'Perhaps you mistake the implications of what I say. I would deny that parliamentary democracy, for all its faults, has failed; being a consensus, it offers its citizens a freer life than the despotisms of either Left or Right. Nor is the world threatened by fascism; individual countries, perhaps. But fascism is always a ramshackle thing which cannot perpetuate itself, whereas the great communist bureaucracies prove to have longer life.

'However, the point I was trying to make goes beyond politics, to forces moving through our evolutionary lives, if I may use that phrase. Evolution still shapes us. Compare Islam and Christianity with the conceptually primitive Aztec religion, where mass-salvation could be achieved by mass-sacrifice. Souls were interchangeable. The Old Testament is a drama of man becoming aware that souls are no longer interchangeable.'

She smiled. 'You speak of the soul, whatever that may be. Yet you are not a religious man?'

'We are all religious. In our day, the Left has all the dialectic, the Right none. Yet lying to hand is the supreme argument that souls are not interchangeable. It is perhaps too universal a truth for the Right to use, too true a truth to fall to the service of any party. Nevertheless it is the vital factor through which the present world struggles towards the future, whether capitalist or communist, Caucasian, Negroid, or Mongoloid. It's our one hope, because undeniable.'

They paused as the waiter brought in their drinks, a cinzano for Ajdini, a vodka for Squire, on a silver tray also bearing two bowls of nuts and olives. The waiter slid the bill to Squire as if performing a conjuring trick.

'I find yours an elitist argument,' Ajdini said. 'Naturally, evolution has no party. People are too busy trying just to live, to survive, to worry over evolution. Who can worry over evolution? Surely you don't?'

'Well, "elitist" is just a worn-out Marxist term of abuse, isn't it? Designed to banish thought. I'm trying to establish some sort of historical perspective.'

'Historical perspective is itself a luxury. People with empty bellies care nothing for yesterday or tomorrow.'

He sighed and raised his glass to her, without sipping, lowering it again to say, 'We are not people with empty bellies, you and I, so we must cultivate those perspectives. Don't try to bludgeon me with fake compassion for the starving. You call my background "deeply privileged"; I see it as carrying deep responsibilities – responsibilities for civilized enjoyment as well as duties. Yes, I have good fortune. That is because I have spent most of my life maintaining those values I live for.' He made a dismissive gesture. 'I do not expect you to accept those values as worth maintaining; perhaps you would rather destroy them, since they are those shared by many in my social stratum – among them, during his lifetime, Aldous Huxley.'

He had made his point. Now he drank.

Looking down at her hand resting on the table, she said, 'You evidently did not care for my paper this afternoon.'

Making a slight effort, he said, 'We're off duty now.'

She put fingers to her delicate lips and said, 'I see you do not want to argue. I wonder why that is?'

'I see you want to argue.'

As they both chewed olives, she said, 'However beastly you may find my politics, I am not a dedicated Women's Libber. Not exactly.'

He said nothing to that, having learnt that either approval or disapproval of such statements provoked argument.

After a short silence, she said, 'Before I was into stylistics, I worked in neurosurgery in Los Angeles. That was when I was fresh out of college, apart from a trip to Mexico, where I saw for myself the poverty and injustice suffered there under American imperialism.'

She went on, and he continued to look at her, but her words no longer penetrated to his senses. He thought about her being a neurosurgeon, and saw her character differently, regarded her not just as a woman parroting ideology, but as someone vulnerable and dedicated. About her remarkable face, the sharp planes cutting back from her nose, there was something of the scalpel; but he detected a sensitivity previously hidden from him, perhaps a sensitivity to things to which he remained blind. Her priggish phrase about Mexicans suffering under American imperialism represented some genuine experience of pain and distancing which she could interpret only in terms of political theory.

She was saying, 'Perhaps you know the name of Montrose Wilder. He was very distinguished in his field. It was a privilege to work with him. A good surgeon. Also a good man.

'When I began as a trainee under him, he had a patient aged about forty, who had been involved in a shooting accident and was suffering from a parietal lesion of the brain. Her name was Dorothy, and she was severely dysphasic.

'Montrose stimulated her hippocampus with an electrode. Dorothy suddenly cried out. She told us that she saw her mother in an orange dress – she relived that forgotten time – her mother in an orange dress walked down a hillside towards her, carrying a basket full of apples. The mother was smiling and happy.

'Afterwards, Dorothy cried a lot. Her mother had died when she was five, and she had lost all conscious memory of her. The electrode had allowed her to relive that fragment of life when she was an infant, untouched by trouble. She was grateful. The memory was a gift from a happier world. A land of lost content . . .'

She looked down at her hands. 'I think I can see now, as I'm telling it to you, that Dorothy perceived a linkage between the mother's death when she was five and the attempt of a drunken and jealous lover to murder her at the age of forty. All succeeding messes flowed from that first mess . . .' She bit her lip.

He said something sympathetic. Ajdini ignored him, lighting another 'Drina' and gazing up into the recesses of the room.

74

'I thought of Dorothy when you spoke about souls. If you have looked into living brains, seen the vulnerable exposed hemispheres, you think ever after in terms of electrical impulses, not of souls.'

'Supposing you look more deeply and see both physiological apparatus and electrical impulses as God's handiwork?'

'Do you do that?'

He laughed. 'No. But I wish I could. I am in the anomalous position of believing in souls yet not in God.'

'So art's a comfort, eh?' She was smiling. 'Not that we don't need comforting.'

'Art's many things, isn't it? A comfort for me, a source of argument for you?'

A warmth in her smile, as she responded to his teasing, touched something inside him. 'In the face of such large questions, really art in the twentieth century has little to say. After Kafka – nothing worth having. The Theatre of the Absurd.'

She indicated the bust which impersonally supervised their conversation. 'Do you think this cross-eyed general is elevated to the Absurd? Just a few pencil lines make a difference.'

'They do to any of us.'

'Will you have dinner with me, please? If I promise not to convert you to Marxism.'

'I'd love to, but I have to go out.' Looking at his watch, he added, 'Now.'

He noted her immediate curiosity, and added, 'I have an appointment. Perhaps tomorrow evening.'

'Are you going to a brothel? I hear there are plenty in Ermalpa. Because of the poverty.'

Laughing, he said, 'No, nothing like that.'

'Oh, don't be all English and bashful. If you are going, can I come with you? I won't spoil your enjoyment, but I'd like to talk to the women.'

'*Die Spitze* might like that but I wouldn't. I'm not in the habit of taking ladies to brothels. For one thing, it's too much like taking coals to Newcastle . . .'

She gave him a long look, estimating him. 'You hardly need to pay for your women, I imagine, Mr Squire.'

He drank the last of his vodka. 'Women don't enter into my plans for this evening, unfortunately. Perhaps things will improve in that respect tomorrow.'

Leaving the hotel, Squire was immediately enveloped in the hot evening noise of Ermalpa's traffic. He stood for a moment, reminded of nights in Rio de Janeiro, where a similar mechanical frenzy had prevailed. Something in the Latin temperament caused drivers to project an extended body-image into their machine, converting it to something between a penis and a clenched fist.

He moved suddenly, turning down side streets which he had memorized from his map, down the Via Scarlatti, down the Via Archimede – very dark and crooked, the Via Archimede – through the Piazza O. Ziino, into the modest avenue next to the Giardino Inglese where the British Consulate stood.

As he walked through the warm evening, Squire thought over what he had said to Ajdini; as ever, he had hedged on the question of religion. One could never get free of religion, yet wasn't it all out of date?

Some three years ago, when Squire was still collecting material for 'Frankenstein', he and Teresa had visited the Britannic Centre for Demystified Yoga, to interview its founder, Dr Alexander Saloman. They drove across London to St John's Wood, where the centre was, and found themselves at a Lebanese house. Two Arab women in white robes, complete with yashmaks, were leaving the building as they entered. A dark man in dark glasses wearing a snappy blue suit was on guard, and let them only reluctantly through a mahogany door.

Inside, all was heavy and sumptuous and dark. Large black plastic sofas, upholstered with the wet-look, greeted them. On the walls hung claymores, nineteenth-century sporting prints, and musical instruments from some obscure corner of the East. A gilded lift took them grandly up to the second floor, and to an audience with Dr Alexander Saloman. Teresa held Squire's arm.

Dr Saloman rose to greet them. He was dressed in black – black shirt, black pullover, black slacks, black shoes, with incongruous blue socks. He wore ebony-rimmed spectacles. He was possibly in his late forties. The skin of his face was dry and folded, his hair had been reduced to stubble, either by decision or natural erosion. He had been born in Vienna, and had lived in Argentina for many years before founding Demystified Yoga and returning to Europe. They shook hands formally.

'What is the purpose of your television series? Is it merely entertainment?' he asked Squire, when they had sat down and Squire had refused a Balkan Sobranie cigarette.

'We hope to be entertaining. I want to show people that there are new things in the world to be enjoyed.'

'Why do you come to me?' The eyes were searching and not unfriendly, though they frequently darted to Teresa, who sat staring at Dr Saloman with her head on one side. One would not trust the doctor with women.

'I practise yoga. I like the way it puts actions before words. To my mind, that's the right priority. Someone told me you might be interesting.'

'Wouldn't you say there are old things in the world to be enjoyed?'

Squire hesitated. 'Isn't that obvious? But my series will not be about them.'

Dr Saloman exhaled smoke. 'Are you ambivalent about old things?'

'Old ideas, yes.'

'Are you religious, Mr Squire?' He spoke almost faultless English, without accent.

'I don't believe in God. Yoga cured my lingering belief. I feel most days that God is within me – if he exists at all.'

He wanted Dr Saloman's response to that, but instead the doctor turned sharply to Teresa and asked, 'Do you believe in God, Mrs Squire?'

She smiled. 'We all go to church every Christmas. As a matter of fact, Dr Saloman, I don't like being asked personal questions. That's more my husband's line.'

'We are persons, Mrs Squire. We must sometimes be personal.'

She laughed. 'Oh, I'm a very personal kind of person, Dr Saloman; but on the whole only with friends.'

As she spoke, she shot a glance at Squire; he thought with some approval that she was always able to take care of herself.

The founder of Demystified Yoga nodded seriously and turned back to Squire.

'So you have a belief in yoga?'

'I use yoga because it creates a stillness I enjoy – a stillness in me, I mean. If God exists, he exists in stillness, or so sages have always imagined. Perhaps *pranayama* is God – the breath of life. Let me ask you a question – do you consider Demystified Yoga a new thing or an old thing?'

Dr Saloman said, without pause, 'Is a young oak a new thing or an old thing?'

'I was asking about yoga, not trees.'

'All things connect. Only we have to look for the connections. I am myself a connection. I have to find if that is why you and your wife seek me out. If not, I will not be of use to you. Among other things, I am a connection between East and West, and that is an important connection for our times.'

He looked squarely at Squire. His mouth was wide and blunt, and bracketed powerfully at either end with lines that ran from the flanges of his nostrils.

'I like both yoga and demystification, Dr Saloman, though I'm not sure whether I like them in conjunction. Why do you see the connection between East and West as important at present?'

Dr Saloman put the end of his cigarette in the glass ashtray on his desk and spread his palms wide, so that Squire could see he concealed nothing.

'There are answers to suit cases. I will put one to your case. In the West, there are many old dead ideas which people still cling to. For instance, the idea that the poor must struggle to overthrow the rich is long dead; yet it is kept alive by many petty demagogues who have no other slogans to mouth. Once-living ideas die and become embalmed into single words – Marxism, socialism, liberalism, democracy. Of course I don't speak politically, that's not my sphere. But this is an age of new possibilities. In different circumstances, we must behave differently in order to think differently. Then salvation is not far away.'

A door opened, and a young Indian woman in a bright blue and orange sari entered, bearing a tray. She placed the tray before Dr Saloman, and smiled and nodded at the visitors. He watched her with his dark eyes and his blunt mouth as she left.

While the doctor poured coffee, Squire looked about the room. There were lace curtains at the two tall windows, making the air dim. Everything in the room, including Dr Saloman's enormous desk, was new, gleaming, foreign. Elaborate psychedelic acrylic pictures adorned one wall; there was also a photograph of somewhere that could have been a clinic in Buenos Aires. Perhaps the birthplace of Demystified Yoga, Squire thought.

His wife rose, walking over to him and placing a hand on his shoulder.

'I don't want any coffee,' she told the doctor. 'I'll leave you two to talk. I have some shopping I have to do.'

Squire rose to his feet. 'We won't be long, Tess. Hang on.'

'I'll see you,' she said. 'Goodbye, Dr Saloman.'

Dr Saloman made no comment. He came round the desk and gave Squire a cup of coffee. The cup was small and gold-rimmed; its fragile handle was difficult to grasp.

'My wife gets rather restless,' Squire said, by way of apology. 'I'm very interested in what you say about our being surrounded by dead ideas. I was born with a neutral mind, and consequently have trouble in deciding which ideas are alive, which dead. How does a meeting of East and West help? There are plenty of dead ideas in the East.'

'Of course. We need cross-fertilization. I'll give you another old idea – racialism. But racialism is really ancient, and still has power. It is a true idea although, like Siva, it can be destructive. We must use its power correctly. We must test ourselves on the diversity that still lives between races – use it like a cold shower for our health.

Increased travel accords that opportunity. My belief is that inter-racial contact can gradually obliterate fascism and communism and the other -isms by generating new ideas. Have you been to India? You should go at once.'

'It's not so easy—'

'Of course it's easy. For you it's easy. I can tell it just by the cut of your suit. I also see that you should take your wife with you, for her inner harmony.'

After their conversation, Squire descended through the Lebanese hall and out into the London street. It was October and the leaves were falling. Everything was tranquil. There was no sign of Teresa. He walked slowly to the car, waiting by a parking meter, and climbed in. He allowed himself to relax and think nothing. Eventually she returned, dangling a carrier bag.

'Sorry if I kept you waiting, darling. I've been shopping.'

She settled herself into the passenger seat and showed him a small glass ornament she had bought.

'That yoga man was too boring. He's a real phoney – you won't use him, will you? I couldn't bear it when he went into religion.' She rubbed against him and kissed him on his neck.

'Did you have to walk out like that? It was impolite. Saloman was okay. He said that we should go to India.'

'Let's go back to the hotel. I wasn't being impolite to him – or you. I just suddenly got fed up with being there. I suppose you would say it was ideological. I went there with you to please you; I sat there to please you. Suddenly I wanted to be *central*. You and he were having a great conversation, and I was just sitting there waiting for you to finish. I couldn't bear being an appendage.'

He looked at her with concern. 'You weren't an appendage. I don't see why you didn't enjoy it. He was interesting, was our Doctor.'

'Not to me he wasn't,' she said.

Squire frowned. 'Really, Tess. Just for half-an-hour? You're as involved with religious questions as anyone.'

She put an arm around him. 'Tommy, be nice to me. Don't be grim. Religion's just not something I wanted to talk about. In any case, I hated the way that man stared at me; he was sinister, and if you'd been a woman you wouldn't have liked it either. He looks like a murderer.'

'That's silly, when—'

She sighed. 'All right, it's silly. Let's go back to the hotel. My feet ache, and I need a drink.'

As he reached the British Consulate, he thought ruefully, 'Well, there was a time when I also found religious talk extremely tedious.' But perhaps that wasn't what Teresa had been trying to tell him.

The Consulate was an unimposing building in greying stucco, hiding behind a number of sabre-leaved shrubs which entirely filled the small garden. The gate was locked. He spoke into a grill; the gate opened. He was met at the door by a solid unspeaking man, and shown into a hall whose chief features were a small chandelier and a portrait of the Queen and Prince Philip.

In a minute, James Rotheray appeared, rubbing his hands and smiling with his head slightly on one side in a manner that Squire remembered from schooldays. They shook hands. Rotheray put an arm round Squire's shoulders and led him through the house to an enclosed courtyard where two men were sitting drinking. Rotheray introduced them to Squire and then led him to another table.

'Lovely to see you, Tommy, you're looking first-rate.'

'And you, Sicily evidently agrees with you.'

'Sicily's splendid, full of antiquities. Getting a bit grey round the temples.'

'Me too. And a bit thin on top. Do you still run?'

'No. Jogging hasn't caught on in Ermalpa. We sometimes manage a scratch game of cricket. I suppose the last time we met was at the Travellers.'

'My Uncle Willie's birthday dinner.'

Squire and Rotheray both belonged to the Travellers' Club.

Rotheray brought drinks and concluded the pleasantries by saying, 'It's frightfully kind of you to come round. We have laid on just a few people for dinner – a dozen, no more – who are looking forward to meeting you and having a chat. It'll all be jolly pleasant, and we have a really good chef. So before we go any further, if you like, we'll talk about . . . what I know you want to talk about. I've got my secretary here, who can give you official advice. He's a first-rate chap.'

He called over one of the men at the other table, a young man with a massive handshake who was introduced as Howard Parker-Smith. Squire recognized the type, or hoped he did: well-muscled body under well-tailored suit, uncompromising attitude under well-bred politeness: and felt pleased that such men still prospered.

'Bring your drink over,' he said to Parker-Smith. Parker-Smith went and fetched a beer.

'Cigarette, sir?' said Parker-Smith, offering a packet. Squire refused, Rotheray took one.

'I'm particularly interested in the two Russians attending the conference,' Squire said. 'What have you got on them?'

Parker-Smith produced a neatly folded sheet of typed paper from his jacket pocket, laid it on the table in front of him, and said, without giving it a glance, 'Georgi Mihailovic Kchevov. We've got quite a lot on him, although he's only a minor ugly. Born 1935, in a town called, encouragingly, Proletarsky, in South Russia. Quite near the border with the Ukraine. Both parents killed 1943 in Great Patriotic War.'

'I don't need a life-story,' Squire said.

'Well, speaks German, some Polish, and Bulgarian. No English as far as is known. First sent outside USSR about five years ago, did heavy work in Gdansk among dock workers, earned promotion. Returned to Russia to KGB Advanced Technical College in Sudzhensk for one year refresher and on cadre there briefly. He played in an orchestra there.'

'What's that?' Squire asked.

'Comrade Kchevov plays the violin. Played in Kursk Youth Orchestra, 1944, for example. Also with him in the Sudzhensk Technical Orchestra was one Luyben Konstantinov, another habitual violin player.'

'I know that name. Konstantinov.'

'Luyben Konstantinov is Bulgarian. When he returned to Bulgaria from Sudzhensk, Kchevov went with him. This year, Kchevov materialized in Bonn a month before the Bulgarian defectors were killed in London and Paris. Kchevov was one of the forward men acting for Konstantinov, who master-minded the killings from Sofia.'

Squire rested his elbows on the table and ran his fingers down the lines of his face.

'Let's have that again, more slowly. What's all this about the Bulgarians? How do they come into it?'

For a moment, Parker-Smith allowed himself to display a little impatience.

'You must surely remember the case of Georgi Markov, a Bulgarian defector who worked for the BBC and Radio Free Europe. Killed by a poison pellet in the heart of London. Konstantinov master-minded that operation from Sofia. He runs Department Two – Counter-Espionage. Of course, it's lousy with Russians. Bulgaria's owned, lock, stock, and barrel, by the KGB. Which is how Georgi Kchevov got in on the act.'

He spoke with the air of one stating the obvious, looking searchingly to and fro at Rotheray and Squire.

'So Georgi Kchevov is quite important,' Rotheray said.

'Not really, James,' Parker-Smith said. 'He was only middleman in a chain of command, probably didn't know a lot of what went on. Certainly didn't do any of the hits. His hands are clean by KGB standards. He's probably here on holiday, more or less. Reward for being efficient. But possibly keeping an eye on Rugorsky to justify the trip. Speaks fluent Italian, of course.'

'Okay. He flew here straight from Bonn?'

Parker-Smith shook his head. 'He's been living in Milan under an alias since May. He didn't like Bonn – the good old Krauts leaned on him. He linked up with Rugorsky only yesterday, at Rome airport. We and the Americans had tabs on him. Chaps like Kchevov know that security's slacker in Italy than north of the Alps, so they aren't quite so watchful here. After all, country's half-communist anyway.'

He caught a glance from Rotheray, fell silent, and sipped his beer.

'Why was Kchevov invited to the conference?' Rotheray asked.

'He wasn't. He just turned up. Nothing unusual in that.' Squire thought for a while and then said, 'Violin apart, Kchevov has about as much connection with the arts as Pavlov has with Pavlova. There must be hundreds of his type crawling round England and Western Europe, worse luck. So what about Rugorsky? He's the one who really interests me.'

'Vasili Rugorsky. Age fifty. Prematurely grey. He met you in London in 1970, according to the records,' Parker-Smith said.

'Correct. Unlike Kchevov, he is a man of genuine culture. I was told he has made liberal gestures in his time. In particular, he spent several years in hard labour in the Gulag, back in Joe Stalin's day, for writing a poem which offended the authorities.'

Parker-Smith nodded. 'Our records aren't precise that far back. We think that Stalin commuted the sentence. If so, that's unusual. Seen in Moscow late 1947, then no notice of whereabouts for some years. Back on *katorga* in 1950. But in 1956 he is working again as a biologist. That's his qualification. Continues at Irkutsk Institute of Biological Sciences until '70, when he moves to Leningrad.'

'Poem forgiven. Conformity achieved?'

'The poem itself is interesting,' Rotheray said, leaning forward in his chair. '"Winter Celebration". They sent us a copy of it in translation with the other details. It likens the Soviet community to a sort of medieval feast with a great hog's head steaming on a platter as main attraction. Stalin evidently didn't care for the comparison. For a British reader, it's difficult to tell whether Rugorsky was being slyly satirical or clumsily attempting flattery.'

As Parker-Smith began reciting more facts, Squire broke in, saying, 'Rugorsky looks a bit like a hog's head himself, which suggests a new line in literary criticism. Rather a fleshy face, hectic colour, protruding nose. He spoke to me at lunch about the duties of those who can still distinguish between true and false. Made what I took to be veiled anti-Soviet remarks. Keen to establish contact. I had the same impression in London in 1970. Despite his history, he moves fairly freely in the West, even if he's stuck with Kchevov as a watchdog this time. He flew here straight from Moscow via Rome, you say?'

'I didn't say that,' Parker-Smith said. 'He had twenty-four hours on the loose in Rome between flights. We don't know what he did. Brothels is the standard thing, of course.'

'Home life?'

Parker-Smith condescended to peep at his sheet of paper. 'Wife and two sons, now aged between twenty-five and thirty, both pukka Party members. Four-room flat in Leningrad suburb near university. He's probably perfectly loyal to the system, if that's what you're thinking about. He knows the bosses and their psychology, they know him, everyone's happy. They accept his style, he makes good propaganda for them abroad as a cultured broad-minded chappie quite ready to criticize shortcomings of government system, just like any Westerner. Or Yevtushenko.'

'Or like some of our buggers, who go abroad and run down the British system in every way, before returning to cushy jobs and free education for the kiddies,' Squire said. A thought struck him. 'Rugorsky's not likely to be a genuine dissatisfied customer, preparing to defect, as far as you know?'

Pursing his lips, Parker-Smith shook his head very slightly.

'Look, if Rugorsky wants to defect – surprising how many Russians at the age of the male menopause do hop it – he'd be best advised to do so in Rome, not Ermalpa. Aeroflot doesn't fly here, so he's booked back to Rome via Alitalia next Monday morning – same flight as you, as it happens. He changes planes at Leonardo da Vinci, where he has a four-hour wait before catching the Aeroflot plane on to Moscow. In that breathing space, he could give Kchevov the shake if he wished, and head for the US Embassy.'

'If he did make a break for it here in Ermalpa,' Rotheray said, 'he'd still be best advised to run for the American Consulate. We don't want him here. Our stock with the Russians is low enough for them to break in here and grab him – aided by fixed local police, let me add. No, as Howard says, Rome's his best bet.' He rubbed his hands together and laughed.

Seriousness prevailed with Parker-Smith. 'I'd guess he's just a hanger-on of the system, Mr Squire. Plays both sides. Likes to make a few mildly anti-Soviet remarks, knowing they go down well with his hosts in the West, and makes him think he has integrity.'

'Good. We know where we stand. Now, did you get me anything on Herman Fittich, Professor of Literature in the University of Bad Neustadt?'

'Nothing exciting. Was conscripted at the age of fifteen into the Wehrmacht to defend Berlin in its last days. Mother raped and killed by Soviet Army of Glorious Liberation during that time. Quiet life since then. Holidays in Britain. Not a joiner, apparently. Good English, papers published in learned American journals. What were you hoping for?'

'Just what you've given me. The detail about his mother is informative. I like Fittich. I think he's just what I think he is, a serious and honourable man who does not much care for the present state of the world. Rugorsky is more of a mystery. But I expect you're right; he's probably harmless.'

Tucking the still-folded sheet of paper back in his pocket, Parker-Smith stubbed out the remains of his cigarette, drained his glass, and stood up. 'If you learn anything of interest, do let us know. It all fits into a larger picture. If I can be of any further help, give me a ring.'

They shook hands and Parker-Smith faded politely away.

'So much for business,' Rotheray said, looking at his watch. 'Now for something more social – more my line, I'm afraid. Anything else we can help you with while you're here?'

'No, thanks, James. It's just a fairly ordinary quasi-academic congress, crawling with Lefties, as you'd expect. There's an interesting American woman who arrived via West Germany, very cool and elegant but underneath very mixed-up, I suspect. Perhaps a real sympathy with the oppressed but it's been channelled into Marxist lines and has withered under a stream of orthodox phraseology. She feels herself in some way trapped and cheated.'

'What age?'

'Oh, she'd be about – early forties. Well-preserved. Has a very cleansed, bare, even barren, appearance. Thinks that just to see a human brain lying in its shell is enough to banish thoughts of God and the human soul. I suspect a deep puritanism as regards sex and the flesh – a feeling she projects onto me. Americans nearly always reflexively suspect the English of puritanism. A strabismus in their history education. She hid it by talking nonchalantly about brothels.'

'There are no good brothels in Ermalpa,' said Rotheray. 'So I'm told. All the attractive whores go to Palermo or Naples or Rome. They return here only when they're old and desperately in need of a re-bore. Anyhow, how's Teresa?'

'Hasn't your secret service been keeping you informed? We broke up last summer, during the heat wave. Haven't quite managed to get things together again since.'

'I am sorry, Tommy. You and Teresa were always such a jolly pair. Why, you knew each other when we were up at King's and she was at Newnham. She's got a slight squint, hasn't she?'

'No.'

'My mistake. Sorry. To be honest, I did hear a whisper, but I hoped it was all over. Difficult creatures, women, I've always found. Is this Marxist American woman nice?'

'Oh, she's nothing to do with me.'

'I thought you sounded interested. Well, let's go and see about dinner. I hope that'll cheer you up a bit.'

Rotheray led the way to what proved to be a pleasant meal, considering that it was a semi-formal British Consulate dinner.

5

She's Only a Sex Symbol

Pippet Hall, Norfolk, June 1977

All the girls cared for was the beautiful weather. They were off early for what they called their 'secret beach', hurrying away on bicycles, with Nellie running effortlessly beside them. Teresa's mother had gone back to her flat in Grantham for the weekend. It was Saturday morning. Teresa and Tom Squire faced one another alone across the breakfast table.

For the past three nights, he had slept in the chief guest room. Teresa was moody and inaccessible.

'I'm going to drive into Norwich to see Uncle Willie,' Squire said, as he folded his napkin. 'Come with me and we'll have lunch in Cutteslow's.'

She looked down at her plate. 'I'd prefer to stay here.'

'I've some business to discuss with him, but I won't be long.'

Teresa had no answer. She prodded a triangular piece of toast in the rack with one finger, rattling it against the silver sides of its pen. The slight mouselike noise conveyed a powerful sense of futility.

'All over the world, poor buggers are being shut up in dungeons or hung up by their thumbs. We've got peace and plenty. Cheer up and come to Norwich with me.'

He studied the silver coffee service, concentrating in particular on the cream jug with its complex reflections of white cloth and blue room which were, in their turn, reflected in the swelling side of the sugar bowl, minutely, distortedly, but with gallant precision. The arrangement reminded him of a canvas by William Nicholson, which his father had once told him was his favourite painting in the Tate, except for the Cotmans.

He sighed. 'I really am sorry about the lady-friend, Tess. Sorry the thought of her hurts you, I mean. It will be only temporary . . . as all things are . . . Don't let it mess up our relationship.'

Her anger burned suddenly like a gorse fire, leaping up into her cheek and eyes. She grasped her knife, as if about to strike him with it. '"Don't let it mess up our relationship!" What do I have to do with that? You've already messed it up. That's your role in life. You can't be relied on. You're always chasing other women – you don't want me at all.'

'That is not so. Perhaps you want it to be so, but it is not. Our relationship is a long and enduring one, I hope.'

She lowered her head, hiding her eyes; the prelude to weeping. He saw with tenderness how the dark roots of her hair were showing through the fake gold.

'Come with me to Norwich and be sensible. We'll stroll round the Tombland antique shops.'

'Another demand!' she said without heat, looking up. 'Don't mess things up. Come to Norwich. Be sensible. I'm sick of being sensible and not messing things up, if you want to know. I'm staying here, as I told you – I have a business associate to see. Go to Norwich on your own. And give up that actress bitch. She's half your age, it's filthy! Give her up at once or I won't be responsible for what happens.'

'I've told you, we're still filming. It will be over soon. Don't try to make me angry.'

'Get her the sack, find someone else for the part, damn her!'

He rose from the table, standing irresolutely with his hand on the back of his chair, aware of the sun outside the windows, chilled by her anger.

'Tess!'

'One of these days, you'll find you've cried my name too late. How much more have I got to stand? John going off as he has – that was your fault – Daddy dying while you were screwing that bitch in Singapore—'

He laughed. 'Since I was out of the country at the time, you can hardly blame me for your father's death.'

'How much more have I got to stand? That girl's only a sex symbol. You're always chasing symbols. I hope she gets cancer like me and dies before your very eyes, blast her!'

'I'm going, Teresa.'

'Go, then, go! She's waiting for you in Norwich, is she, the slut?'

'Excuse me.'

He left the room, moving slowly, hoping she would call him back, would recant, would throw her arms round him and say how sorry she was to hurt him, thus releasing him to do the same. Instead, he heard a plate smash. As he went towards the stairs to collect his wallet and keys from his bedroom, he turned the corner of the corridor and almost bumped into a young man in a denim suit hurrying through the hall.

The young man had long but not very long hair. He wore his sideboards long and cut sharp across the cheeks, so that they appeared to be executing a pincer movement against his nose. It was a harmless-looking nose, but the teeth were large and many, seeming to multiply as he smiled, as now he did, in a rather anxious way. 'Oh, jeez, Mr Squire, you frightened me, lovely morning, isn't it?'

'Who are you and who let you in here?'

'Oh, don't you remember me? Vern? Vernon Jarvis, how are you?'

'What are you doing in here?'

The young man fell back a step. He put a cautionary hand out.

'We met at your party before you flew off to Singapore. I just bumped into that Miss Rowlinson outside, and she said to come in. I heard voices, so I thought—'

He was carrying a smart mock-leather executive's attaché case, incongruous against his green denim-styled suit and fancy shoes with wedge heels. Despite the heat wave, he wore a fawn turtle-neck sweater under the suit, and a gold-plated ingot stamped with a zodiacal sign on a chain round his neck.

'You're the fellow with the brother who runs.'

'Athlete, yes. Hoping to run in Moscow in the Olympic Games. We talked about that, remember?'

'You claimed that sport had nothing to do with politics.'

'You see, Mr Squire, I'm a great admirer of Teresa's – of Mrs Squire's wall trinketry. It's real rinky-dink gear.'

'Wall-trinketry, what's that?'

Jarvis lowered the attaché case, hitherto held in a defensive position, and said with a touch of condescension, '*The* wall-trinketry. Those bugs and creepy-crawlies. Those bugs and creepy-crawlies she *makes*. I aim to invest in them. I'm a director of an exporting firm, and by my calculations—'

'All right, all right. My wife's in the breakfast room. I doubt if she'll want to see you at this hour of the morning.'

Jarvis smirked. 'Oh, she'll want to see me all right.'

'In future, ring the bell before you come barging in, understand?'

'Yes, that's quite clear.' Jarvis smiled at him.

Driving away a few minutes later, Squire saw Jarvis and Teresa by the window of the morning room, deep in discussion. She was leaning against her desk, and did not even look up at the sound of the car. Poor dear, he thought. As if she hadn't trouble enough without having that young oik to deal with.

The sudden death of her father, Ernest Davies, had shaken her. Ernest had been walking home from a friend's house in Grantham one evening, when a car bore down on him as he crossed the road, and knocked him over. He had died in hospital a few days later. The car had been driven by his doctor, heavily under the influence of drink. Astrology had closed over Teresa's head almost immediately.

He switched on the car radio.

He recognized the music at once. The Tom Robinson Band playing 'Long Hot Summer'. He smiled.

Saturday morning traffic into town was heavy. It took him an hour to reach Norwich, but he was in no hurry.

The conversation had come back to him. Jarvis's brother hoped to run for Britain in the four hundred metres of the Moscow Olympics. Squire, as a member of the board of anti-Moscow campaigners, tried to explain to Jarvis that the occasion would inevitably be used for propaganda purposes, like the 1936 Olympics in Berlin.

'No, no, Mr Squire, honest, you don't see, neither my brother nor me are at all political. This is purely and simply a sporting event.'

'Things aren't so simple. It's not what you are, Mr Jarvis, but what you lend yourself to.'

'No, you've got it all wrong, Mr Squire. I know you like politics, but, see, I'm just a businessman, pure and simple, out to make an honest penny, and I hate politics. So does my brother.'

After a drive round, Squire found a parking place in Mancroft Street. Locking the Jag, he walked slowly through Tombland, enjoying the sunshine, stopping occasionally to glance in a shop window. At the bookshop, he walked in and gazed at the books, but saw nothing he wished to buy.

The offices of Challenor, Squire, and Challenor, of which William Squire was senior partner, were built of mellow Georgian red bricks, very similar to the bricks of Pippet Hall. The facade of the building was covered by a venerable virginia creeper, the leaves and suckers of which lapped at William Squire's office window. William had officially retired the previous year, but still worked every morning, looking after old clients of many years' standing, who refused to transfer their business to the brisk young partners who occupied the lower floors.

Uncle Willie's office was at the top of the building. The floors below had been modernized, their small rooms broken down into an open-plan scheme which let in more air and custom, rather in the same way that the fields beyond Norwich – the title deeds to which reposed, in many cases, in the archives of Challenor, Squire, and Challenor – had been stripped of their hedges to let in more air and agricultural machinery. Squire made his way past empty desks and silent computer screens to the third floor.

Uncle Willie's office was a small room on the side of the building, with a window from which the cathedral could almost be seen. Uncle Willie was pottering round smoking his pipe, with the rather sulky-looking Nicholas Dobson in attendance. Dobson was a nephew who had high hopes in the firm. He lived nearby. His expression suggested that he would rather be elsewhere on a hot summer Saturday morning, but he greeted Squire cheerfully enough.

Coughing, Uncle Willie rested his pipe in a marble ashtray and came round the desk to shake hands formally with his nephew.

'You're looking fit, Tom. Gallivanting round the world has been good for you. We're heading for a drought, could be worse than last year, and that won't please most of my clients.' Willie bore a strong resemblance to his dead brother John, Tom Squire's father. He too had a high-bridged nose and a pugnacious set to his jaw. The deep-set lines of the family face had visited him too. So had the clear skin. Although his hair was white, it remained thick.

Thomas thanked his uncle for seeing him on Saturday, although he knew that the old man, a widower for many years, often visited the office on Saturday mornings in order to keep the lethargy of old age staunchly at bay.

The years had hunched his shoulders. He regarded his nephew with a vaguely aggressive air, and then transferred his gaze to the open window.

'How's Teresa?'

'She's fine, Uncle. How are the cats?'

'I've had Nickie spayed. She was turning into a regular kitten-factory. Madge, is she all right? Still staying with you? Terrible about Ernest. Madge makes a pretty widow, poor lady. How's she taking it?' As he spoke of Mrs Davies, he walked over to the window and looked out.

'She seems cheerful enough. It's Teresa who's upset.'

'In my experience,' said Uncle Willie, still gazing out of the window, 'widows are not too unhappy when they are left to pursue their own lives, though they may make a polite show of grief. It's different for widowers.'

He turned and inspected his nephew, to see how the remark had registered.

'Teresa's having a series of nightmares. Always the same, though details differ. Sometimes it seems to be day, sometimes night. She is sitting or lying down when she sees a dark male figure outlined against the window. Someone is trying to break in. Sometimes she tries to scare him away, sometimes she runs from him, sometimes she wakes to the sound of smashing glass.'

'Oh, she's afraid of burglars while you're away.' He went over and picked his pipe up, as if the matter was disposed of.

'There might be another explanation. She complains of back pain. She keeps talking about – well, cancer. She goes to Dr Bell. He gives her analgesics, and she's gone to the Norfolk and Norwich for check-ups. All reports are negative to date.'

From the other side of the room, Dobson said, 'They say cancer's psychosomatic.'

'Nicholas thinks everything's psychosomatic, including taxes,' Uncle Willie said. 'Do you think she's got cancer, Tom? Eh?'

'No, I don't . . . I'm anxious, of course, but the tests, as I say, are negative. People do get these ideas, and I wonder if the dream doesn't indicate something of the force of Tess's obsession.'

'Well.' Uncle Willie shuffled with some papers on his desk, as though he had lost interest in Teresa. 'I hope that now you're back home you'll both settle down, you and Teresa. She's a good girl but she needs a bit of looking after, don't forget that.'

Squire considered saying more on the matter, caught Dobson's eye, and decided against it. He turned to other things.

His London firm had been understanding, and had allowed him maximum freedom during the planning and filming of 'Frankenstein Among the Arts'; now he had to notify them that he would be away longer than anticipated. He wanted his uncle to draft a proper letter, waiving his salary. There were also some long-standing matters which needed attention, such as a protracted argument with the local authorities over a right-of-way across Pippet land. Dobson brought out his file, and they talked for thirty minutes.

'Business over,' Willie said at last. 'Nicholas, leave the file out and we'll go and have a coffee.'

Downstairs, at the side door, he made a great business of seeing that the security bolt was functional. Dobson directed a pitying look over his bent back at Squire. Then they sauntered over to a coffee shop almost opposite St Ephraim's Gate, Dobson walking smartly ahead.

'They're still talking about putting a motorway through to Bury and Chelmsford,' Uncle Willie said, as they selected a table, looking with some dislike at the holiday-makers who surrounded them. 'Then they'll continue it up here. It'll mean the end of East Anglia's isolation, and the end of Norwich and Norfolk as they have been for centuries.'

'Don't worry, Uncle,' Dobson said. 'In the present state of the country's finances, they've stopped building roads. Norwich will be safe for this century.'

'I'm not so sure.' He picked up the menu with contempt. 'Once a planner has planned, and lodged his plans in Whitehall, the abstraction seems to acquire an existence of its own . . . Well, you offer some consolation for our bad trade figures, if they help to protect tradition.'

As the waitress came up, he smiled at her and said, 'I suppose you're still making coffee here in the traditional way – with instant coffee?'

She was young and pleasant-faced. She leaned forward, smiling, and supported her weight by resting one hand on the table. 'I know you're very fond of our coffee, Mr Squire, and it hasn't gone up this week.'

'In that case, we'll treat ourselves to a cup each,' he said, looking up at her in a sprightly way. When the girl had gone, he shook his head and said to his nephews, 'When I was a young man, you were not supposed to address remarks to the waitress. It was bad form. Rigid class structure. I prefer the way things are today. I discovered at quite an advanced age that I enjoy flirting with waitresses. They don't seem to mind, so why not?' He blew his nose on a large white handkerchief. 'The war changed things. Changed everything. Of course, no one knows exactly what waitresses think, doing the job they do.'

'Come on, Uncle,' Dobson said. 'No one knows what solicitors think about.'

'Increasingly, waitresses,' said Uncle Willie, with a laugh. 'This place used to be a Red Cross shop during the war. Did I ever tell you that? Then it became an antique shop. That didn't last.'

'I remember the antique shop,' Squire said. 'I bought about ten garage signs from the dealer, including a Redline Glyco and a Pratt's High Test, enamel on tin. We used them in the Pop Expo.'

'Your father used to chase waitresses,' Uncle Willie said, ignoring Squire's remark. 'There's always been a sort of naughty streak in the Squire family, I'm sorry to say. That is why we don't get on with the branch of the family at King's Lynn – the Decent Dobsons. Except you, Nick. Do you take after your father, Tom?'

John Matthew Squire, his father, had been a countryman, like most of the family in that generation, involved in the affairs of the village and the county. John Squire seldom moved beyond those self-imposed boundaries except when, following the steps of the ancestor whose name he bore, he joined the Royal Norfolk Regiment and went to fight for four years in the assorted muds of Europe, returning home to Hartisham with the rank of major, saying, 'It was quite a good scrap while it lasted.'

Somewhere along the way, John Squire acquired several tastes which led to his downfall. He acquired a taste for art. To the dogs and horses which were his life, he added the Norwich School of painters. They were local men, they painted local things and were faithful to them, not prettifying too much. With his favourite mastiffs at his heels, John Squire became a notable figure as he toured the country, attending markets and, just as assiduously, dusty old shops and attics. Where he went, his son Tom also went. Together, while the dogs prowled round them, father and son acquired a commendable gallery of watercolours and oils by Old Crome, Stoddart, the incomparable Cotman, and others.

'Tractors may drive out Shire horses,' John said, 'but Cotman is permanent.'

Pippet Hall estate, in financial difficulties after the Great War, became more neglected as the art excursions ranged further afield. John's red-haired wife, Patricia, was left to supervise the farm and bring up her other two children, Adrian and Deirdre.

John and his son Tom stayed overnight in country inns as they went on what John called their 'Grand Tours'. The Morris and the mastiffs would be housed in the stables – very few Norfolk inns expected motor cars in the thirties. Tom would often be tucked into a wooden bed in some attic room; his cheek was scoured by a stiff military moustache as his father kissed him good-night, before disappearing below to join whatever company the bar offered; he disappeared with particular promptness if there were women downstairs.

Sometimes the boy would wake in the summer mornings early and run to the window of the strange room, to gaze out at a panorama of rushes and broads, busy bird life, and little boats already launching into the early golden haze over the waters. He always remembered an inn on Hickling Broad, where there was a tame magpie, and he and his father swam naked in the broad before breakfast.

John Squire had a taste also for jazz and popular dance music. Gramophone records began to accumulate at Pippet Hall. Patricia liked that. The records were played on a wind-up gramophone with a huge horn. When Tom and his brother and sister were small, many visitors came to the Hall, attracted by the happy-go-lucky nature of their parents. The visitors sometimes danced to the music of the gramophone, which Tom was allowed to wind. He watched his father as he took his beautiful wife about the waist and whirled her round the entrance hall, where the floor was good for fox-trots.

There was another taste, and one which slowly mastered the master of Pippet Hall. John progressed from being a heavy social drinker to being a heavy drinker. It was that habit which brought about his death, one rainy day in March 1937, when the rest of the family was out of the house.

Tom returned home in the afternoon. The solemn ticking silence warned him that something was wrong. He flung his cap down and ran straight to his father's study. His father lay in one corner of the study, against a smashed picture frame, the glass of which littered the carpet. It was established later that he must have fallen over the mastiffs while the worse for drink. Both dogs had attacked him. They lurked in the opposite corner of the room, chops still bloody. Their master's throat had been ripped away, and the flesh of his face torn off.

The dogs sulked behind John Squire's armchair, knowing their crime. John's son, aged eight, took down one of his father's double-barrelled shotguns from the rack by the door, loaded it, and shot both animals through their skulls at close range. Blood and brains spattered in parabolas across the wallpaper. Then he dropped the gun and ran away into the plantation, where he huddled at the foot of a young oak until one of the farm labourers found him after dusk.

It was hard to tell where Uncle Willie's remarks led, or indeed if they were intended to lead anywhere. He rambled as they drank their coffee, mainly about the 'naughty streak' in the family.

'I don't think I chase waitresses obsessively, Uncle Willie,' Squire said.

'Well, you enjoy a busy life, that I know. When success carries a man beyond family and native heath, he loses his sense of reality. I always say it. A protective sense of reality. A man's achievements in the material world are often seen to be counterbalanced by deterioration in his personal happiness. Supposing our waitress to marry the Prince of Wales tomorrow, she would undoubtedly come to look back on her humble days in this coffee shop as a time of security and happiness. However she may see the matter now.'

'It's not like you to recommend a dull way of life as a paradigm of better things.'

Nicholas Dobson snorted, as if he knew his uncle better, but Willie ignored him.

The old man wiped his lips on the white handkerchief. 'Don't be angry, Tom, I'm only offering a warning.'

'I've managed to look after my own affairs fairly well so far. Why don't you approve?'

Willie looked offended. 'You are making connections between things I did not intend. That's always your clever habit of thought, I understand that.'

'What are you accusing me of?'

Uncle Willie stuck his pipe in his mouth and began lighting it. He said, behind a cloud of smoke, 'You want to stay home a bit more – that was your father's mistake.'

Squire leaned forward so that the people sitting at the next table did not hear what he said. 'Father would have approved strongly of my present work. I care deeply about it, I wouldn't care if I never went back to the firm. It's little enough, but I'm good at it, I think. In me there's a lot of the family's romanticism. I want to make a contribution to the thought of our country, I want to produce a cultural statement which I believe will help England, and maybe the rest of the world, to live more fully despite its present difficulties. I want to make everyone aware of the immense riches round about them in everyday life.'

'Through TV? Through television? What can you do for television viewers? You can't make them switch the set off, can you? I've no time for it. Fat lot it has to do with individual life. Paralysis, more to the point.'

With spirit, Squire said, 'I believe that television has much to do with individual life. Continual box-watching is sad, I agree, sad because it shows you how lacking in opportunities is the average life. But television touches everyone as no art medium has ever done; it represents the triumph of photography, and the wonder is that it's as good as it is. It must be respected. Why not respect it, develop it, now, rather than mourn for it when it is superseded, as no doubt it will be?'

The waitress had brought the bill on a saucer. Squire brushed away his uncle's hand and produced some money.

Willie shook his head. 'I've got a set in my flat. Never switch it on, except for the news. Give me a good book any day. Harrison Ainsworth, he's a good author. I'm just rereading *The Tower of London*. It's full of incident and good description.'

'Very pleasant, I'm sure, Uncle.' He signalled impatiently to the waitress. 'You do not refute, you illustrate what I was saying. Carlyle said people always loved the past and the things of the past because it was safe, whereas the future was dangerous, since it had still to be negotiated.'

'Carlyle was a sensible chap.'

They parted outside the shop, shaking hands. Squire walked briskly in the direction of the Castle. He was angry with himself, he hardly knew why; he had been harsher than he intended with his revered relation.

Nicholas Dobson came hurrying up and fell into step with him. 'You are upset, and I don't blame you. I have to say to you that some of us at least support you. You add lustre to the family, Tom, and God knows it could do with it. We're a miserable lot, the Dobsons even worse than the Squires. We're just lived lives of dull Norfolk monotony for centuries. As for Uncle Willie's moans about TV, he's just a disappointed old man. He doesn't—'

Squire had slowed his pace. Now he halted. 'No, Willie's a fine man. If he's disappointed, it's because most people end up disappointed if they had any guts in them originally. They start out in life with high hopes and high ambitions which maybe circumstances prevent them from fulfilling, or they can't overcome their own limitations. Uncle Willie never quite achieved the career he wished for himself. That isn't to say that he hasn't been an honourable man, and served others well thereby. I admire Uncle Willie and won't hear a word against him. I was too quick with him.'

Dobson put his hands in his pockets. 'You make me ashamed of myself,' he said, grinning and looking far from ashamed. 'But I have to listen to Uncle Willie holding forth a lot more than you do.'

'It was good of you to come after me.' He clapped the young man's arm. 'If you've got time to spare, visit the Castle exhibition with me.'

They crossed Bedford Street and climbed the many steps up to Norwich Castle. Squire got out of breath more easily than once he did. After a word with the keeper, who was an old friend of Squire's, the two men went into the exhibition. It was crowded with tourists.

This was not Squire's favourite way of viewing any exhibition, but he had been abroad when it visited London.

They regarded objects which had come from the Siberian Collection of Peter the Great. Many articles had been preserved by cold, as articles in Egypt were preserved by the dry atmosphere. There were decorations of wood and leather which had once adorned the horses of nomads. All that remained of the dreaded Scythians rested here behind glass: a woollen pigtail case, part of a boot, a child's fur coat dating from five centuries before Christ. Chance survivors of their culture, these artifacts were beyond price; isolated from it, they were inscrutable. Whilst the permutations of chance which brought them to this foreign place were incalculable.

Since Nicholas Dobson still seemed eager for company, Squire took him to his favourite pub, The Pyed Bull on the Market Square, for lunch after the exhibition. The pub was crowded. They bumped into two of Dobson's friends, both of whom were cheerful, out of work, and engaged in touring the country picketing nuclear power plants. They regarded nuclear power as too dangerous to use. When Squire offered them a few statistics on the excellent safety record of the industry, they listened politely, smiling a bit, and then went on enthusiastically about the success they had had at Dungeness.

'There are many reasons why the country needs to develop nuclear power,' Squire said. 'I'm sure you know the arguments, and I won't bore you with them, but it is at present the best practical alternative to coal and oil.'

'We'll just have to go without oil when it runs out,' one of the young men said. He wore a T-shirt with the words 'Sid Vicious' across the chest, but was otherwise well-mannered. 'Get rid of all the cars spoiling towns.'

'And the lorries, trains, planes, and ships delivering the goods we need,' Squire said.

'There'll be something else,' said the other young man. 'Something always turns up, doesn't it? We'll develop Uri Geller powers, telepathy, telekinesis . . . The powers of the human mind are unlimited.'

Almost despite himself, Squire said, 'Unfortunately, history gives no indication that that is so. The mind has its limitations – it's almost impossible to pass on the fruits of experience, for instance. Civilizations make mistakes and fossilize and go under. If we continue to impede latest developments by picketing nuclear plants, or pretend that things turn up of their own accord instead of resulting from hard work and applied intelligence, then we shall go down the drain too.'

'We're down the drain already, aren't we?' The two young men laughed and soon took their leave.

'Sorry about that, Tom,' Dobson said. 'I knew they'd annoy you. They were doing it half as a lark.'

'I wasn't annoyed. They told me what they felt. I told them what I felt. I suppose they regard me as an old-fashioned old man with silly ideas. All the same, you observe that the pendulum has swung dramatically – ten years ago, the man in my position would have been conservative and against nuclear plants. The youngsters would have been calling for innovation. But there, neither you nor your friends could know what the pendulum was doing ten years ago. You were still at school.'

'We were learning about the hazards of nuclear power.' He drained his glass.

'Those hazards have been greatly exaggerated – mainly by the Left for its own interests.'

Dobson smiled. 'I don't want to get onto politics, not my favourite subject. Thanks. Let me buy you another beer.'

'No, thanks. I must get home. Nick, it's sad that your generation should be against such things as nuclear power. My generation believed in the future.'

'It's not so much us that's against it as ecology itself. We want to save the world, not ruin it. You can't go on for ever piling technology on technology with no thought for the consequences. Surely you can see that.'

'Nor can you continue to strip a country of military or economic weapons without suffering the inevitable consequences.'

'People just aren't patriotic any more in the old way. We've learnt better. You are fond of talking about new developments, why can't you see that one development is the junking of old emotions like patriotism which did so much damage? The world is really becoming one – something you talk about but can't understand. I can feel as much sympathy for an oppressed Greek or Chilean as I can for my next-door neighbour.'

'But, Nick, you probably know damn all about the actual problems of people in Greece or Chile. You've just read a paragraph or two in some newspaper or seen something on TV—'

Dobson looked angry. 'I have every respect for you, Tom, but I'm not going to sit here listening to you knock down everything I say. I have a dream of a better, fairer world. Well, let me have it. You told Willie that you believe in dreams, well, let me believe in mine.'

'If you're referring to Teresa's dream, that happened to be a nightmare, and my point was that it was difficult to interpret. So is yours. I believe yours is a dream of evading real responsibilities. It would be nice in a perfect world, to coast along thinking things are somehow improving of their own accord just because you and your pals hope things will work out that way, but in fact the world is filled with powerful enemies who have a rough way with dreams, are quite prepared to step in and impose their own nightmares.'

'I don't believe that either, any more than you believe in my sympathies for the Greeks.'

They parted five minutes later, rather stiffly, and went their different ways.

Squire went to The Nag's Head and phoned Laura Nye at her London address. He could hear the bell ringing in her flat, but it was not answered. On the following Tuesday he was due to go to London to film the last episode of 'Frankenstein Among the Arts', and would see Laura then. Meanwhile, he could only speculate on how she was passing the weekend, as he drove home.

The road north from Norwich, which casually followed the course of the River Wensum, was full of traffic. Squire switched on the radio and drove slowly, blanking out his thoughts by concentrating on the pleasure of the peaceful summer day. Nobody seemed in a particular hurry to reach the coast. Families were going to picnic and swim, no world was dying, there was no invisible and fateful drama such as Solzhenitsyn envisaged being enacted in these unguarded hours. No need for apprehension.

The first sight of Hartisham when coming from the south was the ruins of Hartisham Priory. The priory had been founded in the year 1131. It had once enshrined a relic of the Holy Cross, and had been frequently visited by King Henry III. Now little was left but the ruins of the gatehouse and the south wall, faced with knapped flint. Lumps of masonry stood here and there about the site, now in the care of the Ministry of Works. A few holiday-makers were inspecting the ruins. A child ran laughing through a stone door where the monks had walked in prayer. Squire drove slowly past, then stopped the car on the verge. He walked back to an ice-cream van parked near the ruin and bought three large tubs of strawberry whirl as a surprise for Teresa and the girls.

When he drove up to Pippet Hall, it was to find everything silent, and all windows and doors closed. Carrying the ice creams carefully, he unlocked the front door and went in. He called. There was no response. One of the cats paraded down the stairs, giving a miaow at every fourth step.

In his study, he found a note lying on his desk. He set the plastic cartons down in order to read it, recognizing Teresa's untidy hand-writing as he did so. It was brief.

Dear Tom,
    I have to go away on a business matter that has cropped up. I am leaving the children with your sister at Blakeney. My mother will stay in Grantham. No doubt Matilda will look after you.
    T.

He sat down at the desk, studying the sheet of notepaper, which looked all the stranger because it bore the Pippet Hall address embossed on it. The cat came to sit beside his chair, looking up at him expectantly before turning to lick its left shoulder. The sound of its rough tongue on the fur was the only noise in the room.

At one moment Squire looked up swiftly, thinking he saw a black figure at the french windows, peering in. A bird had flown by. Nobody was there. He was alone.

An early summer day, the sunshine faint on the brickwork of the house. The clumps of rhododendron bushes, which concealed the yard and garages from the front drive, spread a wedge of shadow across the most easterly corner of the house, shading the dining-room window; that window reflected a parade of people approaching the house, and dissected their figures among its glazing bars.

The parade comprised people of various periods, men and women and children. There were men in the three-cornered hats, knee-breeches and tight clothes of the eighteenth century, women in the high-waisted, low-necked dresses of the Regency, or in crinolines with shawls in a mid-Victorian fashion. There were ladies with shingled hair in frocks with low belts, and gentlemen in lounge suits and spats, together with chaps and chicks in jeans and leather jackets. All climbed the steps of the front porch and went into the house, the door of which stood wide to receive them.

Squire asked rhetorically, 'What is man's greatest invention? Some would say the Wheel, or the control of Fire, or cooking, or perhaps the domestication of animals. Some might say the internal combustion engine or the rockets that have taken men across space to the Moon. All these things have been immensely important in the rise of mankind. The list comprises *things* because our culture tends to think in terms of things, although we act in terms of style.

'Not the least of the great inventions of the last two centuries is what you are looking at now, on the other side of this lawn. It is not just a house but an embodiment of style, the style of the Enlightenment which still plays its role in shaping our present.'

The viewpoint moved nearer to take in more clearly the house and the figures entering it.

'There's a vicar going in, one of Christ's representatives on Earth.

He is walking through a doorway which derives its style from a great portico shrine. He probably doesn't care about that, as he goes in to sit beside a hearth designed after a miniature triumphal arch or an altar to the Lares. Do the farmer and his wife over there realize that the facade of the house is conceived in terms of a Classical Order, with the windows on its three floors gradated in height? Does that rather corpulent man – perhaps he is a successful draper – have a clear notion of the ideas of the Italian Andrea Palladio or of the English Lords Burlingham and Shaftesbury? And perhaps that young lady with the patched jeans doesn't realize that she is entering a belated expression of the Renaissance of Roman Architecture on English soil.

'To these people, and to most of the rest of us, this is simply a comfortable Georgian house. There are still thousands of them of all shapes and sizes all over the country, and the style has been imitated on various scales ever since: for almost two hundred years almost everyone had wanted to live in a Georgian house. What all these people do know is that this extraordinary stylistic phenomenon, which imposes on the domiciles of a small Protestant northern island the temple architecture of a long-vanished heathen Mediterranean culture, results in the most pleasant kind of house ever invented.'

The viewpoint had moved to the interior.

'The Georgian house is sensibly laid out, easier to maintain than any previous style of home, comfortable, adaptable, and *homely*. "Home" is an English word, for which Palladio's fellow-countrymen, for instance, have no word; and the Georgian house is a major contribution to civilization and stability. One finds it nowhere but England and Scotland, and Dublin, and its imitations everywhere.

'We cannot live without myth. This house enshrines a myth, the myth that life is subject to constant improvement. The Georgian house is a product not only of architectural orders but of the concept of Order itself, to which the early eighteenth century heartily subscribed.

'Having lived all my life in this particular house, I feel qualified to say that it does promote orderly conduct in the lives lived within its walls – or rather it tends to promote order among the disorderly jumble which constitutes the average life. It doesn't enforce order, class order, like a Victorian house. It is more than a house: it is a style.

'In the eighteenth century, there was agreement about style. There are now more people in the world and a greater divergence of taste. In consequence, we have wide divergences in style. Some would say that there is also a greater range of possibilities. That is true, although youth always tends to exaggerate the possibilities available. We are not creatures of determinism, but, unfortunately, the number of things we can do in one lifetime is limited.

'We observe an example of that law of limitation in the Georgian style itself. I call it an English invention. So it is. But whilst the comfortable English squires and lords of the manor were busying themselves about these homes, the Continent of Europe was about something else – the Rococo. There is no Rococo in England, certainly none of its glories as we know them on the Continent. After the Civil War, we English seem to have settled down to gardening and a limited amount of religion. Instead of the ridiculously pretty baroque churches which grace Europe and South America, we have utilitarian chapels; instead of Fragonard and the great master of Rococo, Tiepolo, we have George Stubbs – what an English name! – and Tom Rowlandson. It's all a question of style.'

As he spoke, he was following the last of the costumed actors to the steps of the house. There, on the upper step, lay a dozen wrist watches, awaiting revelation like hen's eggs in straw.

'Here's an interesting question concerning present-day style. There has never been such a variety of watches cheaply available as there is today. For all we know, there may never be again – the notion of the future as a period of multiplied diversity is another of the cheering illusions of youth.'

He began to pick up the watches, holding them where the sun – reinforced by a conveniently placed spot – glittered on their cases.

'Watches are beautiful objects. Perhaps that is why we are all slaves to them. A watch is really a piece of costume jewellery, one of the few pieces of jewellery society approves of the male wearing, since throughout an average day we can estimate the time to within five minutes; or else we are within reach of a clock or someone else's watch; or else we have escaped routine and do not wish to know the time at all. But for work-oriented cultures, the watch is an essential, like the camera we take on holiday. Both impress us with the precision with which we live: "We were precisely here at precisely such-and-such a time." Living with precision is a modern style.'

Squire began sorting the timepieces, one by one.

'This watch is a Quartz LED, LED standing for Light-Emitting Diode. It presents a blank face to the world until you press this button, when the time comes up on a digital display. For me, LEDs are mean and hostile watches, not unlike those sunglasses people used to wear which looked opaque and reflected back the onlooker's world, so that one could not see the eyes of the wearer. But quartz LEDs are accurate to a degree unknown a generation ago. Armed with such precision, Hitler's generals could have overthrown him before he ruined Europe.

'Do you rate your watches for accuracy, or appearance, or reliability, or sheer razzmatazz? Would you like a Mickey Mouse watch, like this one, or a "Star Wars" watch, like this one?'

The dreaded Darth Vader moved a gauntleted arm to twelve noon.

'*This* watch is a Quartz LCD, LCD standing for Liquid Crystal Display. It announces clearly that it belongs to the nineteen-eighties. It has forsworn the watch's traditional association with gold and gold-casing in favour of a heavy dull metal, the sort of thing we imagine Starship hulls will be made of, three centuries from now.

'It is uncompromising. It does not even call itself a watch any more. It is a Seiko Multi-Mode LC Digital Quartz World Timer, and can give you the time in the world's twenty-nine time zones. It's somewhat specialist, being designed for globe-trotters, or those who fancy themselves as globe-trotters. It can give a twenty-four-hour read-out system, with hours, minutes, seconds, day, and date. It also features a perpetual calendar, so that you can find out whether Easter 1991 falls on a Thursday or a Friday, and is programmed until the year 2009 AD. It is water-resistant, and *features*, as they say by analogy with the movie industry, built-in illumination, so that you can check the time in Rangoon on even the darkest of nights.'

He set the LCD watch down on the step, but it immediately took flight, circled a pampas clump and was lost to view. Squire selected another watch, a more traditional-looking instrument with a leather strap.

'Whatever it may look like, this is not your old clockwork wind-up watch. Nor is it a clockwork automatic. That old phrase about things "going like clockwork" is now long out-of-date, a fossil of language. Clockwork is no longer the most accurate motion, as it was for centuries. The accuracy of a quartz crystal is measured in seconds per century rather than minutes per week.

'This is a quartz watch. Not a quartz digital but what we have learnt to call a quartz analogue. It caters for a public who respect accuracy, but who wish to combine living with precision with living with tradition. You notice that the numerals are Roman, just like the numerals on the grandfather clock in the hall of this house. In spite of its twentieth-century interior, this watch aspires to a Georgian exterior, reminding us each time we look at it of a more gracious, less time-devoured age.

'If you think that makes this watch an example of bad taste, then you are merely being old-fashioned and a little conventional. Good and bad taste are of the past; all that is left us now is multivalent tastes.

'Even the Seiko Multi-Mode LC Digital Quartz World Timer, last seen heading for Rangoon, subscribes to a twenty-four-hour clock system, with sixty minutes in each hour, passed down to us by Babylonian astronomers and refined by Sumerian mathematics some thousand years before Christ.

'The facade of this Georgian house represents a triumph of order and symmetry, but order and symmetry are always under threat. We are a species in evolution and not in equipoise. Consequently, we remain uncertain about numbers. Perhaps that is why we find watches so talismanic; watches appear to have numbers if not time well under control. But numbers continue to give us trouble, not least in matters involving currency. Half the people on the globe cannot understand why sufficient money cannot be printed for everyone. Indeed, the world's present monetary systems have been outgrown, though we struggle on with them, just as previous monetary systems – whether barter or mercantile or purely commercial – have had to be abandoned for more sophisticated infrastructures.

'A Frenchman's word for eighty is "quatre-vingts", or "four twenties", which betrays the spoor of an ancient numerical system, possibly Celtic, based on twenty, such as Mayan and Aztec cultures once used. Our LCD watch uses "Arabic" numerals. Like almost the whole of modern arithmetic, and the decimal system itself, Europe owes its numerals to the Arabs and Indians. The mathematical systems on which our civilization continues to function were not even possible to visualize until we had got rid of the Roman system of numeration.

'The Roman letter-numeral system is now used in few places – at the start of books and films, for example, to remind us rightly that we are confronting something which owes little to originality and much to tradition.'

Squire pushed open the door of the house to enter. He used his right hand, so that his shirt and jacket sleeve fell back to reveal an LCD watch on his wrist. It showed the time in Roman numerals, seconds, minutes, hour, and date. The dial stretched right round his wrist.

'Perhaps one day Seiko will produce a watch like this for those specialists who still study the first *lingua franca* of Europe, Latin. Taste may please itself; it is judgement which is answerable to others.'

The door swung wide. As the focus zoomed in on the hall, a grandfather clock standing there began to strike twelve in stately tones.

The girls and the dog, all strangely excited, were installed in her mother's small town house.

She had used the pretext of going down to the shops for groceries to walk on her own. The sun shone. The pavements were hot and dusty. Tourists stood about in appropriate clothes, some of them licking ice-cream cones. She wore no coat, and felt absurd carrying her mother's stiff shopping-basket. A boy ran up and asked her what the time was. She felt out-of-character, exposed to the world, and could scarcely answer the lad.

Although her open-work shoes were unsuited to walking, she walked. She chose the meaner streets. No one would recognize her, although her father had been a town councillor. The desperation of her thoughts drove her on, an endless disquisition tormented her forward. Someone she passed, staring curiously into her face, reminded her that her lips were moving, in protest, explanation, or accusation.

By the River Witham she stood, staring at its dull pent surface, thinking of all the reasons why she hated rivers, towns, and especially rivers in towns, with their strong flavours of poverty, affliction, distress, aimlessness, winter, death. Backing away, she ran from the water and her thoughts. She walked among trees, glad of a small wilderness, though scarcely conscious where she went. Her father had walked her here with her younger sister, long ago, when they were safe in their innocence. He had been amusing then, amusing and kind: boring only to her adult perceptions.

She blundered into a tree, feeling the dusty bark under her fingertips, calming herself a little before continuing in a less distraught fashion. So this was what freedom was like. Painful and bewildering though it was, at least she was away from Pippet Hall; she was her own self. A doubt crossed her mind – perhaps she would not care for her own company. She found even the silences of the leafy grove an anguish.

Sun shone ahead on a small gravelled clearing, where a bust stood on a central pillar. She went and sat down on an oak bench, sliding off her shoes, lying back so that sunlight poured into her closed eyes and open mouth.

After a while, she took note of her surroundings. She stared at the bust on its pillar. There was an inscription underneath; it read:

In Memory of Ernest Albert Davies
1896–1977
Councillor
He fought for and Saved this Pleasant Place
*

Erected by his Fellow Citizens
*

Her father had spent years fighting both town council and a supermarket chain, who wished to level North Wood and make commercial use of the site. Her mother had written to her, telling her of the ceremony, only a few days ago; she had scarcely taken it in at the time, with more urgent things to occupy her.

Now she sat and gazed at the metal representation of her father's face. He looked sternly beyond her. A thrush alighted on his head.

Setting the empty shopping-basket down beside her on the gravel, she began to weep for all that was bygone.

6

Putting Our Socialist Friends to Rights

Ermalpa, September 1978

By pulling back one curtain, the room could be sparingly filled with morning light. Objects were revealed but, casting no shadows, scarcely acquired reality.

He had slept naked. He put on a pair of blue swimming trunks and stood in the middle of the room in *tadasana*. He breathed slowly, concentrating on the expelled breath, letting the lungs refill automatically, letting air return like a tide, to the abdomen, the ribs, the pectorals; then a pause and a topping-up with still more air. Then a pause and the controlled release.

He went into *trikonasana*, straightening and locking his legs with, first, his right fingers at his right ankle and his left arm raised, and then, second, his left fingers at his left ankle and his right arm raised, head always turned up towards the lifted thumb, knees locked.

After some while, he went into various sitting poses, concentrating on *parvatasana* and, to keep his abdominal muscles in trim, *navasana*. Finally, he went into a recuperative pose, the *sarvangasana*, with his feet high above his head and toes hanging down. He breathed gently, without strain, staying as he was, hanging in the air, for about fifteen minutes, before relaxing into *savasana*, eyes closed, brain inactive.

When he returned to the world, he reflected as always with gratitude on the brief refuge of meditation. Nothing could reach him there, neither his own follies nor the follies of other people. The paradox was that he had banished God by discovering him through the disciplines of yoga; what he had come upon was a timeless region at the back of his own skull: a small chamber shaped by countless generations of blood and perception. It had been there awaiting him all the time. It was as close as he would ever get to Eternity.

Putting on yachting shoes and draping a towel round his neck, he went down through the hotel, still empty of guests, and took a slow swim up and down the outdoor pool. Only one other delegate of the conference was there, an Italian whose name Squire did not remember. They nodded to each other and wished each other good morning as Squire did six lengths and a few dives. As he went back to his room, an aroma of coffee reached his senses.

He felt well prepared to face Thursday and the second full day of the conference.

The dining room of the Grand Hotel Marittimo was full of fresh flowers. Sunshine poured in the far end of the chamber, and the fatherly waiters were moving unhurriedly about their business.

Thomas Squire settled himself at a table with d'Exiteuil, who had managed to find himself a copy of *Le Monde*, the two Frenzas, Cantania, and the Romanian delegate, Geo Camaion. The latter nodded silently at Squire and continued to eat sausages and tomatoes. Gianni and Maria Frenza were chattering happily to each other over plates of fried egg and bacon. Gianni wore a silk sweater; his shaggy black hair, streaked with grey, reached to its collar. His wife looked attractive; she wore a plain brown dress to match the heavy dull gold of her hair. Squire observed that d'Exiteuil frequently gazed at her from behind his newspaper.

Squire ordered continental breakfast from a paternal waiter. He was finishing his orange juice when Geo Camaion, who had reached the toast stage, leaned forward, and remarked in French, 'I found your speech of yesterday, Mr Squire, charmingly insular, as we expect your countrymen always to be.'

He was a small neat man with good features and a nobly furrowed forehead. He spoke in such a friendly way that only a tapping finger on the cloth revealed his inner tension.

'In what respect did you find it insular?' Squire asked.

'We don't expect the English to understand that there are other people in the world – other poets, for instance, than Shakespeare, and other film actors than Errol Flynn.'

The croissants were not good, tasting too oily. Squire wiped his fingers on his napkin and said, 'Surely you fellows haven't been locked behind your frontiers for so long, Mr Camaion, that you have forgotten that Errol Flynn was Tasmanian, not English? Talking of people being locked in, I hear that your President Ceaucescu has finally allowed Peter Doma to leave his native land. Is that so? Wasn't Doma persecuted because he complained about the police system in Romania?'

'Doma! Doma was a client of propaganda hostile to our country!'

'I see. Won't there be more hostility to your country now that you have shown how you persecute an individual, and even his dog, if he happens to disagree with the way things are run? Aren't I right in believing that Doma was even attacked because his wife was Jewish?'

Camaion's eyes were very round. 'How dare you? Isn't anti-Semitism rampant in the United Kingdom?'

'It may exist, lingeringly, I suppose. It certainly isn't official policy.'

The Romanian wiped angrily at his face and rose, flinging his napkin at the table. 'More insular and anti-internationalist remarks, just as one might expect!' He marched from the room.

Maria Frenza said – in Italian, but Squire understood the remark – 'Fortunately the foreign gentleman had finished his meal before walking off.'

An uncomfortable silence fell at the table. Squire poured himself another cup of coffee.

D'Exiteuil said, with forced brightness, 'We shan't have a conference left if we start an international slanging match.'

'He made an error,' Squire said. 'Two in fact. Flynn was one. And I don't believe I mentioned Shakespeare in my speech. The Russian did that.'

'Well, you know, Tom, he's after all only an unimportant critic in a small department in the university in Bucharest, he doesn't carry much weight. You don't have to *eat* him.'

'Your complaint is mine, Jacques. He's only an unimportant critic in a small department in Bucharest University. Had he been Arthur Koestler, let's say, I would have deferred to him. But Koestler would not have spoken as this man did.'

'All the same, you mustn't exactly blame him, you know, for the sins of his government. We'd really all be in the soup if that—'

'Jacques, old chum, pass me over the rolls, will you, and let me enjoy my breakfast. I had no intention of upsetting your apple-cart, and actually I am sorry I broke out as I did.'

Not wishing anyone to see how upset he was by this episode, he retired to his bedroom until it was time to go down to the first session of the day at nine o'clock. He felt to blame over the Camaion affair. He knew that Camaion – a little man, as d'Exiteuil said – was personally piqued because Squire had ignored him at the opening ceremony, or had seemed to ignore him. As Squire now recollected, too late, he had encountered Camaion only a few months earlier at a seminar in Paris. He had forgotten the man's face. His bad memory was at fault. In fact, during the Paris occasion, Camaion had made complimentary remarks in public concerning Squire's work.

At the recollection, a rare blush of shame crept to his cheeks. Some people, and by no means the most contemptible, feel slights very keenly.

From what Squire had been told, in words that now came back clearly, Geo Camaion was quite a brave man. Moreover, Squire had said insulting things about Romania. No matter that they were true. Romania was one of the most authoritarian regimes in the Eastern bloc, yet Squire admired President Ceaucescu's independent stand against Soviet domination. Even at an unimportant conference like this, for Romania to suffer any disgrace could always be seized on in some way by her enemies, of which she had many; or Camaion himself could find his position undermined, and perhaps a worse man set in his place.

A few minutes of thought persuaded Squire that he should apologize to the Romanian as soon as possible.

When he went downstairs, the foyer was already filling with

delegates, many of them indulging in a last smoke before entering the conference hall. By covert glances, by gazes hurriedly switched elsewhere as they encountered his, Squire saw that news of the exchange at the breakfast table was spreading, had spread.

Herman Fittich, a rolled newspaper under his arm, came up cheerfully and said, 'I learn that you have been putting some of our socialist friends to rights this morning. I can't say I found that titbit of news entirely depressing.' He made it plain by his manner that he did not intend to refer to the photograph of Pippet Hall he had produced the previous evening.

Squire smiled uneasily. 'The Romanian called me insular. As one who lives on an island, I'm bound to resent the remark, just as liars hate being called liars.'

'Or communists communists. I wouldn't have said people *practised* living on islands, the way other people practise lying or practise communism. You can live on an island and do other things, whereas if you are a liar or a communist, it's pretty well a full-time occupation.'

Squire smiled again, this time with real humour. 'Then again, if you live on an island, you can stop it just by catching a plane.'

'That's because we have yet to invent airlines which will fly you from moral turpitude.' They both began to laugh, walking together into the conference hall. 'Moral Turpitude – sounds like rather a nice little place, perhaps a desert island in the New Hebrides, named after Sir Harry Turpitude of His Majesty's Navy.'

Slowly, the delegates took their allotted places. Some paused to scrutinize themselves in the tall gilded mirrors, perhaps on the watch for falsehood. Squire sat and chatted to Rugorsky, his neighbour on his left. To his right, d'Exiteuil and Frenza talked together with their heads close, breathing cigarette smoke at each other. Frenza now wore a jacket over his silk sweater. The Ermalpan delegates settled along the left-hand side of the conference room, as neat as a row of starlings perching on a fence. Carlo Morabito was among them.

At ten minutes past nine, d'Exiteuil rose. Smiling and gesticulating, he made a few general announcements before handing over to Frenza.

Frenza removed his heavy spectacles and looked round the room, his face set as if he had something unpleasant to announce. Instead, he made a semi-private joke about the drinking habits of the hotel manager, and the delegates laughed and relaxed, twitching at ties and pens. Frenza then introduced the first speaker of the morning's session, Professor Georgi Kchevov. Frenza said that perhaps the most remarkable feature of this, the First International Congress of Intergraphic Criticism, was the way in which it had been possible to receive contributions from both the West and the East. He felt that this represented a genuine drawing together in the brotherhood of nations, and that here in this congress they could symbolize, among their other important business, a growing unity and understanding and unionism worldwide. He was more than pleased to introduce Professor Georgi Kchevov to address them.

Fittich shot Squire a look across the table while this speech was in progress. It was usual for the chairman to introduce each speaker with a brief listing of their credentials, their institution, their previous contributions, their specialization. Kchevov evidently had no credentials of this kind.

Whilst Frenza talked, Kchevov polished his gold-rimmed spectacles. He rose now, putting them rather awkwardly in place, and then picked up his papers. He smiled at everyone and began to address the assembly in resonant Russian. Squire took note of this; on more than one occasion outside the conference hall, he had overheard Kchevov talking perfectly fluent Italian. But presumably it was politic that Russian should be heard officially at the conference. It seemed to present the interpreters with some problems. A full minute after Kchevov had begun his oration, the female voice of the interpreter came over the headphones, speaking with a hesitancy which in no way matched what Kchevov was saying.

'Yes, accordingly, on the present problems before us – facing us, I should say – I can bear in mind the remark of Delegate Thomas Squire that we in fact explore the familiar, so to say. That's the hope to come up to – with a different picture than the one that we had before.

'We must look ahead concisely, and without being merciful. It's enough to know that many things will not be, where for instance people are exploited with bare bread. They stand in rows now. We can't decide. We have decided. Only the collapse awaits. Leading countries are condemned.

'Many new things will be born. We must decide. We must deal with optimism and only with optimism. I could criticize what has gone previously in this respect, but want only to shed light on the matter, and so refrain in a rather brotherly or fraternal spirit, like a blow on the right place. Shoulder.

'We must not, we should not accuse the pessimism piled in literature whose function is in respect of human problems conveyed in past times, since we now understand better. For instance, I must state in the sociology and political sphere were economics. From all these comes the evolvement of new literature and tokens beyond the word printed. Even to the personality of affairs. Such we may presume to call nowadays in a sense scientific.

'People who are among us and live with us influence the course of events, of course, which is not far in the future. We must not go to bed with them tonight. Orthodoxy of the state can guide us. So we're not able to take a bus to anywhere which is not painted on a card. Sorry, printed in the map. I'm sorry, but that means to concern all of us. The chairs in this hall are, in a sense, filled right up with all human beings.

'Nor should we be very overturned. If experiments of this kind or type, I should say, confirm to literature, if we will have experiments made purely for the sakes of experiments, then we will have no result. There has to be inspiration to confirm, an example being the composer Dmitry Shostakovich, who has a remarkable development which can be seen. It touches men and women alike, not always from behind. We can so be concerned with something fresh coming.'

As Kchevov paused and took a swallow of mineral water from his glass, Squire ran his gaze round the table, looking in particular at the other English-speaking delegates, the Americans, Canadians, and Australians. All appeared perfectly serious.

'In such circumstances, I must add,' said Kchevov, reading from his papers again, 'that we should not take misleading impressions which without optimism makes this huge thing seem not to be real, especially for those of us who had the news in the past, or sometimes a flavour. You don't understand this.

'Only and only if this will certainly give results, confirming to the organic in political spheres can we go to a head. I have nerves about such evaluations when values are discussed on roles of revelation, knowing a musician with a violin, for example, cannot play the drum, when critics speak only of one commitment or something of this work.'

The interpreter's voice ran on in this vein for some while.

Squire scribbled a note to d'Exiteuil complaining that the translation was incomprehensible. D'Exiteuil leant sideways and whispered, 'It must be vexing, but follow the general drift – prescriptive stuff but deeply perceptive.'

'Good.' He concentrated again on what the female voice was saying in his ear.

'. . . according to his word. It is a move forward, declaredly, one we can take without a trip. Why bow to a single person? In a marriage of disciplines, science is not good and bad but neutral.

'What is the way of transposing the over-human values that we have? Sorry, superman. How can everyone unite with us? Doesn't all political science suggest a role? There is a necessity in history which you may all be aware, with the overwhelming rational aspect. That's a question of control when we're talking about science and technology. I don't have to hold this rat in my hand. It's exaggerated in any case because we recently had in our country recent developmental problems now solved, which is a mistaken aspect some took deliberately without to speak their names, since it applies to this century only and after all many others follow it, in what order we shall see presently, with glimpses already if you get out of bed at dawn and dare to look stark. The past will prove less utopian, the future more so. The belief is not a religious one, so to speak, though confused. Some fish we can eat.

'It is not an obsolete thing to speak about the miracle. The individual cannot be completed and put away without any fantasies of hope. I don't qualify for being put away. What I mean here is combining the elements of subconsciousness with political geology to make a reinforcement such is unknown. If the comparison is fair, we could complete it according to the schema existing today, rational for not rational, till someone gets the prize for their body.'

At this there was a murmur of general agreement from the delegates. Kchevov looked up from his papers – rather in astonishment, Squire thought. As the man got going again, Squire wrote a note to Frenza stating that Comrade Kchevov had now been speaking for half-an-hour and should be interrupted, since it was the turn of the next delegate to speak. He pushed it across d'Exiteuil's space to the secretary.

Frenza stared at it, pushed it back interrogatively to d'Exiteuil. The two men started whispering together. Finally, Frenza rose furtively from his seat, came round d'Exiteuil's seat and put his arm around Squire's shoulder in a fraternal embrace. He spoke rapidly in Italian.

'He says that it's agreed that we should never interrupt a delegate if he is obviously delivering something of major importance,' translated d'Exiteuil. 'Particularly in this case where he is clearly building on much of your own work, under the keynote of exploring the familiar.'

'His half-hour is up. You must interrupt him according to the rules, whatever he is saying. Ring your little bell and warn him that he has two minutes left. You've been to these sessions before. You know what to do.'

Looking genuinely anguished when this was translated to him, Frenza began a fresh speech, whispering urgently, his eyes close to Squire's. D'Exiteuil translated, saying, 'What the secretary says is that we must make not only scholarly allowances, etcetera, etcetera, but also diplomatic allowances in the present case. If we interrupted now, the Soviet delegations would be offended and see it as a political move.'

'They can't possibly be offended, they know the rules. What's political about it?'

'Then why did you suggest it?' d'Exiteuil asked. 'It must be political. You get us all into trouble. By the way, Tom, you upset our Romanian friend at breakfast.'

At that moment, another note was passed along. D'Exiteuil snatched it before Frenza could reach, and spread it out. It was in French, and suggested simply that, since the Soviet delegate had exceeded his time limit, he should be asked to sit down. It was signed with a flourish: Carlo Morabito.

D'Exiteuil and Frenza had another hurried confabulation, at the end of which d'Exiteuil signed with two fingers to Squire. 'We give him two minutes more, okay?'

Frenza rang his bell and conveyed to Kchevov the news that he had five more minutes.

Squire listened to the exchange over the headphones. Kchevov apparently said that he was sorry for the interruption and would wind things up immediately.

He spoke on for some while. Frenza sat with his hand on the bell, but had become immobile, staring ahead, perhaps into the political future, like something on Easter Island. He stirred from his daze and invited questions only when Kchevov finally sat down.

A young Italian, one of Ermalpa's smart set and an under-professor in the Faculty of Iconographic Simulation, rose and remarked, according to the translation, that he proposed there was now only the continuous present. History had expanded into everyday life as a strategy for fiction. Fiction was fulfilling its destiny and becoming generally all-pervasive. While the Pope died of laughing, the brows of intellectuals were lined with fatigue.

Good-natured laughter and smart smiling followed these remarks.

D'Exiteuil intervened to say that he accepted Kchevov's interesting talk in the true spirit, although he was fortunate in speaking from a position where the traditional union of church and state versus the people had been alleviated. Nevertheless, he felt that utopianism should now be regarded with a rather large set of reservations in view of its limited temporal applications, though he did see that it had compatibility with their general subject for discussion in certain clearly designated areas. Squire wrote that bit down on his notepad.

One of the Americans, Larry Clayton, rose to say that there was a concealed dilemma in what had been discussed so far during the morning, which was man's inability to mature at a rate compatible with technological progress. There were small and large realisms and he believed that while what his Soviet colleague had had to say was revealing and significant, and a major contribution to the debate, it nevertheless fell under the category of a minor realism.

At the risk of achieving a fascist posture, he believed that his own country, the USA, should pursue a projectory of high technology to the limit of productive capacity. Before the oil ran out – though that was and remained a hypothetical parameter entirely based on relative cost-accounting – it was a priority to establish space colonies on the Moon and on synthetic planets in equivalent orbits, where a whole new nul-g vacuum technology could be developed, using limitless solar energy and maybe demolished superfluous gas planets such as Jupiter, which would provide more power than mankind had so far managed to consume in its total history. Such objectives achieved essentiality.

Concurrently with this admittedly somewhat lyrical scenario, he proposed that all aid to undeveloped countries be embargoed and even that the US become isolationist in intention and trade, the more effectively to gear itself outward to the universe in a receptivity attitude.

If all this sounded like a new version of economic extortion and the Monro doctrine, he would remind delegates that even Karl Marx had admitted that there had always existed a struggle between city and countryside, and that that struggle had proved a fruitful one. Indeed, it was in many of its phases the history of man himself. Now that urbanization was practically global, and the realization of Doxiadis's Ecumenopolis fast approaching, a massive US advancement into neighbouring space would restore that fruitful dichotomy. The urbanization of vacuum was a top priority target.

Clayton admitted to a personal reservation to all this. He knew, none better, how desperately his country needed a new form of government, the present elite being entirely discredited, but he feared that access to new power areas would merely entrench the present elite, even in an altered environment, since those grabbed power who were nearest power. Almost all popular forms of entertainment, including TV and news media and present-day literatures like sci-fi – witness Asimov – were downright reactionary; the texts showed how greatly the masses were held in contempt, and he could not understand how the masses still ate up this stuff and made fortunes for those who so obviously despised them.

Of course, education had been withheld them. They needed a government of the people in an energy-surplus requirement environment, and then maybe mankind would mature along the utopianist lines outlined by his Russian colleague.

Frenza thanked everyone and called for the next paper.

Dr Dwight G. Dobell of San Andreas Baptist University read a well-researched and innocuous paper on 'Abba, Pop Musicals, and Youth Say-So'. The Sicilian morning went by.

When the delegates moved out of the smoke-filled conference hall for lunch, only ten minutes behind timetable, Squire found Herman Fittich waiting for him in the marble gallery.

'Well, that was all very instructive,' the German said mildly. 'Would you care just to take a stroll outside in the fresh air before lunch? I am keen to establish which you think was dottier, the Russian or the American.'

Squire had seen Selina Ajdini in the crowd ahead, and agreed rather reluctantly to accompany the German into the sunshine.

Outside, Fittich said, 'As a matter of fact there is a little modest restaurant round the next corner where we could have a beer. Would you care for that?'

'For a beer, yes. For two beers, even more.'

As they moved rapidly away from the front of the hotel, a voice called Squire's name. He looked round.

The animal behaviourist, Carlo Morabito, was waving a rolled newspaper to attract his attention. As the two men paused, Morabito hurried up.

'Gentlemen, excuse, please, you look like two men possibly going in search of a drink. May I join you in it?' Sensing their hesitation, he added, 'If it is not an intrusion – as another sufferer from all that hot talk.'

'What didn't you enjoy about it, may I ask?' Fittich enquired.

'I did not enjoy anything,' said Morabito. 'Most of all I did not enjoy having red wool pulled over my eyes by the first speaker.'

Fittich took his arm. 'Come along, my dear fellow. You do need a beer.'

The restaurant was little more than a bar. It was narrow and extremely high, and tiled from floor to ceiling in tiles of a sickly green. Gigantic wine barrels stood at the back. A radio played, a Sicilian family ate at a bare clean table, talking animatedly, the adults jocularly lecturing the children, as if they had been placed there deliberately by the *padrone* to advertise the homely virtues of his establishment.

As soon as the three men entered, the patron emerged from behind the bar and showed them to a seat. He took their order for beer, and then asked them in German if they would like something to eat. He had some good fish, just delivered. He promised it would be delicious.

They consented. It would be better than facing their colleagues in the dining room of the Grand Hotel Marittimo.

On the tiles of the table before him, Morabito set a copy of *Frankenstein a 'la Bella Scuola'* which he had been carrying under his arm.

'Perhaps you would be so kind to sign your work for me?'

As he scribbled his name on the title page, Squire said, 'I like the title of the Italian translation. It has a literary reference that the English title lacks. This is still the land of Dante.'

Morabito gestured. 'And also of Mussolini. It's a reminder that the arts in my country still exist in a limbo.'

'We'd say the same in the UK. Even people who regard themselves as reasonably cultivated pride themselves on disliking contemporary music or art or fiction, or all three.'

'You say only "dislike",' Fittich exclaimed. 'But let me assure you that the attitude to the arts in the Bundesrepublik is positively *phobic*. Arts get in the way of decent things like money-making.' He gave them his mischievous smile. 'It's no good chaps from countries like Italy and Great Britain telling a German about the bad state of art. You remember, I suppose, that Hermann Goering summed up the typical German attitude to that little matter – "When I hear the word Culture, I reach for my revolver." Little has changed since dear Hermann's day, believe me; nowadays we reach for our pocket calculators instead.'

The beer arrived. They sighed heavily, raised their glasses, smiled, nodded at each other, drank.

'Gentlemen,' Fittich said, 'I'm glad of your company. Sometimes I feel I am the only man not believing all the lies such as our Russian friend Kchevov spoke. I'm humiliated by my silence so often. Yet if I speak, I'm kicked out. Better to hang on like a rat.'

'"I don't have to hold this rat in my hand,"' Squire quoted. They all laughed.

'You see, a curtain comes down on these matters,' Morabito said. 'I guess there are many delegates like me who think that the talk of that crook Kchevov was an insult, yet they will say nothing. So we conspire with the evil forces loose in the world to silence truth.'

'Agreed,' Squire said. 'It's as though an infection spreads, softening our defences. The power centred in the East paralyses people and year by year evil gains. But why are you immune, Signor Morabito?'

'Do you want I should tell you? Because I have Jewish blood. So simple. My mother was Venetian Jewish. Italy is beset with many, many ills, not least all various kinds of silences because there are deep divisions still among our society since the war. Here in Sicily, still you hear no one speak a bad word against Mussolini. There are many fascists about. Also communists, of course. In my country, I tell you, you can be fascist, communist, Catholic, all in one person. Myself, I tell you simply, I hate them all and I fear for my country. Now is very bad times for Italy. But I talk too much.'

He bit his lips, smiled, gestured at the unavailingness of the word, drank from his glass.

Squire regarded his notepad. 'This chap Kchevov talked about historical necessity and all that. What did you two make of d'Exiteuil's reply? I copied part of it down. He said that utopianism should now be regarded with a rather large set of reservations because – if I understood him rightly – it had shown itself of limited historical applicability. Was he referring to Marxism and attempting, in an oblique way, to put Kchevov down? Or was he trying to say nothing as learnedly as possible?'

'He answered to a specific point made by our Soviet colleague, I believe,' said Fittich. 'It was a passage about imposing superhuman values through the intervention of the state, with a hint about conquering the rest of the world, or something similarly charming, I thought.'

Morabito became excited. He had seated himself opposite Fittich and Squire, and now pointed his fingers at them almost as if about to fire six-guns. 'No, no, such ambitions of conquest are I think out-of-date among Soviet thinking, except maybe on their Right wing. The possibility of a war with the United States is now really excluded. The West will anyhow fall of itself, as did Byzantium, in effect. China is the great enemy for the Soviets.

'Although we could not say that Marxism-Leninism had ever a conscience, it was at least a system. But, in effect, nobody now espouses such beliefs in any country of the Eastern bloc because, as a Polish friend of mine said to me, "Nobody can remain in a communist country and be communist." So this dead doctrine now has power only in the West, on the youth, in effect.'

The patron arrived with the first intimations of fish: cutlery, paper napkins, salt and pepper, a plate of sliced lemon. Morabito fell silent, snatching up his knife and fork as if to defend himself. He spoke again as soon as the patron turned his back.

'Do you gentlemen know of the hatred and bigotry in the Soviet upper echelons? Can you plumb the depths? America is insane, Europe a harlot – that they believe and say. They believe that

Bolshevism unites with Russian Orthodoxy to save the world against – you see I must hesitate before I must speak it – the satanic forces of *World Zionism*.

'That is the new religion that will fill the empty shell of communism – a new anti-Semitism! Anti-Semitism was official policy under the Czars, and soon the calendar will go back and again the Nazi Right wing will proclaim a crusade against the Jewish menace and the builders of the Judaeo-Masonic pyramid in the West. These same neo-Nazis easily combine such racism with a hatred of the Chinese, no problem.'

He tapped hard on the table with an index finger.

'More bad things are in store for the world than ever before. At present, such things are in effect not possible while there is Brezhnev, for he can hold together the Soviet establishment and operate the bureaucracy between managerial and military pressures. When he's gone, we see Stalinism come back – yet even Stalin was not always officially against Jews, though whenever he said the word "cosmopolitanism", then he meant Jews.

'In the Soviet invasion of Czechoslovakia in 1968, "Anti-Zionism" was one excuse. Now more evil propaganda is said in the Soviets against the Jews than ever before. Hitler was only an actor, a – what's the English word? – a *strolling player* in hatred against the Jewish people; soon you will see the performance lived.'

The fish was brought, and again Morabito fell silent, watching with glittering eyes as the patron heaped potatoes on his plate. As soon as the man was gone, he burst out again.

'Do you know the name of Valery Nikolayevich Yemelyanov? Do you? A well-known lecturer to the Party on ideological matters? His claim is that the Gentile world was saved by Stalin's purges from a Jewish *putsch* to take over the world. Now another conspiracy is being staged. Yemelyanov proposes a new front to stamp out every evidence of Jewish culture everywhere. The class struggle is to be replaced by a more deadly and deep one, the struggle against ethnic classes. Of course, it will give the Soviet Nazis the opportunity they need to eradicate anything or anyone opposing them. It will begin when

Brezhnev goes. That will be the history of the twenty-first century, friends – a Final Solution against which Hitler is less than this piece of fish!'

He fell savagely upon the white flesh before him, as if it were the last meal he would ever eat.

The other two ate in uneasy silence, perhaps feeling that Morabito was too dramatic.

Fittich said, 'Well, the heavens are certainly full of portents these days. Nobody can say we haven't been warned when Chaos comes again.'

When it was clear Squire was going to make no answer, Morabito said to him challengingly, 'Do you believe what I am telling you? Because it's true. Here in Italy, we know – the nerves are bare too long. Much worse things are to come, believe me.'

Removing a bone from between his teeth, Squire said, 'Let me tell you the truth, and hope you will not be insulted. I think I can believe what you say concerning Soviet policy, though counter-forces in the Kremlin of which we are unaware may see to it that anti-Semitism does not emerge as you assume at present.

'But I can't quite believe – though in my darker moments I perversely *wish* to – that things in general are getting worse. By and large the human condition – at least in Europe – is improving, particularly if you take the calamitous fourteenth century as your base-line. Or the seventeenth, come to that.'

'You're mincing words,' Morabito said impatiently, thumping his signed copy of Squire's book.

'Well, I'm trying not to. But you are talking politically and I am forced to talk . . . spiritually. Spiritually, I so often feel despite everything that all is well. I don't believe in God, and perhaps it is simply the biological organism telling me that today it is in good balance, that Ego and Self are in counterpoise – or something like that. Whatever it is, I can't help listening to it. It's the closest voice to me. Can you see my difficulty, Morabito? Though worried, I feel content. No offence. It's a character limitation. Even on the day when my wife walks out and leaves me and I am truly miserable, something inside is chirruping to me, "All's well, all's well, and this is the best of all possible worlds." Believe me, many and many a time – for instance when I listen to you – I feel ashamed of that idiot within.'

Tess, perhaps it's that damned complacency in me you can't bear. It's attractive at a distance. It attracts women, or the sort of woman who likes contented men. Close at hand, you may find it intolerable. I've expected you to be content with me, my love, because I was more or less content with myself.

It'll betray me. It has already betrayed me. I believe I've got – God, or whatever it is, tucked in the back of my skull. Maybe that's what betrayed the Jews in Nazi Germany; they couldn't credit for the life of them that the Nazis hadn't also got God in their thick skulls . . .

Truth kills . . . ?

7

Land Full of Strange Gods

Pippet Hall, Norfolk, Christmas 1976

His mother had cared enough for the Jews to do something positive for them.

That was in the early summer of 1938 when, as a widow of one year's standing, she had taken the Normbaum family into the Hall. They were refugees from Hitler's Third Reich, and had fled from Hamburg leaving almost all their possessions behind. Patricia Ann Squire – supported by her sister, Tom Squire's Aunt Rose, who was also living at the Hall in those days – had invited the poor Normbaums to stay indefinitely.

During the Christmas of 1976, Squire thought of those distant pre-war days as he gazed down upon the face of his dead mother.

Patricia Squire had died during the afternoon of Christmas Eve. Her body would lie in its coffin over Christmas and be consigned to the ground on the twenty-eighth of December, at eleven o'clock in the morning, in the church of St Swithun, Hartisham.

The sense of the dead body in the house made for a subdued Christmas when, after breakfast on Christmas morning, everyone retired to the morning room for present-giving and -receiving. Squire left as soon as he could, and went to sit by the mortal remains of his mother.

Downstairs were Teresa, the girls, and her parents, Madge and Ernest Davies; Tom's brother, Adrian; together with Deirdre and Marshall Kaye, Tom's sister and brother-in-law, who always drove over from Blakeney to stay at Pippet Hall for Christmas, bringing with them their three children, Grace, Douglas, and Tom. Uncle Willie would arrive later, after the family had been to church.

An LP of carols from Norwich Cathedral played on the record player. Nellie the Dalmatian rooted among the discarded wrapping paper.

Squire waited upstairs in the small room, furnished with little more than the open coffin. Fragments of scripture, platitudinous saws, floated through his mind.

> We are but little time upon this earth.
> What's done cannot be undone.
> Ashes to ashes.
> Your place is with the living. Join the children downstairs.

And that old quotation from Walter Savage Landor:

There are no fields of amaranth on this side of the grave: there are no voices, O Rhodophe, that are not soon mute, however tuneful; there is no name, with whatever emphasis of passionate love repeated, of which the echo is not faint at last.

John Matthew Squire, his father, dead so many years, had once cried the name of the red-haired Patricia Ann Hodgkins with all the emphasis of passionate love. Now both were gone, and the echo of that cry could be heard only in his own head, and in the heads of his sister and brother.

There was no immortality, of that he was certain, or none in the sense that the Church intended. Yet there was no death, or at least there was a residue of life. For that vast and perennially never-entirely-satisfactory thing, his relationship with his mother, grievously damaged on the very day of his father's death by her savage beating of him, ostensibly for shooting the mastiffs – though even at the time, in his many kinds of grief, he perceived that the beating was merely her pain, her confusion in the face of death, her hatred of this unexpected beastliness, which had driven her to attack him – still hung and would ever hang between him and the phantom domains of his past.

Looking away from his mother's emaciated form, and her closed face splotched by greys and browns unknown in living nature, he gazed with sorrow on the still world of Christmas outside. A light fall of snow, followed by an iron frost, had welded the previous night's mist to the trees. Every bare twig had its nimbus of cold. The grass of the lawns was furred with white. It was a white and blue-grey picture. Death seemed to have deprived the world of colour. The still cold had enlarged the plantation and created a deadness in its depths so that it resembled an ancient forest, or perhaps he saw a spectre of it as it would be a century from now, when his eyes and the eyes of his children would no longer perceive it.

He allowed himself to picture two Shire horses, such as had worked on his father's estate when he was a boy, pulling a great trunk from the forest, of the trunk being set light to, and of cheerful flames leaping to the ashen sky. Truly, one could understand how, long before a sailing ship and a pious old man in monk's habit had brought Christianity to these shores, men had set out with animals to drag in the yule log and burn it, ensuring that the death of the sun in the embers of winter solstice was temporary merely, not lasting.

But the sun was dead, he thought. Every year it did die a little. Though less swiftly than he.

The door opened and Teresa entered in her Sunday clothes. Patricia Squire's body had been brought in its coffin to a small room on the top floor, which had served in its time as maid's room, children's room, and box room. The passage outside was thinly carpeted and Squire had heard his wife's footsteps approaching.

Teresa was dressed in a light coat with fur-trimmed pockets. She wore a fur hat which haloed her hair, and carried gloves. Her smile was warm and loving.

'We're ready to go to church, Tom, if you are.'

He rose hesitantly. She went over to him where he stood by the

133

window and put her arms about him, running her hands through the hair at the base of his skull, murmuring to him.

'I'm sorry about your poor old mother, my darling. It's sad for you, I know. And it wakens up that old wound of your father dying so tragically. I know that too because I'm a part of you. Don't grieve too much, darling – I'll be your little mother as well as your plump little wife. We'll be fine, you'll see.'

They all walked to church as they always did, through the ringing cold, down the drive, over Repton's bridge, along the village street, up the hill, to St Swithun's, twelve of them where there had been thirteen the previous year. Several cars were parked outside the church, including the Porsche belonging to Ray Bond, the flashy builder who had bought the vicarage. The five-minute bell was ringing as they walked between the gravestones, the children, who had led the way impatiently until now, dragging behind.

Inside the church, where worshippers retained their coats to ward off the damp which the massively old-fashioned Victorian heating system did little to dispel, brass plates commemorated the names of the fallen who had given their lives for the country in two world wars. The organ, which was delivering a voluntary based on, or aspiring towards, Holst's 'Christmas Day', under the skeletal fingers of Mr Beaumont, had been presented by the Squire family to commemorate the fallen.

Tom Squire's first sight of the Normbaums had revealed huddled figures in ill-fitting overcoats, staggering into the hall of Pippet Hall, late on a summer evening before the war. Spinks, the Squire's old stableman, brought in a couple of battered cardboard boxes and set them down by the stairs, leaving without a backward look. Young Squire had not understood the alien gestures of the newcomers. He had immediately understood Spinks's unthinking gesture of dislike and disapproval. He stood on the stairs, refusing his mother's invitation to come down, resenting this intrusion of foreign things into his home, this threat of coming war into Hartisham, into his county of Norfolk.

Why should they look so ugly, why should they dress so incongruously, when this super, kind, rich English family was letting them stay here, safe from Hitler, *free*, no charge? Why couldn't they look grateful instead of scared?

He had long since forgiven himself that ungenerous reception of the Normbaums, and his flight upstairs into the bedroom when his mother called him peremptorily down to greet their guests. What had been less easy to forgive, what perhaps should never be quite forgiven, but should lie about in the mind like a dead albatross, a warning for all worse and more subtle situations to come, was the way he had secretly sympathized with Hitler's – well, in those days one did not realize it was extermination – Hitler's extirpation of the Jews.

In the newsprints and on newsreels, ground out in the local fleapit before the appearance of Humphrey Bogart, or Eddie G. Robinson, or Will Hay, or Errol Flynn, Hitler looked rather nice and sensible in his uniform. Tom could not believe what Uncle Robert said about Hitler being a 'villain of the first water'. But he disliked the look of the German Jews, seen scuttling here and there in heavy clothes, dirty, drab, suspicious, the men with matted black beards and strange hats, the women fat and weepy. Their *eyes* were so frightening. Why should they inhabit Germany? It seemed a good idea to get rid of them if they were causing trouble, as everyone said they were.

Now here these troublemakers were in his own house, in father's house, and father would surely never allow that. Already the trouble was starting. He had had to exchange his pleasant big room next to his mother's for a smaller room on the top floor, redeemed only by its stunning view over the rear of the house, the stables, the farm, the village, and the distant tower of Thornage church. Rooks and pigeons were his companions.

Mr Normbaum spoke good English. He was cosmopolitan. But he disappeared almost as soon as he had deposited his wife and children at the Hall. The wife spoke almost no English, the two children, Rachel and little Karl, none. Memory, which after a while proves to have none of the fading properties of the body enshrining it, still held that scene in the hall, under the chandelier, with the door in the background open on sunset sky: Spinks balefully moving away, waistcoated figure averted, mother going forward, arms open in smiling welcome, tall Mrs Normbaum, two ill-clad little children looking up apprehensively into the shadows to where something scuttled away.

It took some days to realize how beautiful those children were, the blue-eyed Rachel in particular.

During the sermon, the Rev. Rowlinson mentioned Patricia Squire, in order to remind his scanty parishioners of the good she had done in her lifetime. He had occasion to mention the fact that she had given refuge to a Jewish family in the troubled days before the last war broke out.

'All times in this realm of earth are troubled. Although it may seem to our eyes that the kinds of troubles vary, that we have to fight against various sorts of evil, that is only because our mortal lives are so short. Could we but look at matters with a wider scan, had we the vision of the Almighty, we would see that there is really only one sort of evil, that evil puts on many guises, yet remains itself, and that it is in us all. Patricia Squire worked all her life against evil . . .'

Limitations of intellect did not prevent the Reverend Rowlinson being a good vicar; indeed, perhaps they helped him. But what he said was only partly true, or only partly useful. For, given the brevity of life's span to which he made reference (a snide but traditional way the Church had of making you depressed and therefore not so actively bad), one had to make *ad hoc* arrangements against evil; so it suited all and sundry to chop evil up into parcels and, by pretending it was divisible, remain able to divide and conquer it. Given a bit of luck.

For instance, there was the evil of ignorance, such as the young Tom Squire showed in his lack of sympathy for Hitler's suffering Jews. That lack had been banished when he was in his teens and acquired knowledge. The dreadful revelation of Belsen and the other concentration camps, which almost coincided with the first flush of puberty, jarred him like the passing of a terrible express train. It had jarred him with knowledge. As an earthquake levels tall buildings, he felt whole edifices of ignorance fall within him. He saw the wickedness of the Nazi regime and – on a par with it if knowledge cannot be quantified, as old Rowlinson appeared to be claiming – his own wickedness. (Yet the wickedness lived even in its own ruins. How grateful he had been when he read Orwell's words, 'I could never find it in my heart to dislike Hitler.' He wondered if all the British felt that way. Hadn't they said, even at the sour end of the war, 'We should have joined up with the Wehrmacht and smashed the Russians while we had the chance'? . . . The things that were said, between individuals, between husband and wife, seemingly so transient, never forgotten . . . '*I'll be your little mother as well as your plump little wife . . .*')

As the sermon laboured on, Squire's attention wandered. His younger brother Adrian sat on one side of him, Teresa on the other, in the family pews. In a niche on the wall just above them stood a bust in white marble of Matthew Squire, 1689–1758, one of the benefactors of the church. Anxious, in his *nouveau riche* state, to keep in with the Church as well as the local gentry, Matthew had endowed the church with a fine wooden pulpit, carved by William Kent, no less, probably from timber left over from the construction of the Hall.

Matthew's bust showed a serious man – but who would not achieve seriousness whilst being carved in stone? The high forehead, the long nose, were echoed in a nearer, living, face: that of Adrian, whose gaze, fixed rigidly on the Rev. Rowlinson, was almost as stony as his ancestor's.

Squire reflected that he probably spent more time thinking about the long-defunct Matthew than about his still-living brother. Although Adrian was rather a dull stick, that was a mistake; blood was thicker than marble.

Adrian was the only member of the family to subside into the civil service. He had been doing worthy and inscrutable things in Whitehall for a quarter of a century and, for most of that time, had owned a flat near the Fulham Road. Whatever his private delights and excitements, the only episode in Adrian's life to stir the family had been when he went on a delegation to Bombay and returned with an Indian film actress on his arm, a lady by the name of Sushila.

That had been almost fifteen years ago. Well did Squire remember how he and Teresa had gone to London to meet Sushila on Adrian's invitation. In theory, Squire thoroughly approved of the match. He too had a taste for the exotic, but had never expected the same to manifest itself in his sober brother; perhaps Adrian's infant imagining also had been stirred by the dark beauty of Rachel Normbaum.

Sushila was beautiful beyond imagining. Squire and Teresa both found themselves silenced before her elegance. 'I wear saris here in London because it is expected of me,' she said. 'At my home, I am more comfortable in jeans.'

'Have you visited London before?' asked Teresa.

Her answer was a silvery laugh. 'My family is pretty cosmopolitan, I'm glad to say.'

Squire had hardly been able to keep his eyes or hands off her, and had deeply envied his brother – an envy that Teresa had infallibly sensed. He remembered the terrible row after Adrian and Sushila were married, when he had acted as his brother's best man. But the marriage was not to last. Perhaps Adrian was too set in his ways. A son was born to them but, within two years, the cosmopolitan Sushila was on a plane back to Bombay, with the child. Adrian had never spoken of her or the boy since in his brother's hearing.

Since those exciting times, the profile had grown sharper, thinner, had acquired a moustache and spectacles with which to regard the changing world. Yet unhappily it seemed no more inclined to exchange confidences than the marble bust behind it.

The Rev. Rowlinson's sermon came to an end, the congregation rose on frigid feet to unite in 'Hark, the herald angels sing'.

After the service, all were cheerful. Everyone shook hands with Edward Rowlinson as he stood in his surplice, a tall and not undignified figure despite the loose false teeth, wishing everyone a Happy Christmas as they filed past him at the entrance. Purple-visaged Ray Bond – an Australian gentleman, some parishioners said – shouted out a 'Merry Christmas' before jumping into his yellow Porsche and belting off in the direction of the nearest whisky.

When the church was empty, the Rev. Rowlinson put on his blue raincoat and gloves. He and his wife and their grown-up daughter Matilda walked downhill with the Squire party to Pippet Hall. It was customary for them to eat their Christmas lunch at the Hall. The children, Ann, Jane, Grace, Douglas, and Tom, led the way, running and calling, keen to get back to their new toys and games, now that duty was done.

The hospitality offered the Rowlinsons was the last drip of a stream of Pippet Hall hospitality which had flowed over the centuries. The sheltering of the Normbaum family, though an act not without self-interest, had been in that good tradition; but taxes direct and indirect, and the winds of change, had dried it. All that was left was an impoverished squire offering a meal to an impoverished vicar. A turkey bone, a game of Consequences, and duty was fulfilled for another year.

The little Normbaums had soon shown themselves marvellous at games round the house. In no time, Rachel was talking a pretty variety of English, and Karl was hardly slower. Rachel was slender and had blue eyes and dark hair, a dashing, brilliant, affectionate child who became Tom's first and unconsummated love. Oh, the delight of having her there, of coming back from school in the holidays and finding her awaiting him, long-legged, at Hartisham station (for in those days the old Great Eastern trains still ran). Those were the happy years, the years of sheltered childhood while the war played itself out below the horizon. And the end of the war – unwelcome in many ways, not least because suddenly the Normbaums were gone to Detroit in a new world, and Pippet Hall became empty and full of shadows, debt, dry rot, servants not returning, old order disappearing in shabbiness, damp, and tarnished silver. Then he had learnt – at the time of the Belsen revelations – that mother had taken in the refugees only to save the Hall being commandeered by the RAF.

Mother had friends in the county, in some cases traditional old friends of Squire's father and grandfather. They helped her. Thomas

Squire had neglected them in their old age, preferring more sophisticated friends in Cambridge and London.

At the Hall gates, Squire paused to let Madge and Ernest, his parents-in-law, catch up with him. Matilda, the pale Rowlinson daughter, went on ahead with Teresa and Deirdre to see how the Christmas lunch, the turkey with all its gallant accessories, was faring. As the party progressed past the artificial lake – frozen but not frozen enough to bear skaters – it could hear Nellie barking from the house, and see Uncle Willie's Austin Maxi standing by the front porch. Like Deirdre and Marshall, Willie always drove over for Christmas Day; unlike them, he would be driving home in the evening, claiming that his cat could not survive overnight without him. He had protested also that Pippet Hall beds were too hard for his old bones.

Despite Patricia's terminal illness, Squire had insisted on the Hall's being decorated for Christmas. The party trooped through the front door, exclaiming at the cold now they were safely out of it, and gathered to admire the Christmas tree, which stood in the hall as usual on such occasions. Its lights seemed to emphasize a dreary negation of light which hung this year at the top of the stairs to the upper regions, where the body lay.

But the tree was grand and glittering, swathed in a glass-fibre called Angel's Breath, which was carefully saved in a hat box from one year to another. The tree had been dug from the grounds and stood in a tub specially constructed for the purpose. At the top of the tree, spreading brilliant plastic wings, was the fairy which Teresa had made; despite its wand, there was about it something of the insect reminiscent of Teresa's more usual creations. A paraffin stove radiated warmth beside the tree, compensating for the uncertainties of the central heating in this area of the house. From a radio in the sitting room came the sound of Bethlehem bells. The thing lying upstairs would not hear those bells this year as, when living, it had done every Christmas since the invention of the wireless. Soon, there would be no one left who remembered cat's whiskers and crystal sets; to Squire himself, they were only stories.

As Uncle Willie came into the hall, smiling, to wish them all a

Happy Christmas, the children disappeared into the morning room to play with Tom Kaye's new Scalextric motor race track. The adults, after removing their coats and scarves, went through into the living room, Squire ushering the Rowlinsons hospitably before him.

'Christmas wouldn't be Christmas without the bells,' Madge Davies said. 'Do you remember how funny it was in the wartime, when the churches were not allowed to ring their bells? I expect you remember that, Mr Rowlinson? I feel so sorry that poor Patricia isn't with us this year – she was quite a campanologist. One can't help wondering who will be taken from us by next Christmas.'

'Don't say that, dear,' Ernest said. 'It's morbid. Besides, we are all in the pink.'

'What about your back? And Teresa says . . .' But she decided not to complete the sentence.

Although the living room struck rather cold, all agreed that it would soon warm up. The room was decorated with boughs of pine tucked behind the pictures on the wall, and with red candles, half-used, which would be lighted again at dusk. To make the fire in the wide hearth burn up, Squire threw onto it elm logs which he had sawn himself. They all stood round the hearth, exchanging idle conversation, except for Adrian Squire, who was silent as usual. He smoked a cigarette unobtrusively, and coughed a little.

'That is one blessing of the Dutch Elm Disease,' said the Rev. Rowlinson. 'It has provided everyone with more wood fuel than they have ever known before. In these days of spiralling prices, it is very welcome.' He shook his head, as if contradicting his own words.

'Wood-burning stoves are very fashionable again. Ray Bond told me so,' said his wife. Dorothy Rowlinson was a large but timid woman with a sharp nose and a memorable amount of grey hair which, though apparently natural, brought to these remote reaches of Norfolk a reminder of the Afro hair-styles affected in Notting Hill Gate. Dorothy Rowlinson's parishioners claimed that spirits could frequently be smelt on her breath; some said brandy or, the more charitable, sherry; otherwise, none had any complaint about this shy and dedicated woman.

'It's fortunate for the look of the countryside that there's more oak than elm in the region,' Marshall said, his sharp Bostonian voice in contrast to the rather woolly tones of both Rowlinsons. 'Northampton and Bedfordshire have been practically denuded of trees. Entire landscapes have changed character in just these last two years.'

Looking mysterious, Uncle Willie took himself off to the morning room, bearing envelopes. He was going to make his annual rather cheese-paring distribution of record tokens to the Squire and Kaye children, and to receive in return their well-simulated cries of grateful surprise.

'People make a lot of fuss about the elms,' said Adrian. 'They'll grow back again.'

'I'm damned sure they won't,' Marshall retorted. 'People don't have time for trees any more.'

'Oh, surely that's not so,' Rev. Rowlinson protested. 'Dorothy and I are very fond of trees.'

Teresa and Matilda entered, bearing trays of glasses and hot negus. Deirdre followed with crisps in bowls. Grace, now thirteen, slipped into the room to try her aunt's drink, and tasted it appreciatively. 'It's lovely, Aunt Teresa, and not at all alcoholic.'

'You just take care,' Deirdre warned her. 'One alcoholic in the family's enough.'

When all present were clutching a glass, Squire went and stood at the far end of the room away from the fire, unconsciously framing himself against a window where a landscape in white and blue-grey led towards distant Walsingham. He took a slim book from a shelf and read *Journey of the Magi* aloud.

> 'A cold coming we had of it,
> Just the worst time of the year . . .'

His voice faltered only once. He kept his thoughts away from the figure of greys and browns lying under the roof with its eyes now always closed, concentrating instead on the magi's account, and on his discomfort at finding – as many men had done – that after returning from a long journey, one's native land was also full of strange gods.

He had read this poem every Christmas morning since returning from Yugoslavia in the late forties, before he married Teresa. His mother would have liked him to continue what had become a tradition. He realized how deeply the words still cut, words of an Anglican poet so much crisper, more uncompromising, than the sentimental consolations Rowlinson ladled out. The real Christian message – which went beyond Christianity – was here, that birth and death were hard, conditions between always unsatisfactory, vision intermittent. Christianity must have been a great religion when it belonged to the underdog.

'Why would you be glad of another death, Uncle Tom?' asked Grace, when he had closed the book and set it back in its place in the bookcase. 'Isn't one enough at present?'

Grace was his favourite niece. She had her mother's fair hair but was going to be taller and slimmer. He smiled at her and said, 'That line isn't a reference to your grandmother. It's spoken by one of the magi, as I suppose you realize.'

'But why did he want another death?'

'I've always supposed he referred to his own death.'

She said lightly, 'I think about God a lot, these days, but I don't know many people who believe in him.' She lowered her voice. 'Of course, the Rev. Rowlinson and Mrs Rowlinson and Matilda all believe in him, but that's their job, isn't it? Of course, I suppose it's easier to believe at Christmas. Do you believe, Uncle Tom, or do you mind saying?'

He hesitated, and immediately felt her interest slip away, saw it in her eyes as they switched their gaze to something happening at the other end of the room. He was tempted to lie to shield her, to say that he did believe. He was tempted to fudge the question, to say that it was a question of perspective. He found himself inarticulate, unable to reply. A thousand answers rose to his mind.

Still with her attention on the other end of the room, where mince pies were appearing, closely followed by the other children, Grace said, 'Someone at school told me that God existed, but he left Earth at the end of the Stone Age because he could see that mankind was getting on pretty well without his help. But I guess that doesn't explain Jesus, does it?'

With a polite smile, she made for the mince pies.

How were Jews treated in the Stone Age? He sipped at his negus.

The question of God was a matter of perspective. It was easier to believe as a child, just as it was easier to believe in Santa Claus. The mere fact of having parents to care for you made a parental God plausible. Then one acquired knowledge, and worse succeeded.

He had a disturbing memory of his mother, throwing a cup down on the flagstones in the kitchen, angry because she was having to do her own washing up. Time, one of those grey years in the late forties when, the tide of war having withdrawn, people were still coping with the effects of the flood. People like Patricia Squire expected the servants to come back after the war, expected that life would return to what it was in the thirties. But the young people of Hartisham did not intend to work at menial jobs any more. They saw their chance: they left Norfolk and went to earn good wages in the car factories of the Midlands. The thirties had been reviled in their time; money was short and nothing was as it had been in grandfather's time, before the Great War. Now, after another war, the thirties were suddenly seen as halcyon. Time gilded them.

The seventies. Everyone complained, comparing them unfavourably with previous decades. Even the forties were now looked back upon with a certain nostalgia. Yet the time would inevitably come when the seventies would themselves be remembered as a time of peace and plenty. So they were, for all their alarms.

He pictured Grace, now munching a mince pie, as a grown woman, saying, 'Christmases are not what they were when old Granny Squire was alive.' And later, to her children, 'Christmases are much more commercial than they were when my old Uncle Tom was alive . . .'

Plain Matilda Rowlinson brought him a mince pie. As he talked to her, his wife filled his glass with more negus. They smiled happily at each other, not needing to speak. The wine, flavoured with cinnamon and nutmeg, ran across his palate, mingling with the rich taste of the mincemeat.

'Do you think God approves of mince pies, Matilda?' Squire asked in sudden mischief. 'Or does he think they're ungodly?'

She laughed. 'I think he leaves it to each of us to decide for ourselves.'

A good answer on the spur of the moment, he thought. All the best gods should leave it to the customer to decide.

It was a question of perspective. Periods of time seemed better or worse according to what followed. When you were young and had seen nothing follow, then time was special. So with God; he was special until you had seen certain things happen, Belsen, authorized murder in Yugoslavia, or your father's face eaten by dogs.

He strolled over to his sister and slid his arm through hers.

'How's things?'

'Oh, extremely cheerful, all things considered. And you? I was just thinking that with a few of these neguses under my belt I could perhaps face looking at mother. Would you come up with me?'

'If you like.'

'Do you remember, people used to say "Bearing up", if you asked them how they were.'

Deirdre filled her glass and they went upstairs. Her boys, Douglas and Tom, were playing with a Slinky on the stairs. 'I'll be down soon,' Deirdre told them, 'I'm just going to inspect your grandmother.'

Her defensive facetiousness fell away from her once they were in the small room on the attic floor. Squire stood by the window, gazing out at the iron landscape, listening to his sister's choked sobs.

He forced himself to speak. 'She went so suddenly when she went. A week and she was gone. Ten days ago, she was joking, and quizzing me about "Frankenstein" . . . Teresa had been having bad dreams. She dreamed that a black figure was trying to get into the house. I told her that we would get a better burglar alarm, but now I wonder . . . Well, it's easy to believe in portents at such a time – death makes everything irrational.'

Deirdre said, with a forced distinctness, 'I blame myself that I never came over to see the old girl when I phoned and you said she was unwell. You know what it is, just before Christmas one's always busy. It was end of term and we had to go over and see Grace in her school play, and Douglas had a cold and Tom had carol-singing and a party . . . Still, I should have bloody well come over. I can see that now. Poor old thing. I don't fancy being a corpse, do you?'

Making the effort, he went over to her and put an arm round her shoulders. 'There's always guilt at these times. Filthy death, filthy guilt. Let it wash round you, don't let it stay. We could all do better by everyone; it must be a cosmic law or something.'

'Old Rowlinson could explain it, I don't doubt.'

He could no longer bring himself to look down at his mother's body. 'I'll put the lid on, if you've had enough.'

'Oh, I don't think I could bear to see you do that. Let me get out of here first.' But she made no move to leave. She adjusted her hair. 'Why haven't you got flowers in here? Why hasn't Teresa put some flowers in the room?'

'A grey Christmas. Do you remember when we were kids and it snowed heavily just before Christmas, and we got stuck on the bridge at Wisbech? And father just laughed. He was enjoying it.'

'They've both gone now. Mother was such a repository of family history – I can feel it already, there's going to be a huge vacuum all down the left-hand side, here . . .' She sketched a large position vaguely in the air.

'Well, there's nothing we can do. Bow to the Grim Reaper, damn him . . . Irrational . . . I keep having an irrational feeling that it's the cold emanating from her that chills the landscape, that she's become a dreadful natural force, that . . . it's as if the corpse erupted out of the dead landscape, the way she keeps bursting into my thoughts . . .'

'What's Adrian said about it?'

'You know Adrian; he never says much about anything.'

'It beats me why you wanted to have the body lying here over Christmas. Bit morbid, isn't it?'

He shrugged. 'It was her home, after all.'

Deirdre went over to the door with a somewhat slack-shouldered walk he had noted in her lately. She put her hand on the doorknob, then hesitated.

'Are you afraid of being alone in this house, Tom?'

'How do you mean? Ghosts?'

She nodded. 'Ghosts and things like that. Father, for instance.'

'That sort of thing doesn't worry me.'

She laughed with a partly derisive note. 'Of course, you're so tough. You've killed chaps in Yugoslavia – I try to forget that rather nasty side to your character. All the same . . . What about Teresa? Isn't she scared? How's she going to be when you're trooping round the world doing your TV series?'

'Oh, that won't take many weeks.'

'It'll alter your lives.'

'Not at all. And I don't think she's afraid of ghosts. She's never said.'

'I'd have thought you'd have asked. It's an obvious enough question, stuck in a place like this. Really, I don't think I've ever liked Pippet Hall, not even when I was a small child . . . I wouldn't care to live here. Won't Teresa be lonely?'

'She keeps very busy. Her decorative insects are really developing into something tremendously attractive, don't you think? Aren't they original?'

Opening the door, casting a last suspicious glance at the coffin, Deirdre said, 'You, aren't you lonely here on your own?'

Hesitantly. 'I am afraid of my own loneliness. But that goes wherever I go. If anything, it's less here, where I belong.'

'I can't stand it when Marsh is away from Blakeney. I'm worse now I'm getting older. He's already put in for, and been accepted for, some bloody dig on some bloody Greek island next summer. I may go with him. Though you can't see me living in a tent exactly, can you?'

'You aren't quite the pioneering type.'

'Me perched on some bloody outcrop of Hellenic rock, while Marsh grubs up bits of broken urn?' She laughed at the ridiculous picture she had conjured.

Squire closed and locked the door behind them.

'What did you do that for?' his sister asked. 'Afraid she'll get loose?'

They descended together to the lower regions, from which seasonal aromas of roast turkey, sausages, bacon, stuffing, and other fleshly delights arose.

The meal took its accustomed course. First, champagne all round and a loyal toast to the sovereign; that tradition must have gone back as far as Matthew Squire himself.

The toast held special meaning, for the Queen was spending Christmas at Sandringham; it was easy to imagine her with her family, sitting down to table only twenty miles away.

After the toast, Scottish smoked salmon, followed by the main course with all its ramifications – the glistening brown barrel of bird attended by a fleet of small china boats containing gravy, bread sauce, cranberry sauce, and blackcurrant jelly. Then came pudding, flaming luridly, amid cries of delight from the children. Lastly, there was a whole Stilton, wrapped in a napkin, for those to cut at who still had room and courage enough, attended by a good port to wash it down with.

Most of the adults collapsed into chairs after the feast, and somnolence reigned. Marshall joined the children in a new card game. Half an hour later, Teresa and Squire put on their coats and went to see their estate manager. Uncle Willie and Adrian came as well, to walk off the effects of lunch.

The air was cold and still, with a slightly smokey flavour to it.

Teresa took her husband's arm. Uncle Willie grasped hers, leaning rather heavily against her. 'Very good lunch, my dear. It's amazing how much nourishment the human frame can withstand.'

Their footsteps echoed on the frosted ground.

The manager lived in an eighteenth-century farmhouse at the far end of the estate, on the Walsingham road. As they returned, an hour later, Teresa pointed to the western sky, where a thin red bar showed between strata of heavy cloud. 'The ghost of the sun!' she exclaimed. A hemisphere of sun emerged from below the cloud curtain, then the whole ball, less lurid than the pudding had appeared two hours earlier. It hung above a furred outline of slope, apparently emitting little light and less heat.

'Tom, Teresa was telling me about her nightmares,' Uncle Willie said abruptly. 'About a dark figure trying to break into the Hall. I suppose I shouldn't ask you this, but are all your cloak-and-dagger activities with the secret service firmly in the past?' He drew himself up, trying to straighten his shoulders, peering past Teresa's furred shoulder at Squire.

Adrian laughed in a way he had, as if thinking better of the humorous aspect that provoked the sound almost before uttering it. 'You don't imagine that KGB agents are tracking Tom down in Darkest Norfolk, do you, Uncle?'

Tom said placidly, 'Be sure there are KGB agents in Norfolk, but they have no particular reason to interest themselves in me.'

To Teresa, Adrian said, 'KGB, my foot! I'd hazard a guess that that figure in your dream was more likely to be a tax inspector than a KGB man, eh?'

Snuggling her shoulder under Squire's arm, Teresa said, 'Let's go back to the fire. Mother's death has made us all morbid. Christmas cake is the perfect antidote.'

As they headed for the rear of the house, Willie said, 'I'm the last of my poor old generation left now. It makes for morbidity.'

She hugged him. 'You're the toughest of us all, Uncle, dear,' she said.

In the waning afternoon light, the side of the house presented an aspect of greyness, as if a blanket had been draped over it. Lights gleamed in the room downstairs, and children could be seen, running here and there, laughing. Matilda Rowlinson was playing a game with them. The last rays of the sun caught the three lower panes of the window of the room where Patricia Squire's body lay; they gleamed with dead colour as the four walkers went below them into the shade of the house.

'Perhaps I'll tell the kiddies a ghost story after tea,' Adrian said. 'I always fancied myself as a story teller.'

Red is the colour of dying light, as incandescence sinks towards invisibility. The bars of the electric fire in my bedroom, dying when switched off, when Rachel lived with us. Long ago now.

Rachel's mother, Rebecca Normbaum, had died some years earlier. Squire was sure his mother had told him as much; at the time, busy with other things, he had paid little attention. He remembered a late photograph of Rebecca, taken in America by polaroid camera when such things were rare in England. A tall elegant woman, still with eyes of blue, though her hair was grey. She stood in a suburban Detroit garden – or 'yard', as she and Rachel would have learnt to call it.

Karl, the son, the uninteresting boy, kept the Normbaum and Squire families spasmodically in touch. He was Charles nowadays, name Anglicized, manner Americanized. He had married a striking blonde Jewish girl in Detroit, and commuted regularly with her to Israel in his prospering line of business, which involved car exhausts and gas filters.

At the beginning of the seventies, before the power crisis, Squire had met Charles in London. They had not found much to say to each other, once the reminiscences had been exhausted. Rachel had made a respectable marriage. She lived in a big house. She had two children, both boys, who were doing well. And a dog. She had shares in a downtown restaurant. She and Charles saw each other about once a month.

So the promise of youth deteriorated into family history.

After their meeting, afflicted by a mixture of curiosity and nostalgia, Squire wrote to Rachel. He received no reply. The following Christmas, a printed card arrived. Little Rachel Normbaum was now Mrs Gary Baxter.

Although Blakeney was so near, Deirdre, Marshall, and their children always slept at the Hall on Christmas night. It was part of the tradition.

When they were younger, this had been a time for drinking too much brandy and port and playing childish games after the children had gone up to bed. Now they were more staid, and Uncle Willie drove himself off to Norwich at nine-thirty in order, as he explained, to look after his flat and his cat.

Squire and Mrs Davies went to see him off at the front door.

'You'd better look after your granddaughter, Madge,' Uncle Willie warned Mrs Davies, as he wound a woolly scarf round his neck. 'Do you know what Grace said to me?'

'I'm sure it was something very precocious, Will. Young girls reach the age of – become young ladies very much earlier than they did in my day. I can't understand it. It must have been something in the diet when we were young.' She smiled at him teasingly.

'Come, my dear, you are still a beautiful lady, and Ernest is a very lucky man. Blossoms that flower late go on flowering into the winter.'

Squire, slightly surprised at this flight of fancy from his uncle, asked, 'What did Grace say to you, Uncle?'

The old man hesitated, then chuckled. 'Why, she told me that she'd had a dream in which she had gone down to the beach, and there she had seen a fully grown male seal sporting in the waves. Although it was a bit rough, she took off her clothes and joined him, and put her arms round him and held him tight. She said it felt lovely. Those were her words: "It felt lovely."'

'She is getting to that age . . .'

'It was her comment afterwards that shocked me. She said, "I expect it's a premonitory dream about enjoying sexual intercourse, don't you, Uncle?"'

While Squire and Uncle Willie laughed, Mrs Davies pretended to look affronted. After Willie had gone, she said as she retreated with Squire from the chilly regions of the front door, 'Willie Squire is such a nice man. Ernest and I have always admired him. A pity he doesn't marry again. I suppose even marriage is unpopular or something these days – so many people seem to be getting divorced.'

151

'Most of them tend to remarry. It's what Dr Johnson calls the triumph of hope over experience.'

'I'm so glad that you and Teresa are happily married, and have this lovely house, full of such exquisite workmanship.'

'Sometimes I am afraid she feels imprisoned here.'

'Oh, no, not Teresa.'

He took her arm and led her into the warm living room, where her husband was already setting out a Scrabble board.

Later in the evening, the children submitted to Adrian's ghost story and then climbed upstairs to bed. Madge and Ernest followed them, and the Rowlinsons left.

Marshall Kaye threw an additional log on the fire and stretched out before it on the sofa, next to Adrian. Deirdre smiled at her husband and returned to the novel she was reading. Teresa trimmed the candles, which were now the room's sole illumination, while Squire poured everyone a malt whisky.

'Not for me,' Adrian said, waving a hand. 'I'm fighting against middle-aged fat.'

'You're very thin, Adrian,' Teresa said. 'A whisky would do you good.'

'It's refusing all the whiskies that would do me good which keeps me thin.'

'Middle age should not be devoted to abstinence,' Kaye said, raising his glass and sipping.

'What is middle age for, Marsh?' Teresa asked her brother-in-law. 'I've yet to find out.'

'Well . . . it's a sort of reprieve-period, in my book. You've finished mating and the furtherance of the species. Your waistline becomes more important than the rat-race . . . I guess it's a time when you're supposed to become wise and good.'

Laughing, Squire brought his glass over and sat down by the fire with them. 'Most people get more awful in middle age, not more good, and take to drink or politics. Although revolutionaries start young, other shades of politician get involved only when they're past the optimal breeding age.'

'Must be a correlation there,' Kaye said, laughing.

'When I was a child,' Adrian confessed, 'I thought that acquiring knowledge would infallibly make one good. Now I suspect it warps the soul.'

'That's a useful bit of knowledge to have.'

Squire said, 'We can recognize distinct stages in a man's life. Puberty. Mating. Family-rearing. After that, with the initial biological directives losing their force, he turns to complaining about the state of the country.'

'Sorry to hear your directives are losing their force, Tom,' Adrian said.

Kaye took the remark more seriously. 'I'm all for complaining about the state of the country. I know it's rather an obsessive British occupation, but in the States it's regarded as unpatriotic, which it shouldn't be. Why, we've had to import Solzhenitsyn to do the complaining for us. That's bad.'

Deirdre looked up from her book. 'Stop grumbling about America, Marsh. Just because they have their own way of doing things.'

'Good old America,' he said. 'So close to God, so far from everyone else.'

'It is disconcerting the way Russian thinking of various types has so greatly influenced the West, on both the Left and the Right,' Squire said, reaching for the decanter. Adrian jumped to his feet.

'I'm going to bed. Politics is something I gave up, along with whiskies that do me good. Thank God that Britain, for all its faults, is not a political nation. To hear you talk, Tom, with your knowing insinuations that there are KGB agents snooping round the grounds, you'd think the poor old country was a dead duck.'

'As to that,' said Squire, leaning back and pointing a hand at his brother, 'as to that, Adrian, old sport, will you dream more sweetly in your whisky-free sleep if I tell you categorically that there is a dedicated band of Soviets and their Warsaw Pact hyenas, all with the most unfriendly intentions towards this sceptred isle, within six or seven miles of this comfortable fire?'

Adrian did his sawn-off laugh. 'My dear Tom, you are getting to be, you know, a bit of a bore with this Lord Chalfontism of yours. Perhaps it really is compensatory fantasy for lack of the old biological drive.'

Squire stood up, set his whisky glass on the table, and raised his right hand, arm extended, to shoulder level. He swung the arm until it pointed almost due north.

'That way's the coast, right? You wouldn't disagree there. Not more than five miles away as the crow flies or the shell whizzes, right? All round our shores, hugging the two-mile limit, are Soviet spy-vessels, monitoring everything that goes on ashore. Five and two make seven.'

'Rubbish!' said Adrian. 'We'd never let them.'

'We can't stop them.' Squire lowered his arm. 'They're seven miles away, sitting in a well-armed ship of modern design. They monitor everything, local radio, police reports, the lot. Plus anything their numerous secret agents ashore like to beam out to them. How come you don't know this, Adrian? It's no secret. Is it that you don't want to know it?'

'It can't be true. What could they learn? Anyhow, we probably do just the same to them.'

'We haven't got the vessels. You know how the defence budget has been pared away by successive governments year after year for thirty years. That's right, isn't it, Marsh?'

Kaye drained his glass. 'We're even closer to the bastards at Blakeney. You can see them through the binoculars. Let's get to bed, Tom. This is no talk for Christmas Day. Maybe, as Solzhenitsyn says, the Third World War is already lost. Just don't quote me.'

'I think you're both being defeatist,' Adrian said, stoutly. 'In any case, even if it were true, they'd never dare attack us.'

'Your trouble, Adrian,' said Kaye, lifting his glass, 'is that you've given up your sense of history along with your taste for whisky. Think *they* care about Christmas, six miles from here? They're for abolishing it for good and ever . . .'

8

Sublimated Coin Warfare

The side street appeared unusually busy. Cream Fiats poured down it like salmon in broken water, bravely plunging into the stream of traffic choking the harbour road. Tyres squealed, brakes whined, a thin blue haze rose from the sun-battered street.

As Herman Fittich, Carlo Morabito, and Thomas Squire emerged from the bar into daylight, they paused to adjust to the noise and glare.

'It's the hour for lunch,' Morabito said. 'What you are viewing are not automobiles but foil-wrapped empty stomachs.'

There was a lot of shouting in the streets. A fat woman was calling from an upper window. Squire was mildly surprised at the activity; the northern myth that people in hot countries were lazy died hard, though it should have given its death rattle, as far as he was concerned, on his visit to Sao Paulo, the busiest city in the world, where the blazing temperatures, far from acting as a soporific, accelerated the pace of life, as a burning building accelerates the movements of those leaving it.

He glanced up at the gesticulating woman framed in her window. In the hard blue sky above the street, an intense point of light gleamed. It moved to one side, stopped, then suddenly accelerated in an arc and vanished behind the shaggy pediments of the Via Enrico Stabile.

It could have been an aircraft reflecting the sun; in which case, its power of acceleration was unthinkable. Even if it was much nearer the rooftops, it was amazingly silent and fast. And what was it?

'I think I've just seen a flying saucer,' Squire said, trying to keep his voice calm.

His two companions made a few jokes as he tried to describe what he had seen. 'I know it sounds ridiculous – I speak in the vein of one who confesses to an idiocy . . .'

'Well, it's always an embarrassing situation to be the sole possessor of a bit of truth,' said Fittich consolingly. 'I remember once I saw ball lightning when I was walking in the Tyrol with a friend. We were in our chalet for the night and not drunk, when this globe about the size of a goldfish bowl entered at the open window. It was completely silent, which was eerie.'

'So was my You-Foe,' said Squire, glancing upwards again.

'It did a tour of the room while we sat petrified, and eventually floated out of the window. I jumped from my bed and watched it sail down among the trees. My girl friend said we should tell no one, but I was then young and foolish in the pursuit of truth, and rashly recounted the incident to my scientific colleagues at the university. They of course assured me that ball lightning did not exist because it contravened natural laws. These days, I believe that ball lightning is quite acceptable, like much else that was once regarded as heresy.'

They walked slowly up the street. Morabito said, 'Italians will believe anything. Sicilians especially are very superstitious people. They can believe in the Virgin Mary, UFOs, witchcraft, Marxism, fascism, and Santa Claus all in one breath.'

'Why should there not be flying saucers?' Fittich asked. 'After all, if there is only one true sighting among thousands which are observation balloons or clouds or passing aircraft, then they exist. It only needs one. One's the miraculous number. The devil only has to appear once for his existence to be verifiable.'

'Wishes shape disbeliefs as well as beliefs, Herman. I believe I just saw a machine, a product of super-technology. A couple of centuries ago, I would have believed I saw a flying man, or a witch on a broomstick. We're too inclined to think of the imagination as an independent function, whereas it is a function like vision, which can be controlled.'

'You may actually have seen a product of super-technology. Why not? Believe your vision, believe your imagination. Wasn't it your Professor Haldane who said that the universe is stranger than we imagine or than we can imagine? That's why I enjoy science fiction as a sideline, because those chaps really try to imagine the unimaginable.'

Squire gave him a questioning look. 'So you do believe in You-Foes?'

The German gestured. 'I think maybe I do. But to declare it so publicly would make a further and perhaps lethal dent in my academic reputation. There are as many orthodoxies today as ever there were, and one defies them at one's peril.'

They fell silent. As they were turning the corner into the Via Milano, Morabito said, 'All this area by the docks was pounded flat by the British in World War II. It has all been rebuilt rather well, because of massive infusions of American dollars after the war.'

'I remember we gave it a pounding,' Squire said. 'This coast commanded the convoy route to Malta and India. There were German batteries here, and landing fields for Stuka squadrons. We blasted the whole place.'

'It certainly was a rather lively time, during the career of our mutual friend Adolf,' Fittich remarked.

He walked at a steady pace, his hands hanging by his sides. Morabito walked rapidly, throwing his shoulders in front of him as his gaze darted from one side to the other. As they came within the shade of the Grand Hotel, he flung a furtive glance upwards.

'At least whatever you saw did not drop any bombs,' he said.

On the marble steps which divided the inner part of the foyer from the outer stood Frank Krawstadt, smoking and pacing nervously.

'There's my colleague,' said Fittich. 'He's not a bad chap, despite his politics, and I must give a little moral support. He's our next speaker.'

'I'll see you later,' Squire said. They smiled and nodded at each other.

Jacques d'Exiteuil came up beaming with Selina Ajdini and two of his fellow-countrymen. He clapped Squire on the back. 'How are you, Tom? You didn't have lunch? A walk on the sea front? Isn't everything going so well?'

'I was just telling Mr Squire how all this area of Ermalpa was pulverized by the British during the war,' Morabito said.

'Ah, the British were doing brave things then, while France was under a cloud of shame,' d'Exiteuil remarked cheerfully, shaking his copper-coloured head. 'You were all Churchills then, Tom, isn't it? I still see a bit of Churchill in you, for instance when you tried to cut short our Russian friend this morning. And at breakfast with poor Camaion – who by the way has much of interest to impart about new restlessness among intellectuals in Bucharest.'

Ajdini said brightly, 'Churchill embodies – in his body, I mean – much that we think of as positive British virtues. Sturdy independence, good vowel sounds, etcetera, etcetera.'

She looked very trim; d'Exiteuil was keeping close to her. The blue spectacles had been removed, so that her blue eyes were unimpeded; at their corners were lines Squire had not noticed earlier. She gazed at Squire in a friendly yet impudent way, as the astute mind behind them speculated on the world. That enquiring look, the uncluttered countenance, the thinly smiling lips, gave a meaning to the ritual of the conference.

'Did you enjoy Comrade Kchevov's talk this morning, Miss Ajdini?' Squire asked, moving fractionally closer to her and clutching his lapels so that his knuckles almost grazed the front of her blouse.

She nodded, and the heavy shoulder bag swung in Squire's direction. 'There was a positive contribution of Marxist science against the philosophizing of Sigmund Freud and his followers. I happen to agree entirely that we are incomplete and cannot make any contribution to society, even a political one, without imagination. Granting that, the miraculous can occur. Of course, it was formulated in a rather unorthodox way. I was reminded of Gurdjieff, both in the mixture of practicality and foxy divination and in "the objective of producing an interesting and beautiful object".'

He marvelled. Even whilst distressing him by her appreciation of the rubbish Kchevov had talked, she was quoting a statement by Gurdjieff which he had appended as motto to his book and used in his speech.

'The miraculous does occur,' he said. 'Nor need we go in search of it. Sometimes it comes in search of us. As an example which springs readily to mind, I have just seen a You-Foe over Ermalpa.'

The Frenchmen laughed heartily. One said, 'I do not think that Sir Winston Churchill would commend himself to such miracles.'

Ajdini was also laughing, perhaps merely at the unexpectedness of his remark. 'You must say we are officially in search here of the miraculous. What we want is a sign, like the early Christians. And it has been – what is that biblical word? – *vouchsafed* to you.'

Again subtle flattery, not unmixed with subtle mockery? He said, 'Perhaps we can discuss the religious implications when we meet tonight for dinner, if you still remember our arrangement. I'd prefer the miraculous in some other guise.'

In his room, he opened up the slats of his jalousie, allowing a little light to stripe the gloom. He intended to do some yoga, but the beer in the café had made him drowsy. Stripping down to his underpants, he sat on the side of the bed and began to make a few notes. Presently, he lay back and fell asleep.

The afternoon session began only five minutes behind time. Gianni Frenza introduced Krawstadt briefly and Krawstadt rose, looking nervous. The female voice of the interpreter on Channel Three delivered her version of his paper, which was entitled 'Pinball Machines: Sublimated Coin Warfare'.

'So far at this date, the SPA organization and also *Intergraphic Studies* magazine have shown severe neglect of a glaring and coloured example of a commercial form of machine-and-art in a combination. It is a pinball table, familiar to all of us. A cult of functionality. Its object is to transfix with emotion a person who will then surrender money for no reward at all. Thus the pintable makes an epitome of capitalist economy in its late stage and will be valued to future students when they come to study this aspect of Americanized and so-called cosmopolitan culture from the early angers of the twentieth century.'

Here Krawstadt cleared his throat and looked furtively about at the audience, as if to check that it had not disappeared. From a distance, he resembled a healthy young man, his slender figure lending strength to the illusion. Closer inspection revealed that his slenderness was the gauntness of ageing. There was a strong frosting of grey among the yellow hairs of his beard, a bald pate gave his head an eroded appearance; even the red of his cheeks was no sign of health but the pitting and inflammation of a long-term psoriasis.

'. . . I am a professor in residence of popular culture. I have some various degrees. Thus I am curator of the newly established Pinball Research Museum at Gottingzell University in Western Germany. There we have an investiture of over five hundred machines – which are being got in working arrangement by mechanics – representing battery-operated and presolenoid models even as far back as 1930 to the present day. Here we see a principle often operative, where an artifact purely of commerce becomes through such market factors as scarcity into a realm of connoisseurship, that is the province of the art historian and exponent of the lives of the people.

'Only during the slump, which is a feature of capitalist economy in gearing the society towards mass-military enterprises, can this little gaudy trap developed from the French bagatelle be born.

'One way of saying it is that this pinball table is an article of commercial exploitation which nowadays contains two elements in bright colours, namely the what we call the Playfield and the Backflash. Usually, the Backflash will have on it a moving score where often vast figures without meaning are available – obtainable to the participant. The Playfield may have such devices as Thumper Bumpers, Roll-About Buttons, Flippers, etc., all brought into action by a plunger which will propel balls precipitated by the insertion of a coin.'

This could go on for ever. Perhaps there is a law about rubbish going on for ever.

It's up to me to behave myself. It was stupid to speak to Camaion as I did at breakfast. Everyone's perfectly friendly and agreeable.

Old Fittich producing that photograph of Tess as he did has upset me. When he took the shot, I must have been in retreat in the Travellers' Club. Matilda Rowlinson was looking after the house. What was Tess doing there that day? And with that little bugger Jarvis. I could kill him.

When I get back to London next week, I'll have to do something decisive; everything is going downhill fast. In the old days I'd have taken up my gun and settled the problems that way.

Churchill . . . Do they think they're flattering me? At least the old man had plenty of guts and the ability to take decisions. They weren't always the wrong decisions, either.

'Backflash and Playfield are united in a theme. Like a bright-coloured flower seeking to attract insects, the manufacturers create many scenes of pop art, drawing for subject-matter upon all types of the decadence of their culture. Most manufacturers are Jewish and based in Chicago. Such scenes may be of rock and roll music, negro musicians, hillbillies, teenage sexuality, railroads, space antics, or many science-fantasy scenes such as time-travel, robots, and future warfare. Also gambling, the turf, pool, baseball, or film stars and of course the exploitation of female figures (as in Gottlieb's *Majorettes*), and funny animals, children of a Walt Disney style, and all other races, in heavy ethnic humour of a Judaic kind.

'Whatever degrades, it will do.

'Also some mythology of an auto-mechanistic kind, designed to attract perhaps those sectors of the populace believing in astrology. An example is from the firm of Bally, called *Fireball*, where a demonic figure in red encourages extravagance, and such imaginary old gods as Wotan and Odin may be released to flash up giant scores via mushroom bumpers, which signify a mushroom nuclear attack of favourite militaristic thinking. This table has a big reputation, and may once be regarded as a classic masterpiece of the 1970s comparable with, say, a landscape by Maxfield Parrish.

161

'Internally, these machines are elaborate. Its circuits and subassemblies are very elaborate, resembling the kind of thing in a Saturn rocket. This technology is a different sort of war game, aimed at nothing less than enslavement of the masses when they escape from their work of the day. We appreciate their beauty as of that of the deadly pitcher plant or rafflesia. They are worthy of a serious study as metafiction or socio-economic artform.'

Krawstadt continued. Manufacturers' names punctuated his talk like a roll call of the illustrious dead. Burrows Automatics, Hardings, Rock-Ola, Gottlieb, Genco, Bally, Williams, Chicago Coin. The Hall was silent, the delegates slumped back in their chairs or sprawled forward over the green baize. Some smoked cigarettes, taking a long while over the gestures of flipping the box, tamping the tobacco, flicking the lighter into action, performing the first inhalation; others doodled with frowning concentration. Some stared at the speaker, some at the ceiling, some into a mysterious beyond.

The paper concluded with Krawstadt pointing out that growing political awareness would perceive that pinball machines were analogues of the capitalist system in decline. Beneath a bright veneer of religion or mythology or sex was merely a cold solenoid-operated system set up by cosmopolitan forces against which no one could win, designed to keep the working classes enslaved.

When Frenza called for questions, Albert Russell Cantania stood up. This representative of the USA was still in his twenties; his book *Form Behind Formula* had already made him powerful in academic circles. He was compactly built, with a lock of hair that drooped over his tanned face. He brushed the hair from his forehead as he started to speak.

'I guess our colleague Krawstadt who has just spoken knows his subject pretty well. Maybe he even has a connoisseur's love of pinball. But I wondered during the time he was talking if he ever got round to slipping a quarter into one of those machines and playing, just for the hell of it. Maybe his politics wouldn't let him, the way puritan morality stops a lot of other killjoys from playing.'

There was a stir in the conference chamber. Those sprawling tended to sit up, those sitting up to sprawl.

'In my time, I've played a lot of pinball, the way I've played a lot of poker. I must have dropped a whole lot of dollars on pinball, like I have on poker. More on poker. But there is one factor our colleague neglected to mention. You play voluntarily, because you want to play. There's no state or federal law saying a man has to play pinball; no one sticks a gun in your back. Another factor, okay, you put a coin in, but you get enjoyment in return. Why not mention enjoyment? Enjoyment is what you get out of pinball machines.

'Pinball machines need skill, they need a quick eye. Exercise of skill and speed yields enjoyment. There's no law against enjoyment either, not where I come from.

'All this talk of exploitation is crazy. You want something, you pay for it; you don't want it, you don't pay. That principle is so basic, and goes back so far beyond the Neolithic revolution in agriculture, that it has nothing to do with politics or morals. I'd say it was a law of nature, human nature. You want a stalk of corn to grow, you plant a seed. No seed, no corn. Everyone ought to get that clear in their heads.

'I mentioned the pinball-table industry in my book, *Form Behind Formula*. I said then and I'll say it again now that pinballs obey the law of supply and demand which drives a vast entertainment industry. Look, pinballs are like a pop song or a paperback novel or a movie or a TV programme – anything to which the general public has easy access. Nobody will ever subsidize them the way opera is subsidized, so they depend purely on popular appeal. That's the basic fact of life – satisfy the public. Happily, in a democracy, there's a big diverse public which gives a lot of artists a living. Some are better than others, some more limited in appeal, some succeed by fulfilling formulas, some by subtly breaking them.

'Same with pinball machines. Let me ask Mr Krawstadt why he thinks Bally and Chicago Coin and the others go on turning out so many models if the whole operation is just a big con foisted on the public? Why isn't there just one standard model which goes on for ever, or maybe gives you an extract from one of Lenin's longer speeches if you put your quarter in?

'The answer, the simple answer, is that people like playing pinball, they enjoy it, and they demand variety. They like their playtables and backflashes big and bright and brassy. They play while consuming a beer, and in a capitalist society they generally have a spare dollar in their pocket they can lay out on entertainment.

'One further point before I sit down. As I understand it, we are here to further the objectives of the Society for Popular Aesthetics – with which I heartily concur, by the way – in raising the cultural estimation of mass art, or future culture, or whatever you want to call it. The sort of attitude we are fighting against is the elitist one which declares that a best-selling paperback is *ipso facto* lousy, a song millions sing is *ipso facto* lousy, a movie that turns a profit is *ipso facto* lousy. The corollary of that attitude says that the novel scarcely anyone reads, the song nobody wants to sing, the movie people stay away from in droves, has to have something special which makes it real art. We fight such pernicious attitudes.

'How is it any different for Krawstadt or whoever to point to all these enjoyable things and say they are merely market devices to put the boot in on the proletariat? All this Leftist crap we're getting handed is just as damned much an enemy of enjoyment as the old structure of aesthetics we're trying to kick out. For God's sake, leave politics out of this and get to proper scholarship, proper appreciation. Else we'll make ourselves a laughing stock.'

He sat down.

Gianni Frenza, who had been conferring in whispers with d'Exiteuil, leant towards the microphone and was interpreted as saying, 'Well, there we have from Dr Cantania an enjoyable expression of typical hard-hitting. Who will like to reply to him?'

Carlo Morabito immediately rose, folding his arms tightly across his chest.

'I will speak in my English and can be translated. I like just to make complaint about the racialist streak in the paper of Dr Krawstadt. When he speaks of cosmopolitanism, he is speaking secretly of the Jews. The whole paper is of course a veiled attack on Jews, against which communist nations have always been hostile, with the honourable exception of maybe Yugoslavia. Delegates should be aware when they are getting poison.'

He sat down again.

'Perhaps Herr Krawstadt would care to amplify after such remarks,' Frenza's interpreter said.

Krawstadt rose, scratching his chin and lower lip.

'These interjections are to cause a confusion in the advisement I need from other delegates. This is a new field, and, as with popular arts, sociology is combined with it. I hear in my ear the familiar cry of the Right that their political beliefs are not political at all but a part of nature. But if I look at a privileged gentlemen's park in America or England or my own country, what's there is for me not just vegetables but I see the exploitive system of privilege behind it. Viewpoints are entirely different.

'With the pinball, the same applies. How is it like a paperback or an LP? It waits brightly painted for when a man is a bit drunk to take his money, like a prostitute. Is prostitution also part of American "entertainments industry" also? At least in the socialist countries prostitution and exploitation of women is abolished, and the sport and games is free of betting and gambling. Pinball is gambling without sport.

'One thing I agree with the other speaker. Let's leave out the politics and get proper scholarship.'

He sat down, to nods of approval round the table.

Squire rose.

'Just a point of fact. Two points. First, prostitution may be ruthlessly repressed, like so much else in socialist countries, yet it still exists. I have been solicited by prostitutes myself in the heart of Moscow. To that I have little or no objection; I'm a big boy; my objection is to being told afterwards that I was *not* solicited. It is that sort of barefaced lie, among other things, which gives communism such a bad name. The end justifies the means always, doesn't it?

'Then that bit about sport. Directly Moscow was chosen as the site of the Olympic Games in 1980, all residential and what we in the West would call private building was halted. The whole ramshackle building industry was forced to work on the stadia and accommodation for the Olympics.

'If you were having a dacha built – no matter in whatsoever state of completion you were left, the builders walked off one morning and left you standing there. Thus the rulers of the country drop the Muscovites in a condition of discomfort or misery to suit their political ends. Don't tell me there are no politics in sport or art except what is introduced by the Right. It's another totalitarian lie.'

He sat down. From the seat next to him, d'Exiteuil rose, smiling down on Squire as he said in English, 'Well, a display of Churchillian fireworks from Tom Squire, as we might expect, and the oratory of his usual high standard – the voice of the man who made "Frankenstein Among the Arts". It is a pleasure on which we can congratulate ourselves that our associations and this conference in particular can accommodate such extreme conservatism as Squire's and Professor Cantania's along with more sociologically oriented items. However, the Olympic Games have little to do with pintables, on which subject Herr Krawstadt contributed much to our enlightenment, and so I suggest we move on to the next paper.

'We must not exercise our prejudices, we must conquer them. I believe with the philosopher Mary Warnock that imagination is important here, and must be applied to our field of study. If we could come to a greater understanding of imagination – which may as likely come through pintables as through anything else – then we should understand a great deal more than we do about prejudice, perception, and such values as aesthetic pleasure. Perhaps we'll invite contributions on the subject of imagination to *Intergraphic Studies*. Thank you.'

The next paper, on the typography of cartography, passed peacefully, although there was a marked increase in small activities during it, both among the delegates round the table and in the spectators sitting in the gallery at the far end. Indeed, the gallery gradually became crowded, as if by some magical form of communication ordinary passers-by in the street had heard that a political argument was brewing and had come in to see for themselves what was happening. After sitting restlessly for a while, some of them departed, finding that the subject under discussion was totally innocuous; yet still the gallery filled as others took their place. Most visitors looked like students. Among them were some attractive young girls, who regarded the spectacle provided with complete assurance. Many of them gazed at Selina Ajdini thoughtfully for a while.

Ajdini was one of the stillest delegates, although she smoked continuously throughout the meeting. The other delegates shuffled in their places, made eye-signals, took notes, tapped at their headphones, drank mineral water, at a greater rate than was usual.

When the afternoon session was over, Squire rose to go, only to be detained by Vasili Rugorsky, who placed a hand on his arm.

'Mr Squire, I have great interest in what you say. Like you, I felt no patience with the dogmatic stance of the man from the Bundesrepublik. Can we have a brief chat, do you think?'

'Of course. Can I buy you a coffee?'

'That would be kind.' The massive head nodded. 'In my country, I would buy you a coffee, but you know that when we travel abroad we have to go penniless for the good of our souls.' He smiled his sidelong smile at Squire. As they walked through the passage, Cantania came up and slapped Squire on the shoulder.

'Not that I needed support, but thanks anyway for providing additional firepower.'

'I wasn't going to let your objection stand alone. All the same, I wish I'd kept my trap shut. It's not the first time I have been out of step today.'

'Keep it that way. What have you to fear? Except now Rugorsky's going to tell you one more time they stopped prostitution in Moscow. Was she any beauty, by the way, the one who tried to pick you up?'

When Cantania had gone, Rugorsky said quietly, 'I was not going to give you a lecture on prostitution.'

He fell into a frowning silence which Squire did not interrupt. The Russian had intensity of bearing which, coupled with the effort it afforded him to speak English, lent weight even to his silences. He moved through the crowds in the corridors with an impassive step, never impolitely, but never allowing himself to be deflected. Squire walked beside him without feeling it necessary to speak.

'You see, the papers are quite entertaining if you listen properly,' said Rugorsky at last. 'Even when they are of themselves boring or trivial or totally mistaken. In a way, you see, they are what Hamlet said of the players, they are the abstracts and brief chronicles of our time. We must use them as we may.'

'As you say, we get out of it what we can. Corporately, these men have a deal of power in academic life; by what is decided here, they can make or ruin reputations. The interest behind the boredom is that we are each of us on trial. The other apposite remark Hamlet made about the players was that it's better to have a bad epitaph after you're dead than their ill report while you live.'

Rugorsky said 'Excuse, please,' to one of the slender Italians who came forward with a beaming smile and ploughed by him in the direction of the bar. He took no notice of what Squire had just said. Either he had not fully heard and understood, or he was pursuing his own line of thought.

'Let us return to the subject of prostitution,' he said suddenly, applying a sly grin over his shoulder at Squire. 'You see, you were not in such a perfect socialist state as China, which the West thinks so very well of just now.

'Maybe you don't need a lecture on why we in Russia feel it necessary to pretend we have vanquished such long-standing social problems. It is a genuine dilemma that we are a new post-revolutionary society and we feel ourselves vulnerable to both the bad examples and the warlike ambitions of the West. To admit that there is a prostitution problem is to open the door to a whole range of evils to which we do not yet feel ourselves strong enough to confess. Do you understand?'

'I'm quite sympathetic to that argument, which I've heard before. But isn't it more the case that there is no one secure enough, no one with enough moral standing, who can even admit that prostitution exists?'

Rugorsky frowned. He removed an aged brown handkerchief from his pocket and blew his nose vigorously. 'Perhaps we should try not to talk morals to each other. You see, frankly, though I see much to admire in the West, in the way of outspokenness, for instance, which we in Russia cannot yet achieve, nevertheless I see what a moral mess you live in. You no doubt see it too.

'I think that Russian society is superior. Not in its rulers, absolutely not – I think worse of them than you do because I have the peculiar advantage of having known them all my life – but in the people.'

'Isn't belief in the morality of "the people", whoever they are, always sentimental at bottom?'

Still pressing forward, Rugorsky ignored the comment.

'You see, these pinball tables – well, we can easily classify and even appreciate to some extent their garish colours, much like the products of fairgrounds and circus, but the truth is that they are wretched traps to make the already miserable more miserable, and their wives also. They are the products of a society in poor health. Krawstadt spoiled truth by doctrinaire phraseology.'

The bar was crowded with thirsty delegates, but Squire and Rugorsky managed to push through to a table for two at the back of the room. In no time, one of the efficient waiters was by their side, and two cappuccinos were ordered.

'I don't wish to talk about pinball tables. It is trivia.'

'Possibly so. Yet everyone round the conference table, you included, has been stirred up by them. Maybe they are important. The SPA should consider the matter.'

Rugorsky regarded him steadily. 'You see, you are quite a clever man. Also, I think, an honest one as far as you can be. But you have had things too much your own way. You do not know real adversity. Maybe you know nothing about the way society operates.

169

When I come to the West, I feel genuine envy and genuine pity, both at once. That's what I felt for you when I first met you, in front of "Hugh Gaitskell", with your delightful wife in her expensive dress. But you don't know where to look for truth. You're a good man lost, Tom.

'Don't get angry. I don't mean offence. Only the truth. If you're angry, reflect that the poor old dog before you drinks coffee he could not afford, and in any case will go back to his terrible communist country soon.

'I mean to tell you another difference between us. I greatly care that the West and particularly your country, the country of Shakespeare and liberal thought, is suffering such ills. You do not care what my country suffers. You are hostile to it. Yes. There is your real resemblance to Winston Churchill, as d'Exiteuil said. You gloat secretly that we suffer because our leaders are bad, because we are communists. That's what you fear, communism, as your ancestors probably feared the Inquisition.

'You spoke of the difficulties with building in Moscow for the Olympic Games. Well, you have a grasp on such a little bit of truth that it turns to lies in your mouth. Why do we have to have these confounded Olympic Games in the first place, do you think? It's to show our progressiveness to our own people, so that they are not discouraged. It's to show the capitalist world that we also can stage-manage the big events, because we are perpetually on the defensive against you. There is no other way in which we can manage except by concentrating all our building potential. The potential is so small that we must as usual make sacrifices – and you're glad. When all's said, we're still a poor country and life for most is hard – and you're glad.' His thick eyelashes came down as he stared at the table.

The coffee arrived.

Looking down at his cup, Squire said, 'My dear Rugorsky, how can I answer all the arguments you put forward? Perhaps the fundamental error you make – forgive me if I speak out as you encourage me to – lies in making such great distinction between your rulers and your ruled. One hopelessly bad, one hopelessly good. That's unreal – and isn't it a very Russian error of thought? Are not your rulers of the people, and have people not conspired to be badly ruled? You threw out the Romanovs, if I remember rightly.

'Every country gets the rulers it deserves. I say that knowing how England has a mediocre team at present. But our system which communists and persons of ill-will seek constantly to undermine, at least allows a chance of changing the team peaceably. Your system is designed to give the people no such chance. So you have a self-perpetuating autarchy, which condones and often perpetuates the crimes of Stalin and his henchmen.

'And if you are a poor country after half a century of Marxism, then it's Marxism and the system it has created which is to blame. Quite simple.'

'No, you see, reality is not so simple.' Rugorsky lifted his cup and placed it to his thick lips, whilst fixing Squire with glittering eyes. 'To give an instance, I did not put forward so many arguments when I spoke; you only say I did. Then you grasped the point of major antagonism, building up explosively the area I tried to defuse, trying to imply I am a member of a criminal nation. You long for a confrontation, I believe. You are fierce.'

Squire said impatiently, 'No, I'm only too bloody polite. Quite honestly, if the USSR's as poor as you say, it is because of the barbarous killing off of the kulaks, and the miserable consequences of the enforced collectivization of agriculture. I listen patiently, but really – a system so criminal and repressive can earn nothing but poverty.'

The Russian inclined his head in a submissive gesture.

'Perhaps you think of my country as one big lock-up, as Solzhenitsyn wants you to do. But I must tell you, you meet many good fellows in a prison, you know. Some may even become your friends and spiritual leaders. So I take the liberty to tell you once more, whilst all the while drinking your coffee, that I care much more about your country than you do about mine. I love England, you see – that's my weakness.

'If you really wish to help people in Russia who work for happier times, then you must do so quietly. You must not make inflammatory speeches, even when idiots like Krawstadt open their mouths so widely.'

The coffee was good. Squire drained his cup and sighed.

'So far, I have kept silent in public. But most of the speakers give vent to a Marxist bias. I was provoked, let's say. How does my keeping quiet further the cause of enlightenment in the Soviet Union?'

'Because . . .' Rugorsky tapped a plump finger on the table top. 'Because it is important that these international gatherings take place. Otherwise, we all get locked up in our own countries. If it is reported that there is political dissension, or if the political system of my country is insulted in public, then we shall not be allowed to leave home again. This is what d'Exiteuil understands. I believe he's a sensible man.

'There's also the personal aspect. If I and Kchevov are involved in trouble, it will be interpreted at home as loss of face. We shall not be allowed again in the West, or maybe even in other socialist countries. I can only live, I tell you frankly, by breathing decadent capitalist oxygen at least once in the year. Perhaps you do understand these things a little, I think. You also travel.'

Looking him in the eye, Squire said, 'You're a charmer, Rugorsky, but I know and you know that you are trying to have it both ways. You admit or pretend you find your own country unbearable, yet you lecture me on the faults of mine.'

'Why not?' The Russian finished his coffee and regarded the bottom of the cup with an amused expression of regret. 'If you can't stand your own wife any more, it doesn't stop you seeing faults in other men's wives. Well . . . perhaps it does. That's not a good analogy I chose.' They laughed together.

They had both been aware that a tide of people was carrying Jacques d'Exiteuil towards their corner. The ever-active conference chairman was talking to two other candidates, patting another on the back, squeezing Maria Frenza's hand, and grinning at Rugorsky and Squire as he approached. His coppery hair and thin features reminded Squire – not for the first time – of a Beerbohm cartoon of the poet Swinburne.

'We will talk more, Thomas,' Rugorsky said quickly, heaving his shoulders forward, so that he leaned across the table almost as if to embrace Squire. 'But not in front of Frenchmen, who are too subtle for simple Russian and English men.'

D'Exiteuil put his arm round Maria Frenza's narrow shoulders and pushed her forward so that she and he together blocked away the table at which Squire and Rugorsky sat from the rest of the crowd. His smile was even broader than before.

'Well, well, well, here in Ermalpa we have really a united nations! After the heat round the conference table, here is Winston Churchill sitting down with—' D'Exiteuil paused for a moment, almost as if he had been going to make an unfortunate comparison. Then he added, 'The Russian bear.'

Rugorsky fixed his glittering eyes on Signora Frenza and reached for her hand. 'Is Madame Frenza also pleased with me because I am being good and not squeezing people to death?'

The question was translated into Italian, and Maria Frenza replied that she understood the hug of the bear to be very enjoyable if one was a lady bear.

This made Rugorsky laugh. He threw his head downwards rather than upwards to laugh, so that his mirth was directed towards the empty coffee cup. Then, with a dextrous movement surprising in one so heavy, he grasped Maria Frenza round the waist and had her sitting on his knee the next moment. He buried his snout in her crop of dark tawny hair.

'You see, I promote you to be a lady bear, with full territorial privileges!'

She laughed politely, making the best of it.

D'Exiteuil dithered a bit, nodding his head from side to side and playing his fingers on the table top. 'I'm sorry I have no lady to offer you,' he said to Squire.

'I'm content, though I'd also enjoy getting my arm round that slinky waist. Perhaps I see politics in everything these days, Jacques, but here before our eyes is a lampoon on statesmanship in the manner of Gillray. You will have to stand in for, say, Harry Truman. Rugorsky

173

and I are Stalin and Churchill, at the conference table at Potsdam. Maria is Eastern Europe, Poland, Hungary, Czechoslovakia, East Germany. You have allowed the bear to grab Maria. See how warmly it embraces her – and how she cannot help responding because she was born that way . . .' James Gillray's pen depicts a crowded cartoon scene. Bright colours and fountains of words issuing from every mouth add to the congestion.

Four principal characters are grouped about a table, which has been laid for a feast and is partly covered by maps and bodies. The scene is a butcher's shop. Carcasses hang from hooks at the rear of the shop, labelled 'Jews', 'Gypsies', 'Finns', 'Serbs', 'Indians', and so on. Blue-and-white striped aprons hang by the door, which sports the name of the firm, 'The Big Three, Pork Butchers and Slaughterers, Potsdam.'

Winston Churchill sits on the left of the picture. He is depicted as a grotesque drunken baby, his eyes small and pig-like, a filthy cigar shaped like a factory chimney causing smoke to pour from his mouth and ears. The cigar is labelled 'British Miners'. The ashen countenances of miners are visible in the wreaths of smoke which coil above Churchill's cap.

The British warlord wears an absurd ill-fitting uniform which bulges over his massive belly. His posterior is covered by a great baby-napkin, made from Union Jacks, and bulging with excreta, some of which, labelled 'Dominions', oozes from the folds of the napkin to the floor. The boots on his feet are tanks. His face is red and mottled with greed as he stretches over the table to grasp at a portion of Signora Frenza.

The signora is firmly within the grasp of the great Russian bear. The bear is massive and hairy, and dominates the whole right-hand side of the cartoon. It has Stalin's features: his stiff upstanding scalp hair, his full moustache, his heavy features and brown eyes, his foul pipe. Blood drips from the pipe, while from its pungent smoke, coiling above the head of the animal generalissimo, emerge wan faces of his victims, labelled 'Intellectuals', 'Peasants', 'Engineers', 'Soldiers', and so on. He does not sit on a throne, like Churchill, but on a model of the Kremlin, from the windows of which Marx, Lenin, Trotsky, Bucharin, and others peer hopelessly.

The bear wears on its upper portions a white tunic, buttoned to the throat and decorated with many medals. Covering its lower portions are military trousers, the flies of which have burst open to reveal – thrusting from amid black fur – a penis of terrifying proportions, the head of which is an ICBM. The bear is about to plunge this weapon into the vagina of Maria Frenza, which has opened in a silent scream. Hence the title of the print, appended in Gillray's rapid lettering below the picture, 'Love and Peace Prevail again in Europe, 1946'.

Maria Frenza is labelled 'The Eastern Territories'. Dragged across the table towards the terrible embrace, skirts in disarray, she creates a diagonal across the picture. Various parts of her anatomy, tastily displayed, are labelled from north to south. Estonia, Latvia and Lithuania, forming her three breasts, burst from an iron corsage. Poland forms her shoulders and arms, Czechoslovakia her trunk, Hungary her hips, Romania her lower abdomen, the protruding delta of the Danube forming the pudendum threatened by the bear's weaponry, and Bulgaria her plump legs and knees.

Pouncing to rescue her across the table – on which carcasses of a revolting feast remain – Churchill has grasped a plump portion of the woman's anatomy exposed by the disorder of her shift, her left buttock, labelled 'Yugoslavia'. Under his grasp, it has broken away from the rest of the body. Trieste is revealed as a rosy anus.

Other extraordinary figures are present in the butcher's shop. The emaciated corpse of Adolf Hitler lies under the table, where a cur labelled 'History' is gnawing its ribs. A little Emperor Hirohito, with an admiral's hat and a monkey's face, swings from a billowing red velvet curtain. Behind Churchill, wearing a lounge suit from the pockets of which money leaks, crowned by an oversize version of the hat named after him, is a cadaverous Anthony Eden. Behind Stalin, green of face, wearing pince-nez, is an enormous Beria, carrying an axe-and-sickle; next to him, slant-eyed, small, with the hindquarters of a jackal, Molotov fawns about his master's chair.

More shadowy figures lurk at the sides of the print. A ragged and unshaven Italy holds out its paw in a beggarly gesture. General de Gaulle sticks his enormous nose through a potted aspidistra to watch the proceedings unobserved. Franco looks on, chuckling. Various generals surge from behind the plush curtain: Marshal Zhukov, General Eisenhower, and General Montgomery are particularly prominent, all rattling weapons at each other.

But the most outstanding figure is the one holding the middle of the stage and standing behind the table between Churchill and Stalin. Although it wears two-tone shoes, a polka-dot bow tie, and a jaunty cap, it is a robot. Its eyes whirl and glaze, steam issues from its nostrils, in its mighty lower jaw stainless steel teeth champ. Its body is formed from turbo-generators, cooling pipes, and printed circuitry. Round its neck is a label reading 'President Truman, Made in Missouri, USA'. Secretary of State Byrnes, evidently carved out of wood and clad only in the American flag, squats on the robot's right shoulder.

Truman is saying: '*We Won the War!* To perdition with these Little Countries! We'll rid the world of the spectre of British Imperialism and then we'll put the Old World to rights with our Yankee Ingenuity. Stalin's an honest man, let him have his fun and then we'll get him when he's exhausted!'

Stalin is saying: '*We Won the War!* Now to Win the Peace! These two hyenas, Churchill and Truman, secretly love me (and so I can deceive them) because I have complete power while they have to be *elected*. One's senile, one's bloodless – I keep young with bloodbaths every night!'

Churchill says: '*We Won the War!* Stalin is such a Nice Man and I hope he likes me, but these Yankees don't see that we have to stamp out Communism now or else we shall all have to bend to that dreadful Weapon. I wish Adolf was alive and on my side. Adolf knew What was What!'

The Eastern Territories cry: 'Oh my Goodness! Oh No, oh Yes! What's a poor girl to do? As if the Huns weren't randy enough! We planted the seeds of Socialism long ago – now they're coming to Coition!'

Zhukov is saying: 'Go on, Joe, give her a stiff bit of Dialectic!'

Montgomery is saying: 'If only Eisenhower and Patton had seen sense, Prague, Berlin, and Vienna would have been completely in our hands and the Russians nowhere.'

Eisenhower is saying: 'Pity the Limeys would not take orders. Now the war has unfortunately finished, we'll have to teach them to toe the line through trade. I hope they make me President.'

Byrnes is saying: 'If only the robot would make some more atomic bombs, we could teach the Bear a few manners. After all, this is a Thanksgiving dinner!'

Eden is saying: 'If this drunken old fool Winston plays his cards right, Russia and America will go to War with each other, and the World will be safe for the British Upper Classes again!'

Mussolini (hanging upside down from one of the butcher's pegs with his throat cut) is saying: 'I'm glad I'm out of it! Things are just beginning to get rough!'

Two little girls, daintily dressed in white muslin, both wearing white gloves and clutching parasols, are examining the Gillray cartoon. One of them, perhaps an elder sister, is explaining the meaning of the allegory to the smaller child.

The smaller child, looking up trustingly with a sweet smile, says, 'I *see*, so the three nasty men are changing the Course of History, is that right?'

'That is correct, dear,' says the older child, smiling in her turn. 'Which proves incidentally that the load of obsolete rubbish sometimes referred to by brainwashed imbeciles of the Left as "Marxist Science" is no more of a science than astrology, because they pretend that individuals cannot influence the tide of history.'

'Oh dear, I'm afraid that I am such a silly,' sighs the smaller child, prettily. 'Cos I thought that astrology was a science. Perhaps I'm guilty of Left Wing sympathies. Anyhow, I think I understand the picture quite well now. Only—'

'Well, dear? Only what?'

'Why does it all have to be so *nasty*?' She opens her eyes wide in a winning way, causing dimples to form in her cheeks.

'It's about bloody *power*, isn't it? And power is *nasty*, isn't it? Cos someone always gets *hurt*, don't they?' She reinforces the lesson by swinging her parasol savagely against the younger child's head, until the muslin is stained red and the little smiling face no longer recognizable. Blood covers children and cartoon alike.

9

How to Get to Ostrow Lomelsky

Singapore, Spring 1977

The shooting in Singapore was finished; tomorrow, the unit would be flying on a Singapore Airlines jumbo jet back to the UK.

Grahame Ash and his team were taking it easy by the swimming pool of their hotel, or shopping in Orchard Road. Squire had hired a power boat which, like a taxi, came with a driver, a Chinese called Sun.

The boat cut through the waters of the harbour, skimming between ocean-going freighters in an exhilarating mingle of spray, sun, and shadow. Squire and the Sex Symbol, Laura Nye, laughed with enjoyment as the warm winds of speed fanned their cheeks. They roared past industrial islands. Ahead were the Roads, the glittering waterways which had brought wealth to Singapore, peppered with islands, many of them crowned with a ragged top-knot of palm trees.

Sun brought them to a small island, curving the power boat in so that a feather of water grew behind them and the craft touched silver sand broadside on. The two Europeans jumped out.

'Oh, it's gorgeous,' Laura exclaimed. 'Just gorgeous!'

'Paradise. Shall we do a Gauguin and stay for ever?'

'I can't believe we're flying home tomorrow. Let's have a swim straight away.'

They had not got the beach entirely to themselves. A large group of Chinese was sitting by rocks some yards away, laughing and eating ice cream. In the other direction, a noisy crowd of Caucasians, men and women, were kicking a football about. Just off the beach, embowered in brightly flowering trees and shrubs, a beach café stood; the sound of its music drifted faintly down the beach. Frank Sinatra-type music.

Squire and Nye went behind a thicket of bamboos and slipped out of their clothes. A minute later, they were yielding to the embrace of the waters. More intensely than on land, they merged with the amniotic flow which pervades and unifies all life. In the cells of their bodies, surges of current corresponded with the waves that broke above their heads.

After the swim, they nestled together in a hollow in the sand. He pressed himself to her.

'My tits are still a bit painful from the sunburn.'

'I've got to see you when the series is over, Laura. Things aren't just going to end. I need you too much. We'll work out something.'

'You know we won't, Tom. There's your wife and children, and I've got Peter. This is just an episode out of time. Don't let's spoil this precious day. Make love to me, go on.'

'At least we've still got the Los Angeles trip ahead of us.'

He rubbed the sand from his hand on his chest and felt her welcoming vagina. Sighs of pleasure escaped them both.

'Never mind a bit of sand. It'll add to the pleasure.'

'Oh, you luscious creature, I could fuck you for ever.'

He slid into her and they lay side by side, scarcely moving, mouths together, tongues linked. He swung a leg over her upper thighs for a better grip, and began to work, feeling sweat run in little channels between their arms and bodies. Flies tickled their burning skin. Little rivulets of sand trickled under their buttocks and shoulders.

They were moving powerfully when something struck Squire in the small of his back. He swung round. A black-and-white beach ball lay beside them.

'Bugger!' he said.

Laura sat up and grabbed for a towel just as a man with a stomach protruding from a Bermuda shirt ran up panting to reclaim the ball.

'Sorry to disturb you,' he said, laughing. He scooped up the ball,

180

booting it down the beach and calling to his friends, 'Look where you're kicking, will you? You're ballsing up other people's romances.'

Squire and Laura looked at each other and laughed.

'Australians,' he said. The football party had moved nearer.

They were sitting up and had come apart. She held his juicy penis in her hand and gave it a few rubs, smiling down at it.

'I'll deal with this later. It was nice while it lasted, but that sports fan has broken me mood.'

He grabbed her suddenly, rolling her in the sand, giving her a playful bite in the crutch and coming up with his chin bearded with sand.

'Come on, cover up all the delicious steaming flesh and I'll buy you a drink.'

Holding hands, they trudged through the yielding sand to the café. On the tiled floor, shade and light lay tied together like smouldering twigs, as rattan screens overhead fended off the brilliant sunshine. They sat companionably together at the bar, and ordered drinks from the barman, a gin and Seven-Up for Laura, a Tiger for Squire.

The bar was unoccupied except for a bald man in shorts smoking a cigar and drinking lager. He scowled as he drank. The only other person present was a woman. The woman sat alone at a table by the bald man. Stripes of light and shade ran over her. She had dyed blonde hair and wore red checked slacks and a black bikini top from which plenty of puckered pink flesh bulged. From her attitude of complete boredom as she stared out at the sea it was apparent that she was married to the bald man. She smoked. Her smoke rose up in stripes and filtered through the rattan bars. Frank Sinatra on cassette sang 'The Good Life', with plenty of backing from Nelson Riddell.

The man at the bar leaned forward and pointed the hot end of his cigar at Squire.

'I can know from your voice that you are not from Australia,' he said.

'True.' To Laura, Squire said, 'I saw a likely-looking Malay restaurant just two blocks from the hotel where we could have lunch. Then a siesta?'

'I don't believe that I could eat any lunch.'

The bald man said, 'Maybe you can know from my voice that I am from Sydney. You from America, you two?'

'Wrong guess, chum. England.'

The bald man was astonished. 'England, eh? You don't sound English, does he, Tinka?'

This last remark was addressed to the semi-blonde woman. She turned her head slightly, waved a slow hand by swivelling it on her wrist, but did not deign to answer.

'What you do in a place like this?' the bald man asked Squire. 'You live here? Your girl – you English too, darling?'

'Where are we having the party tonight, Tom?'

'Grahame's got an open-air place in mind which someone recommended to him. Jenny's booked a table.'

'Grahame's an old sweetie pie.'

The bald man moved over and said, 'Mind if I join you? Can I buy you some drinks? I always am glad to speak with English people. My sister has married an English man in the Air Force.'

Seeing that the man was not going to be put off, Squire and Laura turned their attention to him.

'Were you born in Australia?' Laura asked.

He groped in the pocket of his shirt, brought out a cigar case, took a card from it with clumsy fingers and offered it to them.

'Is me,' he said proudly, as they read 'Andrej Joachimiak: Computers, Micro-Processors'. 'Andrej Joachimiak. I and my firm make the only Australian computer in the world. No one else.' Over his heavy mid-European accent a few flimsy Australian vowels had been laid.

'You manufacture computers?'

Joachimiak screwed one of his temples with what looked like an awkward but nevertheless determined attempt to touch his brain with his finger.

'Know-how. Is all in here. I can make a great success. I am a real know-all.'

'And were you born in Australia?' Laura asked again. 'Is Joachimiak an Australian name?'

'Ah-hark, the lady is a little curious about me, yes. I know, I know it, all lady are detracted by success. Well, I tell you, lady, I was not born in Sydney but in Ostrow Lomelsky. You know Ostrow Lomelsky? Maybe you been to Ostrow Lomelsky?'

Suddenly, he appeared to have lost interest in the conversation.

He turned and lumbered back to his wife, who had produced a paperback entitled *Growing Old Today* and was glaring at one of its pages.

She was smoking continuously. Her cigarettes and lighter lay on the table beside her empty glass. Joachimiak grasped the lighter and blunderingly relit his cigar.

'Can I buy you another lager?' Squire asked the man.

'A brandy. I want brandy. That is kind of you. I'd like to shake your hand, mister. First bit of kindness I've had all day. People don't care any more, do they?'

He shook hands with Squire as the barman delivered three fresh drinks. Sinatra was singing 'What Now My Love'.

Joachimiak edged round Squire so as to be able to address Nye face to face, and returned to his previous question. 'You maybe been to Ostrow Lomelsky?'

'Not that I remember,' Nye said. 'Where is it, exactly?'

He became very cunning, winking and putting one finger along his nose whilst almost laying his head on the bar.

'Ah-hark, so you never heard of Ostrow Lomelsky? Well, you'd like that place. Very quiet. Wide spaces. Only a little village. Very cold winters, all the time it freeze very hard and the horses die.' The mere recollection made his accent heavier. 'Very pain to work, I don't know. The River Bug, it freeze so hard – you know the River Bug?'

'I don't think so.'

'Is not good, in winter is not good, River Bug. So anyhow, I tell you how you get to Ostrow Lomelsky, then you go and see what I say. You know Lublin? Is big city south from Warszawa. From Lublin in a car, if you got a car, drive north-east, only nowdays you don't drive too far or you come to the frontier with the Soviet Union.'

He broke off to laugh, cough, and drink half of the brandy Squire had provided. His wife continued to read, drawing cigarette smoke into her lungs before issuing it into the atmosphere.

'Sounds a nice part of the world,' Squire said.

'Terrible, terrible, I can tell you, Mr Englishman; Sydney is a whole lot better than Ostrow Lomelsky. Not so quiet, no, not so quiet, but a whole lot better.' He shook his head, laughing and wheezing. 'You think Ostrow Lomelsky sounds good? I have to sleep with my parents on top of the stove, you know? Turnips frozen in the ground.'

Wheezing, he turned back towards his wife. 'Tinka, this Limey likes the sound of Ostrow Lomelsky. With the sewer running through the street?' She paid him no attention, thumbing the pages of her book.

'You were telling us how to get to your birthplace.'

'What for you want to know?' He swigged down the rest of his brandy, gasped, coughed, and said, 'So you drive in a car if you got a car north-east from Lublin at forty kilometres an hour, across the River Wieprz where was once a massacre in older days, all the Jews killed off, and in two and a quarter hours you will be in Ostrow Lomelsky, right smack by Krzysztof Gajda's *gasthof*.'

'I see,' said Squire. 'So Ostrow Lomelsky is ninety kilometres outside Lublin in a north-easterly direction?'

Joachimiak took the cigar from his mouth and laid it along his nose, at the same time cocking his head so that it almost rested on the bar.

'Ah-hark, you are pretty fast at calculations, mister. Congratulations, for I see you are a smart guy for an Englishman. But your calculations are wrong, anyhow, or maybe you drive too fast, because the correct distance is only sixty-two kilometres.'

He started to laugh, dropped the cigar on the bar, bent double to laugh, turned back to his wife to try and get her to share his amusement.

'Eh, Tinka, Tinka, this limey guy, he think Lublin is ninety kilometres outside Ostrow Lomelsky! Ninety kilometres! Jesus, Sweet Saviour! This guy'd be in the River Bug before that. How you like that?'

She looked at him stonily. 'You're pissed,' she said.

He redoubled his laughter. 'Yes, but, Tinka, you hear what this guy say to me?'

'I heard,' she said. She regarded him without expression.

'We'd better be going, Sun's waiting for us,' Squire said, slipping off his stool and pulling some crumpled dollars out of his pocket.

'Don't go,' Joachimiak said, grabbing his arm. 'Listen, let me get you a drink. Barman, barman, two brandies!'

They made a difficult exit. Sinatra was still singing 'My Kind of Town'. The woman at the table watched them from over the top of her paperback without changing her expression.

Sun asked them, as he held out a hand to assist Laura Nye unnecessarily into the power boat, 'You have a happy time on the island?'

'It was lovely. Thank you very much.'

She started giggling. 'What was the name of that dreadful village near the River Bug?'

'Oswelsky Tommel?'

'Stromsky Something. Stromsky Lomsky.'

They could not remember, and ended up laughing. As they snuggled together and watched the astonishing panorama of Singapore rise from the sea, Nye said, 'That's broken my dream. I was somewhere on a hillside where I'd never been before. I was walking through a funny sort of garden and there were lights flashing in the sky. Then there was a break and then I was surrounded by little green men. I should have been frightened but wasn't. Everything charmed me – I think I had the idea they were *rescuing* me. They had a UFO parked among trees. They led me there and helped me up the ramp. I was getting very excited to think that I was about to fly to another planet, and then I woke up.'

'Obvious sexual dream. I'm almost twice your age. You regard me as an alien or a time-traveller.'

'Why do dreams always break off at the most interesting part?'

He laughed. 'Good question. I don't know if anyone has answered it. Imagination refusing to go any further? Maybe if the good things always happened in dreams there'd be no incentive to make them happen in waking life. They'd sap your determination if you could get to Venus every night.'

'Like you have to work very hard really to get to Ossle Tomski.'

'*She* was dreadful, wasn't she? Did she make him the way he is or vice versa?'

They were speeding among the freighters by then, heading for the dockside.

After a light lunch, they returned to their hotel. Grahame and the others were nowhere to be seen. With some relief, Squire and Nye took the lift up to their room. It was a beautiful room, cool, well-appointed, smelling of sandalwood, with an ever-interesting view of Orchard Road and the city.

They showered together and sluiced the sand from their bodies. She let the water course over her upturned face.

'Laura, dearest Laura, I can think and breathe nothing but you.'

She pressed herself against him. 'Oh, I do want to be with you. I need you so much, Tom. I can't leave you.'

Squeezing her, he stared painfully at her. 'It'll be different back in England. I can't let you louse up your life with Peter. Besides – oh, Christ I keep telling you, I really am old enough to be your father.'

'You told me also that when your boyhood hero Humphrey Bogart married Lauren Bacall, he was old enough to be her father, and that all worked out really happily. Well, we'll work out something good, too.'

He turned the water off.

'This is just an idyll, my darling. Unreal. Too good to stay true. Don't spoil it with hope.'

She bent down. 'I'm a sucker for you, Tom Squire,' she said, and popped his still dripping penis into her mouth.

They climbed onto the double bed, and began to make love without hurry. Afterwards, they slept.

'Any more dirty dreams?' he asked her when they woke.

'You don't love me, Tom. You only fancied me because I was billed as the Sex Symbol in your Instant Culture series. You only love me as a symbol – and don't start telling me that we all respond to each other as symbols, because I hate that line of chat.'

'You're doubly dear – as yourself and as a symbol. But I can't bring all that misery on everyone. On Tess and the kids, and on your Peter.'

'The other day you were saying that she didn't care for you, only for the house and the possessions.'

'I didn't mean that exactly. Even so, it would still bring her misery. This must just be a beautiful interlude.'

She scowled at him, put out her tongue, reached over to a side table. Grasping a bottle of suntan oil, she began to anoint herself, kneeling up on the bed and shutting him off by her concentration on her body.

'If that sight doesn't give me a hard on, I don't know what will.'

'Oh, Tom, I wish that bloody UFO I dreamed about had taken me away.'

He swung over and sat on the side of the bed so that he did not have to watch her oiling her breasts.

'I just remembered when I first thought of the title, "Frankenstein Among the Arts". Long before I rationalized its use. I thought of all the arts of living, which have perhaps been brought to a higher standard in the West, and to more people, than they have ever been before. And I wondered why the hell we weren't all happier than mankind has ever been. Not that we deserve to be while parts of the world are starving, as moralists would doubtless remark.'

'As if you weren't a stinking moralist!'

'Ah, but I'm not the old kind who was shocked when people enjoyed themselves; I'm shocked that people don't enjoy themselves. And that's what I saw – behind all the benevolent arts of living, a monster looming, blindly clutching and throttling all that comes within its grasp. What I really wanted to do in the series and the book – what I haven't done, what I even lost sight of doing – was analyse not the nature of the arts but the nature of the monster. How would you label it: Morality, Immorality, maybe, Communism, Capitalism, History, or some deep-rooted biological flaw in human stock?'

'Things aren't that bad, darling.'

'You said it yourself earlier today. Why do dreams always stop just as you're getting to the good part? Ever since we were in Sarawak I've been thinking of that cave wall full of phantom hands, palms outstretched in supplication. They may well prove to be the very earliest artwork of mankind that we know – and there we all are, hands lifted, grasping at – something we can't get, something we can hardly even adumbrate.'

She put the stopper back on the bottle.

'Or maybe something we've lost, like the Australian and his Istosky Lemosky.'

The sun was glinting through their blinds with slanting rays. He reached over and picked his watch off the bedside table. 'It's half-five already. In the Pole's case it was no doubt the hostile politics of the century that separated him from his place of birth, awful, cold, and unpronounceable as it was, and set him on that long road to Australia and the noonday brandy. But the monster always calls, through one agency or another.'

She trotted round the room and stroked his hair. He placed a cheek against her glistening flank.

'Stop it. The dice aren't loaded against us. Don't pretend they are or they will be. Fatalism is all wrong. Come on, we found each other, didn't we? That suggests that your monster is on our side, doesn't it? There's no monster. You've just got one of these intellectual ideas like my father had. I'm going to get you out of it, I'm going to be your Lauren Bacall, Bogie, and I'm going to take care of you and mother you like a daughter, and see that no harm comes to you – ever.'

He grasped her teasingly by one labium.

'Laura, you're marvellous. For you I'd swim the Styx, or even the River Bug. Now, drape something over this lascivious little body and let's see how life is progressing down below.'

'Ladies and gentlemen, we're very happy to have you aboard with us for this tour of Singapore by Night, of which we are all so proud, remembering that it is the third largest port in the world. There are many exotic sights to see, for this really is the most cosmopolitan city on Earth, not excluding Hong Kong and other ports you might name, and thus perhaps a pointer for other cities in the future.

'As to the past which is behind us, many many peoples have formed Singapore and still live here now it is an independent republic. That's why it is such a melting pot of the Orient, with Chinese, Malays, Indians, Sikhs, Indonesians, Pakistanis, Eurasians, Japanese, Australians, and also the British and other Europeans, with all different religions, in the pot happily together. So it is a hospitable place.

'It's a great tourist spot, and this year we expect that three million tourists will visit it. All will be welcome, since each tourist spends just about five hundred dollars during an average four days' stay here. Radios, clothing, cameras, electronic gadgets, these are favourite buys for the traveller, along with girls of course, for which Singapore is famous, although prostitution is not quite so rampant as in the days when our city was part of the British Empire and a port for the navy.

'Of course it's not an ideal city, despite what our tourist propaganda says, but maybe there's no such thing as an ideal city – except existing as an ideal. However, if you don't mind if I get a bit egg-headed, I want to draw a parallel between Singapore and Venice, because you'll be able to get a free drink on Four Star Coach Company when we stop at Raffles Hotel in the glamorous heart of the city.

'Both Venice and Singapore depend on the sea, of course. That much is clear even to the thickest tourist from the USA or wherever. As the Middle Ages closed in Europe, it was the golden city of Venice which stood out above all other cities as supreme in beauty and wealth. In its internal development, it showed the promise of a new urban constellation far remote from the old walled cities which till then had existed since Neolithic times. So it was the city looking to the future.

'For many years and centuries, Venice was a symbol and legend of city-state success. We think Singapore is the current example of a demographic urban solution. We are peaceful but energetic.

'Trade was the golden key in Venice. Here in Singapore, it's the same. But much more so. We depend not only on water but also the air. Two hundred ocean-going vessels float in our harbours each day, and sixty countries send their shipping lines here. At the Paya Lebar airport – and soon we will have a newer bigger one at picturesque Changi – we form a hub for international air routes, and over thirty important airlines operate their services through us. If you are male and your hair is too long when you arrive here, then you must get it cut short, but that's a minor detail because nobody wants to harbour hippies in our hard-working republic – they can go on to Bali or India, where nobody seems to care if they shit on the beaches.

'In the future, we will expand also into space if necessary and at all profitable. We can build a spaceport as easily as anyone. There are still a few *kampongs* we could knock down, or we could take over an unused pleasure island. We have to do all we can, because we have no defences and so no crippling defence budget to be paid for in taxes. So we make an appeal to pacifists the world over, but pacifists won't come here to live in case they must work too hard.

'After all, in a hard world, the population of Singapore must work. We've got enemies. Indonesia's a pain at the back of the neck. And all the desperate nations of Indo-China. So here you can work and live comfortably, with dignity. Some of our girls are very beautiful, but sex is an invisible earner and we are realistic. Venice was called The Brothel of Europe in the eighteenth century. We have no danger of a similar label today, not with the Thais about, and Bangkok such a flesh market.

'You know that this whole island was rather a dump, with just a few indolent Malay fishermen and snakes before Sir Stamford Raffles arrived and stirred things up. Well, Venice was much the same until some Italians from Padua escaped from an invader, crossing lagoons and settling on unpromising swamps and islands in the fifth century AD. So was the canal developed and the gondola, which we hear of by the eleventh century. We have created a city out of similar material, due mainly to the energy of the Chinese. It's true we have none of the arts which made Venice great, and no painters or even stars like Piranesi or Tiepolo, but international cabaret stars like Sammy Davis

Jnr often perform here and all the latest films are shown from all over the world. In fact, we're suspicious of art, which is often produced by layabouts or religious maniacs, but it's great *f16* country. Our business men are strictly commercial, yet honourable and look after their families well.

'Perhaps you are whispering to yourselves that Singapore is fun to visit but it must be hell to live in. Let me tell you otherwise, because the health record is so good. Even the President of the Republic is a notable gynaecologist. We have here, I'm proud to say it, the fourth highest urban population density in the globe, which is to say about three million people of all the nationalities I mentioned once, but the GNP figure is about just over four and a half thousand dollars a person, and rising. That's not only because we are industrious and don't allow strikes like in Britain and Australia, to name two disgraceful examples, but because we develop industries and people invest in them, the workers themselves not least. Oil, banking, shipbuilding, all increase.

'Fortunately, we learned something from the appalling state of manufacturing towns in Europe and the USA not forgetting those busy little Japanese people to the north. We have brought in good legislation under our Prime Minister, Lee Kwan Yew, who is certainly no fool. Not only do we avoid a lot of socialism going on, we have strong anti-pollution laws and clean air acts. So the workers have their good health, industry is zoned away from residential areas, and we can generally do without filth and disease. Our record is greatly better than Venice, don't forget, because of the disgusting Italian habits.

'The cleanliness of the Chinese is so well-known as to need no emphasis from us. Often we think our tourists smell bad, but are too hospitable to say it. After all, this is such a clean place, with no diseases such as malaria or plague or smallpox. Syphilis – well, a lot of that is brought in from abroad, and we know gonorrhoea is prevalent in the United States. That's all in all why our death rate is down to 5.4 per 1000 of the population – one of the lowest in the globe.

'French visitors to our shores will be particularly interested to note how we have taken to the English language as the common tongue. The French language is hopeless as it's pronounced. Far more English is spoken here inter-racially every day than in Hong Kong – or in France, for that matter. This is not because we like the English, and anyway Somerset Maugham was decidedly queer, which is not a popular habit in our republic, but because it cools things between the various racial groups, particularly Chinese and Malays, and is used a lot in international trade.

'There's plenty more we could tell, but outside the windows of our coach you see all the lights twinkling in invitation to spend and enjoy, which speak more eloquently than words. So in conclusion I'll say that human beings will always make cities, unless they are just indolent Malay fishermen, and progress has to go on.

'Here in Singapore, fortunately with geography, we think we have one of the best ways of progress, and thank goodness we're a long way from China and the Soviet Union, so we work hard, enjoy play, be kind to our through-put tourists, and hope that you enjoy a pleasant stay here, remembering that our emblemaic flower is the fragile orchid, the symbol of how delicate nature is, and its beauty. Good-night, and thanks for listening. Have a fun holiday.'

As the tourists disembark from the coach, clattering with cameras, past the smiling slant-eyed hostess, night comes on and geopolitical constellations wheel overhead.

Even for the a-political state, time is running out. The lights of Europe may be guttering, but the USSR too is low in the westering sky. As for those stars of lesser magnitude in South America, their light is eclipsed by the brightness of the North American galaxy, which now burns at the zenith. The configurations of the Middle East presage no greater ascendancy for them.

Meanwhile, over the northern horizon, the bulk of that vast planet China continues inexorably to rise, tawny, magnificent, and fringed with an ever-increasing number of satellites.

10

Slatko

A gleaming band of light out to sea separated day from night. Although it was not yet entirely dark, a few stars shone. Thursday was sinking without trace into Ermalpa harbour.

It was possible to stand on the seaward side of the Via della Cala and gaze across a low concrete wall at the old port. Among a muddle of derricks and sheds, the masts of a sailing ship could be discerned. Beyond the masts was the sea, the Mediterranean.

Squire stood with his hands in his pockets, looking across the wall. He let the memory of other seas refresh his mind, but thoughts of the difficulties he faced, here and at home, stayed with him.

Pedestrians brushed past as they hurried home. He glanced at his watch. It was almost time for the last session of the day, at which his friend Herman Fittich would speak; for Fittich's sake, he would submit to being incarcerated again in the mirrored conference hall. As he turned to make his way back to the Grand Hotel Marittimo, he caught sight of Selina Ajdini walking towards him; accompanying her was one of the more cut-glass young Italians, Enrico Pelli, who had earlier delivered a prolix paper on 'Psychiatry and the Popular Understanding of Prehistory'. Ajdini saluted Squire with some eagerness in her gesture, and the customary mocking note in her voice.

'Are you looking for more flying saucers, I suppose?'

'In search of the miraculous? Waiting for a sign?'

She laughed. 'I've seen too many signs in my life. They all point different ways.'

'Ha! "What meaneth Nature by these diverse laws? Passion and reason, self division cause."'

If she recognized a couplet from one of Aldous Huxley's favourite poems, she gave no sign, saying cheerfully, 'If you are about to turn back to the hotel, Signor Pelli and I will walk along with you.'

He smiled warmly at her, suddenly full of affection, loving that naked face, and reflected again on the beautiful curvature of her lips, only made possible by the topography of her lower jaw. How long would you have to live with Selina before you failed to notice those affecting proportions? Enrico was no doubt under the spell of them. He had given Squire no greeting. His face was clouded, his heavy brows drawn together, his back rigid. As he moved reluctantly to walk beside Ajdini and Squire, the latter thought, 'So he's been propositioning her hard, and had no luck.'

And, as his gaze rested on her, 'I wonder what luck I'd have?'

'There's a sailing boat moored by the harbour,' he said, walking on the other side of Ajdini from Pelli, and addressing her left profile. 'How pleasant to sail away now, before the moon is up, to forget all your responsibilities . . . To discover a little sunlit island no one had ever happened across, with a golden beach and no footballers . . .'

'Footballers! How did they get there?'

'They didn't.'

'And on the island . . .?'

'Coconut palms . . .'

'Your dreams are so standard. Better natural products are oil, wheat and whisky . . .'

'I wasn't planning to work or get rich.'

'I'll come with you,' she said. 'I'm not a bad sailor.'

Outside a bar in a side alley, a broken sign burned, advertising a Belgian lager with the words 'STELLA ART' in blurred mauve neon. He took it as a good omen: there were islands somewhere, even if not readily accessible.

'"All I ask is a tall ship and a star to steer her by . . ."'

'It would be a good alternative to listening to Herman Fittich, I'm sure.'

'I like the man. I'm confident he will have something interesting to say.'

She gestured. 'His perpetual irony I cannot stand. A defeated man. But I don't like the Germans in any case.'

'They did make themselves a bit unpopular a few years ago.'

She flashed him a reproving expression. 'Don't you start on the irony. You were safe in Britain when the Germans were killing off Europe. Me, I am Yugoslav by birth, or half Serbian and half Turkish, plus a dash of Persian.'

'So you have reason to hate the Germans.'

She gave a curt nod, and tossed her head.

'I was a tiny girl when the damned Nazis invaded my homeland. Everyone fought them, young and old. No country was more brave, more determined, than Serbia. My father was killed by the Bosch, then my elder brother. So I can't help hating them. An uncle and I escaped to the United States after the war, but one does not forget those times. They leave a mark.'

Pelli said something to her angrily in Italian, but she silenced him with one of her quelling glances.

'The Americans understand little of the rest of the world,' she said. 'But you see I am not like that, although I have American citizenship.'

'Yugoslavia's a magnificent country. If you're so left wing, and you dislike the States as much as it seems you do, why don't you return to Yugoslavia?'

She appeared to undergo a sudden change of mood. As if dismissing the subject, she slipped a slender arm on which bracelets clattered through his arm, and made him look with her in a small lighted shop window. Pelli stood awkwardly by, hands impatiently on hips.

'That handbag's not bad, eh? I bet it was made in Milano. You know Yugoslavia, don't you? You have lived there?'

'Yes, I have.'

'There are more job opportunities for me in the States.'

'Thank democracy for that, Selina. Be grateful for what you've got.'

She sighed and they walked up the street in silence.

'Well, dear, dear. You see, Tom, I do really quite fancy you – much more than I fancy this sulky young man who wants only to go to bed with me and fortunately does not talk English. Well, I go to bed with whom I feel like and maybe tonight I feel like you if you are so inclined. So I don't want to offend you. But you are – oh, so simple. The British are like Americans, they do not know the real world. Okay, there are more job opportunities in the States, but that's only your debating point to be scored. You don't see why there are all those jobs more.

'Jobs are what capitalism's all about – getting people to work for the bosses. That's really why I hate capitalism, because it is just a huge business and industrial machine gone mad, with all the stupid "free citizens", as they call themselves, really mere consumers, chained for life to support the machine, proud of their sharing.'

He seized her wrist and shook it till the bracelets jangled, laughing in irritation. 'At the risk of being left off your visiting list tonight, let me tell you that you are the victim of propaganda – outdated propaganda at that. If the world was as you say, it wouldn't be worth living in! You've got a silly argument, like Krawstadt with his pinball machines. Work's okay, work gives us identity. And do people cease to consume, to need goods, under other systems than capitalism? It's just that other systems are less efficient at producing the goods.'

'That may be, and the other systems may have their faults, but it is the efficiency of the capitalist system I also dislike. It exploits the world for the privileges of a few. Who needs an electric carving knife? That efficiency is itself a crime; I'll give you an example.'

She had got her wrist free from his grasp, and sank her long crimson nails into his arm with a sort of humorous cruelty.

'We were talking about the Nazis. Okay. In the First World War, Germany had three important chemicals firms, Bayer, BASF, and Hoechst. You know all the names today. The Germans managed to synthesize ammonia and nitric acid in a successful industrial process. The British and Americans got millions of tons of natural nitrates needed for high explosives from Chile, and so their chemical industry fell behind Germany.

'The three firms united to become I. G. Farben, a conglomerate which totally identified itself with the Nazi cause. It employed slave labour, it ran its own concentration camp, it manufactured Zyklon B to gas Jews with, as well as manufacturing the usual agents of mass-destruction. I could say its products killed my father and brother.

'The bosses of I. G. Farben were tried at Nuremberg after the war, but they just got cynical sentences of two or three years' imprisonment. Farben was dissolved, but Hoechst, Bayer, and BASF started up again. What's more, they and their subsidiaries got reparation settlements from America, millions of dollars.

'Now they have bought themselves into the American pharmaceuticals industry, so that Bayer, for instance, has forty per cent of its assets in the US. Isn't that an international conspiracy? You see how criminality, murder, become legal as long as they serve the system. Big money is always linked with death in capitalism.'

Squire shook his head. As he stared into the aquarium of the shop window in which five handbags drowned, her words brought a sort of helplessness.

He had a vision of her honed beauty as being formed by flight. In her mind, early terror had separated brain from will. Now the brain worked without further external referent and, seizing on its giant excuse, the shattering experience of war, projected an image of the evil which had destroyed her father leaping from country to country – from Serbia to Germany, from Germany to the USA, ever in pursuit of her. Where would safety be but in the country that had wished to exact vengeance from Germany after the war, and to de-industrialize it entirely?

This interpretation came to him with sudden persuasive power.

The stain of Ajdini's personal bitterness had extended until it coloured her outlook on the whole world. America had become an uncaring step-mother, exchanged for the mother she loved and had left; every pretext which served to bolster her hatred was welcome. The tone of her voice indicated as much.

Tearing his eyes from the sunken handbags, he clasped her arm with his arm and said, 'That's a false perception. A lie. Everyone merchandises death. Don't think otherwise. Supposing your facts are roughly correct – I expect you're loading them – then it proves nothing, nothing except that firms like nations go through good periods and bad. Are Bayer still manufacturing Zyklon B? Ask yourself that.'

'Christ, I give you proof of the evils of capitalism and you don't listen. BASF and the American firm Exxon were linked by trade even in wartime. But you can't see. You're conditioned. It's like living among robots, talking to you people!'

She pulled her arm away and started to march up the street. Pelli caught at her other arm but she beat his hand down.

Falling in beside her, Squire said urgently, 'You told me earlier that you had a belief in the miraculous. Perform a miracle on yourself. You're a splendid woman, Selina – knowing you only two days, I can see such qualities in you.' He was saying more than he had intended, and almost drew back, but the sight of that taut bone-like countenance spurred him on. 'You're poisoning yourself with hatred, somehow, I don't know how, but I sense it.

'Face the fact of your father's death, see it simply as a bitter misfortune of war – and war not as an organized system but as a pandemic at this stage of human development. Try to *blame* no one! Hate cripples us. Don't erect that death into a great structure which will eventually overpower all your happiness and wisdom.

'You've lived in peace in the United States. Try to love it, to accept its vastness – and your own vastness. See the two processes as one. Forgive, let go, accept. Invest in the miraculous. There's no way you can get revenge – from what, dear Selina? – except on yourself.'

They crossed the Via Milano dangerously. She turned an angry face on him.

She opened her mouth, revealing her beautiful lower teeth, her tongue bedded in its clear juices. He was blind to screaming traffic.

'You, what are you doing? Trying some damned Freudian rubbish on me? You know I hate and despise it! Telling me that what I see clearly before me is all in my head! Fool, sentimentalist, bloody Freudian!'

On the pavement, she moved towards him with an attacking movement, then veered so that Pelli bumped into her. Pelli, with no idea what the row was about, tried to grasp her again. Ajdini smacked his hand and almost ran for the hotel door.

'Selina, Marx is a dead duck — neither he nor his creed can help you. He's a damned sight worse than Freud. It's the miraculous — that's what you need!'

She was already hastening through the revolving doors.

Squire turned and looked at the glowering Pelli.

'Life's a bugger, isn't it, chum?' he said.

The traffic screamed by him. What were the drivers all so mad about? Was all of Ermalpa a conspiracy by the Fiat Motor Company?

She fled. One of the displaced, the uprooted, one of the mourners . . . Branded just as surely as the concentration-camp victims.

The modern generation, the generation of his son John, didn't know about that branded generation of which he himself was one in ways hardly less decisive than Ajdini. They might one day have to learn the bitter way.

What was that curious statement of Marcuse, uttered in *One-Dimensional Man*? 'Auschwitz continues to haunt, not the memory but the accomplishments of man — the space flights, the rockets and missiles, the "labyrinthine basement under the Snack Bar" . . .'

Just as the harsh peace terms imposed on Germany at the end of the First World War had paved the way for the second, so the nightmare induced by the second was building up shock waves which would culminate in the third. His inward response to Ajdini's tale of the meshing of German and American pharmaceutical industries had been to exclaim, 'Yes, that's it, that's how the evil gains,' remembering William Burroughs's comment that the paranoid is the man who has just discovered what's going on. What real panacea, what escape, was there, except to advise people not to suffer, and to delight in what they could while they could?

That was no certain way. Pleasure was often the forerunner of trouble. It would be a pleasure to go to bed with Selina, if she was not just a tease, but the unhappy repercussions might be many, as had been the repercussions of his pleasure with Laura Nye in Singapore and elsewhere a year and a half ago. There was no Sure Way. The way of the mystic was not his.

As the civilized world, so called, expanded, driving out the animal kingdom, the labyrinthine chain of cause and effect grew more complex. People became so confused, not understanding the cause of their confusion, that any false prophet like Billy Graham or Karl Marx or von Daniken who came along offering them a thread through the labyrinth was received rapturously by millions. It was not so much the truth the millions cared about, but the thread itself. Something to hold on to.

Thinking his melancholy thoughts, Squire was more inclined to go in search of Ajdini – would she be lying weeping face down on her bed, or smoking a cool cigarette with d'Exiteuil? – rather than listen to Fittich; but a desire to support his German friend drove him into the hotel and towards the conference hall.

'Squire, you're useless. Too well-meaning. It's weak to be well-intentioned. Why don't I face up to how blackly corrupt the world is, and junk my pathetic *thé dansant* optimism? Why not just go and screw Selina, never mind her troubles, get some joy myself, which is what I really want to do, and to hell with Laura and the rest. As for Tess . . . it's just my fool optimism makes me think she cared in the first place . . .'

He went and sat down in his place, between d'Exiteuil and Vasili Rugorsky. The two men were laughing together. Rugorsky said, 'Dr d'Exiteuil owes an apology to you, Thomas.'

D'Exiteuil said, 'You were right about the miraculous, in saying that it can happen. I believe you did observe a UFO earlier today.'

He produced a copy of the local evening newspaper. It featured a photograph of rooftops and a blurred object in the sky. Black headlines proclaimed, 'Flying Hardware over Ermalpa – Have they Come from Outer Space?'

'You see,' said d'Exiteuil, reading, 'Hundreds of people leaving their offices and factories at midday saw bright objects in the sky over the centre of the city. An Alitalia DC-9 landing at the airport sighted a flight of three flying beneath the plane and heading along the coast in the direction of Palermo. The objects were capable of staying stationary and then of moving off at colossal speeds.

'Some of the objects were cigar-shaped, others the more familiar saucer shape. There were similar previous sightings a month ago. The Air Force is correlating all reports and would be glad to receive any photographs of the flying hardware.'

Squire stared at the print and the photograph in silence.

'It's a form of madness,' Rugorsky said. 'You see, these people are well-meaning, but they want to make a drama, like all under-developed people. One child's balloon floating in the sky and they can feel free to imagine an air force of extra-terrestrials. Theatre rules them, not reasoning.'

'But Squire saw one. You didn't want a drama, did you, Tom? I don't know, there were sightings over Paris recently. I begin to think there must be something in it after all. I mean, this has been going on for years . . .'

'There are sightings everywhere. It's a cargo cult merely.'

'I think it's good publicity for the conference. I shall phone the newspaper. Excuse me.'

As d'Exiteuil left, Squire told the Russian, 'I know I saw something. Since I don't know what I saw, it belongs in the category of You-Foe. But now that I see this report in the newspaper I confess I find my belief weakening. Perhaps, as you say, it was a child's balloon – first hanging motionless, then swirled away in an updraught.'

'Notice that all photos of flying saucers show them about the same size, whatever the text claims – and blurred. The cameramen think these things are at infinity, and so they focus their cameras at infinity. Maybe the objects could be only fifty feet away, just above the rooftops.

Then if they move on a wind gust at forty miles an hour, they appear to move four thousand miles an hour because the mind believes them not near but at infinity.'

'Modern cameras focus automatically, Vasili . . . I was immediately convinced that I saw a You-Foe. I didn't want to see one.'

'No, you didn't want to see one. But you were typical in interpreting what you saw as a part of high-technology. The power of the imagination is to create images, and even science progresses by images, images of what is possible. So, the Greeks thought that the heart was a fire, because they knew fire. The heart could not be visualized as a pump until the Renaissance, when pumps were invented.'

'But there are flying saucer visions in the Bible, or what sound like visions. Ezekiel and all that.'

'Hindsight, Tom. You must not believe anything but cause and effect. Always cause and effect. That belief supports all of science and our culture. I may piss on a fire to put it out, but I cannot light it that way.'

This response silenced Squire.

Many candidates were still dawdling at the entrance to the conference hall, as if reluctant to enter. Squire decided on a quick tour of the ground floor, hoping to catch sight of Ajdini. Instead, he was captured by d'Exiteuil, who came bustling cheerfully out of a telephone kiosk and put an arm about Squire's shoulders.

'A reporter from *Oggi in Ermalpa* is coming round to interview me. Perhaps we have a success on our hands after all. How are you enjoying the events, Tom? We have both been so busy that we have hardly made any conversation in two days. I must thank you for your contribution, by the way. And Geo Camaion is okay – don't worry. Aren't there some interesting people here?'

'I wish there was more time for private talk, but one always feels that way at conferences. Rugorsky is an attractive character.'

D'Exiteuil squeezed him. 'And I believe that Selina Ajdini has caught your eye. She certainly catches mine. Ah, Tom, if I were younger . . . While I am here, my dear Séverine is also at a conference on education in New Orleans. We are so often apart, and one does get lonely. It's difficult to be human, eh? Our volume of proceedings will be important. How are you enjoying the standard of the papers? Krawstadt was fiery, yes?'

'You know how difficult I am, Jacques – I believe that many papers would be better and clearer if all the Marxist jargon was dropped. The underlying assumptions that the Western world is about to collapse and a bloody good job if it does is malicious, treasonous . . .'

D'Exiteuil tut-tutted and shook his head decidedly.

'You are not an academic, but you must understand that after all we must speak in a proper rigorous language; you even referred to that necessity in your speech. There's nothing to fear except imprecision. Marxism is our analytical tool, a method of cognition. It's a method, no more, designed for our scientific age. You understand that, I think.'

Squire looked disconcerted. 'You must know a lot more about Marx than I do, Jacques. He bores me. But Marx would not have accepted what you say for one minute. "Method of cognition"? Karl Marx believed only in a crude dialectic which reinforced the inevitability of revolution. That's what Marxism is really all about, isn't it? The overthrow of the established order.'

'Tut, that's old-fashioned. That's *vulgar* Marxism, such as you might find a British trade unionist spouting.'

'Haven't vulgar and academic Marxism, to use your terms, got that much in common, that they sanction anything in the way of aggression or sabotage or repression as long as it ruins society, so that some imaginary classless utopia, of which the ghastly living doppelganger is the Soviet Union, may rise from the ashes?'

'You've been reading the Tory press, Tom. You don't really think that the state of affairs in France or Britain is all that could be desired, do you?'

'Of course I don't. But with equal certainty, I can foresee the sort of blackguards who would grab power if our present social structures collapsed or were brought low. You don't answer my question. You do work for revolution, don't you?'

'Well, capitalism is in decay, you have to face the fact.' He laughed.

'A definitive answer. That it's a lie helps to show the weakness of your case. I might as well say that communism is dead in the USSR and Eastern Europe. Indeed, that's a more accurate statement than yours, because communism *is* dead on its home ground. It has been proved not to work, and its shibboleths are kept going only by force, by the exertion of power by an entrenched gang of criminals.

'Marx said that capitalism was dying over a century ago, and that bit of nonsense has been parroted ever since. He made a mistake, a big historical mistake, because what he observed was capitalism in a raw early state. Our societies have improved beyond recognition since then, and will improve faster if only we shrug off this dead preaching which impedes – it doesn't hasten – social justice.

'If the West collapsed, then we should have not the millennium, as you pretend, but a period in which freedom and justice go to the wall, as they have done in Russia, when the effectively aggressive bastards on the Left would smash up every virtue in the old order and anyone who stood for its values. Which does, incidentally, include all left-wing intellectuals like you.'

D'Exiteuil stood stock still in the middle of the corridor, folded his arms, stroked his beard.

'Please don't provoke me with such nonsense. From you of all people, such paranoia. I expect you to be more civilized. Why are you saying this?'

'I'm not paranoid. I'm probably not particularly civilized either. But it doesn't take a very wise man to see how the contagion spreads. Every strike, every failure in the economy, and you feel the more entitled to declare boldly that capitalism is done for. Every time you do so, claiming the backing of some sort of invalid "scientific" theory, you are assisting the destructive forces who foment trouble inside industries and inside the trade unions. That's how your vulgar and your academic Marxists aid and abet each other.

'You may not dream of revolution personally because I should think you have sense enough to value your skin, but whenever you mouth those ugly phrases you bring nearer the day when it is legal for a thug with an armband to kick you in the guts for as long as he wants.

'If you like that sort of thing, okay, head for one of those countries where your catch-phrases are the going religion, but while you remain here have the decency to respect the civilized blessings, including the rule of law, however capricious, under which you are given the chance to enjoy your life.'

The Frenchman was rigid; his face had flushed a dull red.

'You're crazy, talking to me like this. Are you trying to attack me personally or the entire conference? Every point of view is welcome, yours or Cantania's or Krawstadt's, but we have to aim for some common critical language. It's the diagnosis that has upset you . . . Hm . . . you really are scared beneath the surface. You must be symptomatic of the whole bourgeois world, already sweating at the collar because you know the day is coming.'

Squire grunted contemptuously. 'The day is coming! Listen to your own phrases. "The day is coming." It's a nut-cult slogan. Better to believe that You-Foes are bringing a wise alien race to rescue us from sin.'

D'Exiteuil tucked his hands in his pockets and stood a little taller. 'Well, I just don't happen to believe in sin, not in the sense that you old-fashioned liberals understand it at any rate. Sin is nothing anyone can do anything about, since it's ingrained and presupposes some ridiculous system of divine punishment no one can comprehend—'

'I don't believe in divine punishment either.'

'Maybe you don't, but you behave as if you do.' The phrase was delivered flatly and with considerable contempt. 'What I do just happen to believe in is that a day is coming when exploitive systems will be swept away. Maybe we don't have a working example in the world as yet, but that's no reason why we should not strive for better systems.' D'Exiteuil spoke with spirit. Both men had grown red in the face. Several delegates, lounging about the foyer, watched the argument with covert interest.

'Jacques, I do not believe that you personally hate the past and the present; but such is the attitude that all these old dried figs of cliché enshrine. "Systems" you talk about – typical French intellectual pretension to want to live under a system – but it is all simply materialism—'

'System is just a word! We all have to live under some bloody system, you know!' He rattled his remarkable locks about his head.

'Karl Marx was a nineteenth-century materialist without much historical insight. He saw the miserable condition of the workers, and for that we respect him although he was far from alone in doing so, but he was typical of that progress-obsessed generation. It thought everyone would be happier when reduced to *systems*. He was just one more pedagogue. His idea of a classless society is one more dotty millennial creed. We should all forget about his theorizing, just as we've forgotten about Disraeli's "Young England" movement. Instead of remaining hypnotized by some vain illusion of pie in the future, forget it, junk it, free your mind, and rather try to enjoy and strengthen the present.'

He was alarmed by the venom in his own voice, alarmed by what he had said to his old friend. In the pause, he saw d'Exiteuil gather himself to attack, and feared what was to come.

'You have no creed, no scientific philosophy to guide you. Just "enjoy the present" – that's really the feeble message behind "Frankenstein Among the Arts", isn't it? Enjoyment. How trivial! Sure, Karl Marx made some mistakes; but his is a whole reasoned programme for conduct, now and in the future. You when you speak make out the case against yourself. You think a classless society is dotty – or rather you hope it. On the contrary, it is a lofty ideal. We want men united, not divided, and the honest truth is – though I admit I am not much of a revolutionary – that Britain and France and Germany will have to be *destroyed* before all the old divisions which –' he pressed an index finger against Squire's shirt button – 'which *you* embody in your privileged position are destroyed. I'm sorry that I make you angry, but so were dinosaurs made angry when they saw little mammals trot by.'

'Again an analogy drawn from last century. Evolutionary argument twisted to fit human society. We're trapped by the outworn garments of last century when we should be free to face the future, free to see that enjoyment is not trivial but central—'

'Sorry, Tom, I'll listen to no more. You insult me unnecessarily, I who have fought many battles on your behalf. We have hitherto managed to keep our politics apart from our friendship. Obviously that is no longer possible. I am deeply hurt, deeply offended.'

Squire looked worried.

'I'm sorry, Jacques. Perhaps the conference has been too much for me. I have no wish to offend you personally. We must each stand up for our own beliefs.'

D'Exiteuil spread his hands. 'Didn't I invite you here as guest of honour? Now you call me the worshipper of a nut-cult. Well, we'll see – you observed the flying saucer, not I. There are good men here, your friends and allies, as I counted myself. You really insult and disgrace us all.'

'That wasn't my intention. Forgive me for speaking out. You know I have personal troubles – possibly the strain has told on me. I shouldn't have been personal.'

'Excuse me, I am required in the conference hall.'

Squire stood mopping his neck with a handkerchief. He went to the bar and ordered himself a beer, which he drank standing, conscious of having made a fool of himself. He looked at his watch. He followed along to the hall, where almost all the seats except Ajdini's were already filled.

Enrico Pelli turned a murderous glare on him.

In a minute, Gianni Frenza called upon Herman Fittich to give his paper on science fiction as a modern literary form.

Fittich, soberly dressed in a grey suit, rose, clearing his throat as he looked nervously about him. 'To avoid a few translation problems I intend to deliver my paper in English, since possibly more of you speak that language here than speak German. My apologies to my hosts that I don't try it in Italian, my congratulations to them that I won't.

'When I shall return home, when I will return home, friends will ask me how I enjoyed Ermalpa. "A lovely, fascinating, and complex city", I may answer. I'm hardly going to tell them that I have spent almost all my time in the Grand Hotel Marittimo, and in fact in this very room. But I do know from a study of some guide books before I left Germany that this city is many things. It's a melting-pot, that's a phrase that comes to mind, a melting-pot. A melting-pot of conflicting cultures. Ermalpa has been a western city looking towards the east, and also an oriental city looking towards the west. Many races have made their contributions, from Phoenicians and Greeks to Arabs, Normans, and even the British.

'Melting-pot is a funny description. Things don't melt down that easily in human terms. After many centuries, the various traits remain pretty distinct. But that is what makes it interesting still. We don't want an imposed uniformity of any kind.

'So Ermalpa is a good place in which to hold this first serious critical enquiry into the aspects of the popular culture of our time. My subject is science fiction literature, or *fantascienza*, the excellent Italian word, or *Utopische Romane*, the less effective and in consequence now obsolete German phrase. Science fiction – or SF – is a melting-pot much like Ermalpa. It also contains conflicting cultures. It looks to the future and to the past and, by implication, most searchingly to the present. Many disciplines make their contribution, such as science, of course, notably astronomy and cosmology and the physical sciences, but also any other science you care to name, genetics, biology, down to soft sciences such as sociology and anthropology. Also such more general themes as religion, mythology, apocalypse, catastrophe, Utopia, perfectionism, literature, adventure, and sheer crazy speculation.

'All such things and many more go into the melting-pot. They don't actually melt down, but they all give the brew a flavour. Its contents are so diverse that readers can pick and choose their own specialities. This is why it's difficult for two people to agree on what SF is all about. Despite the popular misconception that it's all about space, it's actually more important than that. It's all about everything.

'It is the modern literature read almost obsessively by the young in all industrial countries, although sadly neglected by their seniors.'

Yes, but what SF's not about is things like this conference. It simplifies, whereas this conference complicates. It substitutes simple aliens for the complexity of nationalities and internationalities. And in the examples I've read, it externalizes evil, making it a menace from without instead of within. Perhaps that's why it's so popular. Even Marxists like it, or use it for their own purposes.

But maybe SF tells the truth in showing how change is everywhere. How the present nations, the current power blocs, will disappear, leaving not a wrack behind – or only a bootee and a bridle. I remember the Scythians and their deep-frozen underwear. In their time, they thought the world was their oyster.

Now I suppose the Marxists feel the same way. What's wrong with all *that*, apart from its high boredom factor, is that it is presented as the Ultimate. There's no ultimate in human affairs, or won't be for many thousand million years, we hope. Surely a proper study of the future would vanquish ideology? There's only a process, forever continuing. Eternal artistries of circumstance.

Meanwhile, on the humdrum level, I have offended Jacques. That outburst was unpardonable. Or was I feeble to apologize? Am I secretly afraid of losing his friendship? I suppose I am. But I did speak badly out of turn. I'll write him a letter of apology, leave it in his letter rack. He is a nice man, I am fond of him. That distinction he made between upper and lower Marxism just made me mad – as it would have done Marx himself.

My affairs are a bit of a cock-up. On Monday I go back to England – to what? Teresa, you will never never know what you've done to me. I kicked out the girl I loved for your sake, didn't I, because I loved you more? What else did I have to do to appease you? . . .

I should have stayed in the bar and had another drink. Why does old Herman look so nervous?

Selina. What did Jacques say about her? Has he been trying to make her?

I suppose he also has his private reasons for being angry. Wife at some conference or other, fears that this one may flop . . .

We're all being ground down by some ghastly historical process. It's better when you're young because you think the process is remediable by action, political action, picketing power stations, or a bullet. I did. My son does. His son will. History in a nutshell . . . Fuck it all. Thighs. Thighs. No wonder that thighs are so perennially popular, and don't get less so as you grow older . . .

No name with whatsoever emphasis of passionate love repeated that grows not faint at last. History is our attempt to retain that passionate love, to commemorate what has gone. Thus we extend our lives. Science fiction, I suppose, extends our lives into an imagined future . . .

How is Pippet Hall to survive? I must keep it on, it must remain a going concern. It enshrines history more effectively than any book, any monument. The present generation, with its inverted snobberies, despises anything of cultural wealth, but surely that attitude, that little ice age of the spirit, won't last. The trouble is, I've no heart to go on without Teresa. Poor girl, poor jade! Terrible to imagine oneself offended.

There is no way in which one can give up in life, short of committing suicide. I've no quarrel with that. Falling on your sword is honourable, if you really have reached a dead end.

But that's not for me. I'm as corrupt as anyone. I'd rather take Selina back to the Hall and fall on her. Iron out her bitterness. She has a fine spirit. She communicates.

Beautiful woman. Damned politics.

Part-Serb. It would be splendid to replenish the Squire stock with Serbian blood, as old Matthew Squire did with German blood. Brave buggers, the Serbs. None braver. I'm not too old to start another family.

But almost.

And sod you too, Pelli . . .

'You may perhaps think my view of a critic's function rather old-fashioned, but I am more interested in appreciation than classification. The reader must be borne in mind. Readers of SF are most struck by its originality although, if they read too much of it, they complain of unoriginality, and find they enjoy it less and less. This is because they have ceased to look for the other qualities SF possesses.

'Goethe's *Faust* is by no means the first story of a man making a deal with the devil; Shakespeare's *Hamlet* is after all just another Renaissance play on the common theme of revenge. Frederik Pohl's *Gateway* is just another tale of a chap who is off-balance getting a ride in a spaceship. But it is only when we look at these works in another light that we see their individual qualities – although we must always remember that they are interesting *because* they are also about a chap dealing with Mephistopheles, a chap trying to avenge his father, a chap getting a trip about the galaxy. Each of these three experiences goes straight down like a taproot of a tree into the awareness of the age which engendered it.

'I should add here, if the remark is not obvious, that it doesn't matter a bit that nobody has had a trip about the galaxy and maybe never will. Neither has anybody held a dialogue with the devil or a conversation with the ghost of their father. But this essence of the unlikely aligns SF with some striking monuments of literature – the imaginative and non-realist vein. I believe that Isaac Asimov is wrong, despite his great authority and reputation, in claiming that the space race justified SF. It needs no such justification. Our admiration for Cervantes's *Don Quixote* would not be heightened if we found that some old knight had actually had a fight with a real windmill. The quality we admire is *imagination*, not realism.

'This is where SF breaks from the old style of the nineteenth-century novel, and where it pleases the young and dismays the old. The novel no longer has novelty, but SF has, though we should maybe despise facile novelty just as we are suspicious of a new model of automobile – the last model may have had better qualities, if less chrome. One indicator of the novel's lost impetus is that novels have become rather inward-looking and a bit provincial, at least in

Germany and England. In the US, things are a little better, though how many new Russian novels have you read with interest lately? . . . Well, never mind. Arts need freedom.

'Critics of the novel of a previous generation, such as Ortega y Gasset, held the idea that one prime function of the novel was to portray character and its development. The view is still echoed unthinkingly in the seats of orthodoxy.

'The fact is, people just don't believe in character, or in development for that matter, in the old way. Two world wars, the inroads of psychology, the increasing fate of man as a statistic, or a consumer, or just as a faceless speck of proletariat so beloved of Marxist jargon – all such factors have transformed us into fragmented beings. The container of custom has been shattered.

'First cinema and then television have also profoundly affected the novel. Also inflationary economies have directed many impoverished novel-writers to more profitable fields. That non-literary consideration must be taken into account when you sum up today's state of play. Yet SF has flourished; ill winds for the novel have proved good winds for SF. That's true especially of this decade, when cinema and television have actually fed the appetite for SF.

'Maybe the secret of all this popularity is that SF puts human character pretty firmly in place. A chap with a name and a lowest common multiple of human characteristics – he may not even have a sex life, poor chap – is set against the cosmos, or against a whole array of inimical technological creations like robots, for example, or against paranoid infrastructures, like multinational companies. Conflict has become more than character – because that's how many people experience life in these days. I guess the population of the world is about three times what it was when Thomas Mann or Thomas Hardy started writing. There had to be a change and SF expresses the change. SF is the change.'

Good old Herman. An attempt to think things out and express the results clearly. Amazing how you can meet a stranger and love him after two days. Quite a brave man, too, under his resigned veneer.

Not a bad fellow to have with you in the slit trench when the shit's flying. That's the acid test. Herman and Vasili.

Rugorsky is a real character. Extraordinary – choosing a German and a Russian to fight with you in a slit trench. How our thoughts have been formed by war . . . Not so many years ago, I'd have been fighting against Herman. And in a few more years will probably die fighting against Vasili Rugorsky.

The idea – even the irony of it – doesn't terrify me, as maybe it should. Better fight and die than give in. You defend your own territory. You fight for your own hearth, your own home, your own country. Something the modern generation believes silly. They'll find out too late when the chips are down. You fight for England. It is atavistic, but the human race hasn't evolved beyond that yet. If you aren't prepared to defend, someone else will attack.

Of course, if the You-Foes are real and contain aliens from another planet, the whole course of human history becomes changed. Perhaps that's why so-called civilized people are reluctant to believe in flying saucers; they are felt to be inappropriate, a discord. The orchestra's playing Borodin's Second Symphony; suddenly more musicians enter and start playing Mozart.

If the aliens are hostile . . . Well, we shall have a situation where Vasili and I will be sharing a slit trench.

I still can't make him out. Wrote a poem called 'Winter Celebration', likening the Soviet system to a medieval feast. Medieval starvation, more like. Exiled by Stalin, then possibly reprieved and disappeared for a while. Disgrace, atonement . . . Sounds like a typical Ruskie existence. That chap at the consulate, Parker-Smith, thought that Rugorsky might possibly defect. Not here, but in Rome when we're flying back on Monday. Interesting. If that's what he intends, he may feel he knows me well enough to flash a warning signal. Perhaps I shall have to help him.

I wonder what Selina's doing. Will she be dining with me this evening? If not, then perhaps Herman and I can rustle together Cantania, Morabito, the two Frenzas, and even d'Exiteuil, if he'll speak to me. We'll have a meal and some drink. Vasili, too. I'd rather talk to him than listen to any Western left-wing nonsense. Actually, I'd rather talk to him than anyone here, except Selina perhaps.

A drink would go down well. Old Herman does go on.

'Charles Dickens's novels are among the first to reflect the atomization of modern society brought about by metropolitan life. The faces in his novels are glimpsed vividly – often with nightmare vividness – but briefly, before they disappear. They are known from the outside. SF carries this process further. We see people only in relation to the unknown. The strangers have moved in.

'Some people praise the logic of science fiction. But I am more interested in the kind of SF which creates mythical beings, robots, monsters, androids, aliens, machines, creatures from the future or the id, revenants, voices from other dimensions, which proliferate in SF as nowhere else. They are a clear indication of the struggle going on within twentieth-century man. In no other form of literature are they so freely allowed on parade.

'Surely in the future men will see SF as the literature of our time. I am well aware that much of SF is rubbish, like much of ordinary fiction, written for retarded children by superannuated children, but there's no reason why we should pay attention to that end of the spectrum. As we still listen to the ancient Greek myths, so men of the future will care for ours, which define technological man. We have no reason to doubt that the first tellers of the Greek myths were scorned in palace and court. The new is never welcome. So SF is scorned today in high places.

'The distinguished founder of the Society for Popular Aesthetics, who is with us in Ermalpa as our guest of honour, has spoken of our task as "exploring the familiar". That clever phrase describes pretty precisely what SF does. In paradoxical manner, the best stories present Today in a disguise which reveals it nakedly as it is. That is a true imaginative function. Emmanuel Kant has shown how the power of our imaginations, the power of mental picture-making, is essential to us if we are to understand the world. Otherwise, we can't recognize any object, for objects are only intelligible as members of

214

a class, of classes of vehicles or of whatever you wish. SF helps us to distinguish ourselves as one phenomenon among many, and our planet as one among many, and our lifetime as one among many. It opens the windows of our fancy and can give us a true perspective. For example, it banishes an obsolete socio-economic theory, which has gained some ground here and there, which claims that human beings can profitably be divided into abstractions labelled "bourgeoisie" and "proletariat".

'But instead of quoting Kant, for I don't want to seem nationalistic, I will finish by quoting the English poet, Percy Bysshe Shelley, because he says something in his *Defence of Poetry*, written at the beginning of last century, which describes with vivid accuracy the plight of today from which a study of science fiction can free us.

'Shelley says,

> We want the creative faculty to imagine that which we know; we want the generous impulse to act that which we imagine; we want the poetry of life: our calculations have outrun conception; we have eaten more than we can digest. The cultivation of those sciences which have enlarged the limits of the empire of man over the external world, has, for want of the poetical faculty, proportionately circumscribed those of the internal world; and man, having enslaved the elements, remains himself a slave.

'I believe we have to live with that slavery, at least for a while. But SF, I know from experience, is one way of making it tolerable.

'Thank you for listening to me.'

As Frenza asked for questions or additional statements to be limited to a duration of five minutes, Rugorsky wrote a note and pushed it over to Squire, making it slide across the green baize, one fat finger simultaneously propelling and holding it captive.

The note consisted of four words. 'But Shelley is dead.'

It was difficult to decide on Rugorsky's meaning. An idle joke. Or perhaps a positivist Soviet rejection of the poet's negative remarks.

Possibly even a threat of some kind. People did die, and that wasn't pleasant. As Selina's Serbian father had died . . .

Inner vision could fly northwards, away from the Mediterranean, over the Alps and France, across the Channel, across England, to Pippet Hall in the heart of the Norfolk countryside, could enter there undetected and find its way up to the children's playroom, the old wooden room now painted white which – in the days when it was stained with brown varnish – had been home for Tom, Adrian, and Deirdre.

Striking in through the windows in the room's brown varnish days, the sun had lit it till it glowed like the interior of a honeypot. Each worn yellow floorboard had an individual character and an individual role. In winter, a coal fire burned in the grate. Next to the grate was a cupboard with a lock mechanism which worked only with difficulty. Inside the cupboard was a secret compartment where Tom stored a few personal possessions. At the back of the compartment was a large tin box with its own lock. The box contained, along with precious things like cigarette cards and postcards and a penknife with bone sides, a fat red notebook on which was printed the one grave word, 'MEMORANDA'.

To the playroom one day, inpelled by grief, together with a certain sense of dramatic intensity, Tom had gone, removing his red notebook from the recesses of the cupboard, and writing in it in black crayon, 'March 12th, 1937. Daddy Died.' From then on, the words being so desperately final, he wrote nothing more in the notebook.

The notebook still existed. So did that entry. So did the death.

John Matthew Squire had bestowed on his eldest son a love of arts and shooting and the countryside which lasted all his life. John Matthew Squire's death had bestowed on the son who found his body a sense of violence and frustration which equally had never worked itself out of his system.

The arrival of the refugee Normbaums, like crows gathering at a battlefield, had proved the herald of a great violence, the war. The war. Growing up, going to school, knowing always that tremendous actions involving courage and hardihood were taking place not a hundred miles away. Hearing the planes roar over the rooftops at night – all of Norfolk was an aerodrome. The intense love for Rachel Normbaum. Puberty. Fondling her in a quiet room, an erection flaming against her thigh and the intense astonishment, mingled with pride and annoyance, when, at the touch of her fingers, semen spurted over his grey trousers. Something to do with being a soldier. Preparing to join the struggle, to leave school, to get into Europe, to taste that traditional harsh life of war – waiting, fighting, killing, marching, winning, going hungry, enjoying the fruits of conquest – women, booze, good companionship, self-glorification. Then Berlin was taken and the war collapsed.

Tom Squire was just too young to fight. He had missed the biggest initiation rite of the century. The allied armies were being disbanded. Detumescence had set in.

On the surface, he was relieved. Below, frustrated, disappointed. Oh, to have liberated Paris!

Only to his Uncle Willie did he make his real feelings known. Uncle Willie had friends in London, connected with the county. Young Tom Squire was on National Service, and completing his preliminary square-bashing at Aldershot, when he was posted for special training at a camp near Devizes. After some tests, he was transferred to MI6 to a department specializing in overseas operations. The Cold War was tightening its grip on the world. Men like Squire were needed.

He was given leave. A friendly man drove up to Pippet Hall; later, Squire met the friendly man in Whitehall. Following a hot tip, Squire applied for a job with a consortium of manufacturers who were interested in new export markets. He got the appointment and went to night school to learn Serbo-Croat.

War-battered Europe was putting itself together again. The Americans, with a gesture of unique generosity, launched the Marshall Plan. Britain, its overseas investments exhausted after paying for the war, set to work cheerfully on an export drive. The war had been won; now they were to win the peace.

The frontiers of the peace were already established. The Iron Curtain had descended across Europe, and the luckless nations of the Continent found themselves either on one side or the other; with one exception. The nation of Yugoslavia.

Although Yugoslavia was communist, there were remarkable differences between it and the other communist countries. Their leader, Tito, was a national hero and had conducted a formidably courageous war against the Nazis; he became a popular peacetime leader, and was not imposed on the country by the Soviet Union. Britain had supported Tito during the war; Churchill had made wise decisions there; so a friendship of sorts remained possible across barriers of ideology.

The BIA (British Industries Abroad) opened an office in Belgrade and attempted to develop trade with the Yugoslavs only a comparatively few months after the official cessation of hostilities. On their staff was a young secretary, Thomas Squire, with a briefing to travel to all regions of Yugoslavia looking for trade. He had the perfect job for undercover work.

'You may not like Yugoslavia very much until you settle in,' Squire's head of department said. 'After that, you'll hate it.'

Squire loved it. There was something in this mountainous country – particularly in Serbia – in its songs, in its turbulent history, which corresponded to the violence trapped in his own nature. Moreover, a war was still going on, a war of minds. As an impoverished and broken economy picked itself up, the nation fended off its enemies. The Yugoslavs were intensely nationalistic, intensely suspicious. Foreigners were constantly watched.

Belgrade, the Serbian and national capital, was at that time a city in ruins. Of the housing that remained, much was old and substandard; the energetic rebuilding was new and substandard. Greyness and cold prevailed. Filth, disease, misery, mud, flowed like blood through the ruptured veins of the capital. Food was short. It was all that Squire desired; here was the harshness and challenge of the world war he had missed.

A Serbian girl called Roša came his way. He knew she was an

agent. He embraced her as eagerly as he did his new life. In her pallor, her treachery, her nakedness, she was a paradigm of her country.

'Obey your operating orders, whatever they are,' he said – he rapidly became fluent in Serbo-Croat, 'but make me part of you. Let's do everything. Be extreme. Involve me, involve me!'

He thought she loved him in a way. She tried to dye her hair blonde, with disastrous results. They both laughed; then she fought with him and wept. Her parents had been shot by Nazis for some petty offence. The country was an armed camp. The army built roads, bridges, bicycle factories. Ferocious drink-parties took place in which people fell out of windows and died. Roša got drunk and sang folk songs about the centuries of Turkish tyranny, the beauty of Serbian hills, and red wine spilt on white tablecloths. Her voice was like zeppelins crashing. It made him weep.

Squire travelled down to wild cities in the south, Titov Veles, Kumanovo, Bitola, Prilep, Skopje. He passed on some information in Skopje, and two Russian agents were arrested. He saw how one of them was beaten up; he only just managed not to vomit, ashamed of his own weakness.

Back in Belgrade. Roša had earned a rare holiday, she said. She took him on an old steamer down the Danube, brown with all the corpses of history. They stopped at Smederevo. Smederevo Fortress was one of the places Roša sang about when drunk. In its time it had been the largest fortress in all the Balkans. Its gigantic and ruinous towers stood against the Danube. It was a cold, depressing place; the wind blew from Russia. Masses of peasants had been forced to pile stone on stone, to erect this monstrous stronghold against the Ottoman Empire.

There was no defence against history and the Turk. When Smederevo fell in 1459, the medieval state of Serbia was quenched like a torch in the river.

A man was waiting for them in Smederevo. He was big and black-bearded. His name was Milo Strugar, and he became Squire's friend. On that first occasion, he was hostile. He drove Roša and Squire away in an old black German car to a wooden-tiled house in the woods. There Squire was made privy to some of the plans of Yugoslav counter-intelligence.

He never saw Roša again after that occasion. The bastards had sent her away, just to show him that you did what you were told. He learned the lesson.

Long before the war, the Yugoslav and Soviet communist parties had forged close links; they were brother Slavs. But Stalin had offered Tito little support in his struggle against German invasion. The old channels of communication were now being obliterated. Yugoslavia had to stand on its own legs or fall under Soviet domination.

Squire saw evidence of how ruthless both sides were. In this corner of Europe, in the broken towns and forests, the Cold War was real. Yugoslavia stood between East and West, mistrusting both; the fight was not merely of words, but of guns, fists and boots.

Living became more complex while its issues simplified. The remnants of the fascist Ustache in Croatia, once linked to Hitler, were allying themselves with the Soviet Union. Their plan was to kill Marshal Tito. They had to be smashed. There were weeks, months, when tank movements on the other side of the frontier suggested that Soviet invasion was imminent.

Squire thought much of his gentle father in those times. He thought of the dogs that had devoured his face. To some acts, there was no adequate response but killing. So in Serbia.

He slept rough, became familiar with the forest. War was not a natural activity of man, but the equations of life forced it on him. He understood perfectly that the Yugoslavs had no alternative but to resist the Russians. Like tigers, they loved their freedom, and would defend it.

More important to the strategists in the West was the fact that here communist was fighting communist for the first time. It gave cause for hope. The struggle was of immense significance for the rest of the world. As he identified with the Yugoslav cause, he saw clearly a parallel between his lonely war at one end of Europe and the role played at the other end of Europe by Britain, only seven years earlier.

After Milo Strugar had tested him, the Yugoslavs began reluctantly to trust Squire. The Serbs preferred him to the Croats. In part, they trusted him because he was British. The label 'Englishman' was sweet in their mouths.

Early in the ill year of 1948. Countries of Central Europe like Czechoslovakia sinking further under Russian ice. Romania becoming more sovietized, and more hostile to Yugoslavia. The USSR beginning to hamper traffic between Berlin and the West.

The BIA sent Squire to the Yugoslav port of Rijeka, where mixed elements in the population caused unrest. Snipers still lurked in the hills above the city. Squire's contact was a Serb called Slobodan, who ran a printing press as a cover for his other activities. Slobodan was a wild and unkempt man, extremely emaciated, who had lost his left eye in the mountains during his term as one of Tito's partisans.

Over cigarettes and slivovitz, and through many curses, Slobodan in his little oily shop explained how a shipment of arms of British manufacture had arrived in Rijeka from the British Zone in Germany. It was delivered in an armoured freight train, and the train was hauled into railway sidings near the docks, where it was guarded by a Special Operations unit of the Yugoslav Army. Regulars, not conscripts, said Slobodan, spitting. After some delay, the officer commanding Rijeka Arsenal – sited some miles inland from Rijeka – arrived with a convoy of trucks to take charge of the shipment. The train was empty.

The major had immediately arrested the captain in charge of the guard unit, the driver and engineer of the train, the train guards, and just about all the officials connected with port operations. But the arms were not recovered.

A full-scale search of Rijeka was in progress when Squire arrived. Slobodan, a true anarchist, had no patience with the blundering military. With mighty curses, he told Squire that he had better ideas of his own.

'I've got orders to contact the major i/c arsenal,' Squire said.

'Screw that, I have more genius in my arse than him in his head. Listen to my report.'

Slobodan had received a tip from an informant that a barge or barges had been sighted off-shore during the previous night, a few miles to the north. The barges were showing no navigation lights. All was obvious to Slobodan – you cut out the floors of the freight cars, remove the crates of arms, and steal them away by sea, not land. Sea is safer by night than land by day or night.

'Barges don't get far in one night. Come, we go see for ourselves in my fast car.'

Squire found himself packed into a tiny Zastava, bumping danger-ously over the coast road, while Slobodan gave him an almost incomprehensible résumé of his family history, in which dismemberment figured rather largely.

After making a few enquiries, they stopped at a small bay west of Opatia, under the humped slopes of Mount Ucka. A black-clad widow-woman who lived up the mountainside swore she could see from her window a newly risen rock or a newly sunken ship under the surface of the Adriatic.

They parked the car and went down to examine the situation. The waters of the Kvarner Bay lapped a line of beach rare on this rocky coast. There were fresh but confused marks in the sand – someone had obliterated tell-tale signs with a sack. The steeply shelving shore-line would allow a shallow-draught barge to pull in to the beach without trouble, and under cover of dark unloading operations could be effected with little risk of discovery: this region, Istra, was under dispute between Yugoslavia and Italy, with parts still administered by British forces; many of the inhabitants had fled, leaving the country almost deserted. The ravages of incessant warfare were plainly seen.

Slobodan and Squire prowled the beach. On trees and bushes fringing the sand they found freshly broken branches, as if vehicles had moved in. They were searching among the bushes when they came on the body of a man dressed in fisherman's clothes. His jersey was clotted with blood. He had been stabbed several times in the rib-cage. His beard was matted with mud and blood. Anger and pain still contorted his rigid face. Ants crawled between his teeth.

'It's Milo,' said Squire. 'Milo Strugar . . .'

'*Jebem te sunce!*' growled Slobodan, thrusting a rampant fist up at the sky. When he recovered, he stuck a cigarette into Squire's mouth and asked, 'What do you know of this man?'

'Milo was my mentor, the first Serb to trust me. As to what he was working on hereabouts, it was secret. I know of it only in general.' He hesitated, not entirely trusting the savage Slobodan, then plunged on, still overcome with shock. 'Milo had a lead given him by a Croatian member of the *Škupstina* [Parliament], an old Partisan pal of his. That I know. I heard only that trouble of some kind was going on in Labin – the Croat spoke of a planned armed insurrection, aimed at getting rid of Tito and manned by disaffected Ustashe elements. Supported by high-level Soviet backing. Where is Labin?'

Slobodan dragged the cigarette from his mouth and pointed inland with fist and cigarette. 'Twenty kilometres up in the hills, not more. Let's go!'

Squire leaned over his friend's torn body, but Slobodan grasped him roughly by the shoulder.

'Cut out that girlie stuff. Weep for your pal later – first, revenge the bugger. Let's get to Labin, stir up things there, find guys who'll help us. These thugs here are desperate.'

Sten guns, magazines, old Cyrillic type-faces, carpenter's tools, and hand grenades mingled on the back seat of Slobodan's car. They had rattled noisily on the road from Rijeka. He threw a blanket over them before proceeding. They rattled again as the car accelerated in a pungent whiff of Jugopetrol. Milo Strugar's body was left lying in the bushes with the ants as they headed up the steep tracks of Istra.

The season was late April. The sun made the hillsides blaze with warmth, exhaling a sweetness that reached them through the open windows of the Zastava. Bumblebees buzzed among short-lived flowers. They drove amid a stand of pines, in which the sun flickered as through a blind, and swerved round a gigantic bend to confront the characteristic landscape of Istra.

Among disorderly and tumbled hills of *karst* were contrasting patches of cultivation, or the thread of a river. Tender green larches shone from broken slopes, backed by darker pines and cypresses.

Fertile and barren lay close, yet distinct. Uncompromising on extravagant bluffs, towns stood out, fortresses as well as villages, each with its Italianate steeple, each dilapidated and without sign of life, each the colour of the hillside it crowned. As the car wound along the road which linked the deserted towns, it passed an occasional donkey, led by a peasant whose ruddy face was powdered by the dust of the thoroughfare.

Squire scrutinized this landscape through field glasses, alert for movement. Istra could provide cover for a whole army. The lorries loaded from the barge could not be far off: they would travel by night, remaining in hiding by day. They drove past shells of houses that bore evidence of the bitter civil war which had still to die completely. Slogans painted crudely on their facades, reading *'Mi Smo Hrvati'* and *'Hocemo Tito'* ('We are Croats,' 'We want Tito'), had provided their occupants with a kind of rough life insurance. The gutted facades threw back the sound of their passage as they roared by; the car could be seen and heard for miles. And the *karst* towered above them in a welter of flowering maquis and broken stone.

Labin appeared round a shoulder of mountainside, grey on the top of its appointed hill. It was perhaps five winding kilometres distant when Squire saw figures on a looming hillside to their right. Not sheep. Men, running. Two of them, three. They dived for cover behind a stone wall and were seen no more. Beyond the wall was a grey-roofed building, slotted into the dip between two hills.

'Turn up to the right,' Squire said. 'Someone's had a moment of panic up there.' He felt his stomach knot unpleasantly. There was no knowing what they would meet.

Some metres further on, a track led off the road to the right. Without hesitation, without decelerating, Slobodan turned up it, belting between stone walls in a cloud of dust. Squire leaned back, grabbed a sten from the rear seat, rammed a magazine in it, and set it on Slobodan's lap, muzzle forward. He selected another sten for himself and held it at the ready. His eyes searched the landscape for hostile movement. Without a word, steering perilously with one hand, Slobodan leaned back and picked up three hand grenades, which he stuffed into a pocket. He winked at Squire. Seeing the point of the operation, Squire also pocketed some grenades.

The narrow track twisted in a manner more suitable for sheep than cars. Twice, metal shrieked as they clipped the stone walls with their mudguards. Then they broke through into a farm yard. Some miserable pullets scattered before their bumper. Ahead and to their left were ruinous buildings. Slobodan braked, keeping the car in clutch and rolling slowly forward as the two men craned their necks for signs of life, stens pointing through the car windows. The farm building to their left had been a mean habitation at the best of times; now the ground-floor windows were roughly boarded up, and the words 'Hocemo Tito' painted on the stonework in inelegant red lettering, with a communist star for emphasis.

In its remote situation, it was a place that had already witnessed violence.

As the Zastava came level with the last window, a machine gun opened fire from the upper room. The rear side window of the car shattered and glass flew. Slobodan swore.

Without hesitation, he spun the wheel and sent the car speeding forward, turning left and shooting round the corner of the farm building. He pulled one of the grenades from his pocket. The car braked just before it ran into a wall of stone. With a yell at Squire, Slobodan jumped out of the vehicle and flung himself behind it. Squire followed, chased by another burst of fire from above.

Squire was still feeling numb. He watched as Slobodan pulled the pin from his grenade, stood to aim, and flung the grenade through the nearest upstairs window of the farmhouse. The grenade disappeared. A second of silence. Then it exploded. Cries and shouts sounded. Tiles clattered down.

Time seemed to move very slowly. Smoke drifted from the window in a leisurely fashion. And Squire regained his ability to move.

Someone was firing at the Zastava from the lower floor, taking pot-shots through the boarded windows with a revolver. Squire left the shelter of the car at a run, throwing himself down against the front of the building. One of the boards blocking the window by the front door was broken. He crawled to a position beneath it. Rising, he lobbed a grenade through the hole. Pressing himself against the stonework, he waited in fierce anticipation, teeth clenched. As the explosion came, he moved to the door. He kicked it in and burst forward, firing his sten, all strictly according to the training manual. It came like second nature.

Smoke, dirt, whirling particles of straw, billowed in his face. Through the filth, he saw that the meagre room contained six men. All were in a demoralized state. The two nearest Squire had suffered directly from his grenade. Their uniforms were torn and bloody. They sprawled on the floor groaning, surrounded by blood and guns. Squire kicked the guns out of the way. At the other end of the room were four men who had been sitting round a table, drinking coffee from a metal flask; one was hurt and clutched his face, moaning; the other three offered no resistance and climbed nervously to their feet at the ferocious sight of Squire, raising their hands above their heads.

Pointing the sten at them, he went forward, satisfied to see them cower back. They were dressed in rough civilian clothes. All were young and pallid of face. They had no guns. It occurred to him that they might be drivers. He made them undo their belts and throw them out of the nearest window, through a broken board. They stood facing him, holding up their trousers and shaking visibly, faces ghastly. They plainly expected to be murdered. He felt no compassion.

He whistled through the board to Slobodan, who whistled back and pointed upstairs. The important people would be up there. Squire blazed away experimentally through the boards above his head. Oaths sounded. Through the loose boards in one of the rear windows, he saw a body go by – someone had jumped for it. Slobodan's sten chattered. He wouldn't let them get away.

There was nothing for it but to rush the stairs, hoping the enemy there were also temporarily demoralized. He ran up the steps in a crouch, yelling, firing from the hip. He flung himself flat as he entered the room. Bits of tile went flying as Slobodan fired from below.

A narrow-faced man with a mole on one cheek, his eyes narrowed, fired point blank at Squire and missed. He was crouching behind a wooden crate. His uniformed sleeve had snagged on a bent nail. As he jerked his arm to free himself, Squire half-rose and swung his sten. He caught the narrow-faced man hard across the eyes with the barrel.

He staggered to his feet. Another uniformed man, who had been taking cover behind an upturned wooden bed, rose and jumped from the window. A shot and a shout sounded. Slobodan was in control out there.

'Okay, Squire?' he yelled. 'Want help?'

Slobodan's first grenade had effectively wrecked the room. Maps and a leather briefcase lay on the floor, against a shattered vodka bottle. In one corner, the walls were splattered with blood; a man lay there, his head hidden. He twitched faintly. Squire went over and kicked him, but he was completely out of action. That left only the narrow-faced man, who had fallen face-down over the packing case.

Squire prodded him in the ribs with his gun.

'Up!'

Despite the blow with the sten, which should have cracked the front of his skull, the man still had fight in him. He had concealed a broad-bladed military knife in his right hand. As he came up from the crate, he struck at Squire with a practised underarm stroke. Squire swerved to save his ribs and kicked the man on the shin. The man fell back onto his other leg, his face suffused with blood, his pupils dilated with the determination to kill. He charged in again, knife first. The bullets from Squire's gun caught him full in the chest. He staggered backwards over the crate and fell to the floor among shards of roofing tiles. His left leg kicked for a moment.

Squire went and leaned against the nearest wall, panting and trembling. He slung the sten over one shoulder and wiped repeatedly at his face with his hand. Sweat poured from him. 'Father, father, I'm sorry . . .' When he realized he was repeating the phrase over and over, like a mantra, he tried to take control of himself. A fit of sneezing overcame him.

He went to the rear window and spat out into the bushes beneath, cleansing his mouth.

'You *finito* up there?'

Slobodan stood below, covering three men with his gun. They leaned, faces inwards, against the farmhouse, hands above their heads, trousers round their knees. Slobodan gave the Thumbs Up sign.

Squire could not speak.

'I've got Zvonko Nedeć here. That's worth something. Who've you got up there?'

Nedeć was a well-known pro-Soviet Croat, high on the Belgrade wanted list.

Squire went into an empty corner of the room and was violently sick. Sweat poured from him. He found himself weeping. The vomit splashed his boots and slacks.

Confused, he realized after a moment that Slobodan was in the room, driving Nedeć before him, the latter with hands tied and face ashen; stains down the front of his trousers showed where he had pissed himself in fright. Only Slobodan was enjoying himself. He clapped Squire on the shoulder.

'Take it easy.'

Squire sat shaking on the rear window sill, mopping his mouth and face. Chill overcame him. He had shot a man down like a dog. Almost without comprehension, he took in the view from his vantage point.

Behind the house ran a ruinous stone wall with a steep drop on its far side. Parked under the drop were three old German army lorries with camouflage canopies lashed into place. No doubt that they contained the stolen arms from the arms train. Beyond the lorries, the broken Istran landscape fell away, giving place to a magnificent panorama of the Kvarner Bay. The sun shone dazzling on the blue water. Resting on the breast of the sea were the islands of Cres and Losinj. Squire stared at the sea with longing, until a movement nearer at hand caught his eye.

Parked under a tree at a distance from the lorries was a white Zastava. A thick-set young man in civilian clothes had broken cover and was running towards it. He climbed in and started up the engine.

At the sound, Slobodan rushed to the window. He pointed at the car.

'Why don't you shoot? That's one of the rats we saw first, maybe!'

Squire shook his head. Slobodan produced his last grenade, pulled its pin, and hurled it at the car, already moving downhill. The grenade exploded behind it. The car kept on going, bumping across the field, and disappeared behind a fold of hill.

Losing interest, Slobodan gave Squire a cigarette. Both men lit up. Squire was ashamed of how much his hand shook.

'Come and look see this. It'll cheer you up. Here's Milo Strugar's killer, okay.'

Slobodan turned and set his foot against the shoulder of the man Squire had shot, so that head and narrow face rolled over in Squire's direction. A further nudge from Slobodan's boot brought the head into a beam of sunlight, which blazed in through a gap in the roof. The features of the dead man were unpleasantly illuminated, so that Squire's stomach lurched again. The features were heavy and sagged in death. On the left cheek was a large mole, its long dark hairs glinting in the sun. It made the man look harmless in death.

There was no doubting his identity.

'You killed Slatko, my clever young friend!'

Squire had studied the dead man's photograph a number of times in Belgrade. Codename Slatko had been active ever since Stalin ceased to be Tito's patron and master; he was the Russian colonel in charge of softening-up operations in Yugoslavia prior to a Soviet take-over. As head of Department XIII of Soviet Counter-Espionage, he was answerable only to the Soviet Central Committee. Slatko's presence here in Istra showed how confident the Russians had become of defeating Tito. Perhaps the stolen arms were to reinforce an intended strike presided over by Slatko, and timed to take place while the West had its energies and attention involved with the Berlin air-lift. If so, Slatko had been over-optimistic.

'You killed Slatko,' Slobodan repeated. He embraced Squire.

'I need a crap,' Squire said.

The official break between Stalin and Tito, marked by Yugoslavia's expulsion from the Cominform for hostility to the USSR, came less than two months later. From then on, the Yugoslavs went their own way, negotiating a difficult path between East and West.

By that time, Thomas Squire had returned to England. He had been too successful – the Yugoslavs feared attempts on his life. They gave him an enormous party in Belgrade and sent him home.

Squire returned to his own country in a curious mental state. What he could confess to no one, and what most deeply disturbed him, was that he had perversely enjoyed killing. It satisfied a black greedy thing in his psyche. For months, he could not rid himself of the vision of Slatko dying, the leg kicking, the Istran sunlight blasting through the broken building.

The department de-activated him, and Squire returned to private life. Following family tradition, he went up to Cambridge, and spent three years there reading Medieval History, without great distinction. Among his friends were James Rotheray and Ronald Broadwell, later to become Squire's publisher.

He invested the money paid by the BIA, and a legacy that accrued to him on his twenty-first birthday, in a directorship in a city insurance firm. Then he settled down to pretending that he took himself for an ordinary man. Several years passed before he could realize that he was an ordinary man.

'By the way,' d' Exiteuil said, turning an unfriendly face to Squire as they were leaving the conference hall. 'You said yesterday in your opening speech that we had to forge a methodology for the future. Well, we have one, despite anything you or Fittich may say to the contrary. It's Marxism. Academic Marxism. And it's already started to run future culture. Popular arts, after all, can never belong to reactionaries like you. We have to shape them to the needs of society. You will be out of it from now on, as I expect you will discover after the conference.'

11

'The Strong Act as They Have Power to Act'

Blakeney, Norfolk, July 1978

Two women stood at a window looking out, one intently, one restlessly.

The house was low-built of red brick, with seven bays and two storeys. It dated from the Regency period. Even in the sunny days of this fitful Norfolk July, its rooms remained shady.

Pink flowers of tamarisk pressed against the window, growing in sandy soil. The house stood on a spit of land at one end of Blakeney quay, with long perspectives of sea and marshes to both the back and front. The rear of the house was sheltered against winter winds by trees and a high wall.

In the front of the house, the windows were square casements, low to the ground, with white-painted shutters on the inside. The two women stood together at the living-room window, Deirdre Kaye with her arms folded, Teresa Squire with binoculars to her eyes, searching the distance.

The linked circles of Teresa's vision passed over the lively scene of the harbour, with its porcupine-quill quota of masts of dinghies, with near-naked children fishing for gillies at the harbour-edge. They lifted slightly and passed beyond the main channel to the distant sea, the glittering mud of low tide where terns fed, the bars of sand, the marshes and dykes, to a pale stretch of beach backed by the blue North Sea. On the stretch of beach four ponies moved.

Even from this distance, the glasses enabled Teresa to distinguish the copper heads of Deirdre's two boys, Douglas and Tom, Deirdre's husband, Marshall, and her own estranged husband, Tom, riding in a line by the water's edge. She stared for a long while at Tom's image, wavering in the heat rising from the land. He resembled a phantom progressing underwater. He had drowned in heat and absence.

'Well, *I'll* go and knit a doormat or something,' Deirdre said.

'They're out on the point – coming back here, I expect,' Teresa said, lowering the glasses and turning to her sister-in-law. 'The boys look terribly brown. So do you, Deirdre. How long have you and Marshall been back from Greece?'

Deirdre went over to a low table and lit a cigarette from the lighter standing there. 'A week. Sorry I didn't send any cards. The house still smells shut up, doesn't it? It's almost as hot in Norfolk as it was on Milos. I can't believe it.'

'There was nothing but rain and cloud here all June.'

Deirdre swung round to confront Teresa.

'Look, let's not beat about the bush, Tess. How much longer are you going to keep the children over at Grantham with your mother? It's bad for them and for everyone. You know Tom's still willing to have you back. I think you should stop acting up and return to Pippet Hall at once.'

'That's really our private business and nobody else's.' The words were said defensively. Teresa clutched the binoculars and looked anxiously at Deirdre, who was a head taller than she. Deirdre promptly wreathed herself in smoke. 'It's not simply a question of his "having me back", as you put it. I just can't take his unfaithfulness any longer. Sorry, but I just can't.'

Grace came into the room, carrying a large cat.

'Get out, will you?' Deirdre told her oldest child. 'I'm having a row with your aunt.'

As Grace faded from the scene, pulling a face, Deirdre said, 'I wanted to say this to you before they return and Tom finds you've arrived. I personally am baffled, completely baffled, by how you are behaving. This talk about Tom being unfaithful – I mean, you realize that's old-fashioned for a start?'

'You'd probably call it by a nastier name. It hurts me, as it does most women. Men think they can get away with too much.'

'Well, Tom doesn't think that because Tom isn't that kind, though he may have had a bit on the side occasionally. I want to say two things to you. First of all, you ought to try and realize that he's experienced difficulties in life – well, so have we all; but last year and this are in a way his great years. As I see it. They've come a bit late, but they're wonderful for him. Last year, the excitement of conceiving the "Frankenstein" series and getting it filmed and the book written; then, this year, the tremendous success of the book and the series. The book's reprinting and they're now re-running the series, in case you haven't bothered to watch the box, with all your other enterprises. It's a triumph for Tom and for the family. You realize that he thinks he's doing something for England, for the West – silly though you probably find that. And in the middle of it all, you – you have to muck everything up, so that he's left Pippet Hall in despair and gone to live in his club in London. How do you think he feels? You're his wife – haven't you more sense of him as a person than to let him drift like that?'

'I didn't make him leave Pippet Hall, did I? Nor did I make him go with that woman.'

'Laura Nye, do you mean?'

'Oh, I expect he's brought her here often. You probably know her well, which is why you take her side.'

'Don't be cheap. That's *my* role. I met Laura twice last year. But that's all past – you've been told it's finished, over and over again. That was your excuse to muck about yourself, wasn't it? My God, how you grabbed it with both hands! So what if Tom did have it off with Laura Nye? She was one of the actresses in his drama. She was literally a passing fancy. He's got to do something while he's travelling to all these fancy locations, Hollywood, Malaysia, and so on. If I were in Singapore now, I'd be having it off with the nearest Chinaman, I can tell you!'

Teresa put the binoculars down on the window sill, carefully, to conceal her trembling. 'I don't want to have this discussion, Deirdre, sorry. I came over here to see Tom, not you. How you would behave in Singapore is nothing to do with it. Tom obviously preferred the girl to me. He's old enough to be her father. You speak as if the tragedy's all his, but believe me it's mine too—'

Coughing angrily into her fist, Deirdre said, 'What thought processes do you use? Your mind is stuck on clichés. "He's old enough to be her father", indeed! Just try and understand what that may mean in real terms. Tom'll be fifty next year. That's not a very comfortable age for men. He probably saw this fling as his last chance, as something to bolster his flagging libido. I don't know, he doesn't confide, but I can make intelligent guesses about the situation, and you should do the same. You should ask yourself why he needed that reassurance in the first place.'

'Oh, stop it, Deirdre! Talk about clichés, you sound like an Agony Column yourself. A successful man like Tom needing reassurance from me . . .'

'Of course he does! You're his wife. Don't be so blind. He kicked Laura out and returned to you, didn't he? You turned your back. *Agony!* – You think he's not lacerated by your unhappiness? Why aren't you lacerated by his? *And* he bailed your business out earlier this year – to the tune of several thousand pounds, I heard.'

'He was obliged to, Deirdre . . .' She put her chin up. 'I don't want to sound ungrateful, but Tom was legally bound to sort that out. If I hadn't been so upset, my business would have flourished. You think I don't suffer? I just don't make a fuss about it. After all, *I* was the one left at home alone. It's humiliating to have your husband chasing some bit of goods, humiliating, and then you watch them laughing together on TV, and know everyone else is watching, admiring, too. And you expect me to catch the repeats . . . Do you think I can get over that? I'm disgraced.'

Deirdre stubbed her cigarette out in a shell ashtray. 'Of course you were hurt. Okay, then you had your consolation and got back at him. Put your claws away, stop erecting all these items into an ideology of grievance, and be a proper wife.'

'There's just one difficulty you prefer to ignore . . .'

Teresa paused. Deirdre looked at her suspiciously. 'What's that? You've got another bloke?'

'I don't love Tom any more.'

Deirdre sat down. 'Don't say that to Tom.' She got up again. She moved over to one of the windows and opened it a trifle wider.

'You're no chicken yourself, Teresa. You're four years older than me. "You don't love him . . ." That's a bit more ideology of grievance, if you ask me. I mean, at your age, you and Tom should steadfastly continue to love each other. By rote, as it were. You're not in your twenties. When a man goes a bit haywire at the male menopause, okay, his wife stays by him, supporting him through a year or two of rough water, and after that they become closer than ever; his gratitude will ensure that. But if you lose that chance – which you've already bungled . . . You've got the wrong idea about love, deserting him when he probably needs you more than ever.'

'Deserting . . . Oh, Christ, it's like being in a trap of words . . .' said Teresa, moving unhappily round the room.

'Don't rush about. We've only got words since you've turned down actions.'

'Tom's fine, just fine. It's only his pride that's hurt – he's mad because I actually dared to go away with another man to Malta for Christmas, because I pleased myself for once. *He's* off to Sicily in September. He'll probably find a woman for himself there.'

'God, you bitch, what a mad round of pleasure you make it all sound!'

'Look, Deirdre, maybe you hate me. He doesn't need me. He needs me *at home*. That's different. He just needs me at home, keeping Pippet Hall in order. The wife in her place. You know he is proposing to open the place to visitors, now he's such a big success?'

'Well, the bloody estate is broke. Be reasonable. You're so vituperative: why should he want to forgive you?'

'You can't see that aspect of things as clearly as I can. After all, you're a Squire too. Tom just wants me at Pippet Hall. That satisfies his love of order. He'll forgive anything, anything, to get me back, because the Hall is the most important thing in his life. Any messy divorce, or anything like that, and he could lose the Hall. I've got him by the short hairs and he knows it. I'm being kinder than you think, driving over here today to see what he has to say, especially with my health delicate.'

She stopped before the anger in Deirdre's face.

'Don't dare think that way. You'd even use his love of the Hall against him? Just watch it. Marsh and I may have been away, but we also have an interest in the Hall. I have witnesses to prove that you have been back there on several occasions, and have taken that little rotter Jarvis with you. And you had him over when Tom was away filming, before you found out about Laura.'

As they stood there confronting each other, they heard footsteps and voices outside in the back yard.

'Don't bring Vernon Jarvis into this,' Teresa said. Her face and lips were pale. 'He's not around now. He had nothing to do with this quarrel—'

'He has fleeced you and hopped it?'

'I said, he is not around. Tom started the quarrel and Tom has to mend it. Money doesn't mend quarrels, if you think it does. Tom's the one in the wrong.'

'Well, get him out of the wrong, then. You certainly owe him that.'

The ponies were hired from Old Man Hill, who had run a stable in conjunction with his fishing boat for longer than anyone in Blakeney could remember.

After walking along in the shallows of the sleeping sea, the animals were reluctant to be turned towards the land. Douglas and young Tom rode ahead, wearing only swimming trunks and trying to steer the animals with their knees. Tom Squire and Marshall Kaye followed behind.

For two summers in succession, Kaye had been digging in Greece. He was tanned a deep brown behind his spectacles, and presented a striking appearance. His drooping moustache was yellow, his eyebrows dark brown, his hair brown fading to blond on top, where the Aegean sun had bleached it. So the years had baked him, Squire reflected, from a brash young Yale graduate to a seasoned and renowned archaeologist. His eyes, fringed by dark lashes, were light blue. Above his shorts was a worn windcheater of a similar faded hue.

He was giving Squire an account of his and Deirdre's stay on Milos, making both it and the excavations sound rewarding. Squire envied the stability of the younger man's life.

'Despite everything, despite that amazing sense of being surrounded by the history of your own culture, I find Greece and the islands depressing,' Kaye said.

'How's that? I thought the Greeks were getting into their stride again, now that the colonels have departed.'

Their mounts negotiated low swelling dunes through which some first spears of grass appeared.

'They are, kind of. I suppose I mean that the denudation problem is depressing, and the way nothing's being done about it, or is ever going to be done, as far as I can see. Not more than two per cent of the entire country retains its original topsoil . . .'

'Not more than two per cent!'

'Nope. That's the fact at the root of all Greece's problems. From the Peloponnesian wars onwards, the forests have been ruthlessly hacked down and the timber used for ships or fuel. Rain and wind soon does for naked topsoil. You never see a damned bird in Greece. A few mangey sparrows round the tourist spots. Ravens. Nothing else. It's a dead place, killed by man, his lust for war, and his domestic animals — mainly goats.'

He was silent, then he said, 'Political stability is impossible until you get your agriculture right. I'd hate to calculate how many billions of dollars the US has pumped into Greece since World War II in order to keep it safe for democracy, without once worrying whether it was safe for corn.'

They were off the beach now, moving inland, the boys still leading. They travelled in single file along the top of a dyke, water and rushes setting up their perpetual rustle on either side. Where the land rose from the marshes ahead, there stood Blakeney, distinct in a medley of whites and umbers, its church crowning the rise and dominating all other buildings.

Squire rode at the rear of the file. Addressing his brother-in-law's back, he said, 'Considering its significance for the West, it would be a sad day if Greece became communist.'

'But not necessarily fatal, to my mind.' Kaye twisted in the saddle to add, 'I'm slowly altering my opinions. The West has been reluctant to realize how nationalism remains a safeguard against the monolithic aspects of communism. Your experiences in Yugoslavia show how nationalism triumphed over ideology there. So it will elsewhere – China for example. Maybe Eurocommunism is a genuine new direction. The Eurocommunists in Bologna make noises like decent uncorrupt capitalists.'

'Don't weaken, Marsh. That way the rot sets in.'

'Maybe. Maybe not. I like to talk, Tom, but I was always a dove, not a hawk. That's why I quit the States during the sixties. More aggressive we get, the more trigger-happy the Russians become.'

'That's an attitude they want us to adopt, certainly.'

After a pause, Kaye added, 'I appreciate that Britain's position is far more vulnerable than that of the States. We're just as open to sudden armed strikes here as Western Germany. But I discover I have ceased to believe in the concept of sudden strikes.'

They were moving among sailing craft lying on their sides on muddy banks patterned by bird feet.

'Despite events in Czechoslovakia in '68?'

'Of course, there are many people in the States, mainly of the older generation, who would feel about the collapse of the UK much as you would about the collapse of Greece.'

Squire laughed. 'Well, that's a consolation.'

The sun enveloped Squire's body, bathing it in summer. He felt the heat on his sparsely protected head and the occasional runnel of sweat down his chest. That suited him well. Yet he felt uneasy, he did not know why.

He was sorry to hear his brother-in-law speak as he did. The world was a dangerous place – that was the open secret a younger generation of Englishmen resolutely refused to learn; they believed that as long as everyone earned the same wages, all was well. Marshall's generation of Americans knew better than that. But everyone, of whatever nationality, seemed to prefer to forget that certain ancient laws were not revoked simply by the setting up of trade unions and health services: predators were about. The world was a dangerous place: for the individual as well as the nation.

The patient ponies carried them to the flat ground by the harbour.

'We're going to grab some ice creams, Dad,' Douglas called.

Squire and Kaye handed the ponies over to Old Man Hill's daughter, a gnarled woman, who sat patiently by the artist's van. The men looked in at the paintings displayed for sale inside the van, and were confronted with a conventional array of windmills, churches, cows, and willows. They strolled together towards Marsh House, which faced them from the other end of the quay. Along the quayside, they passed the hotel where Squire had dined with Tess, Grahame Ash, and the camera crew a year ago; it seemed a happier time in retrospect.

'You gain a different perspective on the world when you're engaged in a dig,' Kaye said. 'In a sense, you live in the past, the present becomes remote.'

'Professionally, that must be a good thing . . . Your salary is still paid in 1978.'

Kaye laughed.

Without any change in tone, Squire said, 'We'll have a beer when we get in. But I see Teresa's car parked outside your front door.'

Kaye shot him a swift glance. 'She must have driven over from Grantham to see you. Is that a hopeful sign?'

'It depends what you mean by hope. I want us to be together again but, as time goes by, I inevitably want it less. As you with Eurocommunism, so I with separation: resignation masquerading as wisdom sets in.'

They both laughed.

'Deirdre and I are sorry you suffer all this trouble, Tom. I just hope you have something by way of consolation.'

'If you mean Laura, no, I haven't. We broke it up to satisfy Tess almost a year ago. Perhaps that was a mistake. Tess remains unsatisfied.' Bitterness crept into his voice.

As Kaye and Squire entered the gate of Marsh House, Teresa appeared at the front door and waved to her husband. Something misplaced inflated the gesture: it was designed for someone considerably more distant than Squire. He went up to Tess, took her hand and kissed her cheek.

They regarded each other with reserve, like military commanders looking for ground cover. Teresa's gaze held that elusive suggestion of a squint which sometimes lent even her serious moods a touch of mischief.

His nostrils received a warm perfume from her.

She wore a light dress suited to the weather, low-cut and showing the cleft between her breasts. She was tanned as far as the eye could see.

'Tess, you're looking well. How are Ann and Jane?'

'That's good, because I'm feeling rather terrible, having just been given a good going over by your sister. The girls are fine – at school today. They break up later than Doug and Tom.'

She turned to speak to Kaye, who kissed her. They all moved into the house.

'You drove over from Grantham just to see me?' Squire asked.

'I happened to ring Deirdre and she said you would be here for the weekend.'

As they moved from the hall into the living room, Teresa's mother appeared, and greeted Squire. Mrs Davies was wearing an uncharacteristic costume, a kaftan in orange and lemon, and dark glasses.

'Tom, it's charming to see you. So you've managed to tear yourself away from London? I was taking the sun in the back garden – we've only been here an hour, not more, have we, Teresa? And the traffic was so thick on the A17, is it?'

'You're looking very summery, Madge.'

'Do you know, I've had this old kaftan for years, but haven't dared to wear it. I hope I don't look too much like chicken dressed as lamb, or whatever that phrase is. We're driving over to Norwich to see Willie. He's coming back with us to Grantham, to stay the weekend, as I expect Teresa told you.'

'No, I didn't, Mother,' Teresa said, in some exasperation. 'I've hardly said a word to Tom.'

'Well, you mustn't let your silly old mother interrupt you. You talk nicely to Tom and I'm sure you can get back together again. Tom, your misdeeds are in the past, or so I hope, and I want you and Teresa to kiss and make up. Remember that you're both my children. Let's have an end to this silly, pointless quarrel, for the sake of family harmony. Your Uncle Willie would say the same if he were here.'

Deirdre appeared in the archway of the living room. She tucked a thumb under her ample chin. Grace also materialized, still bearing the tabby.

'This meeting does promise to be a shining example of family harmony, I must say,' Deirdre remarked. 'Marsh, you'd do well to get us all a drink – the sooner we're tanked up, the better. As for you, Grace, I think you'd better make yourself scarce.'

'Oh, Mummy . . .'

'Go on, go and bully your brothers. You know too much already.'

'You do chase the poor girl,' Mrs Davies said to Deirdre as Grace disappeared. 'Of course, I know I'm only an old woman and it's none of my business.'

'Quite so,' agreed Deirdre, blandly. 'All the same, Grace can look after herself. She told me yesterday that she is going to be an aircraft designer, and I believe her. She has some fantastic ideas about airliner loos and galleys which could revolutionize aviation history.'

Kaye entered through the french doors from the back garden. 'The drink trolley's outside. I thought you'd like to take a drink on the terrace while the sun shines.'

As they trooped out, Grace reappeared in a crimson beach robe, and curtsied to them one by one, cat under her left arm. Mrs Davies came last, taking the opportunity to grasp Squire's wrist.

'I just wanted to say to you – you're at a responsible age, Tom. I think that your Tess would come back to you gladly if you gave up that younger woman. She can't be good for you.'

'I have given her up, long ago. I believe it if nobody else does.'

'Don't be cross. What I mean is, you must understand Teresa. I think it is the idea of – well, of this sex business that scares her off. Your Uncle Willie and I wouldn't have anything like that. We have discussed the subject, oh yes. At your age, Tom, you're nearly fifty, it is disgusting. Undignified. Ernest and I gave up all that sort of thing on my fortieth birthday, and neither of us were any the worse for it. Funnily enough, we were talking about it in the spring of last year, just before he was killed – when you were away in California, or wherever it was.'

Abandoning the cat at last, Grace sidled up to them and let out squeals of suppressed laughter. 'Grannie, that's awful! I'd have thought that you and Willie would be a bit more swinging. After all, what's the point of getting married unless . . . Well, anyhow, I think it's just terrific that Uncle Tom is the age he is and is still able to mate. Bully for him! It's wonderful.'

'But not exactly unique in the annals of medical science, Grace,' Squire said, laughing.

Mrs Davies looked reproachfully at Grace. 'My nerves are all to pieces. I've had my say, now I'm going to have a cigarette. To hear you talking so brazenly about sex, my girl . . . We never mentioned it, or thought about it, when I was your age. I don't know what the world's coming to.'

Kaye poured them all drinks. 'Your beer at last,' he told Squire, handing over a full tankard.

He raised his glass cheerfully. 'Here's to us all. Good to be back home, good to see Madge and Teresa and Tom here. Let's hope the family will be a little more stable now.'

'That's a bit optimistic,' Grace said, *sotto voce*.

'Quiet, child, it's only a toast,' Deirdre said.

'The country's been going to the dogs steadily while you've been doing your archaeological work in Greece,' Mrs Davies reported. 'The unemployment figures are still rising, and the inflation rate. It's this terrible Labour government of ours.'

'Don't despair, Madge,' Kaye said. 'Deirdre and I see a different aspect of things, coming from abroad. After Athens, England seems remarkably stable, sensible, and prosperous.'

'That's because we're having a heat wave, Pop, you nit,' Grace said. 'People only go on strike in winter, when it's cold.'

A lull fell over the conversation. Everyone became preoccupied with their drinks, or looked at the sails glittering far across the wilderness of marsh.

'So how did you enjoy your trip to this Greek island, where exactly was it, Marshall?' asked Mrs Davies, in a palpable attempt to blanket the difficulties in the room with words. 'I kept meaning to look it up in my atlas and then I never did so. It seems years since Ernest and I had our Greek cruise. It is years, alas . . . The weather was lovely but I didn't care for Athens at all. So noisy, even then.'

Squire and Teresa were standing awkwardly apart. 'Grantham always reminds me of Athens,' he said, but she did not take up the small joke.

Marshall Kaye began to deliver an archaeological lecture, ostensibly to Mrs Davies. Tom and Douglas appeared, licking ice-cream cones, took the temperature of the terrace, and slipped rapidly away.

'The great days of Milos ended when the Athenians, who were at war with Sparta, invaded the island in 416 BC. Eventually Milos had to surrender to the Athenians, who took all the women and children into slavery, and slaughtered all the men of military age.'

'What a terrible way to behave!' said Mrs Davies severely, as if some of the discredit reflected on Marshall Kaye.

'Yes, and it still happens. It happened also before the days of Athens. We could learn lessons from the Athens–Milos encounter – except that lessons of history are never learnt. The Athenians demanded that the Milians surrender, in which case they would not be destroyed. The Milians tried to get out of a difficult situation by offering friendship. That wasn't good enough for Athens. They made a resounding speech to the Milians, which Thucydides reports, or possibly invents.

'They said, "You're weaker than we are, so you'd better give in. We have concluded from experience that it's a law of nature to rule whatever one can. We didn't make this law, nor were we the first to act on it. We found it in existence, and we shall leave it in existence for those who come after us. We are merely acting in accordance with it, and we know very well that if you had our power, then you'd act in the same way to us."

'And they also said that the standard of justice done depends on the equality of power to compel. "The strong act as they have the power to act, and the weak accept what they have to accept." It is a lucid exposition of *realpolitik*, and often applies to situations in the world today. It's also applicable to individuals.'

He looked round to address this final remark to Squire and Teresa.

'And to Eurocommunists,' Squire said. He took Teresa by the hand and led her upstairs to Deirdre and Marshall's bedroom, where half-unpacked suitcases skirted the walls.

'Let's talk,' he said. 'Forget Marsh's lectures. You're looking summery.'

'You needn't flatter me.' She looked as if she was going to say more, but nothing more emerged. In Squire's eyes, she appeared smaller than before, perhaps because she was wearing flat seaside shoes. Her shoulders were vulnerable. Her face looked as if it had tanned unevenly, and her wrinkles showed. Her gaze had gone to the carpet under his anxious scrutiny; he saw the dark roots of her dyed hair.

'At least you came alone,' she said, almost in a whisper.

'I'm living in London because I can't bear to be in the Hall without you and the girls.'

She made a gesture, perhaps thinking he missed her point.

'Matilda Rowlinson is looking in every day, to see it's all shipshape . . . How's Nellie?'

Teresa smiled. 'A bit of a nuisance in mother's flat. The girls love her . . . Oh, I'm looking after the girls properly and feeding Nellie regularly, don't worry, while you're playing the great successful man. I shop at the corner supermarket and talk to mother and play cards with her and her friends and all that – not at all the life you imagine I'm leading, I'm sure, while you're being feted as Guru Number One all over London.'

244

'The English critics have been a bit hard on "Frankenstein Among the Arts". Didn't you read the reviews?'

'You know I don't read reviews.'

'Teresa, you can't be jealous of my limited success. It'll all be over soon, forgotten. But it is a sort of culmination of my life. I'm uncertain myself of its value but I want to share it with you. I have been able to express and demonstrate elements of popular culture in perspective, in such a way that it gives pleasure and – well, perhaps *hope* to a lot of people.'

'Ha! It hasn't affected us that way, has it?'

'As a nation we've become defeatist. I hope I have somehow made us that bit stronger. Let everyone see how much we have, things precious to our day, how much we have to lose – how we should value the beauty of which technology is capable, the richness of an expendable plastic cup or a match-box, the visual delight of a traffic jam at night . . .'

She walked over to the door, looked out on the landing, and closed it. 'Grace is such an eavesdropper. You don't have to lecture me. You treat me as if I was stupid, do you realize that? Ever since we've been married, you've been telling me things, things I just don't want to know, things about your damned family, about art, Pippet Hall . . .'

He broke in. 'Tess, dearest, please do not say that. We need a grand reconciliation – talk like that will reduce me to silence, utterly.'

'I want your silence. I'm sick of your talk.'

He stood and stared at her. 'If I've talked to you . . . I don't lecture you. I – of course I talk to you, I've always wanted to share everything. Isn't that the purpose of marriage?'

'All this talk about your book and your television series . . . It's not my thing, any more than your farm is. You address me as if I was one of your viewers. Oh, I can see how you think the series in some way squares you in your father's eyes, eases that chip on your shoulder, makes you famous, as you discourse so cleverly about things you imagine he would have enjoyed. Really, at your age, it's pathetic!'

'Why pathetic? My father remains a strong influence. Why be

ashamed of that? He'd understand that there is idealism still today, waiting to be freed—'

'I'm sorry, I think that's all rubbish. You see yourself as some sort of knight of old, a one-man crusader—'

'But that's not true—'

'Tilting against nostalgia, or received values, or – I don't know, and I didn't want this conversation anyway. They're always your bloody conversations, not mine. Damn and blast the art of today. God, if your father only knew . . . Your mother was lucky, she died just in time to escape the mess we're in.' She shook her head wildly, so that her hair flew. 'It's too late, Tom, it's too late. I don't know. You've hurt me, I do know that much.'

He moved towards her. She moved away. A box of Silk Cut lay on Deirdre's side of the bed. Squire slid a cigarette from the packet and lit it. He never smoked.

'I'm trying to make amends, Tess. Just let me try. You know Laura is out of the picture.'

'You'll get cancer, smoking. Where did you catch that habit? I've warned Deirdre but she takes no notice of me. No, as a matter of fact it's not Laura, it's *you*. The way you are. Only three years ago, you were having a mad love affair with that dreadful art-historian woman, Sheila Lippard-Milne. I never told anyone about that, not even mother and father. That hurt me bitterly, but you didn't care. How could I escape what I felt? How could I escape? And what am I supposed to do this time? If it's not Sheila or Laura, it'll be someone else. Am I supposed to be sorry for you because you won't grow up? What's the matter with you? No, don't tell me, I know you'll tell me. All I really want's your silence from now on . . .'

'You know that Sheila—'

'Let's not hear her name.' Teresa raised a hand in caution. 'I don't intend to go into all that again. Your bloody sister downstairs and your uncle think that you're at the male menopause. Did you ever hear anything so silly? I defy you to find that malady in a medical dictionary! They don't know about Sheila Lippard-Milne. I never told anyone about you and precious Sheila Lippard-Milne. How long's this male menopause supposed to go on for, eh, how many years? As long as it suits you? Till we're all in our graves? My nerves are ruined, do you wonder I sought refuge with the first likely man who came along? I had to build up my dented self-esteem. No, don't say it – I know he turned out a rascal, but you can laugh, my moral judgement was at zero, I paid in blood for every drop of pleasure I had.'

'Yes, people do, you know.'

Sighing, she went over to the window which opened on the front of the house. The lower part of the sash window had been pushed up to let in sea breezes, presumably in Deirdre's desire to clear the house of its closed-up smell. Teresa leaned out with her forearms on the sill, as if she could not bear her husband's proximity, and gazed towards the boat-filled harbour.

She was wearing a flimsy summer dress, low-cut round the shoulders. Squire had a good view of her shoulder-blades. From behind, she looked slender and youthful, almost thin, for her cramped attitude made the shoulder-blades project. His fancy saw her as a member of a mutated species, developing wings and about to fly away from him.

The tender bones, so functionally shaped, protruding under the flesh. The skin itself, clear and fair, roseate with a touch of the summer sun. The bumpy little tract of her backbone, leading down under the material of the dress, and there glimpsed in outline. The downy line of hairs following the track. The curve of her neck up into her dyed bright hair. At all these things Squire gazed during the silence, heavy with their frustration.

And said to himself, 'Whatever arguments I put up, however I attempt to reason, however unreasonable she is, she will win. Because she has that beautiful body.' Biology was always going to win in the end.

He walked round the room, and stubbed his cigarette out in Deirdre's ashtray, hardly aware of what he was doing. Stuck into the side of Deirdre's mirror, beside other treasures, was a card he had sent her from Tinjar Park in Sarawak, showing ancient supplicatory hands painted on a cave wall. He felt gratitude to his sister for caring enough to keep it.

'Tess, I know how you must be distressed,' he said to her back, moving unhappily behind her.

She brought her torso in from the window and slowly drew the sash down.

'Depressed! You're joking.'

'I said distressed. I'm trying to tell you that I understand. I won't say what I think about Jarvis, but I have bought him off and paid the debt to your Italian packaging firm. I've settled all the financial side of things. Now I want to look after you and see you happy again. We are too old for this sort of emotional jag.'

'Oh, Tom,' she said wearily, brushing a curl of hair from her eyes. 'You're being superior again.' She sat down on the foot of the bed; her back to him.

'Well, I'm trying not to be superior. I'm trying to keep my temper. Perhaps you think I'm complacent – that's simply because mainly I'm happy, most of the time. Despite the male menopause . . . Or perhaps I'm not . . .'

'You're only interested in yourself,' she said feelingly. 'That's more to the point.'

'Did you drive over from Grantham just to insult me? If you won't make our quarrel up, then what more do you want from me?'

She regarded the carpet, inspecting the grains of sand on it. 'I want nothing more. Mother persuaded me we should look in here. I hoped . . . Oh, hell. I know I sponged off you, and that kept me quiet. I hate myself, it's not just you. Life's so bloody difficult. Everything's gone wrong. Besides – you turned me out at New Year. A fine start to the year that was. Don't deny it.'

'You were with Jarvis, Tess. Don't forget that. You were with Jarvis.'

'That dreadful row. In front of the Broadwells . . . Now my business ruined on top of everything.' She produced a handkerchief and wiped her nose. 'You've paid up generously. I know. I'm supposed to be grateful and come creeping home. But you're not really sorry. The truth is, you *bought* me. I'm another Squire acquisition, like the furniture. You just want me standing around while your life goes on.'

He stood looking helplessly down at her, wondering what to do.

'You needn't stand around. Come back and start up your business again at the Hall.'

She stole a glance at him. 'Those dreams I used to have. A dark figure trying to break into the Hall . . . It was you all the time breaking into my life.'

'Or Jarvis, disrupting our lives?'

'You would think that . . .'

'Actually, I *don't* think it. It's too glib. If you remember, I used the dark figure in the TV series . . .' But it was no good trying to talk to her about that, no good trying to cool the temperature. Like God, the dark figure was a part of the lives of all men and women; sometimes it merely waited in the wings, idly; sometimes it came marching in boldly through the french windows. Like God, it lurked in the attic at the back of the skull, the space created by generations of blood and perception; the trick was to acknowledge its existence and yet manage to live sanely. At the moment, Teresa could not bear to live sanely; and that was still his responsibility, whether he wanted it or not.

She stood up, confronting him with slightly downcast face, regarding him through her eyelashes, one hand resting pensively on the brass bed-end.

'You know I'm sorry, Tommy.'

Unwished, the memory came back to him of their first encounter outside his tutor's rooms in Cambridge, when he and Teresa were both undergraduates. Later, he had said to his friend Rotheray, reporting the meeting, 'Either she was giving me the old come-on, or she has a slight squint.' There the fugitive thing was again – rarely seen, the slight strabismus lent her helplessness in his eyes. He reached for her bare arm. Her hair had been dark in Cambridge days; she had been the first girl he knew to wear a sweater under a shirt.

'Well, you'll have to help me, Tess, or I can't help you.'

'That's what you said three years ago.' She shook her head.

'It's as true now as it was then. You bring up the name of Sheila Lippard-Milne. I admit I loved her, though amazingly I didn't realize it at the time, but I gave her up, as I have Laura. I chose *you*. I've not seen Sheila since, or written to her. I felt at the time I was making a considerable gesture, proving my love for you. Yet it honestly seemed as if you never noticed.'

'Oh, I remember how miserable you were. You made it pretty obvious.' She was silent, and went to stare out of the window at the sunshine, resting her finger-tips on the glass. 'Perhaps marriage is always a cage . . . What do you want me to do?'

He stood up. 'Let's have a grand reconciliation. All back to the Hall, you, the girls, the dog, try and get John to come back, at least for a day or two. Celebrate, throw a party. Make love to each other. Both say we're sorry – all that kind of thing. Start again, see if it's possible, *make* it possible.'

Still looking out of the window, she said, 'The horoscope in the paper this morning said I should look out for a betrayal by someone close to me.'

'Did you hear what I said?' Angrily.

'Oh, I know you think they're rubbish. Anything I believe in is rubbish. But they were right about Sheila. "A disruptive influence", they said, and I remember it was that very day I discovered that letter she wrote you from New York. Don't tell me there isn't something in it. I date the start of my cancer from then, you'll be interested to know.'

'Perhaps tomorrow the horoscope will mention a grand reconciliation, then you'll be convinced.'

She said, turning to confront him, 'Supposing I want to go off and get screwed by any man who happens to come along. How will you like that?'

'Would you like it? Is that what you want? You could have been more enthusiastic with me.'

'You were bound to throw that in my face sooner or later! I suppose you've forgotten that the doctor said after John was born that I was to take things easy and avoid exertion?'

He began pacing about the room. 'You went off with that sneak Jarvis, you brought him into my house when I wasn't there, more than once. You've more than evened things up, Teresa. You've treated me like shit. There are historical and biological reasons why men are less likely to be faithful than women, less able to endure monogamy . . . I've done my best in that respect, so you can keep quiet and do your best. Otherwise we'll get nowhere.'

'Is that what you call a grand reconciliation?'

'I hoped for something better.' He regarded her narrowly, his expression closed. 'When two countries are hostile, they make what peace they can. So with us. Do you wish to come back? Are you prepared to make a go of it? It's now or never.'

'Don't start laying down conditions. Maybe it's too late. My heart isn't as soft as it once was. Things will never be what they were.'

'How I wish it was possible to turn the clock back . . .'

She asked, 'What is this grand reconciliation you talk about, anyway?'

He attempted lightness. 'As I say, maybe a housewarming at the Hall, friends round, celebrations, flowers, champagne, Nellie going mad, the girls back in their own beds, you and I in ours, kisses, violins, apologies, forgiveness. You name it.'

She shook her head. 'I'm sorry, Tom, you're being unreal. If you think that after what's happened we can just fling ourselves into each other's arms, you're mistaken. It may appeal to your sense of drama but not to mine. I'm not one of your actresses, however much you may regret the fact.'

That evening, Teresa and her mother were waved goodbye as they continued on their way to Norwich. Squire, restless after the fruitless encounter, decided to drive himself over to Pippet Hall. The Society for Popular Aesthetics was expanding rapidly; the secretary was even able to take on a secretary; and Squire needed documents relating to its foundation for an article he was writing. The Hall was only six miles from Blakeney.

He had been staying permanently in London, either with friends or at his club, since the New Year, when the shock of seeing Teresa in the company of Jarvis had discouraged him from returning to Norfolk. London was more convenient, and provided more than enough work for him. So the Hall was closed down, and Matilda Rowlinson and the farm manager looked after it. He had been back only twice – once for a day, once for a solitary weekend – in the last half-year.

The grass on the lawn looked rather long. The downstairs windows of the house were shuttered; that would be careful Matilda's work. Caught by the peace of the evening and the surroundings, Squire strolled across the side lawn before entering the house, to gaze at butterflies circling round Teresa's buddleia. Here The Who had once played to delighted crowds, and local rock'n'roll groups like The Bang-Bang. Pop was truly an international language.

Teresa and he had had a language in common in those happier days. But now. *Your silence is all I need from you.*

He tried not to resent the cruel things she had said that afternoon. She was, in her own way, uttering a cry for help.

His shoes were damp from an early dew as he unlocked the front door and entered the hall. He stood, closing the solid oak behind him. No children called except spectrally. No Dalmatian came up at a run, scattering mats. Only a cat appeared, yawning and stretching, to dissolve into the shadows.

Light filtering through the tall windows on the staircase filled the hall with a dim beauty. He stretched his arms and walked about with pleasure. The portraits of Matthew and Charlotte looked benevolently down. His footsteps echoed.

'*All I need from you is your silence.*'

In his study, the darkness was so intense that he opened one of the shutters. Outside lay the meadows where once had nested the pipits who gave their name to the place; now only a few blackbirds hopped amid the grass, mechanically perky.

When he had finished at his desk, and collected the papers he needed, he went over to his refrigerator, which stood on a filing cabinet under Calvert's painting, and poured himself a vodka-on-the-rocks.

Her anger, her vindictiveness, had seemed so personal. He could not tell how much of it was impersonal – directed at some mysterious target before which *he* happened to be standing – yet what he hoped was reason told him that she nursed some grievance beyond any folly he had committed.

His behaviour to her was, in a sense, the opposite of hers. He tried always to respond to her as a person, personally. Yet he was aware of the *impersonality* of his and of all experience. That was where mysticism crept in: he saw how he was not only living but being lived. Well, that was not necessarily a mystical perception so much as a biological one. He was not only an individual but a link in the totally impersonal chain of life, a torch-bearer for the selfish gene.

Which did not by any means absolve the individual from morality. It made the individual important beyond any influences in his own brief lifetime, for by his behaviour for good or ill he helped shape (yes, in a small way) the needful moral improvement of the human race in time to come. Improvement of the whole damned species could only come through the striving of each individual; at that point moralities and biologies met.

He could not seem to explain to Teresa – though he had tried in happier days – that his appreciation of her as an individual was enhanced by his awareness of the impersonal forces in her, that his life experience was most directly read through her being, that it was precisely their sexual and mental closeness that enabled them to explore the richness of being alive. However mistakenly, he had concentrated his life increasingly on that exploration in recent years; both 'Frankenstein' and his fatal love affair sprang from it. It was a quest for that richness of experience, an intensification of it before it died from beyond his clutches, which turned him to Laura: and Tess's subsequent rejection of him that had left him isolated.

The vodka was cool in his throat. He was not acutely unhappy. Isolation was nothing new to him. Perhaps he could soon face the fact that reconciliation was not possible between him and his wife.

In which case – he would have to sell up Pippet Hall.

He closed the shutter and walked from the room, taking the papers he needed with him.

'*All I really want now is your silence.*'

Silence had a sinister quality. He equated it with death, and only rarely with spirituality. The silence Teresa demanded from him was death, not spirit. And silence was unique in this respect; it was something one could demand and unfailingly receive. Ultimately, inevitably, he would become silent under her indifference.

If he dreaded silence, there was something he dreaded more: forms of language which masked silence, the absence of feeling. Teresa still *felt* intensely; he could still hurt her. So there was hope. But all around him he encountered defensive lack of feeling. Official language, the language of the military or of bureaucracy, Marxist jargon – all these were enemies of simple human experience. Instead of conjuring experience, they annihilated it in their repressive structuring.

At least Teresa had spoken to him directly. The worst thing was a woman talking Marxism or one of those other desiccated male languages. One good reason for continuing to love women, even when the going was rough, was that, on the whole, they stayed too human to go for ideological language.

He climbed the stairs, hesitated before their bedroom, and went instead down the passage to the old nursery. He opened the door, half-expecting to find the interior a glowing brown, as he remembered it from childhood, with the warmth of the stained floor and walls enhanced by a coal fire. Instead, he was greeted by Dulux high gloss white paint.

John's old red wooden fire-engine stood on top of the cupboards. The dolls' house stood on the table by the window, where he and Adrian had played for long hours with their Meccano.

He gazed blankly out of the window. A rabbit had joined the starlings on the lawn. What would become of the old place if he gave up? Fall into ruin? Wrenched from its purposes and turned into an *institution*?

Laura had visited Pippet Hall only twice. Once with the film team, before there was anything between them, to play the Sex Symbol in the Georgian House episode. Once last autumn for a weekend, just before they separated for good, following the party at Claridge's.

As Teresa complained, he had managed to defer that inevitable parting for a month or two, but only because work on 'Frankenstein' had continued for longer than anticipated. The break had been final. He could not bear to see her again, to speak impersonally to her. He had dived back to work, she had gone on to play a more interesting role; he had watched her on television recently, as an injured wife in a Play of the Week. Damned good she was.

And when they had parted, nine months ago, she'd been damned good then. Nothing to complain about.

Delays and hesitations inseparable from creativity occurred. Some incidents had to be re-shot. Some of the scenes involving the CSO process had not worked as well as expected. A model had to be re-made. 'World Dream Design Centre', the episode they filmed in Hollywood and Los Angeles, had its troubles. Ash fell ill. August turned into September. Definite boundaries became blurred. An electricians' strike further delayed progress.

But by the first week of October, all thirteen episodes of 'Frankenstein Among the Arts' were completed to the satisfaction not only of the British but of the German, American, and Australian interests involved in the production. Everywhere, quiet and sometimes noisy confidence grew that something special had been created.

After a grand farewell party at Claridge's, attended by all the crowned heads of television, and some from the arts world, Squire drove with Laura in her car, back to her flat.

'Jesus,' she said. 'I realize for the first time that we're all a stunning success.'

'Wait till you read the reviews . . .'

The flat was tiny without being cosy. It occupied part of a house on the run-down fringes of Canonbury. Laura's husband, Peter, was away on a photographic assignment, she knew not where. He had left a scrawled note without saying.

They bought pitas on the way to the flat, stopping at a kebab house in Essex Road. They ate standing in her narrow kitchen as they said goodbye.

Both of them trembled. Laura leaned against the breakfast bar, unable to touch him. Both of them dropped pieces of lettuce, tomato, and meat, in their anguish at facing this final moment.

The mansion, once moderately grand, designed for a prosperous middle class with servants, had been divided into several flats. It was always full of mysterious young people, designated of course as 'students', whenever Squire was there. Bicycles blocked the hall passage. Laura's flat was decorated with her husband's photographs, framed in metal. Generally shots of streets, taken from ingenious angles no one else would have thought of. Never a shot of Laura in the nude, or even dressed. Silly bugger.

The furniture looked cheap but was expensive, Laura said; it was too low to get out of easily. Laura and Peter quarrelled all the while, she said, excusing a general neglect.

When he went to pee in the toilet, his eyes came level with a packet of sanitary towels lying on the window sill. The sight of them moved and obscurely hurt him: though on this evening of parting everything brought him close to tears. He thought of her vulnerability. Didn't vulnerable and vulva derive from the same Latin root? She would have taken care to keep her Tampax out of sight a few months earlier. They were both of them going down the drain – like the Tampaxes, eventually – and he had to remember that she, at twenty-six, felt acutely that youth was passing.

He returned to the kitchen and his half-eaten pita.

'I've really fucked things up for you, my love. It's as well I'm disappearing at last.'

'You haven't fucked anything up. I was just a mess till you came along. Your dear steadiness – you have been that way all your life, I can tell. I didn't need an older man, I needed you.'

'It goes too deep for me to say. I was muffled for so long. With you – no guard possible, no guard needed . . .'

'We've had something so worthwhile together. In that sense, I don't mind parting, though I'll hate myself for saying it when you've gone . . . I'll never forget you, Tom. You've changed me, given me so much, so many things . . .'

'Nothing – nothing compared with what you've given me. With you I've been aware of the whole world again. You've made me whole again . . .' A piece of mutton fell to the floor. He kicked it in the direction of the sink.

'You're such a dear, dear person.' She reached out and touched his neck. He clutched her wrist, still brown from the summer they had had.

'Don't be hurt. Grow. Continue. My love and gratitude will always be with you, for whatever that's worth. Laura, dear Laura . . .' He spoke indistinctly, munching the bread.

'We've had such travels together, gone so far.'

'I'll never forget what a weight you were when you fell asleep on me on the plane back from LA.'

'And try not to forget how many miles it is to the River Bug.' Her lip trembled as she said it.

'Perhaps one day we'll meet in that little romantic Polish village whose name we remember so well.'

'You mean Molly Naggy?'

'I think it was Lolowsky Molehold.'

'Anyhow, we'll recognize it by all the dead horses.' She started to laugh and cry a little.

He put an arm round her waist. 'You're rotten at geography, incredible at everything else.'

'You'll always be my lovely man.' She rubbed her face against his jacket. 'My standard. Let me give you a last cup of coffee. Instant. And there will always be "Frankenstein" . . . Something worthwhile we did together.'

'And your lovely photograph in the book. I'll send you a copy before it's published. Lasciviously inscribed.'

'To hell with Peter. Bring it round in person.'

'I'll see about that. No, no coffee – I'd better go, my love.'

'My love.' Her beautiful gaze engaging his.

'Oh, dearest Laura . . .' They clung tightly to each other for the last time.

It was autumn. He felt the chill as he blundered down the garden path, the chill a younger man would not have noticed. He thought, as he went blindly into the street, 'From now on, there's only autumn. Then winter. Fifty next birthday. Old age. I was lucky to have a Laura in my life, bloody lucky. Just that short while – not so short, either . . .

'Well, somehow I've done what I said I would, at last. Now I must go back and make amends. The great renunciation . . . I hope it counts for something . . .

'Oh, Laura . . .'

He unlocked the secret compartment in the nursery cupboard. Only a few treasures there these days. A little framed pencil sketch his father had made of him when he was a child of four, just after Adrian was born. Not very good, when considered dispassionately. A school magazine dating from only a few years back, in which was his son John's article, then considered both daring and amusing, on why the monarchy should be abolished. A couple of letters from Laura – notes, really. He smelt the envelopes, but enclosure in the cupboard had made them fusty. Two letters dating from last winter from Tess, and a rough copy of his response.

Grantham
6th Nov.

Dear Tom,

Thanks for your letter. There's a reason why I have not returned to Pippet Hall as you request.

I do not have to do as you say. Honestly, what you think or say is not so important to me as it was once. You know that even a worm will turn. You did not keep your promise about leaving that girl at the end of August, did you? Have you really left her as you say, or do you still pine for all the things she gave you . . .

I am doing well here. I have my own flat and workplace and my company is now exporting to the USA. You don't have to feel sorry for me, and the girls are fine. So is Nellie.

They send love.

Teresa

My dear Tess,

Matilda forwarded your letter to me. I'm in London, being unable to tolerate the Hall on my own. I am not, as you may imagine, 'having fun' here, although there are one or two old male friends to support me, so I am not utterly desolate. I've also seen John on two occasions; he's much as always.

I am delighted to hear that your company is flourishing. I've encouraged the idea from the start, you may recall. When I asked you to return to Pippet Hall, it was not an order, but a simple hope that you would come back to me. I still have that hope. Do so, and we can convert the barn into a studio for you.

As I told you in my last letter, I have renounced Laura Nye. That I did as soon as 'Frankenstein' was completed, as promised. In fact, on the very day of the farewell party at Claridge's. I admit to feeling lonely; I need your dear love and comfort. There are two schools of thought about how a wife behaves towards an erring husband, but you must let yourself be guided by your feelings, rather than fashion or friends. May I suggest you don't treat me according to my deserts but according to your capacity for sweetness.

Thanks largely to Grahame Ash, the series looks extremely handsome – I think you'll approve, especially the design side. It is to be shown at 8.10, prime viewing time, every Friday evening, starting on February 23rd next. Ron Broadwell will publish the book as his great New Year title, and is planning a signing tour, round the country, on which I hope you'll be able to accompany me; it should be fun and easy to do. VIP treatment guaranteed.

Christmas is approaching, as the meretricious glitter of the shops in the West End painfully reminds me. I hope that this angst can be quelled soon, and that we can all spend Christmas happily together at the Hall as usual. It's almost a year since mother died

– how fast this hectic year has gone. I hope you and your mother have fully recovered from the shock of your father's death.

Your loving

Tom

Grantham

2nd December

Dear Tom,

In your latest piece of optimism you outdo yourself. What makes you think I wish to tramp round England as part of your menagerie, promoting your book? What makes you think I want even to hear about it, or the series, knowing your fancy woman is in them both?

Can't you realize how you hurt me? I've got feelings too you know.

As for Christmas, I'm sorry but I'm making my own arrangements. I'm going somewhere where I can find some sun and peace. Worry is making me ill. Once I thought I could trust you, but disillusion has crept in. *Burst* in.

I'm writing this in bed. Unwell.

Teresa

Under the letters lay a little red book bearing the impressive word '*Memoranda*'. In it, in his eight-year-old hand, he had inscribed the bare fact of his father's death. He did not open the book.

There was also an official letter in an envelope with a Belgrade postmark, congratulating him on his services to Anglo–Yugoslav understanding. Enclosed with it was a message scrawled in pencil from a man called Slobodan. He did not open the envelope.

Under the envelope and red book lay a little folder with covers made from wallpaper. Inside were three stories, each under a page long, written in a childish hand and illustrated with pictures done in crayon. They were by Rachel Normbaum, and had been presented to him almost forty years ago. He did not open the folder.

He cleared the secret compartment of all but the pencil sketch, and stood with its contents in his hand. Time went by.

Outside it was growing dull.

He locked the cupboard and went downstairs to the kitchen.

There, an unpleasant smell distracted him from his purpose. He set the documents of his past down on the table and went over to the tall windows, opening a shutter to let in a ray of evening light. For a while he stood peering out.

The room appeared sombre and dead. It smelt as if it had been closed for a long while. The large red enamel Aga, which he had had installed in place of the old range when he and Teresa were married, was cold for the first time since its installation. He walked round the room, familiar since childhood, today chill, unfriendly. In one corner were mouse droppings, in another by the scullery door, a damp patch along the floor, where the wallpaper was peeling; the damp had always been there, and looked no worse than before. In the scullery, a tap dripped intermittently. Squire went through to turn it off.

Back in the kitchen, he prepared a small fire in the Aga. He stuffed some old newspaper and cardboard into the grate and set light to them. He piled the letters and '*Memoranda*' book on top of the flames. The past no longer meant anything. It had died. He was free, whether he desired to be, or not. 'I'll be happier, once this is over,' he promised himself.

'*All I really want is your silence now.*'

As he waited there dumbly, gazing at the blue flames, a key grated in the scullery door. He stood alert, with the door of the Aga open and smoke escaping into the room. Matilda Rowlinson entered the kitchen. She smiled, more composed than he. Squire felt guilty without knowing why.

'Hello, Tom. Lovely to see you. I saw your car in the drive.' She came and shook hands.

'You're keeping everything in good order. I'm burning some old stuff.' He heard the guilt in his voice. 'Old papers, actually.'

'It's a pleasure. I love coming over to the Hall. I come every day without fail – generally about this time of day. I like it when evening's setting in, not being the kind who's afraid of ghosts.'

'I've never seen a ghost.'

As she went over and closed the door of the Aga, she said, 'I'm only sorry that you and Teresa aren't still here together.'

She had turned from the cooker. They were close. Squire looked with pleasure at Matilda's pale, honest face. It was slightly spotty about the mouth. Her hair was more attractive, richer, than he recalled. He sensed the warmth of her spirit as she regarded him with shining eyes. Something in her bodily gesture, an eagerness, appraised him of her mood; the knowledge must have shown in his eyes, for she suddenly became embarrassed and dropped her gaze, moving away defensively.

'I thought perhaps you'd like a cup of tea. That was why I came over.' She started to busy herself with preparations, filling the kettle, switching it on, getting out cups and saucers.

'It's been a gorgeous day . . .'

'I remember you when you were a baby, Matilda.'

She put the milk bottle down and regarded him seriously.

'I'm a grown woman now, Tom, as you are probably aware.'

He smiled. 'Yes, I am aware.'

'What are you burning?'

'Just a few old documents. Records of my past. I suppose I have their contents by heart well enough.' He stirred the pages with a poker. The school magazine was slow to burn. He watched it blacken.

There was a long silence, in which she stared at the Aga with him.

'Your heart can't be very easy at present.' Another silence. 'I wish there was something I could do.'

She took her coat off and laid it over the back of a chair. Her neat and modest figure was shown at its best by her green cotton dress.

'I am very grateful for what you are doing.'

'I suppose I meant more personally.'

As the kettle boiled and switched itself off, he said, 'You could pray for me.'

Matilda frowned. 'There's no need for you to be ironical.'

'I wasn't.'

Filling the teapot, she said with a sigh, 'I suppose it's my sheltered upbringing, what else, but human relationships – I do find them difficult to handle.'

He laughed dryly. 'We all do. It's believed that the human race was once endogamous. Ever since exogamy set in, everyone's found relationships a bit sort of difficult. Fascinating, of course, but difficult to handle, as you say.'

Accepting the cup she offered, he walked round the other side of the table and took a chair. They sat facing each other. As they sipped, the paper in the stove turned to ashes.

'Would you care for a biscuit?'

'No thanks.'

'You're not – are you going to sleep here alone this weekend, Tom?'

'I must get back to Blakeney before dark.'

'There's a whole hour and more of this lovely twilight before it's dark. And it was Full Moon last night.'

The kitchen was filling with dusk already, making of her face a pale blur. He felt her personality, tender and sensible, radiating across the scrubbed table towards him.

'I'm glad of the tea,' he said. 'And I'm glad you came. But I've got to be going.'

'Let me know the next time you're coming up. I'm always at home.'

She drew the one open shutter into place, and the kitchen faded into darkness.

12

Tribal Customs

Ascot, Berks, New Year's Eve 1977

Near Ascot, and not far from the famous racecourse, lies the area of Hazeldene, a developer's paradise of the thirties. It remains far enough from London by road and near enough to it by train to serve as a refuge for the semi-rich. Half-timbered leather-work shops abound and, on Saturday afternoon when the Jags are parked in front of their mansions, children and adults appear on well-groomed horses, to canter through stretches of bracken which have somehow survived among the desirable residences. Here Tom Squire's old friend and publisher, Ron Broadwell, had his home.

It was the last day of the year, cold and windy, and the weeping silver birches tossed behind neat beech hedges. At seven in the evening, it had already been dark for two hours.

As Squire drove towards the Broadwell house, he recited a poem aloud:

> 'Tis the yeares midnight, and it is the days . . .
> The sun is spent . . .
> The world's whole sap is sunke,
> The generall balme the hydroptique earth hath drunk.

He had once been able to recite the whole poem; now parts were gone from memory. He had recited it long ago to a Serbian girl called

Roša – who had laughed heartily – as they stood on the steps of the Avala memorial outside Belgrade, one midnight, drunk. He smiled at the recollection. When Squire was at Cambridge, Donne and Eliot had been the fashionable poets, and he had never lost his love of them. There were no poets like them.

The Broadwell mansion, 'Felbrigg', was visible from the road, sprawling tentatively behind its paddock and a white ranch fence. A tarmac drive with real old-fashioned streetlamps burning at each end led to the house. Lights blazed in the windows. As he drove up, he caught the twinkle of lanterns on a Christmas tree; it held promise of a pleasant evening ahead.

Both Ron and his wife Belinda came to the door to greet him. Ron was a large solid man with a cheerful florid face, a crop of shaggy dark hair tinged with white, and a predilection for the good things of life. He appeared with a big cigar in his mouth. Belinda was a tall lady running unhurriedly to fat, a smiling woman with a miller's face who, despite many years of marriage to Ron, still spoke with a slight Virginian accent. She wore a long black velvet gown with the air of one humorously aware she was doing something typical of her.

Belinda had previously been married to Ron's partner in the publishing house of Webb Broadwell, but that marriage had lasted no more than a year. 'Webb was great stuff as a publisher,' she confided to Squire once. 'But not so damned hot when it came to handling a shy virginal wife. I guess he performed better between bawds.'

They greeted Squire heartily, as he handed over to Belinda's safe-keeping an enormous box of Swiss chocolates. In the large bright hall, the Christmas tree glittered. Ron's dogs barked excitedly in a distant part of the house. The air was spiced with the flavour of good things.

Squire gave Belinda a big kiss. 'Mmm, good old Virginny – I feel better already.'

'Very pleased you could make it,' Broadwell said, hanging up Squire's coat. 'All the Broadwell tribe cleared off the day after Boxing Day, having eaten us out of house and home. So this evening we have plenty of room for the Squire tribe. Teresa phoned me from Malta this morning, and she hopes to join us about nine.'

'Fine. At least there's no fog to delay flights.' They stood in the hall, smiling at each other.

'Teresa said Malta was pleasant,' Belinda said. 'We hope that you and she will get things together again this evening, Tom. If she can enjoy Malta, she can put up with you.'

'New Year's Eve – ideal time for New Year resolutions,' Ron said. 'I'll get her to one side and tell her about all the royalties you're going to earn.'

'Forgive our tribal customs. It's kind of you to put up with us and act as neutral ground.'

'Oh, we're not all that neutral,' Belinda said.

'Come on,' Ron said, ushering Squire into the living room. 'We can get in two good hours' drinking before Teresa arrives.'

'Don't overdo the booze,' his wife cautioned, adding to Squire, 'Keep your eye on Ron. The doctor told him to cut down on those cigars, and on the whisky.'

'I'm as fit as a fiddle, lass. Played a round of golf this morning, didn't I?'

'Just behave yourself, that's all I ask. Tom, we have a couple of house guests, and I believe you already know each other. Come say hello.'

In the fireplace, a cheerful log fire burned. To one side of the fireplace sat a woman, painting. She was a petite dark-haired lady in her forties, neat, plump, magnificently groomed and manicured, with a gold ribbon in the back of her coiled hair. She wore a biscuit-coloured terylene lounging suit and amber rings on her fingers. She was painting a very small picture on a small sketching block, using acrylics from a tiny palette lying by her right hand. She used a brush as delicate as a grass snake's tongue. As Squire entered the room, she smiled resignedly at her work and laid aside the sketchpad.

Her husband, sprawling opposite her on a chesterfield, was totally immersed in a newly published Webb Broadwell coffee-table book, entitled *The Sower of the Systems*, a collection of apocalyptic paintings through the ages, by Leslie Lippard-Milne. He wore a crumpled brown suit, with brown-and-yellow striped socks showing between trousers and slippers. Squire knew the couple well. The man was the editor of *Intergraphic Studies*, Jacques d'Exiteuil, whom Squire had last seen, with his wife Séverine, only a few months earlier in Paris.

Becoming aware of approaching bodies, d'Exiteuil jumped up abruptly, dropping the Lippard-Milne book on the chesterfield and beaming at Squire. For a small, thin man, he managed to convey a lot of stature. Squire shook his hand till d'Exiteuil's coppery locks trembled.

'You didn't bring your son John along?' d'Exiteuil enquired. 'He was with you last time we met in London, if you recall. He impressed me with his knowledge of the music of the Genesis pop group.'

'I saw him a few days before Christmas. This evening, he is seeing the old year out with Fred Cholera and the Pustules. They're a bit more punk than Genesis. Tomorrow, he sees the New Year in with a demonstration outside a power plant.'

He laughed and crossed to hold and kiss Séverine d'Exiteuil – always a pleasurable experience. She smelt delicious, as ever.

'Dear Séverine, you smell like an orchard!'

'You are as always so conservative, Tommy,' she said. She was one of the few women outside his family who addressed him with the diminutive. 'Whatever are nuclear power stations for but to demonstrate outside?'

He pretended to look astonished. 'I've never voted Conservative in my life, Séverine. Couldn't bring myself to do so. In the sixties, that happy time, it was fashionable for everyone to be radical, whether they combined it with seriousness or frivolity, whether they worked for Apple or the Beeb. But Conservatism lacked *chic*.'

Séverine laughed; they liked to tease each other as a substitute for anything more earthy.

'All the same, whatever you say . . . I'm sure that as a privileged landowner you are just an old Tory at heart!'

'Yes, Séverine, if Ruskin was a Tory, if William Morris was a Tory, then I also am a Tory.'

She was silent for a moment, regarding him smilingly but absent-mindedly. In that pause, her husband said crisply, from his side of the hearthrug, 'I'm not so surprised that you link yourself with the names of Morris and Ruskin, Tom, because there is something lordly about you. We're products of our environment, and you're owner of Pippet Hall. But, from my viewpoint, Morris and Ruskin are practically Tory. You remember Herbert Wells's dismissal of them – in *A Modern Utopia*, I think – as Olympian and unworldly, "the irresponsible rich men of a shareholding type". A good phrase.'

'Don't knock shareholding, Jacques,' Belinda said. 'It's a responsible job.'

After a warning glance at her husband, who lapsed into his wine glass, Séverine remarked, 'Jacques and I have always been *Communiste*, as long as we have known each other. It was once the smart thing in Paris, thanks to de Beauvoir and Sartre. Now the trendy people opt for anarchy instead.'

'Well, I've voted Tory all my life, and I certainly don't intend to change now,' Broadwell said, laughing. 'This is a Tory country until publishing is nationalized, and I'm the Last of the Small Time Capitalists.'

'Yes, but you aren't *chic*, darling,' said Belinda affectionately, draping an arm round her husband's shoulder. 'You eat and drink too much to be *chic*. If all these strikes continue and we run out of food, that could be good for you. Now why don't you get that gift we have for Tom – but fast – and then pour us all another drink?'

'Don't you long to go back to the States, with all this trouble in Europe?' Séverine asked Belinda. 'We had a strike on the Metro, and then when we arrive at Heathrow the baggage men are striking and messing up everything. Last time, it was the computer men. The excitement has been put back into travel with a vengeance . . . When Jacques and I spent our year in San Francisco, everything was so smooth and nice.'

'England's a very nice place for Americans, even when it takes on some aspects of a banana republic,' Belinda said. 'It still has civilized virtues you don't find elsewhere, except maybe in France. I remember all that the country has suffered this century in two world wars, and how it has lost an empire – given it away in a fit of absent-mindedness, more like; that helps me remain patient with the economy. I just wish you'd speak to the Reds in the TUC who disrupt industry.'

'Those poor men really only strike for a better wage. Wage rates in England are shockingly low.'

'Well, I guess I'm just an imperialist at heart, Séverine. If I had my choice, I'd be reincarnated and marry Curzon.'

'You have enough trouble managing me, darling, never mind India,' Broadwell said consolingly. He started distributing drinks and passed his wife a Cinzano Rosso and Squire a vodka-on-the-rocks.

Squire was studying Séverine's miniature painting. It showed part of the room, with Jacques sitting on the sofa with his feet on the arm. On his shoulder rested a gigantic parrot, with beak of stone and brilliant plumage.

D'Exiteuil came over to Squire's side, grinning and smoothing his little beard. 'She's a talented painter, but that bird is slightly menacing, to my mind. Tom, you know why we're here? Ron will publish a special selection from *Intergraphic Studies*, the best essays, and lots of illustrations. It could lead to publication of the magazine over here. The hope is that we'll catch a little of the lustre emanating from your good works when they appear. We also hope to persuade you to write the Introduction. Of course we will also be including your Humphrey Bogart article in the book. Is it a possibility?'

'I should think so. If I can find something useful to say, and not merely write a vague endorsement. I feel written out of things to say at present – you know I'm just an amateur in this field.'

'Not at all. I told Ron that it might be possible as a commercial venture to produce a limited edition especially for members of the SPA.'

'Are you getting any further with arrangements for the conference you mentioned when I was with you in Paris?'

D'Exiteuil clutched his head. 'My God, the trouble I am having! I am trying to get a grant from the International Universities Foundation, which exists mainly to bestow grants. Will they coop-erate? No! They say the subject is not a subject. I think their secretary is mad, judging by his letters . . . But just before Christmas I had a communication from a Dottore Frenza, at the University of Ermalpa in Sicily. He's a philosopher.'

'Ermalpa! What do they know about future culture?'

'No, no, the situation has possibilities,' d'Exiteuil said, shaking his head sagaciously. 'Ermalpa University has a Faculty of Iconographic Simulation, with a few bright young men like Enrico Pelli. They are determined to run a conference in September, just to put themselves on the international map, so we at IS may join in. I will send you details when anything tangible results. You will have to be there.'

'Can you persuade people to go to Sicily?' Broadwell asked, arriving with a brightly-wrapped package.

'Anyone will go anywhere if you pay their air fare,' d'Exiteuil said, 'Ancient proverb of the nineteen-seventies.'

'Present for you, Tom,' Broadwell said, thrusting the package forward.

Squire unwrapped it. Inside the Christmas paper was a ten-inch 78 record, with Irene Taylor singing 'Everything I Have is Yours' on the Decca label. On the other side, she was singing 'No One Loves Me Like That Dallas Man'.

'Lovely, thanks very much, Ron. Taylor has a perfect period voice.'

'Like to hear it now? I picked it up in Bristol market just before Christmas. I don't think it's been played.'

They were sitting round the fire peacefully, sipping drinks and listening to the Irene Taylor record. Elm logs crackled, drowning the surface hiss – it was apparent that the record was much beloved by a previous owner. Stereo made it sound as if the lady was singing in her shower.

Squire sat beside Séverine, basking in her delicious aroma while she continued to paint. Seville in summer – perhaps it was just the association of names. Oranges, sunlight, a bed for two in an attic.

The Broadwell living room was decorated in rather a florid taste, the perfect extension of Ron Broadwell himself. Three Piranesi *Carceri* were mounted with wide green mounts and framed in exuberant gilt. The wallpaper was green-and-gold stripe. At the rear of the room, sliding glass doors opened into an extensive conservatory, most of the work on which Ron had done himself, aided by a son; there, a collection of exotic finches fussed from bough to plastic bough. Beyond the birds, in a wintry garden, lay an oval swimming pool, floodlit – presumably more to impress than invite guests.

The Piranesis excepted, the pictures in the room were modern. Two nice Mike Wilks fantasy cities, an alarming Ian Pollock, an Ayrton minotaur, all framed in aluminium. They hung above a long bookcase filled mainly with Webb Broadwell books – Squire identified the spine of his own *Cult and Culture,* it was the book which had persuaded the despots of television to invest in 'Frankenstein'. It and *Against Barbarism* were the only other books he had written or was likely to write. An Introduction for Jacques he could manage.

The fireplace was declamatory but certainly knew how to burn logs. The semi-pornographic nineteenth-century Japanese woodcut over the mantelpiece was not a good idea. On a side-table were silver-framed photographs of the children, mostly smiling, now grown up, and their children, mostly waving, and dogs, mostly begging, interspersed with little silver articles which must have had utility in one culture or another – say before the invention of side-tables. It would have been more fun for visitors to have a random collection of plastic mazes available; there were brilliant mazes and puzzles on the market now which had so far escaped serious comment. But that was not exactly the object of furnishings and bric-a-brac. They existed more to make the householder feel secure and the visitor insecure. Not that Ron and Belinda actively thought that way; they simply followed *Vogue* and *Homes and Gardens*, a rack of which stood behind the piano.

When they had played both sides of the record, Broadwell showed d'Exiteuil an advance copy of *Frankenstein Among the Arts*.

'We are also doing a limited edition, five hundred copies, all signed, with one hundred extra plates, bound in full crushed blue morocco, in slip case. Sixty quid a time.'

'All very elegant, Ron. How many examples of the ordinary edition do you publish?'

'We have a first print run of sixty thousand, almost all already subscribed, and a reprint under way, and the book club have taken another fifty-five thousand. That's how we managed to include so much colour and keep the price within bounds. Nice, isn't it? Publication day, Friday, 3rd March.'

D'Exiteuil shook his head ruefully, 'Ah, success, success . . . You know that my sole book, a collection of essays, in English, called *The Stupidity of the Rich*, was merely a *succès d'estime*. Oddly enough, I see some of my more absurd ideas cropping up in this book, *The Sower of the Seasons*, which you published.' He turned to Squire. 'Tom, do you know Lippard-Milne?'

'I know his wife quite well.'

'Well, you see he has no guiding principle in criticism. Being English, he has a good critical eye, and is observant. That's because you English all read your Bibles so much until a generation ago. You attended to the details, which were expressed in a fine language. Now the Bible has been rendered into civil servant English, and you are left without direction, and the whole perpetual instrument of Marxist analysis has yet to be taken up with the same expertise as it is wielded in France.'

'Marxism naturally doesn't suit us, any more than absinthe, garotting, or *lederhosen*,' Squire said. 'We have a monarchy, if you recall.'

'Do you pretend that the Queen is obstructing literary criticism, Tommy?' Séverine asked, and they all laughed.

'No politics allowed here tonight,' said Belinda. 'Let's all sink our differences at least until next year – which is only a few hours away. Come and eat now. I have just a little snack for you to keep the wolf away. We won't wait for Teresa in case she's late, but I've kept something for her.'

The little snack proved to be a pocket-sized banquet. They had just finished, and were returning to the living room, when there were sounds of a car engine in the drive, and the front-door bell chimed. The Broadwell hounds barked furiously from the kitchen.

Ron Broadwell opened the door. Teresa was not there as anticipated. Instead, her mother walked in, smiling. Madge Davies was smartly dressed in a brown wool coat trimmed with fox. With her was Squire's Uncle Willie, dressed in his customary navy blue overcoat but wearing what, even on close inspection, was a rather snappy tweed hat.

As the two of them shook hands with everyone, and removed their outer garments, Uncle Willie explained that they had intended to meet Teresa at the airport, but her plane had been delayed.

His cheeks were reddened by the cold outside, but he was very brisk; Mrs Davies seemed at first unusually subdued.

'Teresa managed to phone through to us from Rome airport,' Willie explained. 'For some reason, she chose to return from Malta via Rome. Madge and I guess she had some business there, because she's doing very well, selling to the US and so on. We think she's arranging some special packaging. The Italians are good at packaging. Her Rome–Heathrow plane was delayed because of a strike of fuel-tender men. As soon as she gets to Heathrow, she'll catch a taxi here.'

Séverine raised one of her immaculate eyebrows at Squire. 'You remember what I said about putting the excitement back in travel. It soon won't be safe for a woman to travel alone. I can't wait for that day . . .'

'It's just a handful of communist agitators in each country,' Willie explained.

'The capitalists will go on saying that until their system finally breaks down completely,' d'Exiteuil said. 'May we play that charming little Taylor record again, Ron?'

'Go ahead,' Belinda said. 'I suppose you think "Everything I Have is Yours" is some kind of commie signature tune, Jacques?'

'I certainly didn't expect to see you, Mother,' Squire said, touching his cheek to Mrs Davies's cheek. She was wearing a perfume he identified as one of Teresa's. 'Uncle Willie even less. I thought he'd be in Norwich, tucked up safely in bed with his cat.'

'Well, dear . . .' She looked embarrassed, and allowed the Broadwells to usher her into the living room. 'What a charming house you have here, Mr Broadwell, and so wonderfully warm. I suppose that as a *publisher* . . . I don't believe in economizing on the heating, but my flat in Grantham is always so chilly. Double-glazing doesn't seem to help. You're all double-glazed here, I expect, of course.'

'*Tell* them, Madge,' Willie prompted.

Madge adjusted her white hair, and said, looking mainly at Squire, 'Will, at my age, I'm quite . . . I feel it is rather an imposition to come into a strange house and immediately . . . sort of . . . what was that poem about it? Anyhow, Tom, you know that Ernest and I were always very fond of your Uncle Will. Ernest especially. I remember the occasion when we first met him in Norwich, that was in the old Haymarket, no, in the Carlton Hotel, which was then very smart – it's been pulled down now – and Ernest said afterwards, "I trust that man", he said. Well, Tommy, old as we are, Will and I have decided – it's almost a year since poor Ernest was knocked down and killed – he was never what you'd call a strong man – to get married and live together.'

As everyone clapped, Squire put on a puzzled expression and asked, 'But which are you going to do, Mother – get married or live together?'

Amid the laughter, Willie said, 'Madge and I are determined to start anew, as far as that's possible at our advanced age. She'll sell her place, I'll sell up mine, and we'll buy a little bungalow, possibly in Hunstanton. Settle down like Darby and Joan, whoever they were.'

Shaking his uncle warmly by the hand, Squire offered his congratulations. He embraced Mrs Davies.

'Tom, I hope you won't find anything too . . .' She hesitated for a phrase which had vanished without trace.

'Does Teresa know?'

'We told her before she went off to Malta. I mean, your uncle and I are just going to be close friends.'

'I shouldn't trust him if I were you, Mother.'

'It's thirty-four years since Diana died,' Willie said defensively. He brought out his pipe and lit it.

Broadwell moved to get more drinks. Mrs Davies's news was received with amused pleasure. She herself became flustered and apologetic and reminiscent and flirtatious.

When Broadwell returned with champagne, she thanked him and said, 'If Will and I are to be united, it is important to us that Tom and Teresa – you see, she's still a child to me, Mr Broadwell, although she's in her forties, and she and I have always been very alike in our tastes. Not all perhaps, but many. She's always been artistic. Next year is going to be a good one for Tom, I know, so he can afford to be kind to Teresa and try and understand her point of view. As his publisher, you can exert a good influence on him, I'm sure.'

Ron Broadwell laughed. 'That's not a view people generally have of publishers!'

'It's dreadful how everyone seems to quarrel nowadays. I'm sure it was never like it is today – I don't know what's happening in the world. I heard just this morning that the Persians are demonstrating against the Shah. That man's done so much for his country, it does seem ungrateful. I saw him in London once, several years ago, and he looked so distinguished.'

They all drank a toast to Madge and Willie.

'I must remind you that Teresa will not return to Pippet Hall,' Squire told his mother-in-law a little later. 'You must understand my position. I will not eat humble pie for ever, although I would like our life to resume as soon as possible. Do you have any notion of my present difficulties? I think you should speak to Teresa, Mother. She can manage her new business from the Hall, if that's the problem.'

'Oh, dear, that's not the problem. I'm afraid you brought this on yourself, Tom, all this unfaithfulness, it's dreadful. Such things never happened in the twenties, when I was young.'

'Really, Mother? You surprise me. Historians regard the twenties as a period of noted licence, if not licentiousness. Twenties, forties, sixties, the even-numbered decades, all periods of so-called low morals, separated by outbreaks of so-called morality.'

She smiled placatingly at him.

'Well, whatever it is, I think it's all wrong. You've only to read the papers. They're full of it. Something's gone wrong with the nation. People don't know their places any longer. All your encouragement of these so-called arts doesn't help, either. You should know better in your position. I don't blame you especially, Tom, but don't you think all this dreadful rock and roll demoralizes young people? When Ernest and I got married all those years ago, we started out with such high hopes. We worked hard, we went to church, we kept ourselves properly to ourselves . . . Now, oh, England has become – well, I feel it is hostile, I don't recognize it. Some mornings I feel the world's going to collapse. Now you and Teresa . . .'

She left the sentence dangling, as being too dreadful to finish.

He regarded her with sympathy. 'I feel just the opposite. But perhaps the instability of the world was demonstrated to me rather early in life. I think everything's all right, despite the newspapers. It's true we confuse material and moral values. It's true husbands and wives fall out. It's true the divorce rate is going up and the birth rate down. It's true there is a quality we call evil in individuals, which gets magnified by theories and ideologies which have power to rule our common sense. But still humans aren't bad, and we're rather lucky to be living together on this snug little planet. Your announcing your engagement to Uncle Willie makes us all feel even luckier.'

Mrs Davies pursed her lips. 'I don't understand you, Tom. How you can be so happy away from your wife, I don't understand. You used to be so loving. Make it up with her this evening – to please Willie and I.'

Squire took a judiciously deep drink of his champagne.

Mrs Davies set her glass down on a side-table, among small silver objects, resting her ringed and wrinkled hand over it. 'I don't understand what's happening. But then, you always were a mystery to me. You're so intellectual, I suppose. Then there was that rather unpleasant business in Yugoslavia you were involved in – I never could understand that. And I remember when you got married you insisted on having that red Aga installed, whereas poor Teresa had set her heart on a white one. She's not happy either. Her business is going wrong – she and her partner are in trouble, and I know she owes lots of money all over the place, even New York. Isn't New York bankrupt, too? I don't pretend to understand these things, and she won't confide in me any more. I even have to feed the dog.'

As if the word had been a signal, two enormous spaniels, liver and white, burst into the room. They made straight for Mrs Davies, springing on her with the mindless abandon of their kind. As her hand was knocked, the champagne glass went flying, to finish in pieces against the wall. She lay back on the sofa with her hands before her face, and the dogs trampled over her as if over a small muddy hill. Belinda appeared among them, dragging them off by their collars and cursing them cheerfully.

'Oh, you canine delinquents! Mrs Davies, how can I say how sorry I am? I hope you like dogs. They were shut in the back hall, weren't you, you bums, and they made a spirited dash for companionship, freedom and you, not necessarily in that order. Would you like something to eat?'

Willie appeared chivalrously to assist his bride-to-be, the broken glass was cleared, the dogs were returned to captivity, more champagne was poured, and, as the fuss died down, Squire managed to deflect his uncle into Ron Broadwell's study.

'I should have written you a note, my dear Tom, but you have been rather elusive. I do hope our news doesn't come as too much of a shock? Madge is a good woman.'

'Not at all, no.'

'We're going to stay in town tonight. At Brown's. Haven't stayed at Brown's for years. It's still very comfortable. Separate rooms, of course.'

'Of course. Now, Uncle, I want a little plain talk with you. Perhaps I've been rather slow on the uptake—'

Willie looked unhappy. 'Do we have to talk personally, Tom? After all, it is New Year's Eve. Doesn't your publisher have a telly?'

Squire stuck his hands in his pockets. 'My present position is unsatisfactory. I cannot endure it much longer. My life is no life. I'm in a grey area. I shall be under general scrutiny, no use pretending otherwise, when the "Frankenstein" series starts its run at the end of February; the gossip columnists are after me already. You know all about Teresa's and my situation – and about Laura Nye. Well, in case you didn't know it, I renounced Laura as promised. I did so in September, three months ago.'

Uncle Willie had become cautious and took refuge behind his pipe. He sat down on the arm of a chair, adopting a lawyer-like attitude.

'October, the way I heard it.'

Making an impatient gesture in the air, Squire said, 'October, then, for God's sake! That's still two months ago, Uncle. Whenever it was, I renounced her. I loved Laura, Uncle, and she loved me.'

'You're your father's son, Tom. She was half your age.'

'And you're getting married again in your bloody seventies. Try to understand. It was real. And I gave it up for Teresa's sake.'

The older man shook his head. 'In my experience, no good ever comes of renunciations. No good at all. They have a reputation for being noble, and I suppose it's made you feel noble. But my experience in law has shown me that renunciations lead only to bad blood and recrimination, often over years.'

The words took Squire by surprise. He sat down opposite his uncle.

'Anger, disappointment, a trail of disaster,' Willie said. 'Sorry.'

'Very well, Uncle, I am angry, I am disappointed. Laura gave me a great deal – qualities I don't get elsewhere. I admit, I have admitted to Teresa, that I was in the wrong. I feel very bad about it. Yet Teresa still plays difficult, still will not come back. Do you know why not because, if so, I want to know too.'

Willie chewed his lower lip and looked embarrassed. 'My dear Tom, Madge and I now naturally want you two youngsters back together again more than ever. You must understand that, and it's more than sentiment. There's the fate of the Hall and everything—'

'I don't wish to talk about the Hall. Answer my question, please. What is Teresa playing at?'

'Don't start bullying me. That won't help, just because you've messed up your affairs.'

'Give me a straight answer, then. Madge has just told me that Teresa's business is virtually bankrupt, and that she and her partner are broke. All news to me – bad news. I didn't even know she had a partner. Who is it? Who's the partner?'

'I thought you knew.' Evasively.

'Who is it? I'm asking you.'

'Look, Tom, keep your voice down. Oughtn't we—'

'Who's the partner, Uncle? Tell me. Not her mother?'

'Vernon Jarvis, of course.'

'Who's Vernon Jarvis?'

'You know who Vernon Jarvis is. You've met him. Teresa told me you'd met him.'

'Jarvis? Christ, that little sod whose brother wanted to run in Moscow. Yes, he sneaked into the Hall once, one morning, shortly after I got back from Singapore. I bumped into him in the passage . . . Uncle, are you telling me that that fellow is screwing my wife? Is that what's going on? Jarvis?'

Uncle Willie rose, put his pipe down and started shaking his head and rolling his eyes. 'Tom, Tom, don't get excited. You must already know all this. Why ask me? It's none of my business, only what I've heard from Madge. Why pretend not to know? First you were away, then you went off and gave him a clear field.'

'He has been screwing Teresa? He still is? That's what she's up to . . . God, I didn't know. I never suspected – why should I? . . . Has that little bastard been in Malta with her? Oh, God, no . . . She was so bloody self-righteous, so bloody self-righteous about the way I carried on, spying on me with field-glasses, and all the while she was getting him up to the house. I can hardly believe it of her. Teresa. In our house, our rooms . . . God, I'd have killed them both, I swear, shot them like dogs, if I'd have caught them . . .'

He choked. A bottle of Bell's whisky stood on Broadwell's mahogany bookcase. Squire went over to it, poured a generous measure into his empty champagne glass, and drank it neat.

'It's too much. The husband's always supposed to hear these things last. Why didn't you warn me?' His cheeks blazed red.

Uncle Willie was also flustered. 'Damn it, I did try to warn you. In summer of last year, June or whenever it was you came up to my office in Norwich. And other times.'

Squire let out a long groan. 'My guilt, I suppose; I remember – I believed you were warning me to watch my own behaviour. I thought you were laying on a few preachments. Why not simply say outright, "That little shit Jarvis is fucking your wife"? Then it might have got through to me.'

He stood calming himself, stretching his arms, gazing bitterly out at the darkness beyond the window-panes.

His uncle came behind him and put a hand on his shoulder. 'She doesn't mean anything. She still loves you. She just needed comfort. Jarvis is what you'd call a temporary measure, I'm sure of that.'

Turning, Squire said, 'So she doesn't mean anything by it? A few fucks are neither here nor there, is that it? Well, I'd accept that theory, you see, I'd be bloody well prepared to accept that theory – but how come when *I* had a few fucks here and there she made my life such a misery? All that moral gush I had to wade through? And you damned well siding with her, you utter hypocrite, just because you're planning to get your leg over her mother!'

'Tom, Tom, I'm only saying—'

'The bitch! There's no excuse . . . God!' He drank off the rest of his whisky and started pacing. 'The promptness with which she must have got back at me. As if she was waiting for the excuse . . . You don't have to be a male chauvinist to see through Women's Lib and all that tripe. Biology takes care of that. There are biological and ontological differences in sexual behaviour between men and women which no cultural cosmetics can disguise. It's a simple fact of existence that a man can father far more offspring than his mate can bear. A woman is limited in her potential for reproduction by her capacity to nurture her young – not to mention those long tedious months of gestation.'

'But that's—'

'Throughout the history of the human species, males compete to fertilize the bloody females, and not vice versa. You may have observed as much yourself. Why else do men always look at women and women at themselves? We've got no instinctual investment in fidelity as a sex – we sow our seed whenever the opportunity arises. If it wasn't so, the bloody rats would be strutting about in charge of the planet.'

'Oh, calm down, Tom. She could be here any minute. She's still your wife.'

'Fucking well try telling her that!'

'Don't spoil New Year's Eve! Think of these other people. I'm going. I've had enough of your Army language.'

Squire took to pacing again.

'Take Teresa's and my case. We married, we had children. We had four children. I suppose you remember Georgie, who died at the age of two – that was in 1956, of all miserable years – because Tess and I still do, if you don't. We cared for them, educated them expensively – so that they could turn anarchist and bugger up the country and consort with the likes of Fred Cholera. All that represents a considerable existential investment on the part of this male!' He struck his chest. 'So I am under evolutionary pressure to protect myself against being cuckolded, and to reject other brats, fat devouring cuckoos, sired on my spouse by any passing male who fancies her, never mind some little shit whose brother plans to run the four hundred metres in Moscow.'

'Don't get worked up again. Where did I put my pipe?'

'For these reasons, deep-seated, deep as artesian wells, the male has a far greater concern than the female in the fidelity of his mate. For these reasons, the male suffers from his partner's infidelity more strongly than the female does. For these same reasons, the male often responds to external interference by shooting the unfaithful female and the offending interloper, if he can catch him. Aren't most murders sexual murders? And I've bloody well been apologizing to my unfaithful female!'

In an attempt to mollify his nephew, Uncle Willie clasped Squire by his arms, and gazed at his dark face.

'There now, no talk of shooting and killing people! You're not in Yugoslavia now. It's terrible to hear you carrying on like this at your age. I told you that renunciation was not good for the soul. You must forgive Tess – she wants to come back, despite everything.'

'Take your hands away, Uncle. I'm not going to forgive her for your asking. Indeed, I'm not sure I can forgive her at all, after the way she went at me for a lesser offence.'

'Well, dear boy, the same offence, the same offence. Be fair.'

'I've told you why I think infidelity is a lesser offence in men. I don't care what the libbers say – it's subscribing to silly wishy-washy ideas like that, or opposing nuclear energy, or believing communism can solve human problems, which has got the country into its present rotten position. In any case, she's now going to come running to me for money to bale her and her lover out of trouble, isn't she?'

'It's nothing to do with me, is it? Be reasonable.'

'I won't give her a penny, he can pay up or bloody well be declared bankrupt. Imprisoned, with luck.'

More shaking of the avuncular head. 'I have advised Teresa on financial matters, I admit, and the position as far as I understand it – which isn't far, by the way – is that you, her legal husband, are responsible for her debts . . .'

Squire looked round wildly, as if hoping to see a pair of loaded duelling pistols hanging conveniently on the wall.

'There's no way in which I will take the bitch back or settle her debts for money squandered on behalf of that nasty little sneak, Jarvis. When I think of the way she has humiliated me . . .'

They heard the distant chime of the front-door bell.

'That – that may be Teresa now,' Uncle Willie said. 'Tom, my dear boy, I know this is most upsetting for you, and I'd have felt just the same in your position, once upon a time. But please don't make a scene in someone else's house.'

'Why not, for God's sake? Ron's only my bloody publisher, isn't he?'

Squire went to the study door, flung it open, and advanced along the passage. He paused before entering the front hall, gathering himself, checked at the sound of his wife's voice, that familiar voice so poignant that his anger faded before it. She was explaining something to Belinda.

'. . . and then there was a bomb scare at Heathrow and we all had to be searched . . .' Hearing her voice, he recalled her once-and-eternal innocence.

He continued into the hall. Beyond Belinda's plump back, he saw his wife, wrapped in a shortie Swedish coat with hat to match and looking tall in crimson high-heeled boots; with her stood a young man, grinning slightly, in a Russian-type fur hat and ankle-length grey tweed coat. Whiskery sideboards made a pincer movement across his cheeks, in an attempt to cut off his nose from his mouth. It was Jarvis.

Squire had not expected that. He stopped as Teresa saw him.

'Oh, darling, there you are!' cried Teresa. 'We are so late, I thought you'd be gone.' She moved towards him in a tentative way: so tentatively that Jarvis, also coming forward, overtook her, sticking out a boney hand.

'Glad to see you again, Mr Squire. I've been taking care of Teresa.' He smiled with all the teeth at his command. 'What a journey we've had!'

So overcome was Squire by this effrontery that he accepted the hand before realizing it. The touch of it immediately roused him and he withdrew his own.

'So you're the creature who's been fooling around with my wife and sneaking into my home when I was away! Get out immediately!'

Jarvis opened his mouth rather wide and stuck his fists on his hips.

'If you're going to be unfriendly, two can play that game.'

'Don't you dare make trouble here, Tom,' Teresa said.

'Oh, don't mind us,' Belinda said, closing the front door. 'Feel at home.'

Squire said, 'Teresa, you're mad bringing this fellow here!'

'Don't you order me to get out, Mr Squire,' Jarvis said, his confidence returning. 'It's not your place any more than it is mine. I've got every right to be here. I'm looking after your wife, and so what? You weren't so much of a success in that line, gallivanting round the world.'

He showed signs of continuing his discourse, but Belinda said coolly, 'You do not have as much right to be here as Mr Squire, young man, whatever your name is. Just for the record, Mr Squire was invited here and is our guest. You were not invited and you are not our guest.'

'Belinda! I was going to introduce you. Vernon has brought me all the way back from Malta. We've been travelling for hours . . .' Teresa looked close to tears.

'No doubt he took you all the way to Malta, too,' said Belinda. Ron Broadwell appeared in time to hear this last exchange.

'Any trouble?' he asked.

'Ron, this fellow has the impertinence to turn up here with my wife on his arm. I shall not stay if he does. You've arrived with her, Jarvis, you can take her away again – back to Malta, for all I care.'

Jarvis said, 'If you weren't old enough to be my father, I'd bash your face in.'

'You can try if you like. You'd get a few surprises.'

'For two pins I would, you self-satisfied—'

Broadwell moved forward, his bulk making the advance an impressive sight. 'I'm not having an intruder spoiling our evening. You must make up your own mind what you are doing, Teresa. Of course, you're welcome to stay on your own.'

Teresa stamped her foot and shook her fists. 'My God, Tom, how you disgrace me – in front of friends. Vern only wanted to be your friend . . .'

Turning to Jarvis, Broadwell said, 'You aren't welcome here. Get out and go home. Close the door behind you. Go on, vamoose!'

Glaring angrily at her husband, Teresa said, 'We came here in perfect innocence. I wasn't going to turn Vern away after all our troubles today. You ought to try Alitalia some time. I knew it was the wrong day to travel; the stars were against it, but I wanted to see you on New Year's Eve. Now you show how little you care, telling Vern to take me away, treating me—'

He had swung away in disgust, but now he turned back. 'What did you want to see me for, Teresa? You've shown no inclination these last months. I suppose you want to borrow money?'

She grasped Jarvis's arm. 'I'm sorry, Vern, I didn't mean to drag you into this. He always tries to humiliate me. I loved and trusted you once, Tom. As for you, Belinda, I knew you were never a friend of mine—'

'Oh, yes, I was,' Belinda said sharply. 'I was a good friend of yours, because I've never hinted to you that not for one moment did I think you did at all a good job of being Tom's wife. Now you've found someone of your own kind, perhaps Tom can find someone to make him happier. That's what we all hope.'

Ron laid a hand on his wife's arm. She glared like a cat about to pounce, and then put an arm round him.

'Such fun to be totally honest for once,' she said: 'Sorry, Teresa.'

But Teresa had already turned back to her husband. 'You of all people accusing Vernon of fooling around with me behind your back. Why can't I invite him home? He only came for coffee and a business chat. I'll invite in who I like. I wanted him to see my work. I'm not going to be cooped up while you do what you please with any woman you fancy.'

Jarvis was also talking. Squire found he had ceased to listen. Before the spectacle of his wife attacking him and defending Jarvis, all the fight had gone out of him. He was thinking rather abstractedly about closing up the Hall, perhaps even selling up – why not? Maintaining it was just a struggle – and going abroad somewhere, living on capital and royalties. Maybe California. Or one of the Adriatic islands. Mali Losinj. But even if they were Yugoslav, they were still communist. Singapore? Malaysia. Without Laura?

Jarvis was still talking, wagging a finger, maintaining a long self-righteous discourse, chiefly concerned with how his popularity with women was sustained because he treated them right, although he didn't think it was fair to marry. Furthermore, he cultivated Teresa because she was good at her craft and they would make a success of the business they were developing if only their capital hadn't run out unexpectedly. Even that was because of his generosity. He was too generous.

Squire realized that Séverine and her husband were listening with fascination – the scent of her perfume reached him. Much as he hated this occasion, he recognized that he could laugh about it with her afterwards. Possibly rather a long time afterwards.

He noted also that Teresa's mother and Willie had made themselves scarce. His dry mouth reminded him how welcome alcohol would be.

'Perhaps we should go and have a drink somewhere,' he said, cutting in on Jarvis's speech. 'We'll sort this false nonsense out once and for all. There's bound to be a pub open in Ascot tonight. I won't impose this disruption on my friends any longer. But if you are determined to consort with all and sundry, Teresa, then we must make arrangements accordingly.'

'I didn't say—' Teresa began, but Jarvis silenced her. 'I'm not drinking with you, Mr Squire. Not after the way you've insulted me in front of these people. And damaged my reputation. I intended you no harm.'

Squire laughed with a poor parched sound. 'You'd better understand that you've done me considerable harm – and Teresa also. If you don't want to talk, why not simply blow back into the night, the way you came?'

At this point, Ron Broadwell heaved himself forward, clapping his hands. Belinda took Squire's arm and squeezed him. 'I don't believe it,' she said.

'Did you two come in a taxi?' Ron asked Teresa, flinging open the front door.

'Of course not. Vern had his car at the airport. And where's my mother? Tom, you're turning me away – realize that, you're turning me away. I warn you, I don't like it, and I shan't stand for it.'

'Goodbye, Teresa,' he called.

'Terry, let's scram out of here,' Jarvis said, tugging at his coat. He added menacingly to Broadwell, 'And I'll plant one on you if you shove me.'

'Do you wish me to turn the dogs on you?'

The front door slammed. Broadwell ushered his wife and Squire into the living room to the fire, ostentatiously wiping sweat from his forehead.

'I thought the blighter was going to attack me, I really thought he was going to hit me. You heard what he said? Well, Jacques, Séverine, you see how we English live. It's all drama – the land of Shakespeare.'

The French couple smiled and shrugged and expressed their sympathies with Squire. 'It happens all the while in France,' Jacques said. 'Maybe with stabbing in addition.'

Broadwell went to the window, drew back the curtain, and watched to see Jarvis drive off. Uncle Will and Mrs Davies stood by the fireplace, holding hands without speaking.

'We'd better leave after all that,' Willie said, glumly.

'I never thought she would actually go with him,' Squire said. He felt his lips pale and sat down. 'I never thought to see that. She sided with him . . . I need a drink.'

Mrs Davies began to weep. 'Take me away, please Willie . . . I never expected to hear a daughter of mine treated like that by her husband. We ought to go after them. Oh, oh, how awful everything is . . . Tom, you're so cruel . . . Poor Teresa . . .'

'I'll get you a drink, Mrs Davies,' Ron Broadwell said. 'We all need one. Big ones, at that. And – Happy New Year, everyone, by the way!'

It was midnight. Distant bells began to peal.

13

Illegal Currency Charges

Ermalpa, September 1978

It was midnight; Thursday, 14 September, was passing into history.

The lights in the corridors had dimmed or had been switched off. Francesca da Rimini and Paolo, their nudity and guilty love shrouded in decent shadow, stood like sentinels over the dark foyer of the hotel, staring towards the Via Milano. Down that thoroughfare, last Fiats were fleeing, travelling all the faster in their comparative solitude, like the remnants of a school of fish escaping from a vast maw.

In the bar of the Grand Hotel Marittimo, lights still burned, the skilled waiters still waited, smiling and polite, pocketing their small tips. The tables were still encircled by conference delegates, most of them drinking and smoking, all of them talking.

Herman Fittich, buoyed by the success of his talk that evening, was laughing as he compared teaching experiences with members of the French delegation. Rugorsky was at another table, arguing with Morabito and some Italians, though turning every now and again to pat the arm of Maria Frenza, who sat next to him, smoking and smiling exclusively into the night air.

Dwight Dobell sat with Frenza at another table, discussing the vagaries of the American academic system. Squire was at the same table, half-listening; he had sat through many similar discussions in his time, yet the American academic system remained incomprehensible to him. Each conversation added a mite more incomprehensibility. He got up as if to go to the toilets, but turned instead to the lift, and travelled to the second floor. It might as well be bedtime.

The long melancholy corridors with their high arched ceilings were dim; every other light was off. A few trays lay uncollected outside doors. The silence was as thick as a blanket on a hot night. A vacuum cleaner, entangled in metres of its own cable, stood awaiting morning; its heavy fake streamlining suggested that it was a survivor from the regime of Mussolini; with its jutting black rubber prow, it even looked like Mussolini.

Before he reached the corner of the passage, Squire heard voices. A woman's first, sharp, protesting. Then a man's.

He turned the corner. The first door on the left was open. Light poured into the corridor from a bedside lamp.

A man bent over a woman. He was in trousers and shirt-sleeves. His jacket had been flung down on the bed. He was holding the woman fairly gently and speaking persuasively, not in English. She had reached the door, and was leaning backwards, to get as far away as possible. She saw Squire.

At the same moment, he recognized d'Exiteuil and Ajdini. D'Exiteuil turned, poking his little beard over his shoulder, looking extremely displeased by the interruption. Ajdini waved enthusiastically.

'Ah, Tom Squire! I must simply have a word with you. There is rather an abstract question needing to be resolved.'

She moved fast, eluding d'Exiteuil, turning deftly to wish him good-night, smiling, linking her arm with Squire's, adjusting her coiffure, thanking d'Exiteuil for his kindness.

D'Exiteuil stood at his door, his brows gathered darkly, pulling at his cheek as he folded his arms across his chest.

'Good-night, Jacques,' Squire said.

Squire walked briskly along to his room, unlocked it, ushered Ajdini in, followed her, and locked the door behind them. He was laughing more openly than she, as he stood beside her. She was a tall lady. Colour had mounted into the normal pallor of her cheeks.

'I see that look in your eye,' she said, pushing him with extended arm, 'I hope I just didn't step from the frying pan into the fire.'

'What a gorgeous voice you have, Selina, and how lovely you look when a little ruffled. Was Jacques going to rape you?'

'Of course not. Jacques? He is harmless. I simply changed my mind, that's all. I simply changed my mind. Now I'm going to bed and I hope that you will be an English gentleman and not present me with any difficulty.'

'Don't insult me with the English gentleman bit. Regard me as Serbian, just for tonight. I've got you here and I won't let you go till morning.'

'I'm not insulting you, I'm praising you, for heaven's sake. You're not another little Enrico Pelli, I know that. Now, I'll have a drink with you while you calm down a bit, for friendship, then I will go to my room.'

'Your room's not lonely. I am. You promised me that you would sleep with me tonight. You must keep your promises. You've whetted my appetite, Selina.'

The fine bone features became finer, turning almost to porcelain. She commenced to prowl about the room looking about her, as if bored by the conversation. He stood and watched her slender buttocks moving under her dress.

'My belief in the miraculous doesn't extend to quite that extent.' She sighed. 'Let me go, Tom. I don't like to be your captive. This is boring. How'd you like to be a woman and go through this same scene so often? I was going through it only just now with Jacques, except that as yet you have not laid a finger on me. But that will come, eh?' She looked at him with contempt, yet with a half-smile; there was a coquetry she seemingly could not suppress.

'You must continually plant yourself in the same scene, mustn't you, Selina? The role must give you a little titillation and pleasure, isn't that so?' He heard anger and banter and lust, spiced with a mite of sympathy, in his own voice.

She stopped pacing and faced him. 'Give me a cigarette.'

'Don't smoke.'

'It's so late.'

'You look fresh.'

'I will not have any of your phoney psychiatry such as you gave me this morning. That was an insult, I consider. That Freudian stuff . . . That's why I avoided you and would not eat dinner with you this evening, in case you wondered.'

'I didn't wonder. I guessed. But my remarks weren't meant to irritate. I simply had a moment of perception regarding some of your troubles, or thought I did. I don't want to pry, why should I? But if I can help I'd be glad to.'

'Because you think you can get me into bed that way.'

He laughed. 'Does it hold such fears for you that you dread it? It's pleasant. Precious, if done for its own sweet sake, not as some sort of – bargain. Often exciting, sometimes consoling, occasionally – miraculous.'

She flushed. 'Okay. That's enough. I'm not a kid, you know. I can't be talked into what I don't wish to do. I'm not just a bloody body, you know.'

'True.' He pulled the door key out of his trouser pocket by its plastic label, walked over to the door, and opened it.

'You're free to go if you wish.'

She gathered herself up, breasts, stomach, handbag, between her arms, then suddenly changed posture, raising a finger.

'Wait! Maybe I have a cigarette left after all, let me just look.'

She opened her handbag and produced a packet, which she flipped open and proffered, letting Squire see the label. 'Drina'.

'You can buy them in Germany now. So many poor Yugoslav *Gastarbeiter* are in the Bundesrepublik, working away to keep democracy going.'

'And maybe to prop the tottering communist economy back home?'

As he accepted a cigarette, they both laughed. After they had lit up, she closed the door gently with her back and smiled at him.

'Wicked Jacques may still be lingering in the corridor with intent. I am afraid to go from your room.'

'If not sex, I've only got vodka to offer.'

'Fine.'

She consented to sit down on the bed. After a drink, she allowed him to kiss her. Then she drew away her lips and smoked in silence. He watched her, admiring the line of her neck, its feather of dark hairs, her lobeless ear.

'How could there be any possible connection between the death of my father, so long ago in Kragujevac, in a country I no longer visit, and my political sympathies?'

'It's just an intuition, and my intuitions aren't reliable. But I also lost my father at an early age, and am aware of the stresses such bereavements bring with them. Otherwise, I had only your extraordinary reading of Aldous Huxley to go by. In his most enduring book, *Brave New World* – which I suppose Herman would classify as science fiction – Huxley dramatizes the battle between the state and the individual or, to define it more narrowly, between a bureaucracy and sexuality. Do you hate Huxley because he was on the side of sexuality? Doesn't sexuality and all that goes with it challenge the Perfect State – or any state that claims perfection and therefore classifies all who criticize it as criminals? Remember the words of the Savage in *Brave New World*. He claims the right to be unhappy, to grow old and ugly and impotent, to catch syphilis, to be tortured, because then he can get a glimpse of freedom and poetry. I'd say on the basis of our very slight acquaintance, that you might be alarmed by the Savage in all of us, including the Savage in yourself. By opting for a repressive system, you repress the Savage.'

'More phoney psychiatry! You insult me. You treat me as if I were a child.' She puffed smoke at him.

He put an arm lightly round her waist.

'You just see it that way. I only offered you an intuition. Marxism sounds bad in your pretty mouth, but I've no business speaking to you like this.'

'That's true!' she said with spirit. 'It's immoral – interfering. Someone described you as a self-appointed critic, that I know. They were right!'

'Would you rather critics were appointed by the state? The self-appointed ones are best, kindest, most disinterested . . . Were you happy as a child – I mean, before the massacre at Kragujevac? Can you remember so far back?'

She turned the fine bone china of her face towards him and regarded him searchingly with a pure glance which came close to making him quail.

'No – yes. One always remembers.' She looked at him, playfully, slid her spectacles down on her nose to regard him better. 'Let me tell you this – since it's late – my secret. My father was a desperate man, desperately poor, desperately everything, like a character from Gorki. There were trees behind our house where he would go to *rage* . . . He often beat me when he was drunk, with his hand or with poles. Yet after he was shot, I knew I loved him dearly, needed him, and I longed in despair to see him once more and even be beaten by him. I would be utterly degraded, as long as he came back. There, that's the truth.'

She exhaled blue smoke and waved it away.

'Your mother? You don't mention her.'

'She died giving birth to me. Another woman looked after us then.'

They sat without speaking, smoking together companionably, occasionally sipping vodka. She said, 'Of course there's more to it than that. There always is. The world changed, that day he and my brother were shot by the Germans. It wasn't only them I lost, but a less tangible thing . . . A.E. Housman's land of lost content. You can never get back there.'

She quoted,

> That is the land of lost content,
> I see it shining plain,
> The happy highways where I went
> And cannot come again.

'You will think I'm very self-pitying, when you get to know me.'

'We all need pity.' He stroked her dark hair, and she rested her head against his shoulder. He remembered her anecdote about Dorothy, the woman with the brain injury.

'One day, I'll tell you about the death of my father.'

A simple exchange of stories . . . The promise appeared to please her. She rested a hand with its bright nails on his shoulder, whilst continuing to gaze into the shadowy recesses of the room.

'It's the night, Tom. When we're changed, somehow . . .'

'I don't really know you at all. It's a cheek to pretend to . . . Why don't you go back to Serbia?'

'Oh . . . The pain, or something. Let's not talk about it. Kiss me again, if you'll kindly go no further than that. In a way you're right – I hate sexuality.'

'Your beautiful lips, Selina . . .' He poured kisses on them, removed her spectacles, held her tightly, relished the taste of her mouth, the warmth of her breath, began pressing his body with its erection against her thighs. She pushed away, gasping.

'Look, Tom, be kind, promise, *promise* – I know how you feel, but promise you will just do no more than kiss me. Will you? Just kiss . . .'

'No more? Come on, no one knows we're here together.'

'Tom . . .' She wrapped an arm around his neck, whispering, 'Then I'll feel safe . . . Promise . . .'

He began to kiss her, pressing closer, forgetting himself, becoming just a warmth, sensing her delight. Her arms tightened as she sank back on the bed, their lips still together. Then her body began to heave under him, her leg hooked round his. Her tongue darted into his mouth, low gasps escaped her. He lay on top of her, eyes closed, 'Drina' burning his fingers. She ceased to move.

Rather than disturb her, he pinched out the cigarette stub with his fingers.

Gradually she stirred. She sighed. Judging his moment, he sat up, breathing so deeply he almost trembled. He took a small sip of the vodka. It was warm.

'I must go, Tom, dear. I won't stay.' It was a faun's glance she gave, there and away.

'I'll see you tomorrow.'

She stood up. Her mood had changed; she was gentle and not exactly downcast, although her eyes perpetually sought the floor.

'Yes . . . Oh dear . . . It is tomorrow . . . That's serious.'

He kissed her on the cheek, with care in case she did not wish it. She appeared not to notice. As she moved to the door, she said, 'Perhaps we'll have more time together.'

When she slipped into the dark corridor, she said, 'Tom, the miraculous does sometimes happen.'

Squire stood listlessly at the door until she had disappeared, before moving back into the room. An envelope lay at his feet. As he stooped to pick it up, he thought that Selina must have dropped it, and instantly his mind conjured up a scene where he went to her bedroom to return it and found her undressing. But the note had his name on, written in a foreign hand; it had been slipped under the door. He immediately lost interest, and flipped it onto the table.

Locking the door, he went and lay on the bed, hands behind his head, his meditations possessed by Selina Ajdini.

In a moment of vision, succoured by the silence of the hour, he saw no mystery in personality. He perceived her with clarity, and the circumstances which surrounded her. The clarity neither magnified nor belittled her; it was cleansed even of compassion, for one condition of the vision was that his own personality, with all its limitations and potentials for growth, was also clear to him – a distortion in one would have implied a distortion in the other.

Within those linked visions burned his understanding of human nature, of its ramshackle structure, its transience, its quality of light.

There was nothing inscrutable about personality or relationships between people. These matters could be perceived, divined; in a sense he knew Selina fully. There was no puzzle. The puzzle came when such things had to be translated into words. Words belonged only to the cerebrum, the part of the brain that made man specifically human; but the mysterious world inhabited by whole understanding occupied all of the brain, and the nervous system beyond it, and the blood cells and body beyond that. It could not be reduced into words. Any system of understanding built purely on words – such as an ideology – was an impoverishment of the human being. Selina tried to live in her words, her ideology, because, for specific reasons, she was afraid of the whole world of her personality. Pain lurked there.

With patience and love, it would be possible to make that proscribed area accessible to her again. But not by words alone. Words alone could not defeat pain.

He climbed off the bed, assumed *tadasana*, and performed some steady *hora* breathing in order to clear his mind still further. Moments of meditation and vision could be encouraged, developed. They enlarged life. They created stillness.

The stillness was in some miraculous way eternal within the frames of a human life. Squire had experienced the first such perception at the age of four. He still recalled it: it had remained with him. The nursery with a coal fire burning, firelight reflecting on all the shining brown surfaces of the room. The child at the window, face half-turned to the outdoors, realizing the lure – the wilderness – of the world, as dusk filtered in. Realizing the unknown was limitless. It had been the first of his escapes beyond time, and in a way the most vivid. He had felt his own containedness and greatness. He had reached to an oceanic content within his own being.

There had been other similar moments before his father died; they continued after the watershed of that event.

The death had killed his tentative reaching towards the orthodoxies of the Christian religion, though not towards an unspoken mysticism. He saw only now that the unspokenness had preserved its freshness. He hated the very word 'mysticism'; but of its flesh he was not in doubt, for he felt it inside him.

Even these reflections visited his mind without a cloud of words, as he slowed his breathing and set aside the hotel room.

With placid amusement, he detached himself from his body, rising above it to see a man, recently embraced by a woman, standing in still posture, mind clear of logical thought. That stillness, that balance, was a triumph, achieved within – the image always charged him with excitement – within the violent explosion that was the universe. He visualized the curdling galaxies, the stellar bodies, whirling away from each other, still fleeing from that primal explosion, that ejaculation of matter which began everything. The cosmos was still inexpressibly new.

All human experience was a brief dawn affair; more comprehensive experiences would be possible later in the cosmic day. Meanwhile, it was possible to develop towards greater understanding.

The sparks flew forever up the chimney. Turmoil was all that could be expected. There was evil in man, in men and women; only a fool would doubt it when he had the privilege of living in the twentieth century – as a being confined to a lunatic asylum would be the maddest of all inmates if he refused to believe in lunacy – but that evil was a flaw wrought by the holocaust of the physical world. That was where religion falsified the situation. Flames had no morality. If evil was a human creation, so was the concept of perfection. Wasn't perfection always visualized as somehow static? And stasis was an impossibility in the exploding universe. It was a good idea to recognize the instability of all things, and to breathe deep and slow.

He threw off his clothes, brushed his teeth, and climbed between the sheets.

His mind would not let him sleep. He lay there for some while before realizing that sleep was not going to visit him yet. Some factor just beyond his grasp was worrying him.

He sat up with sudden impatience, saying into the wall of dark before his face, 'But anyone who could speak so ill of Huxley cannot be a good person.'

Impatiently, he let his head thump back on the pillow.

Again, he tried to make himself sleep, concentrating on slow breathing. But the moment of rapture had curdled into a mood of self-distrust, sucking him back into the past with its regrets.

Images of disquiet flooded him. His father's savage death. His mother's dead countenance, patched with hitherto unknown browns and greys. The long estrangement from Teresa. Even the savagery with which the English critics, unlike those abroad, had attacked 'Frankenstein Among the Arts'.

From serenity, he fell into despair.

Near at hand lay his doubts about the conference in Ermalpa, and his quarrel with d'Exiteuil. One of his beliefs was that, as the nineteenth century cultivated optimism, often of a rootless kind, so that century's impoverished heirs and assigns of the twentieth cultivated a pessimism possibly as rootless. The art of enjoyment was lacking. He had always hoped to contribute to the general enjoyment; not as an entertainer – he had no gift for that – but as an appreciater, one who could enhance other people's lives, as his father had enhanced his. That had been the driving force behind his great television series and the book related to it.

('Tottering between playing the common man and the intellectual, hopelessly fumbling both roles, Thomas Squire – even now no doubt expecting a knighthood for his services to a TV-zapped nation – tries to camouflage a lack of content beneath a middlebrow concern with the surface of trivia; his compulsive dashes about the globe, which reduce all space and time to a corner of the studio, are physical analogues of his efforts to cover dozens of subjects in order to conceal the fact that he has no subject. As he points in astonishment at things with which we are all too familiar, it is impossible not to feel that the new Renaissance on which he lavishes his laboured epigrams is our Untergang in thirteen episodes.' Leslie Lippard-Milne, 'Frankensquire Among the Parts', *New Statesman*)

There were no Lippard-Milnes in Ermalpa. The conference paid him homage – although one accepted that homage never meant what it professed. But the delegates were also busy destroying the things he held dear, the things they held dear. Could poor Krawstadt ever *enjoy* a game of pinball now he had written so villainously on the subject? Well, perhaps one hoped not.

These unembarrassed arts, why should they wilt so easily beneath scrutiny? Another law was emerging. Pick a flower and it dies.

What was he going to do next? How was the rest of his life to be lived? He thought of the sailing ship moored at the harbour, ready to slip away to sea. There was no escape, only the appearance of escape. That depended who else was in the boat with him. The opportunity to begin again often presented itself, no doubt of that. But the blowfly in the human heart ensured that one went on making the old mistakes.

He had no complaints. Things were as they were. If the conference was a failure, he was not responsible; he would never be one to admit it failed. If ideology killed it, there again he had no complaint. In his time – it was curious to look back on it now – he had killed for the sake of ideology. He could remember the savage triumph he felt when, in a farmhouse in Istra, he looked down at the broken body of Slatko, the Russian colonel. That had been no timeless moment of vision; whenever the episode rose to mind, he pushed it from him, not wishing to recognize any more that part of himself.

Now Slatko's brutal face pursued him. Squire sat up and put the light on, feeling ill.

He padded over to the bathroom to get himself a sip of water – he had been warned that Ermalpa water was contaminated, but he had heard similar tales wherever he went. He caught sight of the unopened envelope lying on the table. After drinking, he took the envelope back to bed and ripped it open.

Inside was one sheet of paper with the hotel's crest. The letter read,

Dear Tom,

For reasons you know well, I can bear no more of the talk round the conference table. Let me get away just in the morning. You must come with me and pay. We can take a No 9 bus to the little town called Nontreale. It is a cheap fare but you know our government keeps us poor as saints – which we otherwise are not – when we are out of our country. Besides, you are rich.

Tell nobody our plan. I must not tell my 'comrade' Kchevov. We will play truant, and talk like men, and view Nontreale cathedral to educate you and make me thirsty.

The bus leaves at 9.05 in the morning. Meet me just outside the hotel at ten minutes to nine tomorrow and I will take you to the bus stop. Nobody shall know where we go, so please be safe and flush this sheet in your toilet bowl (we Russians have a passionate admiration for secrets, you know that). I trust you.

Yours

Vasili Rugorsky

Squire laughed. He laid the letter by his bed, switched off the light, and in a moment was sound asleep, worries forgotten.

The No 9 bus was crowded, but they managed to sit together. Rugorsky's mood was somewhat withdrawn. He had missed his breakfast in order to get away from the hotel without questioning.

'I am a man who likes much to eat. But more I like to see foreign countries. When shall I again be allowed outside the sacred frontiers of my own country? It is naturally cosy in there, because it is so well guarded. But I feel a necessity to store up some images of Sicily, other than that room of mirrors and electronic equipment in which we sit.'

He lapsed into silence. Both men sat staring out of the windows as the bus wound through the suburbs of Ermalpa with many a stop, a pachyderm surrounded by flocks of Fiats.

On the outskirts of town, the buildings became drab and decrepit. Squire was reminded of the older parts of Cairo. Coppersmiths and saddlers and vulcanizers worked in tiny open-fronted shops beneath the room in which they and their families lived. The bus had transported its passengers from a twentieth-century city to some outlying byway of history. People, animals, and scruffy fowls were everywhere. Piles of refuse filled yards and gardens, spilling into the street. Here and there an elderly tree defied its destiny by sending forth bright blossom, carmine on purple.

Squire made an idle remark about the filth.

'No, you see, you are a man of the world,' said Rugorsky, looking at him askance in his teasing way. 'But your world is limited. Here it is no real filth. It is merely untidy. That's all. Merely a little untidy.'

He sank into silence again.

Outside the city, the bus turned onto a good dusty road and began forging steadily west. The way wound upwards, yielding increasingly fine views of the Mediterranean. At every broken-walled village *en route*, the bus stopped, and women and goats ceased their activities to stare at it.

Half-an-hour later, they arrived in Nontreale. The bus nosed along narrow streets hardly wider than the vehicle, entered the main square, and stopped with a protracted sigh. All the passengers climbed out.

The air was cooler than it had been in Ermalpa. Squire and Rugorsky stood together while the latter wiped his brow thoroughly with a brown handkerchief.

Nontreale held two points of historical and aesthetic interest, a ruinous castle and a cathedral. The cathedral filled one side of the small square. As they stood looking across at it, the crowd generated by the arrival of the bus slowly disappeared. Most of the people appeared to be locals; it was early as yet for tourists. In front of the cathedral, shopkeepers were setting up stalls loaded with bright tourist goods.

Rugorsky nodded and grunted. 'Byzantium. A common heritage of East and West, you see. It looks promising, Tom. Perhaps we shall enjoy it more for having an ice cream first.'

'There's a bar over there. Would you prefer a drink?'

'I don't wish for a bad reputation. Let us proceed first to an ice cream.'

They sat down at open-air tables to one side of the square, and the sun shone on them. Rugorsky asked, 'You don't mind to pay for me?'

'I'm pleased to do so.'

'It does not make you feel too superior to me?'

Squire laughed. 'You are not the sort of man one easily feels superior to, Vasili.'

'That's good – but be careful. I am aware of the terrible sinful power of money. Well aware. Money is very corrupting.'

'So people say. The lack of it corrupts, too.'

They ordered *cassati* from the waiter.

Rugorsky reopened the subject. 'You perhaps assume that as a good socialist I naturally preach about the evils of money. But that is not all my meaning. You see, I also feel on the personal level, and not just as a theory, that money corrupts. It has corrupted me. I am a corrupt man, Tom. Very corrupt, unfortunately. It's not my wish.'

'I don't see you like that.'

An impatient gesture, made slowly to remove any offence. 'You do not know me. You see, Tom, I do not wish to argue about how corrupt I am. That a man must decide for himself. The scale in such judgements is merely internal. You agree?'

Squire was silent. Howard Parker-Smith had phoned him from the Consulate earlier in the morning, catching him just before he left his hotel room. Rugorsky certainly had money problems. Squire wondered with some apprehension what exactly Rugorsky was planning to do.

He ate the ice cream slowly. It had a delicious flavour and texture. As they ate, they watched the life of the square. An old woman had brought two donkeys down from the hills, and was tying them to a railing a short distance away, talking to them loudly as she did so. 'I was speaking with the Italian Morabito last night,' Rugorsky said. 'He has been once to your house in England. It is in the country.'

'Yes. Norfolk. Only six or seven miles from the sea.'

The Russian sighed. 'Perhaps I may myself come there one day and stay with you, as I have stayed with Lippard-Milne and his wife. They live in Sloane Street, in London.'

'Yes, I know. I've been there.' Squire had caught sight of Howard Parker-Smith. At least he was certain he recognized those well-knit shoulders, clad in an English blazer, and the sleek well-groomed head, before the figure disappeared down a side-alley off the square. He glanced at his watch; it was before ten-thirty. He and Parker-Smith had been talking over the phone less than two hours earlier. What was the man doing here, if not keeping an eye on the two of them? Perhaps he was expecting a sudden move by Rugorsky.

Squire paid the waiter. He and Rugorsky rose, and they strolled across the square to the cathedral, soon entering into its grand shadow.

The main part of the building was twelfth century, with a grandiose porch built on four centuries later in a Gothic style. They stood for a while before moving into the great shell of the interior. Here, all was shadowy, the slanting bars of light from the high windows creating a sense of space and mystery. The shell was full of dusty scents, as if the departed still breathed. Squire stood gazing into that majestic space, seeing it as a convincing rendering of the true reality in which all things had their being, as well as an unwitting representation of that luminous hole in the rear of the skull, the lantern hidden in bone in which alone he believed – and in which, he reflected, he probably believed alone.

Rugorsky was much more interested in the famous mosaics, which he regarded fiercely, striding about in his shirt-sleeves, his arms folded. His white hair streamed as he gazed upwards at saints, both meek and warlike, who floated upwards to the roof in a haze of gold. He moved gradually towards the great commanding figure of Christ Pantocrat, eyes staring, forehead creased in an all-too-just frown, which dominated the apse behind the high altar.

Neither man paid attention to the faithful just leaving the cathedral after mass. A man and his wife still knelt in their places, elbows touching, staring up at the great silver cross, their dark faces seeming to glow with worship; like Christ Pantocrat, both frowned, perhaps aware of the injustice of their lot, against which their lips moved in prayer. Old ladies beyond anger, clad in Mediterranean widows' black, went away bow-legged to light their sweet-smelling candles before returning to the workaday world outside.

Rugorsky walked back to Squire's side. 'A remarkable expression of medieval Italian art. These people had to be on guard against God. The relationship was understood on both sides to be formal. By reputation these mosaics are the equal of Ravenna. Those I have never seen and may never see.'

'They are splendid,' Squire murmured, vaguely. The two men walked apart again, Rugorsky to resume his staring at the stones above his head. Squire went and sat in a chair, slowing his breathing, experiencing the extent of the cathedral.

'Shall we go?' he asked, when Rugorsky eased his bulk into the next chair.

'No. Wait, you see. Waiting is important. Keep the minute while you can, in order to remember. It's a long bus ride. Just be still. That's important.'

They sat where they were, both men immobile.

Finally, Rugorsky stood up. 'Now we can leave. Perhaps something has sunk in.' He tapped his head. 'You do not have religious feeling?'

'No, not really. Frankly, I was glad when I got rid of God.'

'I see. I have not outgrown a religious impulse, despite all examples I see of godlessness all round. I mean, at home. Without God, I can see no meaning in anything.'

'The meaning lies within us.'

Once they moved outside the cathedral, Rugorsky appeared nervous again. He used the sticky brown handkerchief to mop his brow, and looked pale.

'Are you feeling well, Vasili? You surely won't be in trouble just because you took a morning away from the conference? A lot of the other delegates have been taking, or plan to take, days off. Herman told me he was going down to a beach for a swim.'

He stood gazing back at the stonework rising above them. 'It's Friday, yes. I forget which day it is. In just three days, you see, I must return to Russia. To be frank, I don't much relish the prospect. Tomorrow night, the conference is finished.' He shot Squire one of his telling glances as they strolled across the square, from shadow into sunlight. 'Do you ever experience the feeling that you have come to a dead halt in your life? Do you understand what I mean?'

'Yes.'

Rugorsky ran a hand through his white hair. He stood still, gazing about him as he spoke.

'Maybe you do, maybe you don't. You see, I am a man with a weight upon his mind. It would be impossible for me to explain everything, and without explaining everything, then I can't explain anything.' He was silent. He clutched his shirt sleeves, looking up at the cathedral for a while.

He laughed shortly. 'You see, I tell you nothing what I mean. Even so, I tell to you more than I tell to anyone I know in Russia. It must be the mark of a generous man, don't you think? I don't know what to do.'

Squire said, 'That feeling of a dead end. Perhaps it's characteristic of the age of fifty. One does run into difficulties then.'

'Of course. Circumstances accumulate at the age of fifty; possibilities are fewer than they once were . . . It's really a beautiful cathedral, mainly because it can still be used for the purposes for which it was designed many centuries ago, in confidence. There would be worse fates for a man than to have one room to live in across the square there – and watch the cathedral and see the people – wicked people no doubt, be sure of that – going in and out all the time.'

He regarded with longing the crumbling buildings across the square, where children played in doorways, and a woman languorously arranged a garment on a balcony railing. At that moment, another grey bus lumbered up from the plain in a cloud of exhaust fumes, and expired with a sigh under the central palm trees.

'Are you having trouble with Kchevov?'

'It's a mistake to throw out God.' He patted his white forelock into place, turning as he did so to scrutinize Squire. 'I speak as a member of a country or nation, so to say, which has experience in that area. It's a mistake to throw out God.'

'Difficult, painful – not necessarily mistaken. Maybe the evolution of the human race demands it . . . Although God is in many ways the greatest human idea so far.'

Perhaps Rugorsky did not care for the remark. Turning to walk on, he said, flatly, 'Georgi Kchevov can make trouble for me. I don't wish him to know more than he must do. Did you destroy the note I put under your door last night?'

Squire patted a pocket of the jacket he was carrying over his arm. 'I must admit I didn't. I've got it here with me.'

Another heavy silence. Then Rugorsky said, 'Now we must look at the Castle.'

They walked past the tourist stalls. Out of habit, Squire stopped and bought some postcards. He would send a card to Teresa, damn her, and to Deirdre, and possibly one to Willie and Madge in their new home. Rugorsky stood solidly by his shoulder, breathing hard, bored by the transaction. Squire also bought some little toy Sicilian carts for souvenirs, and tucked them in his jacket pocket.

Surrounding the cathedral was a maze of mean streets, through which Rugorsky led confidently. The alleyways were full of people, some selling vegetables, sentimental religious baubles, or toys. Sunshine blazed through an archway; they went towards it, emerging in a small square behind the cathedral. Ahead was the Castle of Nontreale.

The great stone walls of the Castle, tufted with fern here and there, were fringed by white Fiats, nestling together round the ramparts like fleas round a cat's ear. The Castle had withstood many attacks throughout the ages, before eventually succumbing to the internal combustion engine. Although it lay more or less in ruins, and the lizards flickering over its hot stonework were its chief occupants, its two great towers remained intact, looking towards the distant sea.

The towers faced northwards, the direction from which all invaders had come. Nontreale was poised on the brink of a great basalt core of rock which loomed above the plain as it had done ever since prehistoric times. Its Castle stood on the very edge of the precipice, with the road far below, then – below the labouring road – plain, studded with vines and villas, across which the shadow of the eminence was flung.

A narrow and crumbling path, fringed with wild flowers at which butterflies sipped before fluttering away into the abyss, led round the base of the northern wall and the two towers. 'Let's go that way,' Rugorsky said, pointing.

'It's only a goat track,' Squire said.

'We get a good view. Come on.' He gripped Squire's arm and led him forward.

It seemed to Squire that they would have enjoyed a better view from the top of one of the towers, but he followed the Russian. It felt cold as they entered the shadow of the fortress.

The chill entered Squire. As they moved forward with their right hands steadying themselves against the rough wall, he found himself dwelling uneasily on Howard Parker-Smith's early morning call. Parker-Smith had more information concerning Vasili Rugorsky. Rugorsky was in trouble back in Leningrad.

'He's been embezzling public funds,' Parker-Smith said. 'All these Russians involve themselves in graft as they rise in the hierarchy – it's a disease. The authorities probably allowed him a visa to Sicily so that they could turn everything over while he's away. I guess there's not a shred of paper left in his office by now. They'll bag him when he gets home again.'

'How do you know this?'

'Same way Rugorsky now knows it,' Parker-Smith said. 'A friendly colleague of his at Leningrad University got the word to him yesterday via the grapevine. We tapped the grapevine.'

'What happens next?'

'Depends. The friendly colleague may stand to gain if Rugorsky does a bunk. His friendly message may not be so friendly. Keep your eye on Rugorsky. One thing's for sure – he's in a spot. We must see which way the cat will jump.' He rang off.

The path became narrower. Rugorsky went forward more slowly. A little roll of fat at the back of his neck glistened, and the ends of his white hair were dark with sweat. Far below them, a bus laboured up the road they had come, the sound of its engine frail in the still air. Below the road were tiny trees, shrubs, fields, roofs, stretching all the way to the distant sea, where a peninsula of rock pointed its finger towards Italy.

Squire thought, 'All these things will I give thee if thou wilt fall down and worship me.'

Rugorsky turned round, steadying himself against the wall of the Castle. His eyes were narrowed; he was a man in the grip of a strong emotion. He reached forward and grasped Squire's arm.

'You were in Yugoslavia in 1948 . . .'

Immediately, a blaze of images was released in Squire's mind. Once again Slatko died on the floor of an Istran farmhouse, even as he himself plunged into the precipice. Rugorsky was sent in belated vengeance for

307

that ancient killing; by killing Squire he would acquire enough virtue to cancel out the embezzlement charges awaiting him in the USSR. Sometimes the figure falling was not he, but Rugorsky, or some more mythical figure, falling into a plumbless gulf.

He slipped and regained his balance, leaning with his back against the ancient stonework. The alarming images faded. He and Rugorsky stared at each other, ringed by wall and blue sky.

'Come,' Rugorsky said. 'We're safe here.'

'Safe . . . ?'

'No person in the world can hear what we speak. As I wrote in my letter, we talk together like men.' He shuffled nearer.

'Keep your distance, Vasili. You were going to push me off the cliff. What's this you say about Yugoslavia?'

'So in your heart you really believe we are all murderers and criminals after all? You think I'd be so naughty? It's not so. Maybe I can convince you of it, you see. For you and I have met once before. More than once. Twice. When we first spoke at the conference, I reminded you that we had met previously, with Leslie Lippard-Milne and his pretty wife, in front of Richard Hamilton's picture at the Tate Gallery, yes? You had forgotten the occasion, because you are slightly an egotist, I believe, and so do not easily recollect other people. It's just a slight punishment. But – I knew I had set eyes on you previously.' He paused, adding with distinct emotion, 'Many many years ago, Thomas, when you and I were young men, and much more inclined to push people off cliffs than we are now – then I saw you. I had a good look at you. It was in a region of Yugoslavia called Istra.'

Hearing the thickness of his own voice, Squire asked, 'What were you doing in Istra?'

With a gleam of his self-mocking humour, Rugorsky said, 'What do Russians do anywhere abroad except foment trouble? My government had something against me, and so I was sent abroad to work on their behalf. I was being punished for writing a silly satirical poem about our beloved late leader, Comrade Stalin.'

'"Winter Celebration".'

'You are properly informed in our literature. My poem circulated in *samizdat*. When the authorities caught up with it, they were not amused. They are never amused. So after some training I was sent to Belgrade, where I became – I suppose you would say a *gundog* for a very important KGB high official who had the codename Slatko. The word is Serbian for "sweetness". You remember that name, I am sure.'

'I remember,' Squire said. 'Slatko . . .'

'You see, it was important to our Comrade Leader that all socialist countries should appear in agreement before the outside world. Just to have this one little country, Yugoslavia, disagreeing was bad for his sleep every night. Yugoslavia must be crushed. Therefore this evil man Slatko was sent in, with orders direct from Stalin. It was easy to send him in secretly, and many others like him.'

'And you?'

'Slatko was not sweet. He had many murders to his credit. He had especially the ambition to kill Tito, so he proceeded very cautiously. But he was also a drunken sot and, one spring morning in Istra, when he had hit the bottle and his actions were slow . . . well, Thomas, you drove up at the place where he was hiding, and by good fortune you managed to shoot him. It was the luck of the beginner, as we say.'

Squire imitated the Russian in giving his face a mop. 'That's thirty years ago.'

'Do we ever forget such moments of our youth? Time's nothing.'

He gestured out towards the sea. 'Here we are, almost in a similar situation, you might say. Here I stand, speaking with the man who assassinated the evil Slatko. I am proud.'

He sat down on the narrow path, gazing across the panorama before them.

'I wanted to speak these things to you, because I doubt that we will ever meet again. All my possibilities are closing.'

After a moment's hesitation, Squire came and sat beside him, his shoes pointing out over the drop.

'Where were you that day? You were at the farmhouse?'

'Before dawn on that day, I had driven an old German truck

containing crates of British machine-guns from the coast. I was resting in the sun. Writing another poem, to be exact. When I saw your car approach the farmhouse, I jumped over a wall at the back to hide. So did two others with me. There were explosions of grenades and shooting for some while. I kept my head down.

'When I dared to peep up, there I saw you standing by an upper window of the house, only a few metres above me. I studied your English face. I could have shot you easily. Instead, I sneaked away, keeping behind the wall. There was a little car we had stolen, a Fiat. I ran to that and drove off in it. As a matter of fact, I believe you unkindly threw a grenade after me, but I kept going. What I felt then I'll never forget.'

'Nor I.'

'Well, it's impossible to forget. I was so scared, but also glad, because that cruel ogre was finished. At great danger to my life, I made my way back to my native country, aided by Soviet contacts I knew in Belgrade. What foolish loyalty to Stalin and my country! When I reported back, I was rewarded by ten years in the Gulag. That term was miraculously reduced after Stalin's death.'

He sighed heavily.

'Now you are in trouble again,' Squire said.

Rugorsky smiled. 'But I don't do anything so serious as pushing my friends from cliffs.'

'The world's a dangerous place.'

'You don't need to tell me that. I brought you here because I wished to speak of those distant times in Yugoslavia. I longed to tell you of the extraordinary bond between us over many years, across the East–West struggle. To be frank, I thought if I told you that you would remember me in future times.'

'I expect I shall.'

'When we met before the Hamilton picture in the Tate Gallery, I had to work through my memory for many hours before I recalled you. This charming English critic was Slatko's executioner. He had shot the evil man who had been chilled by the breath of Stalin. Then I believed in the miraculous.'

'Of course you checked up on me through the KGB.'

'I don't deny. You also checked up on me – you know I am in trouble again now. That's how the world situation is – we must check up on each other. We didn't make that situation, you and I.'

'The charges in Leningrad – they're serious?'

The Russian pulled a stalk of grass and bit it. 'All things are serious, you see. Unfortunately, such is the state of morals that we all get involved with some form of graft as we progress upwards. There is no other way. Perhaps you will remember the case of Madame Furtseva, Minister of Culture and the late Khrushchev's lady-friend. I knew her slightly – she was disgraced for such things. But that's another tale . . . When I arrive at Moscow, I shall probably be tried, sentenced, and returned to the camps. My poor wife . . . I will never survive. I'm old, my kidney is weak. It will not be like living in a civilized English prison. Even if I could survive – even if the miracle happens and I am cleared at my trial – but that is not how they conduct trials in Moscow – I shall never again see the pleasant places of the West.'

'Let's get back to the square. I'll buy you a drink.' He got cautiously to his feet. This time, he extended a hand to Rugorsky, who took it and struggled up. They edged their way back along the narrow path.

Addressing Squire's back, Rugorsky said, laughing slightly, 'You see, Thomas, we two are not such bad fellows, after all. We have managed some communication. There is always division between East and West, and always has been. So much mistrust. But just this afternoon we spoke like men.'

As they rounded the base of one of the towers, Nontreale again materialized; the shadowy abyss lay behind them. Squire found his legs trembling as he stood on firm ground, staring up the narrow side street, where life was lived among overhead balconies, drooping telephone wires, eaves that almost met overhead, and stalls selling portraits of Christ and the Virgin with luminous eyeballs which glowed at night.

They pushed their way into a bar in the main square, opposite the ice-cream parlour where they had sat earlier. Men in rough clothes were crowding the counter. Squire almost spilt the beers as he carried them to a small table.

'Quite a scrum,' he said.

'No. It's not so at all, you see. Here, nobody pushes at all. Everyone is decent and polite.'

As they sat down, Squire said, 'Whatever you have been up to in Leningrad, you are short of money when you come abroad.'

Rugorsky looked searchingly over his glass at Squire. 'It's a privilege for you to buy me this beer. We shall think of it many years ahead. What little money I have, I keep. It's possible a little bribe may help me at Moscow airport, because if I can fly on to Leningrad, then there's a chance for me. In Moscow, none.'

'I'm sorry. I am glad to buy you a beer. Is Kchevov keeping an eye on you?'

'Of course. I'm sure you know it. But we will speak of such things no more. Instead, tell me about your Pop Expo. We are being watched by a friend of yours.'

Turning, Squire saw that Parker-Smith was toying with a glass of wine and reading an Italian newspaper behind them.

They caught the bus back to Ermalpa. Neither Squire nor Rugorsky spoke much on the way. Squire watched the Russian drinking in the outside world, storing away what he saw, possibly reflecting that even the dirtiest vulcanizers, carrying on their trade and their private life in two rooms, enjoyed a freedom they had no way of evaluating. And he thought, 'The impulse to push me over the cliff in order to gain some small political advantage in Russia was in his heart. I'm sure of it, even if he denies it. Otherwise, why should I have felt threatened as I did?'

They climbed out of the bus at last, only two blocks from the Grand Hotel Marittimo. The vehicle disappeared in a snort of grey exhaust fumes. Outside the swing doors, they paused.

'I thought I might get to England from here,' Rugorsky said abruptly. 'But something tells me that I would not be welcome at Pippet Hall. You have a mistrust. Perhaps you still think in your mind that I had

an intention to do something a little serious on the cliff at Nontreale
. . . Well, really we are stuck with the nation we are born into, you see,
and must play out its game of consequences.'

'I'm sorry I can't help, Vasili. And I didn't lob that grenade at you
in Istra.'

'That's a small cause for celebration. If you're not feeling too
unfriendly, perhaps you would like to buy us a bottle of champagne,
or at least a beer.'

He smoothed down his white lock of hair and smiled ingratiatingly,
showing broken teeth. Scratch a Russian . . .

'I'm going to my room to have a shower, Vasili. I'm sure you'll
find friends in the bar.' They stood scrutinizing each other.

Rugorsky shrugged. 'Well, I understand your meaning.' As they
pushed through the swing doors into the cool of the foyer, he gave
Squire one of his sly looks. 'You do still think partly that I would be
wicked enough to push you over the cliff, don't you?'

Looking him in the eye, Squire said, 'If you were once one of
Slatko's men – yes.'

Rugorsky nodded and rubbed his chin. 'I see, Thomas. It's because
you're not sentimental enough.'

14

An Ideological Decision

The taxi-driver talked all the way from the airport. He was eloquent on the subject of immigrants, for which he did not care. Immigrants made London dirty and refused to work. They bred like rabbits and ruined the country. Squire made little response; he did not wish to be turned out of the taxi as had happened to him once when he tried to persuade the driver that 'the blacks' actually contributed something to Britain's tottering economy.

'You look tired, squire,' said the taxi-driver, familiarly, as he pulled up in Bouverie Square.

Cheered by being thus addressed, Squire agreed he was tired.

'What, been abroad then?'

'That's it.'

'It is tiring abroad, innit? Dunno what people go there for.'

Squire stood on the pavement. The taxi-driver reluctantly lifted his two cases out of the vehicle and set them on the pavement, while glancing up at the building suspiciously. 'Can you manage them cases, squire? They look a bit posh for round here, don't they? That'll be twenty-five pounds, thanks.'

It was, if not nice, recognizable to be back in England.

As the taxi moved off in a cloud of exhaust, and Squire bent to pick up his luggage, a pudgy man, dragging a wheeled suitcase, came along the street and cried Squire's name.

Squire responded to the man's smile and shook his outstretched hand. The pudgy man wore a tight pair of faded jeans, a worn leather jacket, and a light blue silk sweater marked with beer or coffee stains. His long straggling grey hair surrounded a brown bald patch on the top of his head. He was perhaps sixty years old, and panted a good deal as he paused. He wiped his mouth on a blue spotted handkerchief.

'Mustn't stop. Just going to catch a train, but it's lovely to see you. How're you getting on?'

'Fine,' Squire said. 'And you?'

The plump man flung his arms wide. 'I've had it, really had it. Finished. The BBC didn't get the increase it hoped for and they wouldn't renew my contract. They're broke, the bastards . . . I can't get a job to suit me – *me*, of all people! The country's going down the drain fast, it's terrible. No room for people of talent any more.'

Suddenly the name came back to Squire. Grahame Ash, the director of 'Frankenstein Among the Arts', skilled, inventive, dedicated.

'What are you going to do?'

Ash grabbed Squire's arm. 'Don't laugh. I've accepted a job with Aussie television. They offered me something – not much. I'm on my way now, just going to say goodbye to an old friend first, then I fly to Sydney in a couple of days. Terrible, isn't it?'

'Very enterprising of you, Grahame. I wish you the best of luck.'

'After all I've done . . . "Frankenstein" and all the rest of it. But the oil crisis isn't going to go away. Inflation isn't going to go down. I believe, if you ask me, that the Arab world is going to squeeze Europe and the US by the throat. Nothing's ever going to be the same again. We're going to go down the drain, till we end up like a lot of little Uruguays and Paraguays. This country's had it, that's my belief, I tell you frankly. We'll have to team up with the Soviet Bloc in the end, just to keep going. Trading in furs again, before long. Well, I must dash.' He looked at his wrist watch. Summer was closing, and the day; the light thickened in the narrow street.

'I hope you find things better in Australia. They've got massive economic problems too.'

315

'Don't tell me. I'll find out soon enough. But I've got a younger brother in Sydney, haven't seen him for fifteen years. I'll be okay. I'm talented, you know, Tom. I've got faith. Remember the times we had in Singapore, and Sarawak?'

'Of course. All the best. I'd always be glad to hear from you.'

'I'll drop you a card. How's Laura? See anything of her?'

'Not lately.'

'Lovely girl. All the best, then.'

'All the best.' Squire watched Ash's departing back before taking up his cases.

The flat suited Squire well enough. He had no objection to the Paddington area. A Greek hairdresser worked at his trade in the basement of the house; sounds of clippers and bazouki music drifted up the stairs. On the ground floor was an old woman of mysterious nationality who occasionally walked a fat pug to the corner lamp post. The Iranian professor of metallurgy on the first floor was also very quiet. The young men in frilly shirts who visited him most evenings were also quiet, if not downright taciturn.

Squire rented the top floor. It was modest, and the furnishings were not even dreadful enough to be worth joking about. But the front room was large and had once been good. He found himself not displeased to be back. A sepia photograph of his parents, and a colour photograph of John, stood on the mantelpiece; otherwise the room was anonymous.

From the window, he could see the corner shop, a grocer's run by a Pakistani family which remained open most hours of the day and night. Mr Ali Khan was the only acquaintance Squire had made in the neighbourhood; the two men now knew each other well enough for Mr Khan to confide his suspicions concerning the Chinese who ran the 'Hong Kong Restaurant and Take-Away', only three doors from his shop. They worked too hard and were secretive.

Having dumped his suitcases in the middle of the room, Squire went back downstairs to collect his mail, which had been thrown into an old Bovril box on the hall floor. Most of the letters were re-addressed from Pippet Hall in the firm round handwriting of Matilda Rowlinson. He had given the flat address to few people.

There was no letter from Teresa. Most of the mail looked like circulars or fan mail. He opened one letter as a kind of spot check. It came from a gentleman in Carlisle who claimed to have spent twenty years in the RAF. He had watched the 'Frankenstein' programme (sic) on television, and was disappointed to hear no mention of Irving Berlin, the best song-writer of this or any other century. It was time some sort of justice was done.

Squire was carrying clothes about in a rather helpless fashion, sorting out dirty items to be taken to the launderette in Praed Street, when his doorbell rang. He went to the door and dragged it open.

His brother-in-law, Marshall Kaye, stood there, bronzed, slightly ragged round the moustache, and smiling.

'Hi, Tom, glad to find you back home. I rang your number several times. From a news item I caught, I feared the flying saucers over Ermalpa had got a hold of you.'

'Marsh, come in.' They shook hands. Squire indicated the muddle in his room. 'As you can see, I'm just back. Care to sample some eight-year-old duty-free malt?'

'Try me.'

Whilst Squire was breaking open the whisky carton, Kaye asked him about the flying saucers.

'I saw one, Marsh. I'm convinced. I saw it, yet I still don't believe it.'

'Okay. It's like seeing a damned ghost – it may scare you, but it can't affect your life in any way. Just suppose whole squadrons of flying saucers landed, and we were up to here in little green men. It still wouldn't affect our inner lives one bit.'

'You think not? Would you say that as you scavenged through the ruins of London?'

'What I mean is, some people are toppled into misery by what may seem minor factors. Others triumphantly survive the most terrible tragedies and come up smiling. Like some of the characters in Solzhenitsyn's *Gulag Archipelago*.'

They drank, exchanging more idle remarks. Kay asked about the conference, and Squire gave him a brief account of the Rugorsky affair.

'Sounds pretty hairy!' Kaye exclaimed. 'Was the guy flying back to Moscow today?'

'Yes. I bought him a drink and a meal at Rome airport before we went our separate ways. Kchevov was with him, keeping close, so I had to stand him a meal too. Rugorsky was naturally cagey, because he was not absolutely sure that his *friend* was unable to understand English. Otherwise he was calm. He was convinced that he was going back to Moscow to face absolute destruction. He didn't think he would see his wife – who's in Leningrad – again.'

'Can we do anything from this end?'

'We can and will send letters, stressing his international importance. D'Exiteuil will help too; he has powerful friends in government, and the French, as you know, exert a bit of a pull in Moscow. But fraudulent currency transactions are a criminal offence.'

'Guys who defraud criminals are not necessarily themselves criminal.'

'A point of view it would be rather difficult to sustain in a Moscow court of law . . . Someone, probably Solzhenitsyn, spoke of the lack of character among men in the West, and the corresponding stature of so many characters in the USSR under that oppressive system. Of course, the remark is one of prejudice and can have no statistical validity, but I thought of it when parting from Vasili. He is a terrific guy. Good to have in a slit trench with you when the shit's flying.'

'Not so good on a cliff edge.'

Squire looked down at the worn carpet and rubbed his knees.

'You know what I was thinking in Rome airport? He and I between us could have clobbered Kchevov in the toilets, and tied him up like a mummy with strip towels. Then I could have brought Vasili back here. The uncertainties over Pippet Hall deterred me – that's my excuse. He would have been safe there for a while, and then we could have found him somewhere a bit more secure, in Canada, or the good old US of A.'

'You'd have been mad. Would he have played along?'

'Oh, probably.' Squire looked at his watch. 'He did his share of toilet-fighting as a young man, I'm sure . . . He'll be in Moscow by now, poor sod. I feel like a worm for doing nothing.'

'But he did try to knock you off?'

'Maybe.'

They drank in silence for a while. Kaye rose and ambled about the room. Something in his bearing told Squire that he disliked the flat with all its shabbiness, and felt caged within it; layers of time in a Paddington room held less appeal for the American than the thicker strata of an old Greek palace.

With surprising force, amounting almost to anger, he turned suddenly on his heel to look down at Squire, who sat in a worn cane chair. 'So here you are, lurking in a seedy flat in Paddington. I don't understand, Tom – this must be some brand of British behaviour that eludes me. What the hell goes on?'

'It was so damned uncomfortable at the Travellers'. My room was half the size of this. It made sense to move here.'

Kaye tugged his moustache down over his mouth. 'You know what I mean. You don't belong here. This isn't your thing. Is it the mid-life crisis, have you got a black woman stashed away in the jacuzzi, or are you in search of God?'

'Come on, Marsh, there are other explanations for living in Paddington. And there's nothing wrong with this flat. I've always imagined that if anyone goes looking for God they can find him easily – he's only an image in the mind. Do you know, one of the most interesting places we went to while we were making the TV series was the Tinjar National Park in Sarawak. We visited a cave where there were some paintings made over forty centuries ago – you may remember it from the first episode, "Eternal Ephemera". There was a whole wall covered with paintings of hands, hands facing palms outward, hundreds upon hundreds of them.'

'I remember. You sent Deirdre a postcard of it. What about it?'

'I often think of that wall. It may be the earliest human painting that survives. Those hands aren't making supplications to God. In all religions, people making a supplication to God turn their palms

319

either upwards, unconsciously indicating thereby that God resides in their skulls, in the uppermost part of their anatomy, or else inwards, thereby unconsciously acknowledging that he is an inward quality.

'Those hands were extended outward, in supplication to other men. It's a pity that throughout human history God has got in the way of that gesture. Even as I say it, I become aware that Rugorsky would perhaps relish the perception. I can't get him out of my mind.'

After a moment's thought, he asked, 'Do you believe in God when you're doing one of your digs?'

'Never. I believe in history and logical deduction. And any palms I saw outstretched to me in Greece, or on Milos, belonged to beggars.'

Silence came between them again. Squire looked at the shabby carpet, Kaye stared into his glass. At last, Kaye cleared his throat, a look of discomfort on his brown capacious face.

'Well, er, I'd better tell you what I'm here about, Tom. I'm here in the thankless role of peacemaker.'

'Thanks.'

'It was June of last year that you and Teresa fell out, right? That's fifteen months. A long time. Your friends feel that if the two of you don't team up again soon, you'll never make it. So we've agreed to get together and try to push. I couldn't have some more whisky, could I?'

He stood up as Squire gestured to the bottle.

'Switch the light on too, will you? It's getting a bit dark. What makes you think I any longer want Teresa to come back?'

'Cigarette?'

'I've got my own.' He reached into the open suitcase and fished out a half-empty packet of 'Drina' cigarettes. He lit one without offering the packet to Kaye, who smoked his own.

'You've caught the habit? Those things'll kill you, you know that? I've figured out that you do want Teresa back. Just one look at this apartment convinces me. I've heard of a hair-shirt economy but this is ridiculous. The famous Tom Squire dossing in some dump in

Paddington, for Christ's sake? The gesture is too ostentatious, too obvious. You're punishing yourself, Tom, you're displaying your sores.'

'It's cheap here. I can get my hair cut in the basement.'

'Don't be difficult. Things are difficult enough. Teresa wants to come back to you.'

'That's a decided policy change. Has her lover-boy deserted her?'

'That's what's difficult. Yes. He has. And she's broke. But that's not her primary motivation for wanting a reunion.'

Squire smoked the Yugoslav cigarette and waited for Kaye to continue.

'Look, Tom, I know that she doesn't want to come back just because the Jarvis guy walked out on her. She loves you. You hurt her pride, that's all, and she had to show how independent she can be.'

'She's always known how independent she can be.'

'You know what I mean. Hell hath no fury and all that.'

'Marsh. She was not scorned. I know I upset her with the Laura affair, but I never deliberately insulted her feelings. She then set out to make me feel as bad as possible. She succeeded.'

'Shit, I'm no good at this. I'm going to put my foot in it. I told Deirdre that she should have talked to you, but she sent me instead.'

'Oh, why's that?'

'Well, er, Deirdre's round the corner in the pub, The Plumes, I think it is. She's looking after Teresa. The plan is for us to go down and join them. Talk things over. Feel up to it?'

'Deirdre's keeping Teresa from making a fast exit, no doubt.' He stood up and went to the window. Mr Ali Khan's lights were on in the corner shop. 'I will smoke this cigarette and in that time decide whether a) I will come down and speak to Teresa and b) I will accept her back. If the answer to b) is *nyet*, then plainly the answer to a) is *nyet*, since there'd be no point in seeing her.'

He stood looking out at the street. Kaye examined the toy Sicilian carts.

'Think of the Athenians at Milos, Tom. 'We have concluded from experience that it's a law of nature to rule whatever one can.' Teresa is surrendering after her tiny revolt. You must reclaim her and Pippet

Hall and the family as part of your domain, though I know it sounds chauvinistic. Rule what you can. That's what you must do – and make her surrender as palatable as you can.'

Not turning round, Squire said remotely, 'I am thinking of the Athenians at Milos. I am also thinking of Vasili in Moscow. They should be getting the first punches in on him about now.' He lapsed into silence, smoking with folded arms.

Quiet lay in the room. From below came the faint sound of bazouki. Somewhere a man was shouting. Marshall Kaye sat tight and sipped his malt.

Finally, Squire turned and walked across the room to stub out the butt of his cigarette in an ashtray. He breathed the last lungful of smoke into the air, watching as its spirals moved across the stained ceiling.

'Okay, Marsh,' he said briskly, rubbing his palms against the seat of his slacks. 'I've come to an ideological decision regarding Teresa. Maybe we in the West make too much of our personal problems.'

As he spoke, screams and furious barking broke out below stairs.

'Hang on, that's Deirdre's voice,' Kaye said, running over to the door in alarm and throwing it open. Angry female voices rose from the dimness, punctuated by the shrill yaps of a dog.

'You keek my dorg, I report you at the RSPCA!'

'Is it a dog or a shark? It nearly bit my leg off!'

The two men hurried downstairs, bumping into the Iranian professor of metallurgy, who shuffled out of his room, clad in a yellow silk dressing-gown, to find out what the noise was about. On the ground floor, the woman of mysterious nationality was bundling her pug-dog out of the door; each, in its fashion, maintained a continuous complaint as they disappeared. Deirdre Kaye began to ascend the stairs, stumbling in the thick dust.

'Marsh, that you? Tom? What is this place? Doesn't it possess any lights? Gas lights? Candles? Where are you? Who was that dreadful creature with the captive coyote? Is she a denizen of this –' by now she was face-to-face with the Iranian professor of metallurgy – 'this multi-national lodging-house?'

'Come on up and stop complaining, Deirdre,' Kaye said, seizing his wife by the arm and dragging her past the Iranian professor. 'You just encountered another tenant, that's all.'

'Tenant plus wolf-hound, thanks. Tom, what on earth are you doing in these squalid surroundings? I need a drink. Plus a tetanus injection.'

They sat Deirdre down in the best-upholstered of Squire's armchairs, and Kaye tenderly inspected her ankle while Squire poured them all whisky.

'No ice, I'm afraid,' he said, handing his sister a glass.

'Plenty of dog biscuits, I'm sure,' Deirdre said.

Deirdre was dressed for summer and the city, in a smart spotted dress and jacket in pure silk. She was heavily made up. When she had calmed down slightly, she said, 'I wondered what had happened. You've been so long, Marsh. I had to come and see, little thinking this place doubled as kennels. Here you both are, sitting boozing, while I've been stuck with Teresa in the pub.'

'Also boozing, I hope,' Squire said.

'Frankly, your wife is not my favourite company. She's been a bitch to you, and I don't mind saying so.'

'Funny you should say that, Deirdre. Tom was just about to tell me that he is going back to her.'

Deirdre pulled a face and clutched her ankle, as if hoping that injury might excuse her speaking out of turn. 'There is the Hall and all that to think of. Don't take any notice of anything I say.'

'You're misjudging Tess,' Squire said. 'She has her harpy-like aspects, but I understand how she feels; her life has been thrown out of kilter. That's my responsibility, in part at least, unless I kick her out – which I'm not disposed to do. You must help by sympathizing with her position. It is not characteristic of Teresa to get mixed up with little shits like Jarvis.'

His sister took a large gulp of her whisky. 'Glenfiddich – saved! Tom, you idiot, you don't have to go through with this goody-goody altruistic stuff for our sake. Be yourself. Kick her out, call up Laura. Laura's smashing. Obey your impulses. No renunciations. Uncle Willie told you that ages ago.'

Kaye said, 'You realize we have witnesses to prove that Teresa invited this guy Jarvis up to Pippet Hall on several occasions when you were away. Photographic evidence as a matter of fact.'

Down in the bowels of the house, bazouki music started again, louder than before. The Greek hairdresser's evening was hitting its stride. Squire went over to the window and leant against the sill, looking inward at his sister and brother-in-law, arms folded.

'Everyone's so involved with their little transient private lives. Perhaps as sucklings of a materialist culture we really do try to possess each other too much. Perhaps we really are flabby and deserve to go under.

'You come up here and tell me Tess still loves me, Marsh. Now you say you have photographic evidence of her carrying-on. You can't make up your own mind where you stand. But I've made up my mind. Let me quote the Athenians right back at you – "It's a law of nature to rule whatever you can." Teresa's making a fresh approach. So I am going to take her back to the Hall – tonight, if possible. On such good terms as we can contrive.

'I will try to retain the Hall and my wife. It would be foolish to lose either, just because one primitive part of my brain wants me to get revenge on her for ill-treatment. At the Hall, I can work my best. I have to protect my society, SPA, and to fight for the various things I find myself capable of fighting for. Ermalpa's taught me that even quite everyday things need to be defended.'

'Well, you have made up your mind,' Deirdre said. 'Seeing you standing there, I can't help thinking of mother's old advice to us – "Always look first-rate." You're doing your Squire stuff again and being first-rate – I hope it makes you happy.'

'Well, Deirdre, I am basically pretty happy. I'm puzzled why that's regarded as such a strange statement these days. Don't drink any more; take me down to the pub and let me chat with Tess – if she's still there. We can drive up to Hartisham this evening, if she feels so inclined. She has to behave not too impossibly with me, and recognize herself as a native of Milos, in the capitulating position.'

Deirdre stood up and smoothed down her dress. She made a wry face at Kaye. 'Life goes on. That's the silly thing about it.'

'I'll put on a sweater,' Squire said. 'It's cooler here than it was in Ermalpa.'

Exotic Iranian odours greeted them as they made their way down the dim stairs. Kaye paused on the landing and looked back at Squire.

'Tom, I want you to know I respect what you're doing.'

'Marsh – don't go all American on me. Having let my enemy off the hook, I can hardly do less for my wife . . .'

'I know it's not going to be easy for you, Tom. But Teresa's horoscope said this was a good day for reconciliations, you'll be glad to know.' He grinned. 'Make it all happen.'

'That's what's known as looking for the miraculous.'

Kaye rubbed the back of his neck.

'Maybe what's always needed is an act of faith.'

The way to the front door was impeded by push-bikes. In the basement, the Greek barber was singing loudly. Deirdre walked diligently, on the alert for foreign ladies and fat dogs.

Daylight still lingered in the street. Squire, Kaye and Deirdre walked along together. They turned the corner by Mr Ali Khan's shop.

The Plumes was in front of them, doors open to admit the summer air and emit smoke. The interior looked welcoming, with its oak panels and dim lights. Black men and white, in T-shirts and jeans, stood out on the pavement, talking and lifting pint mugs of beer to their lips. As Squire approached, he saw Teresa sitting waiting alone inside at a little table, with a drink in front of her. Teresa saw Squire.

She waved. The smile that accompanied the flutter of the hand was hesitant. She had a new hair-style.

He waved in response. He knew, as he entered the lighted space and became merged with the bustle of early evening drinkers, that

Teresa – and Deirdre, and he, and everything of which they were a part – were changed. Things would never be as they had been; that must be accepted.

Even to speak to her, so familiar, so loved for all she was and symbolized, a new language was required.

'How was Ermalpa?' Teresa asked, as he sat down beside her, looking at him slightly squint.